KT-432-764

Clifford Hanley is something of a Scottish institution. His working life began in journalism, and branched into radio writing, the music hall, the legitimate theatre, songwriting and television. His first published book, *Dancing in the Streets*, an affectionate evocation of Glasgow childhood, was hailed as a classic, and in a score of novels and non-fiction works he has acquired a mass of happy readers. His thrillers under the pseudonym of Henry Calvin have a cult quality.

His lyric to the ancient pipe tune *Scotland the Brave*, written absentmindedly one Saturday morning, is the undoubted national anthem of Scotland – much to his surprise.

Hanley is married, with three adult children. His hobbies are talking, language, music and golf.

Also by Clifford Hanley

DANCING IN THE STREETS

and published by Corgi Books

*This book is affectionately dedicated
to Glendon*

# 1

His mother's fingers were like steel digging into his scalp and he kept his eyes tight shut as soapy water ran down his face. When she wiped them he blinked. The edges of the kitchen range glinted in the light from the gas mantle and the fire was dull red in the basket. He suffered the fierce scrubbing of his neck with a scratchy flannel.

His sister Henrietta was at the kitchen table, bent over a book. Bobby had a chair pulled as close to the fire as it could get without moving the zinc bath, and he was crouching forward on it with both hands stretched out to the heat.

'You'll get tartan legs if you sit as near as that to the fire, Bobby,' Mother said. Bobby shrugged and slid his chair back an inch. He could never get enough heat. Peter stood up obediently and stepped out of the bath and on to the towel, and his mother hoisted the bath with an easy swing that carried it over to the sink to be emptied in a swirl of steam. Then she plucked the towel from under him and he stood meekly for another scrubbing.

Bobby slid his chair into the space where the bath had stood.

Mother pulled Peter's shirt down over his head and left him, red and tiny, in front of the fire while she went to wipe out the bath. Bobby pushed him to the side and edged nearer the heat. Henrietta glanced up from her book and pursed her lips, and returned to her book.

Peter didn't mind. His skin was blazing from the towelling, and now it was nice to be warm. But he sensed that Bobby had something on his mind. Bobby had some new trick. Already, at five, Peter had learned to sense the workings of Bobby's mind. And like Mother's savage scraping of his skin, they were something that had to be suffered. Bobby picked up a teacup from the kitchen range and turned it upside down.

'What's in this cup?' he asked Peter.

'Nothing.'

Henrietta turned round briefly from her book and said, 'Don't pay any attention, Peter, it's another of his silly tricks.'

'You shut up, Henrietta, it's got nothing to do with you.'

Mother turned from the sink, and shook her head.

'Don't talk like that to your sister, Bobby.' Her voice was soft. Even when she was being sharp, there was always music in it.

Bobby glowered and said, 'Well!'

It meant, Well, it's none of her business, or Well she shouldn't interfere; or Well it was somebody else's fault; or anything else Bobby meant it to mean.

'What's in the cup?' he insisted.

'Nothing,' Peter said. 'I said nothing.'

'Ha ha. There is something in it. Something invisible, see?' He held out the cup for inspection and Peter stared into it.

'I don't see anything.'

'Stupid. You can't see invisible things, they're invisible, it's no use looking.'

Peter kept staring into the cup.

'Angels?'

'Angels! That's just stupid. You're stupid.'

Mother turned from the sink and said, reasonably, 'I suppose if there are angels, Bobby, they would be invisible.'

'In a cup? What would angels be doing in a cup?' Bobby was aggrieved at the interruption of his game.

'Well,' said Mother, 'they used to say long ago that ten thousand angels could dance on the point of a needle. I never understood that myself, why they would want to be dancing on a needle. But God moves in mysterious ways. I suppose there might be some reason for it.'

Bobby shook the cup angrily, as if to shake out any angels who had invaded it.

'What else?' he demanded. Peter imagined streams of tiny angels falling on to the waxcloth, and shuffled back in case he should stand on them. Bobby couldn't delay his triumph any longer.

'It's air. AIR. Stupid.'

Henrietta raised her eyes to heaven, put her fingers in her ears and went back to her book. Meg, the mother, wondered why Bobby was forever thinking up things to tease the child. Jealousy, perhaps, because he had no mother of his own. But she was sure she loved them all equally, though it was sometimes hard not to be impatient with Bobby, always crouching into the fire and doing nothing much else except prod prod prod away at his step-brother. Little Peter took the cup from him and shook it upside down.

'Now there's nothing in it.'

'Stupid, the air's still in it, it never comes out.'

'I'll get it out,' Henrietta said.

'No you'll not, nobody can get it out.'

Henrietta took the cup from Peter, took it to the sink and filled it to the brim with water.

'There's no air in it now because there's no room, see?'

'You cheated.'

'That is very ingenious, I would never have thought of that,' Meg said.

'It's a cheat.'

'It's called using your brains, Bobby,' said Meg. 'Now come on, it's time for bed if you've got the school tomorrow.'

'School?' Bobby was angry at all Cassidys. 'He's too stupid to go to school.'

'Well, that's why Henrietta and you will have to take him, isn't it?' Meg asked placidly. 'And anyway, if he was stupid, it's all the more reason to go to school. It's the great cure for stupidity. Come on now, bedtime.'

She kissed the boys, carefully giving Bobby an extra hug, and they went into the dark front room, to the bed-couch. With any luck they would be sleeping before Andy and John came in, to sleep in the box-bed beside them.

'Sometimes I could slap that Bobby,' Henrietta said absentmindedly.

'A wicked thought is as bad as a wicked deed, Henrietta. He's your brother, and he's only a wee boy.'

'He's a bully.'

'He's only a wee boy, boys are always up to something.' In her soft island voice it sounded like 'poice are alwiss up to some-sing'. 'Bed for you too, miss, you need your sleep at your age.'

'Can I read in bed?'

'As long as the book's away before your father comes in, you know what he's like.' This sounded disloyal. 'I mean, about you getting your sleep.'

'Yes.'

In the bed-couch in the front room, Bobby was still

peevish at the way Henrietta had spoiled his trick, although he was thinking that he would remember the bit about the water next time he tried it.

'I'm not taking you to school tomorrow,' he told Peter.

'Henrietta'll take me.'

'Maybe they'll not take you.'

'They'll have to take me.' Peter was slightly alarmed.

'What for? They'll tell you you should be in a Fenian school.'

'What's a Fenian school?'

'Stupid. A school for Fenians.'

'What's a Fenian?'

'You're a Fenian.'

'I am not.'

'You are sot. Shut up, I'm sleeping.'

He did seem suddenly to be sleeping. Bobby always slept first, while Peter lay and thought about the strange things he thought about when he wasn't even trying to think. After a few minutes he felt Bobby's feet moving against his bare calves, and he knew Bobby was asleep because when he slept, his toes curled and uncurled and scratched against Peter's legs. He moved his legs away, but the toes crept after them, and he had to curl up in a ball to escape them.

In the kitchen, Henrietta's eyes were beginning to droop over her book, and her mother came quietly to pick the book from her hands and pull the bed curtains. Henrietta opened her eyes wide and said, 'The cat.'

The cat had no name. It was just The Cat. It was dozing on the shelf below the oven door on the kitchen range, and its tail had waved in a dream till the tip nearly touched the firebars. There was a faint singeing smell from the little fur that remained on the tail. In an exercise long practised, Meg swooped, plucked a damp cloth hanging from a string along the mantelpiece, gripped the cat by the root of the tail and lifted it to let the tail slide down through the cloth. The Cat protested feebly and crept under the bed.

'It'll be the death of me,' Meg muttered, and closed the bed curtains. The cat mewed resentfully from the darkness under the bed.

It's just like Bobby, Henrietta thought. A real Mason cat. She pulled the blankets over her face to stifle a fit of the giggles.

# 2

The classroom was the most enormous place Peter had ever been in and from his little chair near the window the teacher's desk seemed miles away. Miss Wales. There were forty other children in the class, in little wooden chairs with arms. It was all strange, so it was wonderful. Bobby had warned him that he would hate it. Henrietta had promised him he would like it. It was new. He liked it. He had never been in a room with so many people before either. How would he ever get to know them?

Nothing seemed to be happening for a long time. Miss Wales sat at her desk and wrote in a book.

A girl near the front suddenly screamed, a long piercing scream followed by wailing and sobbing. Miss Wales looked up angrily.

'I told you not to put your hands on the arms of your chairs!' she shouted. Quite different from his mother, who never ever shouted. He couldn't remember her saying anything about chairs. The only thing she had said to him when he first came in, in a long slow queue, had been Name and Address. Some of the other children handed her a bit of paper and she copied it into a book. The boy in front of Peter had his bit of paper fastened to his jersey with a safety-pin and Miss Wales had to unfasten it. Peter wondered if his mother should have given him a bit of paper, and had forgotten. But when Miss Wales scowled at him and said Name and Address, he said Peter Cassidy Fourteen Cumbie Street.

'Cumbie Street. Hmph.'

It sounded as if there was something wrong with Cumbie Street, and that puzzled him. He liked Cumbie Street. But he didn't say anything else, and when she told him to find a seat he gripped his schoolbag tightly and found a seat. She had never mentioned putting hands on chair arms, or if she had, he hadn't heard.

The girl who had screamed was standing up waving one arm, and Peter half-stood to see her better. His fingers, on the arm of the chair, were squashed with a piercing pain as the boy next to him shuffled his chair closer. He nearly started to scream, just like the girl, but he knew it would

11

only annoy the teacher. He pulled his hand free and clutched it under his armpit and screwed up his eyes till it got better.

Do what you're told, listen and learn, and don't annoy the teacher, his mother had told him. In the street outside there was the muffled clip-clop of a horse. A shrill male voice yelled, 'Coal, coal,' and Peter, without thinking, joined in the chorus, 'One and fourpence-hapenny coal!' He had been doing it since he could talk.

'Stand up the boy who shouted!' Miss Wales was furious. Peter stood up. Three other boys had shouted as well. In the street, in the world where he lived, everybody did it. He wondered why they hadn't stood up too.

'Come out here, boy!'

He went to the front of the class, still clutching his schoolbag. He had annoyed the teacher.

She had funny glasses with no rims, and her eyes were unnaturally big behind them.

'You will stand facing the board till playtime, boy. What's your name?'

'Peter Cassidy, Miss.'

'Cassidy. Hmph. I'll remember that name. Hurry up. Stand facing the board. And you'd better remember this is a classroom, not a bear garden. I suppose that's the way you behave in Cumbie Street.'

'Yes Miss.'

'Don't be insolent.'

'Yes Miss.'

He hurried to stand right against the blackboard, stiffly, with his bag held to his chest.

'There will be no more noise, or talking,' he heard her warn the class. 'Sit straight up. Put your hands on your heads. And no noise, or you will be severely punished.'

He had never heard the word punished. He thought she meant punched. He put his hands on his head and his schoolbag fell to the floor. He prayed that she hadn't heard it. He was terrified at the thought of being punched by Miss Wales. She was enormous, bigger than his Da, with great big hands. He thought Bobby had probably been right. He didn't like school very much.

After a long time, the bell rang.

'All right,' she said. 'Go out to the playground. Slowly.

Don't run and don't push or you will be severely punished. The boys will wait till all the girls have left. No talking!'

He dared to squint round to see the girls filing out, and then the boys. Miss Wales was still writing something. He picked up his bag and tried to tiptoe after the boys. She turned and glared at him, but didn't say anything. He was free.

The playground was paved in concrete. The school building was on one side, a high brick wall on the second, a long dark open shed on the third and a low wall topped by high iron railings on the fourth. It was full of yelling. None of the girls was there. A group of boys were playing a chasing game. Another group was in a ring, throwing a rubber ball. He saw a boy from his own class, who stood, doing nothing, and then ran a few steps and stopped again, and then ran, playing some game inside his head. Then he saw Bobby, talking to bigger boys, eight-year-olds. He ran to him in relief. Bobby looked embarrassed.

'Beat it, stupid.'

'Zat the wee brother?' one of the boys asked. Bobby just shrugged, and took a bite out of a roll. The piece, the piece! Peter had forgotten it. He pulled a paper bag from his satchel and brought out the roll his mother had packed for him, lightly smeared with margarine and jelly. He bit into it and dropped the paper bag. 'Stupid,' Bobby was exasperated again. 'Pick that up or you'll get the belt!' Peter picked it up in a panic and stuffed it back into the schoolbag.

'Who did you get, son?' the other boy asked quite kindly. The bigger boys didn't seem to mind new kids, it was only brothers who were ashamed of them.

'Miss Wales.'

'Jesus God. Walloper Wales, eh? Has she skelped you yet?'

'No.'

'Just you wait. Oh Jesus God. Eh?'

'Aye, she'll sort you, right enough.' Bobby didn't seem too unhappy at the thought.

'She said she would punch us.'

'Her?' The other boy groaned. 'She could punch Elky Clark, eh?'

Peter knew Elky Clark was a famous boxer. Bobby was right. He hated school.

The days drifted into one another in a dream. He wasn't conscious of whether he had been at school for days or months as the routine became routine and familiar, and letters and numbers began to make sense. They too were new, and wonderful. When he went home, Henrietta would sometimes take him through his reading book, and imitate Miss Wales. Even Bobby laughed.

'Put your hands on your head and sit up straight and read the next bit right or you will be severely punished.'

'I thought she meant punched, Henrietta.'

'You will be severely punched, right on the nose.'

'One two one two, an uppercut.' Bobby shouted, prancing round the kitchen and flailing his fists.

'Less noise, or you will all be kept in and punched on the nose.'

'Punch punch,' Bobby yelled. 'Punch punch punch.'

Peter was in an agony of laughter.

'You shouldn't make fun of your teacher,' Meg said. But her heart wasn't in it. 'She's only doing her best, and a terrible job she has with you hooligans.'

'Punch punch punch!'

'You will all settle down at once and read out loud. Bess had a rabbit in a hut.'

'It got out and the bad dog bit it. Bess was sad and Jill got a bun for her.'

It was miraculously funny. It was never funny in Miss Wales' class, but with Henrietta and Bobby chanting it, Peter couldn't control himself.

'I wish you were my teacher, Henrietta.' He spluttered and sprayed the book.

'Oh, I would punch you harder than Miss Wales.'

'Maybe she will be,' Meg said from her regular stance at the sink. 'Maybe you'll be a teacher when you grow up, eh Henrietta?'

'A teacher!' Bobby was horrified.

'There is nothing wrong with a teacher, good pay and respect, Bobby. Maybe you'll be a teacher too if you work hard at your books.'

'I'm going to be a car driver. Ding-ding, ding-ding.'

'We'll see. I want you all to get on, that's what matters. I want you all to do well.'

Peter chewed over the knowledge that he wouldn't

always be five years old, and it was strange. One day he would be as old as Mother. Old. As he looked at her, sunshine through the kitchen window lit her brown hair and put a line of light down her nose and mouth and chin.

'Mother,' he said in astonishment.

'What, son?'

'You look awful nice.'

'Well. So. Do I, now? Well I never.'

She turned away and scraped hard at a potato, and drew the back of her hand across her eyes. Bobby looked blankly at Peter.

'She does, as well,' Henrietta said briskly, in her teacher's voice. 'Now pay attention, the next bit is very hard.'

'And you'll be severely punched,' Bobby cackled. But the mirth was forced and he had lost interest. As Henrietta and Peter went through the next bit, Bobby apathetically bounced a ball on the floor and tried to land it on the cat. The schoolbook was put away when Andy and John came in from their paper round and went wordlessly to the dresser to hack themselves thick slices of bread.

'Did you get the *Rover*?' Bobby cried. Andy dug into his pocket and threw him a tightly folded paper.

'This is the *Girls' Own Paper*,' Bobby wailed.

'That's for Henrietta, John's got your *Rover* all right.'

'His *Rover*?' John protested. 'It's mine. Oh, all right, you can read it for a wee while.' Bobby fell on the *Rover* and buried himself in the Merry Mac joke page.

'You didn't . . . *take* these comics,' Meg said.

'No, no, mother, you could never get away wi' that. Mister Convery lets me have the extras. Well, I had to pay for the *Girls' Own Paper*.'

'Oh, Andy,' Henrietta protested.

'Och, it comes out my wages.' Andy waggled his head cockily.

'You shouldn't, Andy,' said Meg. 'But it's a very kind thought.'

'Oh yes, Andy,' said Henrietta. 'Thank you very much. I'll *always* read the *Girl's Own Paper*, even when I'm a woman.'

'A lot of pansy stuff,' Bobby dismissed it. 'Stupid lassies at school.'

'Sawright,' Andy said generously. 'Quite good, for lassies.'

'Oh aye, sawright.' Bobby eagerly agreed with his big brother. 'St Hilda's, but. Sounds like a Fenian school.'

'Bobby, I will not have that word spoken in this house.'

'What's a Fenian, Mother?' Peter asked.

'Fenian is a very disagreeable word that some people apply to Roman Catholics, and it's not nice. They are Christians the same as ourselves, but they go to a different church.'

'They go to the Chapel,' Bobby added.

'That's right,' Andy said. 'The pineapple.'

'Am I a Fenian, Mother?'

'No, you are not, you're the same as your father and me and your brothers and sister, and I don't want you using that word.'

'Bobby said . . .' Peter saw Bobby's fist clenching, and stopped, and Meg looked quickly from one to the other.

'Bobby says more than his prayers, and we'll hear no more of it. Don't eat too much of that bread, boys, or you'll spoil your appetites.'

The thing would straighten itself out when the child was old enough to understand. It must be perplexing to grow up in a house where he and his sister were Cassidys and his father and brothers were Masons – his mother a Mason for that matter. But plenty of families were in the same boat, especially with the war only eight years over and all those fathers destroyed and women left with children and lucky if they could find another man to start another family. But even without the war, in the midst of life we are in death.

Her own Paul had survived the war unhurt, to be smashed to death by a motorbus in the vigour of his youth. She still sometimes wondered, but always suppressed the thought, if she had taken on too much with Andrew and his three motherless boys, young Andy hardly thirteen years younger than herself. But the purpose of life was to get on with it, and accept it, and make it better for all of them.

'How was school today, kid?' Andy was asking.

'All right,' said Peter. 'Just the same.'

'Punch punch punch.' Bobby, still reading Merry Mac's joke page, giggled reminiscently.

'Anybody punches you, kid, you let me know.'

16

Andy was a good boy, even if he wasn't too clever at his books. He could be better if he was only interested, he was bright enough at other things. The trouble with Bobby was that he was too near Peter in age and he couldn't help pick-pick-picking at the child. He would grow out of it. I'm as bad, always pick-pick-picking at myself, she thought, thinking thinking thinking all the time, wrapped up in my own mind. Half the time I don't hear what's going on round about me.

'What was that, Andy?' she asked.

'I said it'll be great to chuck it next year.'

'Chuck what? Not the school.'

'I'll be fourteen.'

'That doesn't mean you have to leave school. You want to make something of yourself.'

'I can get a right job in Convery's, serve in the shop, Mr Convery says it's all right.'

'Oh, Mr Convery would say it's all right. All right, getting one of my boys to do his work for him for next to nothing. You can do better than that for yourself, Andrew, with a proper schooling, a clever boy like you.'

'Me? Clever?'

'Yes, you, clever. Look at that toy fort you made for John and Bobby, do you call that stupid?'

'Och, that was only a wee . . . I just did that for fun.'

'Your father and I will talk about it. About school.'

'Awright.' A year was a long way off. But even as Meg promised to discuss it with his father, she could see the discussion as trouble.

# 3

The real trouble about discussing anything important with Andrew senior was that there was no trouble; because there was no discussion. It wasn't that Andrew was immovable. He moved constantly.

Lying in the box bed in the kitchen, with the curtains closed, Henrietta was supposed to be asleep, but even when her mother and stepfather talked in low voices, the buzz would steadily bring her awake and sometimes alert. This time they were discussing something less important, but important to Henrietta, because Henrietta had decided she would like to kill Miss Wales.

So had Andrew.

'I'll kill the bitch,' he said.

'Now you don't mean that, Andrew.'

'She should be in jail. A teacher. Hitting a kid with a stick.'

'It is certainly no proper way to behave.'

'She should get a dose of her own medicine. I'll fix her barrow, let me tell you.'

'You can't do anything violent, Andrew, it would be quite wrong.'

'Are you not worried about it?'

'Oh, I am, I think it is just terrible, a child of that age, his wee hand is still swollen.'

'He must have done something to deserve it.'

'Yes, he was talking. Is a baby of five supposed to sit like . . . like a stooky for hours on end?'

'He must have done something worse than that.'

'What if he did? What are you to think of a grown woman, and an educated woman at that, striking a tiny child with a blackboard pointer?'

'Och, she would never hit him with a pointer. It must be against the regulations.'

'There's no reason wee Peter would invent such a story. And I saw his hand.'

'Och, you know what kids are, they'll say anything, Meg.'

'I don't think the child was saying anything but the truth.'

'Anyway, least said soonest mended, Meg.'

'A minute ago you were going to kill her.'

'It's you that told me to do nothing about it.'

'I only said we couldn't do anything violent.'

'It's the same thing.'

'We can't just let it go as if it didn't matter.'

'What else can we do? I don't want to get into any trouble.'

'Maybe you could talk to the headmaster.'

'Huh. You know what they're like. They take care of their own. They'll never admit anything. Anyway, I can't miss my work to go to some school.'

'There's your dinner hour, the school's only ten minutes from the stickyard.'

'I would look sweet, chapping at his door in my dungarees.'

'It isn't much to do for a child that's been cruelly beaten.'

'You think I don't do enough for them?'

'I never said that, Andrew, you're very good to them.'

'Well, it's only right. I mean I gave you and the kids a home, kids need a father. I've never complained, have I?'

'No, Andrew, you're very good.'

Henrietta, fully awake, couldn't make it out. She knew she had lived in this house all her life, and so had Peter, and Da and the boys had only moved in when Da married Mother. She couldn't understand how he could say that he had given her a home. But adults had funny ways of saying things.

'Well,' said Andrew, 'It's time for bed if I've got an early start.'

'Are you starting earlier tomorrow, then?'

'No, but it's early enough, God knows.'

'Very well, Andrew, I'll just bank the fire and do your boots for the morning.'

As she slid towards sleep again, Henrietta rehearsed her resentment of the boot business. It was all right for her mother to polish Da's boots. A wife promised to love, honour and obey. But a stepsister never promised anything, and she hated having to join Meg every evening, or sometimes rising early in the morning, to polish the boys' boots too. It was woman's work, her mother said. Everything that men didn't want to do was woman's work. She

19

embraced her familiar dream of living in a big house, with a room of her own instead of a box-bed in the kitchen with her parents in the other box-bed. She drifted from there to the other dream of being one of the girls at St Hilda's, with a study, and adventures with the other girls, and laughing at Bessie Bunter, and no boys with dirty boots anywhere.

She was awakened half-an-hour before the boys, to help with the boots while Mother gave Da his breakfast and made up his midday piece to take to the stickyard. Da said nothing, which was usual. Mother, who usually had plenty to say, or would often sing to herself, was silent too; not angry-silent, but thinking her own thoughts.

Meg supervised Peter in washing his hands and face, and unobtrusively examined his right hand as she held it under the tap. The swelling was well down, but she had to control herself tightly to avoid mentioning the thing again. Least said soonest mended, maybe, in the case of the child. Best that he should forget it if he could. He hadn't even cried. He was a strange wee creature, Peter. Her heart ached for him.

As soon as the children were out of the door, she washed and changed into her good dress and shoes and tidied her hair and put her coat on, then sat impatiently for fully twenty minutes so as not to arrive at the school when children were still about in the playgrounds. If they saw her they would only be embarrassed. But it was still barely after nine when she found the headmaster's office and knocked at his door.

Mr Manderson was a florid overweight man in his forties, with broken veins across his cheeks and his nose. A man with a quick temper, Meg judged, and groped for the word she wanted. Choleric. She loved words and enjoyed finding the right one. But he was nice enough, and came round to place a chair for her. She had been tight-clenched and nervous. Now she found herself calm and easy. So he had an eye for the women too, this Mr Manderson, and if she wasn't a raving beauty she was still young enough and not ugly and she recognised the look he gave her, and it gave her the upper hand.

'And what can I do for you, Mrs Mason?'

'My little boy has just started school, Mr Manderson. Peter Cassidy.'

'Cassidy?'

'I was Mrs Cassidy in my first marriage.'

'Of course.'

A girl from the Highlands, or the Islands, by the voice. They were often pretty but usually simple. Maybe hysterical too. He hated hysterical women, and he got plenty. He was not over-fond of parents of any kind because they always meant trouble.

'The boy is in the class of a Miss Wales.'

'Yes. Miss Wales. A very good teacher, very experienced.'

'I cannot judge of that, though he seems to be doing well with his reading and his counting, it's true.'

'We do our best, we do our best.' Manderson grew jovial.

'Yesterday, she struck Peter on the hand with the blackboard pointer.'

'Never, never, Mrs . . . Mason. A . . . a playful tap to call his attention. Their minds do wander.'

'No, it was not a playful tap. She made him hold out his hand and struck him on the palm with her full force. With the blackboard pointer.'

Christ, there was nothing hysterical about this one.

'The boy told you that?'

'Who else would tell me?'

'Children do exaggerate.'

'That is true. I did myself as a child.'

'Well . . .'

'They even tell straightforward lies, Mr Manderson, I know that, and I don't suppose my own are different from any others. But I had the evidence, of the state of his hand when he came home, and it was surely brutally beaten.'

The woman was so calm and reasonable that Manderson was slightly alarmed, floundering in the effort to turn her aside.

'He may have been attacked by some other children. There has been some bullying in the school. We do our best, but we can't see everything.'

'I think that is quite absurd, Mr Manderson. Yon swelling was not the work of little boys, it was coldly and deliberately inflicted, and I am as sure as sure that it was done by the teacher.'

'I can't believe such a thing of Miss Wales. She's been with us for ten years.'

'All that time. And all these children. And never a

complaint before, in all these years.'

'Never a complaint of this kind. I just can't believe it, Mrs Mason.'

'And what she said worries me too. She called the boy to the front of the class and left him standing by the board for some time, and then she said, "Get out your arithmetic books while I thrash this boy."'

'I don't quite understand.'

'I'm saying that that is not the kind of thing a child would invent. And I'm saying that a person who would say that is not what you would call a kindly person. In fact, I'm saying you would almost think she was enjoying it, putting fear into the child as well as beating him. That she was sadistic.'

'Seditious? I don't understand.'

'No matter. I know that naughty children are punished, but I will not have this, I will not have my child used like this. He is never beaten at home, and he behaves well enough there. And I will not have it, Mr Manderson.'

'I'm really perplexed, Mrs Mason. I'm quite flabbergasted. But there must be some exaggeration in the story. I just can't believe that Miss Wales, a teacher of her experience, would ever strike a child with a pointer.'

'Well, I have said what I came to say and I am satisfied.'

She stood up. Manderson, enormously relieved, hurried round to open the door for her. His ordeal was not quite over.

'The only thing,' she said, halfway through the door, 'is that if Miss Wales has never done this before, she would be wise not to do it again, either.'

And she was gone before he could answer.

As she passed through the school gate, Meg looked round the playground with distaste, at the grim grey building and the high walls and the iron railings. What were the railings for? To keep the animals in, or to keep human beings out? She remembered the schoolhouse on Duna, with the hill and the heather for a playground, and old Mr McAllister, who would reduce the rowdiest child to silence and obedience with no more than a wave of his hand and a lift of his eyebrow. Glasgow was no place to bring up children, with the dirty streets and the concrete and the prison bars. But then, Duna had memories worse than a cruel woman with a pointer in her hand. Meg put them from her.

22

For a moment she felt weak. Her own ordeal was over, and it had not been the ordeal she had feared. She couldn't believe she had done it, that she had said everything she would have wanted to say, had never lifted her voice or lost her control. She found herself shaking. She breathed deeply and lengthened her stride and the weakness gave way to a sense of exhilaration. She had done it and maybe she had made the world a better place, a bit. She realised she was passing the road that led to the stickyard, and for a moment she was tempted to go and tell Andrew, to share her triumph. But she knew, as she was tempted, that she could never tell him because it would diminish him. He could never have the courage to face the headmaster out, he still had his boyhood loathing and fear of schools, and it would never do for him to know that she could do what he could not. She had nobody she could ever tell.

And the headmaster didn't even know the word sadistic. She had only read it, had never heard it spoken, but she was only an ignorant housewife. She had always thought a teacher would have read everything, would know all the words in the language. Maybe it was simple ignorance of the world that had given her that idea.

Her elation changed to a heavy sense of frustration. There was so much she wanted to do, maybe there were even so many things she *could* do, instead of cooking and washing and sewing and trying to do the best for two families. If she had never had Henrietta, the whole of life might have been different.

She was horrified at herself. She loved Henrietta, she adored the girl, she saw herself and the father in her face, she often felt like weeping just at the sight of her, for joy.

You think too much, Meg Macrae, you should think yourself lucky to have what you have.

She decided to make stew and doughballs with thick gravy for the evening meal. Andrew and the kids loved it.

When Miss Wales obeyed the summons to the Head's office at lunchtime she expected a friendly chat about things in general. She was stunned by his cold fury. She denied everything. She explained that the Cassidy child was a born troublemaker and a born liar, and Irish Catholic

23

stock at that, and just what could be expected from that kind of background in Cumbie Street.

'I spent this morning with his mother. She's a Highland Presbyterian, and she's harder than granite.'

'Huh. They're not much different.'

'I would swear that woman has never told a lie in her life, and she's brought her family up the same way.'

'I never met a kid in all my years teaching who wouldn't lie like a trooper, Headmaster.'

'I'm sorry I didn't ask you in to meet her. She would have put the fear of death in you. She was as cold and calm as a prosecutor in a murder trial, and she knows what evidence is all about.'

'You don't believe this story, Headmaster?'

'It doesn't matter what I believe, Miss Wales. That woman could make mincemeat of you in front of any jury in the country. And I think if you look sideways at that kid again, she'll have your job. You'll be in the street. Just you make sure she never has to come back to this school again, that's all. Jesus Christ, she would have my job as well.'

'I know my job, Headmaster. I'm not afraid of any of these Cumbie Street scruff.'

'Scruff. Aha. She uses words I had to look up in the dictionary. Did you know you were sadistic?'

'There's no such word.'

'Oh aye. We'd better all just watch our step. And if you come across any kids called Mason, watch your step with them as well.'

'Why?'

'They're another litter the same tigress is defending. Now not another word, I've heard enough.'

Henrietta went secretly to her mother while she was cleaning the front room.

'Were you in school this morning, Mother?'

'Why would you ask that, what made you think that?'

'Jenny Arbuckle said she saw you in the corridor.'

'Maybe it was another woman with the same coat, Henrietta.'

'Oh.' Henrietta was downcast.

'Now it's nobody's business where I go when you're at

school, Henrietta, nobody's business at all, not even your Da's.'

'No, Mother.'

'Oh, Henrietta, wherever I was this morning, I had a lovely morning. Oh, I did enjoy it fine.'

'Oh, good, Mother.' Henrietta's face crunched up in delight and complicity. Meg hugged her tight.

'Oh, I love my children, Henrietta.'

'I know, Mother, I know. Oh, good!'

# 4

The house was one of three doors on the second storey landing. It was a kitchen, with a window overlooking the back court, and a front room overlooking Cumbie Street, and between the two rooms a dark lobby with the coal bunker and the lavatory. To Meg, it was a miserable cramped little box. To Peter it was as big as any house he had known, even big enough to hide in. He was standing at the front room window staring down at Cumbie Street and discovering that there was something he could do with his eyes so that the picture turned vague and blurred, and then when he brought his eyes back it got sharp and distinct again. His mother poked her head into the room.

'Are you all right, Peter?'

'Yes. I can make my eyes go funny,'

'Can you now? Here's some lemonade and a biscuit.'

'Oh good.'

He took the glass of lemonade and a biscuit with one corner broken off, and stared out of the window again. Meg looked at him and wondered what went on in his head, but knew she could never know. She went back to the kitchen to talk to Annie Miller. She had taken him with her on her weekly trip to the Public Library, where he sat absolutely silent staring fascinated at the thousands of books while she looked through the shelves, and on the way home she sent him into McKean's for a bag of broken pastry. It was the cheapest way to buy biscuits, but it was a kind of rule that the bargain bags were bought by children, whoever might eat them after they left the shop. Then they had met Annie Miller on the way upstairs from the close and she had come in for a cup of tea and a crack.

'Don't know how you can find the time, Meg,' Annie said complacently. 'I can hardly get a minute to look at the paper, and there's nothing but bad news in that.'

It was true Annie could never find time. Always in a hash. She wore an overall even when she went out for messages, there had been no time to take it off and put on a coat. Instead of walking she moved at a despairing shuffle because the kids, or her man, would be home at any minute and there was nothing ready for them. She carried a duster hanging out of one overall pocket, and a packet of five Woodbine in the other. She smoked. Meg had never seen a woman smoking until she met Annie. The right-hand pocket of the overall was full of little holes where she had nipped a cigarette and stuck the dowt away still smouldering. Her house was only a single-end, a kitchen with no front room, but there was never time to clean it up properly. She spent her days shuffling round it waving her duster.

Meg put an extra saucer on the table as an ash tray. The Cat leapt lazily on to Annie's lap and fell asleep.

'He never does that with me,' said Meg.

'You haveny enough room for him, Hen. Oh, it must be nice to be thin. I canny abide the creatures, but they make a convenience of me. That's right, Pussy, Liberty Hall come one come all.'

'We always had cats on the Island, he makes me feel like home. But never any as silly as that. Look at his tail, if you turn your back for a minute he sticks it in the fire.'

'Maybe he thinks he's a poker, do you think you're a poker, Pussy? Oh, this'll never pay the rent, Meg, I should be in there scrubbing hell out the place, except I've lost the scrubber, I put it on the windowsill to dry and it fell into the back court. Never saw it again. I think there's something down there that eats brushes.'

'Och, stay just where you are and have your tea in peace, you can't be at it all the time, Annie.'

Annie's company was soothing, for all she was feckless and raggle-taggle. She reminded Meg of Henrietta McGillivray on the Isle of Duna, and her scatter of bairns and the work never done. She found herself smiling, remembering what Billie McGillivray, Henrietta's husband, had said to her when she was just a girl.

A man should never marry a girl from the Islands. He can take her to Glasgow and get a wee house four stairs up in the sky, and when he comes home for his dinner she'll tell him it's not ready because she had to feed the hens and milk the cow and hoe the turnips.

But there had always been plenty of laughs in the Mcgillivray house. Her smile gave way to a small sigh.

'What's this?' Annie picked up one of her books. 'Kipps? Is it some kind of fish?'

'No, it's H. G. Wells, he writes odd stories about the

27

future and flying through space, but I don't know this one. Oh, I could never get by without a bit of time for reading.'

'If I laid a book down next door I would never find it again. You would never think you could lose things in one wee room. Bert's top teeth went missing for two days last week, he had to live on mince and mashed tatties.'

'If it wasn't for books I would have died when I was in service. Working like a slavey six days a week for six shillings. She was a widow woman and her man had been a schoolteacher. Books by the hundreds all round the house, it was just sublime.'

'It sounds like an awful lot of stuff to dust.'

'Oh aye, you would have loved it, Annie.' They laughed together.

'I had a rare one last week by a man called Frood, all about dreams.'

'Oh, I had a dream book, they gave it away wi' *Peg's Paper*, it was a real pantomime. I can't right mind where I put it away.'

'It seems there is all sorts . . . I mean there are all sorts of things we don't want to know, and we push them to the bottom of our minds and they come out all mixed up when we're dreaming. I believe it, there's a lot of funny things in my own mind.'

'If you dream about a wedding it means a death.'

'Oh, tommyrot, Annie, that's no better than reading teacups.'

'Oh, I believe in teacups.'

'Aye, well, maybe I do too. There are more things in heaven and earth.'

At the front room window Peter recognised Henrietta in a group of girls playing ropes, and at the same time heard the doorbell. He ran to open the door.

'It's Auntie Alice, Mother,' he announced. 'Can I go out to play?'

'Alice! Come away in, the tea's just on. All right, Peter, but don't you be crossing the main road.'

Andrew's sister Alice came into the kitchen smiling her wee smile, eyes flicking round the room; like an auctioneer, Meg always thought, or maybe a bailiff. She sat in Andrew's easy chair, her handbag clutched tightly against her stomach.

'You shouldn't bother, Meg.'

'It's either that or pour it down the sink, Alice.'

'Here, I'll away and let you get on with your visitor,' Annie said, but standing behind Alice, Meg shook her head, and Annie added, 'after I've finished this cup.'

'Is that a new teapot?'

'Aye, Woolworth's best, Alice. It makes a good strong cup.' Meg took out a good cup and saucer for her sister-in-law.

In Cumbie Street, Peter stood and watched, rapt, at the whirling skipping ropes, a girl at each end working them while the others dashed in and out of them in turn. It was dazzling, like staring at a fast river from a bridge, and it looked impossible. Henrietta was one of the girls swinging the ropes, one in each hand, swinging them in opposite directions, flushed and panting.

'Is it your wee brother?' one of the girls asked. Henrietta glanced round without breaking her rhythm.

'Hello, Peter.'

'Hello.'

'Do you want a shot, son?' the first girl asked him, as she bobbed up and down to time her run into the ropes.

'They're too fast.'

She shot into the whistling ropes and out again at the other end, and ran round to him and took him by the hand.

'We'll try pavey-waveys,' she shouted. The ropes stopped and the girls stood gasping. She led him into the middle and held him by both hands.

'It's all right, Peter.' She smiled down into his face. She had a short blue dress and long black hair caught back in a blue ribbon. She hopped and half-carried him up and down with her. The rope began to swish back and forward beneath their feet.

'Right over this time,' she shouted. The rope swung over their heads and they jumped together as it came down. He didn't look at it. He gripped her hands and looked up into her face.

'Faster, faster!' The buildings beyond her face were jerking and blurring and he jumped heroically to keep in time. She stopped, a bead of sweat running down her nose. He heard the other girls cheering.

'Well done, Peter.' She stooped to hug him, and without

thinking he kissed her on the lips.

'Ooh! Jeannie's got a boyfriend, Jeannie's got a boy-friend . . .'

'Look at the wee jessie.' It was Bobby's voice. 'Playin' wi' the lassies!'

Peter was still looking up at Jeannie. She was nice.

A shouting match broke out as the girls shrilly ordered Bobby and his pals to go and play somewhere else.

'Cissie ropes,' one of the boys shouted, and the others took it up as a chant.

'All right, have a shot,' Jeannie screamed at them.

'Cissie ropes!'

'You're a crapper!' Jeannie had turned from a soft dark-haired girl into a warrior. 'Come on, let us see you. French ropes. Come on.'

The double ropes started to swing at a terrible speed. Girls bunched at one end and rushed through. One of Bobby's pals stood beside Henrietta, jerking back and forward, and finally made a run for the centre. One rope caught him on the shins and the other across the neck. There was a scream of female joy.

'Steal the ropes!' Bobby shouted. The boys advanced warily. Jeannie stepped forward with fists clenched.

'Just try it, you.'

The wounded hero rubbed his neck, lips clamped shut.

'Aw, who wants their rotten ropes?'

He walked away and the others backed away after him, some of them with tongues stuck bravely out.

'Are you comin'?' Bobby asked Peter.

'All right.'

'Don't bother, Peter,' Henrietta said. But he shrugged. Bobby had never asked him to play with him before. He had only a momentary regret as he heard the swish of the ropes again, and the shouts of the girls.

The boys wandered into the Gallowgate, aimless, looking for trouble.

'We'll run across the road,' one of them said.

'Mother says I've not to cross the road,' Peter objected.

'Aw, "Mother says, Mother says." It's easy.'

Peter took it for granted that anybody who ran across the tramlines when his mother had told him not to would be mangled by a car. They lined up on the edge of the pavement, and the boy with the sore neck suddenly shouted, 'Me!' and bolted across to the other side. There were no trams anywhere near, not even a bus or a lorry. He reached the other side and jumped up and down. Bobby looked both ways and then ran, yelling all the way. Peter was caught in the excitement. He flung himself off the pavement but was dragged back by another boy.

'Dummy, there's a caur!'

'Oh.' As the tramcar clanked past, the driver shook his fist at them.

'Right' said the big boy, and ran. Peter scurried behind him. It was wonderful. He was on the other pavement and nothing had happened.

Bobby ran back first. Peter looked up and down and ran after him. He tripped on a granite sett and fell flat on the first tram track. His head was ringing and he couldn't breathe.

He could hear the angry clanging of a bell.

Meg was glad of Annie's company during Alice's visit. She had never been able to feel comfortable with her sister-in-law. Conversation fell dead in Alice's presence.

'Weather's quite nice.'

'Oh aye,' said Annie. 'There's always plenty of it.'

'I like it better, this, than yon rain.'

'Oh aye, aye.'

'Mind you, the rain's good for the farmers,' Alice said thoughtfully.

'Oh aye, you're right there,' said Annie. 'It fair washes the mud off their boots.'

Meg had her back turned to shield the bag of broken biscuits, groping for a few reasonable specimens to put on a plate, and trying not to laugh.

'Mind you,' Annie said, 'See snow? I cannot be doin' wi' snow.'

'Well, it's not the time of year for it.'

'Ah, but see yon Yukon? They get it regular. Oh, it would drive me melancholy. See my man? He gets frostbite if I leave the door open.'

'Oh.'

'See in the Yukon? His nose would break right off before your eyes.'

31

'It must be cold there, right enough.'

'A wee biscuit, Alice?' Meg proffered the plate, and Alice looked at it doubtfully. There was only one entirely whole biscuit in the collection.

'Wee Bobby tripped and dropped the bag when he was coming up the stairs.'

'Ach, they'll be broken worse than that by the time they get to your belly,' Annie said brutally. 'Aye, I think I can manage another cup, Meg.'

Alice was visibly irritated that Annie wasn't leaving, but once the signal had passed, Meg knew she could depend on her feckless neighbour to stick it out to the end.

Alice abandoned the confusing topic of Yukon weather and scanned the kitchen again.

'You've got some nice things, Meg.'

'Well, I wouldn't say it was Buckingham Palace.'

'Away you go,' Annie said. 'The King would be delighted wi' it. Imagine the coal it takes to heat a place that size.'

'I don't think the King's worried about things like coal,' Alice said severely.

'Well, some poor bugger's got to worry about it.'

A bad word. Meg was privately delighted. Alice was still pricing the bits and pieces in the kitchen.

'Of course, the Com Pen would be a help,' she said.

Oh? So that was all Alice was after. Now she was carefully fingering the piping along the arm of Andrew's chair, to show that she was concentrating on that and was just talking idly.

'Of course, they say money can't bring anybody back to life.' She sighed heavily. 'It must have been a shock, losing your first hubby like that.'

'Aye, it was.'

'But the Com Pen's always a wee help at a time like that.'

'Not enough to notice.'

'Oh?' Alice was sharp. 'Was it not all that much, eh?'

'No.'

'I've heard of widows getting hundreds of pounds.'

'Is that a fact?'

'Oh, it's a known fact.'

'Oh well.'

'I've heard of some widows,' Annie said gravely, 'that hardly got a run round the table and a kick at the cat.'

There was a hammering at the door and Meg hurried to let Peter in. Blood was pouring from his nose and there was a sticky line of it down his jersey.

'I fell.'

'Oh Peter, your poor wee nose.'

'I can't stand blood!' Alice wailed. Meg, who had been about to whisk Peter to the sink, brought him instead to the fireplace, beside Alice. Alice pushed her chair back and started up. Peter turned and looked at her.

'How can you not stand blood when you're full of it?'

She backed away twittering.

'Eh, well, it's been nice, Meg, I'll really have to away, tell Andrew I was asking for him.'

She blundered out, and Meg and Annie listened till they could hear her feet down the stairs.

'My God, she's a warmer!' Annie guffawed. 'Is she wi' Scotland Yard?'

Meg was kneeling by the unprotesting Peter, sponging his face.

'I was running across the main road,' he said.

'I told you not to!'

'I'm sorry, I'll not do it again, Mother.'

'You'd better not.' She started to laugh. 'But you couldn't have done it at a better time.'

Annie roared with laughter. Peter couldn't understand grown-up people at all.

# 5

It was some weeks before Peter became aware that Miss Wales had stopped using the blackboard pointer as a weapon. He had not been the only victim, but now there was none. He was able to put his whole mind to his books.

There wasn't even any punishment for Sadie Gourlay when she committed a deadly sin. It was a Friday, and the lessons had somehow petered out, and Miss Wales did something quite unusual, asking the class if anybody could tell a story. Sadie had her hand up, snapping her fingers madly. He couldn't snap his fingers. He had his hand under the desk, twisting them in vain and getting no sound. He could see Miss Wales looking to the ceiling and inviting Sadie to tell her story, since there were no other offers.

'It's a story about Pat and Mick.'

'Yes.'

'Well, Pat and Mick were walkin' on the road and they fell down a stank, and here, a wee dog came along and shit on them . . .'

'Go back to your seat!'

'I haveny finished the story, Miss.'

'We don't want to hear the story. Go back to your seat.'

Peter wondered how Sadie could be so stupid. There were words nobody said, and she had said one of the worst ones. But she didn't get the pointer on her hand. There was something about Sadie, something wild and reckless. She wore white knickers. He had seen them and she hadn't cared.

'Does anybody know the alphabet?' Miss Wales demanded. Peter put up his hand very cautiously, after weeks of not trying to call attention to himself.

'You think you know the alphabet, Peter Cassidy?' The idea was ridiculous.

'Yes Miss.' He recited the alphabet.

'Who taught you that?'

'I don't know, Miss.'

'You didn't make it up by yourself, boy!'

'Maybe I heard my sister saying it, Miss.'

He could feel a quiver in his stomach, and his eyes strayed to the pointer. He had done something wrong again.

34

'Very good.' She clamped her jaws. 'Very good. You should all know the alphabet as well as Peter Cassidy.'

She wasn't going to give him the pointer. But she was still the same Miss Wales.

'And what is the alphabet, Peter Cassidy?'

'It's all the letters, Miss.'

'All the letters what?'

'I don't know, Miss.'

'In the right order, boy! In the right order! Everybody knows that, you stupid boy. Now, what is the alphabet?'

'All the letters in the right order, Miss.'

'Sit down.'

He felt Joe Henderson jabbing a finger into his back, heard his hoarse whisper.

'Teacher's pet.'

'Was that you talking, Peter Cassidy?'

'No, Miss.'

'Who was it?'

'I don't know, Miss.'

'Teacher's pet.'

When the bell rang at three o'clock and they escaped, Joe Henderson trotted along behind him, jabbing him in the back and wailing 'Teacher's pet, teacher's pet.' It went on right across the playground and into the street and there, safely away from supervision, Joe danced up and down and yelled at him. Peter looked round carefully to check that no teachers could see them.

'You leave Peter alone,' Sadie Gourlay shouted.

'You shurrup. Teacher's pet, teacher's pet.' Jab jab. Peter punched him on the nose and Joe staggered back with blood showing.

'I'll tell the teacher!'

'If you tell the teacher you'll get another one.'

Joe ran away, wailing, 'Haw Maw, Haw Maw, Haw Maw.'

Other boys crowded round Peter as he walked away, thumping him on the back and saying the Champion, the Champion. It irritated him. He hadn't wanted to punch Joe Henderson, and his fingers were still sore from the impact. But he began to believe them. He had done it, like Elky Clark or somebody in the pictures.

Somebody shouted, 'Here's Joe's Maw!'

In the distance, a big woman with hair askew was coming at speed, with Joe's hand in hers, and his feet dragging as she pulled him along. At Peter's side was the wooden fence that walled off the old coup. He squeezed through a gap and ran in terror to the other side of the coup. When he got to Cumbie Street he found his way into the wash-house in the back court and hid there till it was dark and his mother was frantic.

'Where were you?'

'Out.'

'Come straight home from school in future.'

'All right.'

Fighting was wrong. As long as Mrs Henderson hadn't tracked him to his home, and he was safe, he would never do it again.

As long as Joe left him alone.

He would never tell his mother. His memory of the fight confused him. On one hand it was quite good to think about it, to treasure the instant of triumph when he had conquered the baddie. On the other hand, he knew how it felt to have his nose bashed and bleeding and he could feel Joe Henderson's shock and pain as if it had been his own. What surprised him most was that the fight completely changed his life with Bobby. On the next morning, he walked to school with Bobby and Henrietta. Andy and John always vanished to find their own friends. Even Henrietta left to join a group of girls, and walk up to the school with them, talking and whispering and laughing about the mysteries girls laughed about.

Bobby always walked too fast, and Peter had to trot to keep up with him. But as they caught up with three of Bobby's friends, the confident sophisticated eight-year-olds, one of them put a hand on Peter's head and ruffled his hair.

'The wee champ, eh? Best wee fighter in the school, wee Peter.'

Bobby hadn't heard about the fight, but he held his peace while his friends re-enacted the scene, and began to enjoy the second-hand pride of being the brother of a champion. Peter was buoyed up by his first feeling of importance. Two of them carried him the last hundred yards to school by the famous Fireman's Lift, hands linked for the hero's seat, and he willingly demonstrated the Killer Punch; fist clenched with the thumb stuck through between the index and middle fingers. It was well known that this would floor the biggest opponent. He was formally appointed Mascot, and even after the great fight was forgotten, the habit lingered, and Bobby took the part of his proud protector and actually took him out to play with the Big Yins and introduced him to the adventurers of the wider world. Bobby always laughed first at the funny things Peter said, even if Peter didn't know they were funny.

It was a different life Bobby and his pals lived, furtive and aggressive, finding excitement and sometimes terror among the tenements and the back streets and the closes. Meg often worried about the grime and the congestion of Glasgow and yearned for a place with an open sky and a bit of green where children could grow up decently and play the games she had played on Duna. But to them, the tenements were the known world. If they ever pined for something different, it was the Wild West, but they made up their own. Peter learned the trick of being both cowboy and horse, galloping through the streets with shouts of Whoa and Gee-up and slashing at his own calf with a rolled-up newspaper. When they played the other horse game, Bobby was horse, and automatically claimed Peter as his rider. The combination of the stocky, belligerent Bobby and his featherweight stepbrother was made for victory as two horses drew themselves together in a shoulder charge and the riders tried to pull each other off. Bobby and Peter were champions. Instead of watching Bobby warily for the next trick he might play, Peter was in complicity with him against Meg, because what they did in the streets was not for parents' ears.

Sometimes they relented and played with the girls in Cumbie Street, in games that swung from one pavement across to the other. Peter's conscience was clear about these. He liked Statues. One of the gang stood in the middle of the street, and turned his back for an instant while everybody else tried to run across and then had to freeze when he turned round again, crouched or balanced on one leg. 'Maggie moved, she's oot!'

*Charlie Charlie may I cross the water?*
Peter was quick at picking up the chants.
*Not today but yes tomorrow.*
*How cold is your water?*
*Too cold for you.*
*How deep is your water?*
*Put your hand in and see.*
Dabble hands in imaginary water.
*Oh I've lost my golden ring!*
Mad dash to the other side while Charlie tried to catch the laggards. When the girl Jeannie was playing Charlie she would sometimes deliberately let Peter escape safely. At other times she would swoop on him and throw her arms round him and pick him up.

When somebody had a ball, the boys liked King, because it gave them the chance to throw the ball deliberately at a girl and even hurt her, or cannon into a girl during the mêlée. Some of the girls were just as eager for aggression.

When there was no ball, it was always a girl who shouted for *Bee Baw Babbity*, and the boys always shouted in disgust – but they always ended up playing it, prancing in a ring with a boy or a girl in the middle.

*Bee Baw Babbity, Babbity, Babbity*
*Bee Baw Babbity, a lassie or a wee laddie*
*I wouldnae ha'e a lassie-oh, lassie-oh, lassie-oh*
*I wouldnae ha'e a lassie-oh*
*I'd rather ha'e a wee laddie . . . laddie . . . laddie . . .*

And the boys chanted apathetically and contemptuously as they waited for the girl in the middle to pick one to take her place in the middle, and even kiss him if he was clever enough to try to dodge her but fail.

'Good job she picked him and no' me. I wouldnae let her kiss me. Yugh.' The boy who spoke would sneer coldly, bright eyes darting about for his chance.

Away from the girls, the gang would roam the streets, aimless marauders in a private war.

When they hunted for cigarette cards they used Peter as the beggar because he was built for it.

'Any cigarette cairds, Mister?' And the man would pull out his cigarettes and take the card from the packet and hand it over. Sometimes, especially if he was drunk, he would add a penny. They combed the area in search for drunk men. When they had individual hoards of cigarette cards they gambled for them.

The game was simple. Two of them faced each other, then one turned his back to slip some cards between his hands, with a face or a blank at the top of the pile. When he turned round again, hands tightly pressed together, the other shouted, 'Face', or 'Blank' and won or lost. But there were tricks in it. If two of the fingers pressed down on the cards were slightly apart, the other gambler might catch sight of the top card and see clearly that it was a blank.

But if the card glimpsed between the fingers wasn't the top card, he had been caught. If he was an old hand he would see through the trick and shout Face.

But if the other gambler was an old hand he would deliberately show a blank between his fingers and have a blank on top too.

And if his opponent knew he was an old hand he would reverse the trick. Bobby explained it all to Peter and Peter's mind reeled. It was like standing in Capaldi's chip shop, between the two mirrors facing each other, and reflections of reflections of reflections running away in each direction to the end of the world. It even had the same frustration as the chip shop, where you knew your reflection was there, but you could never look round your first reflection to see the one behind it. Peter sometimes lay in bed at night trying to think of a way to jump aside so fast that he would catch the other reflections before they could jump out of sight.

He was nervous of mentioning this to Bobby in case it was stupid, but Bobby and his friends were delighted at the idea and had serious discussions about how it could be done, maybe on a very fast horse like Tom Mix's; or a motorbike.

Or a train. Or an aeroplane. They preferred a train because trains were faster. When they watched a train it went past like lightning, but aeroplanes crawled across the sky. Peter got cocky about the way his stupid ideas were earnestly considered by the Elders. He wondered about bananas and water too. He saw that if you put bananas in a paper poke, they stuck out at the top because they were too big for it, but even if you put too much water in a cup it refused to stick out at the top. He had stood doggedly at the sink trying to make water from the tap pile itself up in a heap above the rim of the cup.

When he mentioned this eagerly to the Elders, Charlie Dunn said, 'That's stupid. Water . . . water is water, it's FLAT.'

'What about a fountain?' Bobby demanded, defending his protégé.

'A fountain's different.'

Charlie was the biggest.

'Aye, right enough,' Bobby agreed. 'It's stupid.'

'Ach, he's too wee to know any better,' Charlie dismissed the subject. Peter accepted his failure and his stupidity.

When they were bored they went to another street where they slipped into closes, rang doorbells and ran away. At first Peter was given the safe job of standing near the close as lookout, but even this was so exciting and jittery that he thought he would almost prefer the real thing, and they let him take a chance in a close in Soay Street. As they pelted down the street in flight, Charlie Dunn was laughing and shouting.

'He couldnae even reach the bell, he just kicked the door!'

This was killingly funny and Peter was a wee hero. Charlie was the boldest of the bold. While the others stayed on ground level, he had the nerve to run up to the first landing and ring two or three bells before he ran down. Once he even swore to run right to the top landing, three flights up, and ring every bell in the building. The gang huddled round the mouth of the close exhilarated and petrified. He crept into the close and upstairs; or tried to creep. His tacketty boots rang and echoed on the stone stairs. They waited, looking round fearfully for passers-by who would know they were up to something. They waited and waited.

There came the sound of Charlie's boots clattering on the stairs, and his wild yell, possibly of triumph. They bolted. When Charlie caught them up he was disgusted.

'Crowd of crappers!'

'You done it, Charlie.'

'Christ, I got a kick right in the erse. It's bloody sore.'

'Did a man catch you?'

'Naw, a wummin.'

'A wummin kicked Charlie in the erse!' they yelled to one

another. Even the bad words gave Peter a delicious guilty thrill. Playing with the Big Yins was rich with fear. It was worse when they decided to test their nerve running along the walls of a back court and dropping fearlessly to the ground. In the feats of courage, Bobby withdrew his brotherly protection and Peter had to trail at the end of the line. He couldn't force himself to stand upright on a wall, but sat astride it and inched forward while the gang trotted farther and farther away into the dusk. When they had disappeared he realised he couldn't get down, and he thought he might be stuck all night. It was Charlie Dunn who came back and found him and helped him to the ground.

'You're too wee for this game,' Charlie said impatiently. But he added, 'You're right game, though.'

Always at the back of his mind was the thought that the polis might catch them some time, and that his double life would be revealed to his mother. One evening, Charlie proposed a raid on Blaney's fruit shop. They kept baskets of potatoes and turnips and cabbages on the pavement, outside the shop, to attract passing customers, and it would be easy. Peter didn't think it would be easy. Charlie went first, to demonstrate how easy it was. From the corner of Soay Street, twenty yards from the shop, he dashed along the Gallowgate and snatched a potato without breaking stride. Bobby went next, and got away with another. Peter waited to the end. He could see Bobby standing well beyond the gaslit shop window, waving him on. He trotted towards Blaney's, saw Bobby turn and run away, and his courage failed him. He ran past the shop, waving his left hand towards the basket of potatoes, and kept going.

His feet were off the ground. He had been seized from behind and swung in the air. He was swung round and put down, and he was staring up into Mr Blaney's furious face.

'Where is it?' Mr Blaney demanded.

'I never done anything.' He was being shaken. He lost control. He could feel a hot wet stream down one leg. Mr Blaney was confused, but he still had the impetus of his annoyance.

'I'll send the polis to your mother. Away you go.'

Hideously uncomfortable, Peter tried to run away, clutching his wet trousers at the front. They were nearly dry by the time he went home, and he didn't tell Bobby that he had disgraced himself. He sat through tea waiting for heavy footsteps on the landing. They didn't come. After tea he said he was going to bed. Meg looked slightly surprised, but made no objection. He felt that if anything awful did happen, he would be safer tucked in bed in the dark. If he escaped the police this time he would never go out with the Big Yins again.

The next afternoon, when Bobby asked him if he was coming out to play, he dropped his book, jumped up and dutifully followed him.

# 6

On Saturdays they all went to the matinée, but the children went to the Lectric, across the street, and Meg and Andrew went to another one in the middle of the Town. Peter couldn't imagine the Town except as another world where people walked about in good clothes and ate things. While the parents were away, Henrietta made the tea for the others.

The Lectric was a bare brick barn with bench seats, and long before it opened there was a mob of kids at the door yelling and eating and shoving to be first in case the hall filled and there were no seats left. Peter tried to worm his way to the front, but Henrietta always held him back by the hand to prevent him from being trampled. When the door did open the panicky customers filled it like a log-jam. Big Tim the doorman roared and shoved savagely to force them into a line. The line turned back into a squirming mob as soon as his huge hands were withdrawn.

'Maybe we'll not get in, Henrietta!'

'We'll get in.'

When they did get in, every seat seemed to be filled, and Big Tim was still roaring for silence. He picked Peter up by the waist and deposited him in a square hole high in the wall, a shuttered window with a deep sill. He was going to pick up Henrietta too, changed his mind and held his clasped hands for her to step up. He ignored John, who climbed up beside them on his own. High above the crowd, Peter could see everything, with the comforting security of Henrietta's arm round him, see the huge form of Tim striding up and down the aisles, waving a finger, pulling wrestlers apart, roaring for silence. He could see Andy and Bobby sitting in the middle of the crowd, Bobby throwing peanut shells in the air till he saw Big Tim staring at him. The customers began to stamp their feet, Tim roared for quiet. It was the same every Saturday. The lights went out and the pictures began.

The noise didn't matter because the pictures were silent. While other children scuffled and yelped down below, Peter was completely absorbed, in the words as well as the pictures, muttering them to himself as they appeared.

Blake of Scotland Yard.

'BLAKE OF SCOTLAND YARD!' The roar of the crowd, always a second late.

Get Your Hands off that Gold.

'GET YOUR HANDS OFF THAT GOLD!'

Little shadows sometimes shot across the screen; lumps of orange peel or peanuts flying about the hall.

'No monkey nuts!' Big Tim was yelling, as his feet crunched up and down the aisle on a thick carpet of nut shells.

'MIND YOUR BACK – MIND YOUR BACK!' The goodie never noticed baddies creeping up behind him with guns, even when the customers screamed to warn him. Peter was swept into the panic, bobbed up and down while Henrietta tightened her grip, and screamed with the rest.

'SHOOT! SHOOT!'

'No monkey nuts!'

Crunch crunch crunch.

The goodie won in the end and clasped his bride in a long embrace.

'WAH! AWAY YA BIG JESSIE!'

A wedding ceremony. A wedding cake four feet high.

'HAUFERS. HAUFERS. GIVE US HAUFERS!'

They all had an animal lust for sweet cakes, they would have eaten them for every meal.

After the pictures, the Gallowgate was painfully bright with sunshine. Peter would blink and stagger, hanging on to Henrietta's arm among the shifting crowd. Andy and John were now a group of their own.

'Have the tea ready in an hour,' Andy said grandly. 'We'll be back.'

'What! If you don't watch you'll have to make it yourself.'

'What? Away with you.' He swaggered away with John, and with Bobby bobbing and trotting to keep up with them. John looked back with a funny smile and waved his hand.

'You can help me to make the tea, Peter.'

'All right. Where are they going?'

'Oh, away to play at something daft.'

In fact, Henrietta enjoyed having the kitchen to herself and playing housewife, and Peter fetched and carried for

44

her, put knives and forks out in the wrong places and poured milk into the jug. It was his favourite tea, tinned salmon and sliced tomatoes and bits of lettuce, and thin thin slices of bread and margarine cut into triangles. When Peter got bored he sat in his Da's chair and tried to read the *Rover*, a finger running along each line as he spelled the words.

'What's a Mackinaw, Henrietta?'

'A jacket.'

'Why do they not call it a jacket?'

'It's a special jacket called a Mackinaw jacket.'

'Oh. Will I ever know everything as well?'

'I don't know everything, Peter.'

'You do sot.'

'I do not. Will we have a biscuit while the boys are out?'

'Oh, great. What's a whirlpool?'

'It's a hole in the sea and boats fall right down it.'

'That's terrible. I'll dream about it.'

'You will not.'

'I will sot.'

'Eat your biscuit and don't be daft.'

When the boys came in, Andy said, 'Hey, salmon, the jinkies. This is mine.'

'You'll not sit down till you've washed your hands,' Henrietta said primly.

'Hey, where do you get that? You think you're Mother or something?'

'You should be setting an example. You're the man of the house, aren't you?'

'Oh, all right. You two see you scrub your nails, see?' Andy went to the sink with a swagger. Some day, Peter thought, he would be able to walk like that, like Andy.

'Eh, what about the chips, well?' Andy demanded.

'What do you take me for, a skivvy?'

'Aw come on, the man of the house needs chips.'

'It would take half an hour.'

'Sawright, I'll have a piece on jam while we wait.'

'All right,' Henrietta said. 'I'll make chips, if you polish your own boots for the next week.'

'Me? I don't know how to polish boots. Men don't polish boots.'

'No boots, no chips.'

'I'll polish mine, Henrietta,' John offered.

'All right, you get chips.'

'You can give me hauf,' Andy told him. Henrietta snorted and started to peel potatoes.

The doorbell rang and Angy went to answer it. He came back waving an envelope.

'It's a telegram. For Mother. I gave the boy a penny,' he added complacently.

'Oh dear. Will we open it?'

'Sure.'

'No, it's for Mother. Oh, I hope it's not bad news.'

'Aw come on, make the chips. It's nothing to do wi' us.'

She fried the chips on the fire, constantly glancing at the envelope on the mantelpiece and working it into a harrowing drama like Sons of the Sea.

'What's a telegram, Andy?'

'A message. A boy brings it on a bike.'

'Right up the stairs?'

'No, he leaves his bike in the close.'

Since Meg wasn't there to check him, Bobby had six spoonfuls of sugar in his tea. Meg came back so excited that there was no time to tell her about the telegram.

'We saw the talkies!'

'What?'

'Talking pictures,' Da explained. 'There he is up on the screen, and he opens his mouth, and you can hear him singing.'

John was sceptical.

'It'll be somebody at the back of the screen singing.'

'No no, it's a machine attached to the picture, and you can hear everything they say.'

'It's astonishing,' said Meg. 'We live in a wonderful age.'

'Oh hey, Ma, there's a telegram for you. I gave the boy a penny.'

'You shouldn't have, Andy. A telegram!' She turned white, and shook as she tore the envelope open. She sat down.

'Oh,' she said. 'I forgot, we brought a box of cream cakes for your tea, here.'

'What is it?' Da demanded. Her lips quivered.

'"Alastiar dead. Funeral Tuesday. Henrietta." That's Henrietta McGillivray on Duna.'

'Oh. Well.' Da was uncomfortable, trying to wish it out of existence. 'It's not family.'

'It is, Andrew.' She was weeping softly. 'They were the only family I had till I was fourteen. Alastair was like a brother, my own brother. I'll have to go.'

'You canny go all the way to Duna. What'll we do without you?'

'Oh, you'll manage. Henrietta can take a couple of days off school.'

Henrietta glowed with importance.

'So can I, Ma.' Bobby offered.

'You can not, Bobby.'

'But the money!' Andrew protested.

'Och, money, money. I've got some sewing money and I can borrow from the rent this once. I have to go. But there'll not be a boat till Monday now.'

'Well, you've got time to think about it.'

'I have to go.'

Andrew sat heavily in his chair and Meg stood staring at nothing and wiped her eyes. She became conscious of him again, and there was a sudden conjuring trick between her purse and his hand.

'I'm not fit company and I have a lot to think about, Andrew. Why don't you go down to the Afton for a pint? It's been a shock for you too.'

'Aye, it has . . . Oh well, the walk'll do me good. Are you sure?'

'Oh aye.'

He rose and patted her clumsily and went out, not quite on tiptoe.

Peter lay in bed that night thinking about the day. He had forgotten about holes in the sea that swallowed boats. He felt strangely exhilarated that somebody was Dead. It was important. People sitting in carriages drawn by beautiful black horses while other people stopped in the street and took off their hats. Then there was something else at the back of his mind.

The pictures. That had been funny. While Henrietta had been hugging him so that he wouldn't fall off the window-sill, he had felt John's hand hugging Henrietta. And something had happened between them that he couldn't see, because John was on her other side, but she had muttered, 'Don't be silly, John.' And he said, 'Sorry. I wasn't thinking.' And she had muttered, 'It's all right, there's no harm in it.' And then, Peter was sure, she had kissed him. And then she laughed.

Girls were strange. He saw himself at the front room window, looking down at the skipping game, and feeling that they were different, they were all by themselves as if they all knew something that boys didn't know, and they didn't need boys to share the secret. They were always whispering about something.

He saw Jeannie's face coming down to his, and he was kissing her mouth as if it were his mother, but it wasn't the same as his mother, it was funny. Bobby's sleeping toes began to curl and uncurl against his bare calves and he drew his legs up and curled into a ball and drifted away.

# 7

The warm sunny day was a small blessing. There were too
many mourners to crowd into the McGillivrays' kitchen,
and Mr Ferrier held the service in the yard outside. On the
other hand, a touch of rain or chill wind might have
persuaded him to cut it short. He was the same as Meg
remembered, a man who seemed to have been born white-
haired and heavy and middle-aged and full of endless
words. From infancy she remembered the interminable
effort to keep awake while he repeated his text four times
and then dissected Scripture with a fine fine knife while her
head nodded till her mother's sharp elbow jolted her into
reverence and alertness.

*And ninthly . . . and twelfthly, and fifteenthly, and the sin
of Pride, the sin of Absalom, did not die with Absalom, for
it still stalks the earth, it is here in this very congregation.
Oh Brethren, we are steeped in sin and we shall never find
Salvation until we pluck it from our hearts as we would
pluck out our own eye if it offendeth us. The sin of
ostentatious raiment, yea, even like Absalom's sin of pride
in his golden locks, the sin that is visited with the awful
judgement of the Lord. The sin of intellectual pride, of
those who presume to interpret the holy word of God, to
dilute the Holy Scripture of God, to bend God's holy word
to their own convenience, nay, who question the very
Scriptural truth of the Divine Creation, given to us by our
Father in Heaven that we may read and reverence his great
works, we who are as dust or as the grains of sand upon the
shore, ignorant and defiled.*
*And seventeenthly . . . and twentiethly . . .*

She had tried to imagine God, on His hands and knees,
patiently filing every grain of sand on the shore beside the
harbour, and had once asked her mother how long it had
taken Him. Her mother had been inexplicably angry and
told her not to make jokes about her Heavenly Father, not
even to mention His name, and Meg had gathered that God
was a Bad Word except when Mr Ferrier used it.
    Now, she only wished he would come to an end. The

longer he went on, the more Henrietta was racked with pain and grief. And the old man didn't even have anything comforting or kindly to say about poor dead Alastair. 'Defiled with sin . . . all miserable sinners unworthy of Thy grace . . . offended Thee in thought and word and deed . . .'

Even if it was all true, it didn't need an hour of repetition.

When it was over at last, and the men lifted the coffin for the long walk down the hill, Henrietta fell into Meg's arms and sobbed. A few of the neighbour women even found her open emotion unseemly.

'It is the will of God.'

'Yes, the Lord giveth and the Lord taketh away.'

'The will of God.'

'It must just be borne.'

'Aye, aye.'

'It's true enough,' Meg said impatiently. 'But that isn't much comfort to a woman bereaved.'

'They're right enough, Meg,' Henrietta sobbed. 'We must put up with it.'

'Aye, aye. There, Henrietta.'

There was, too, a faint sense of disapproval in some of the neighbours at Meg's presumption in usurping the role of comforter, and her not even living on the Island, intruding on their ceremony from Glasgow itself, where people got up to heaven knew what abominations.

'Pious old bitches,' Henrietta whispered, and Meg had to swallow a wild laugh.

She had time to feel sorry for the men, away at the graveside, suffering another hour of Mr Ferrier's joyful proclamations of doom and damnation. In the kitchen, the women were busied with laying the table and the dresser, and Meg and Henrietta were briefly left outside. Henrietta wiped her eyes and shook off her grief.

'They canna help it, Meg, for some of them a funeral is the only fun they get from one year's end to another.'

'I know, I know. I don't know what to do myself, I don't know what to say.'

'I know, there's nothing anybody can say. Oh, my beautiful wee boy.' The tears came again. 'I'd better stop this.'

'Och, have a good greet, Henrietta. It maybe helps.'

Henrietta braced herself.

'Ach, there's no sense in it, there's no sense in anything. It was enough that you came back, Meg, we've missed you sore.'

'Me too.'

'I hope you're happy in Glasgow.'

'Happy enough. I've got a decent man and I keep busy.'

'There's more to life than keeping busy, Meg. If there's no joy in it it's not worth a damn.'

'Oh, there's enough, there's enough. We can't expect too much.'

Henrietta read a whole life story into the answer, and grieved for the girl she had reared after she was orphaned, but she let the subject lie.

'When you were wee I sometimes thought you might marry Alastair one day, you were so close.'

'Ah, too close, Henrietta. He's still my brother.'

'Aye, aye. Well, I suppose we'd better go inside and look holy.' And she winked. At that, Meg burst into tears.

It was clear, from Meg's vivid memories of life in the McGillivray cottage, that most of the china on the table and the dresser was borrowed from neighbours less feckless than Henrietta; the houseproud women who Kept Things Good. But that at least was a simple act of neighbourly kindness, even if they felt complacent and superior in being able to lend it. Mr Ferrier was right, the sin of pride was hard to escape. The minister came back with the men from the burial, and went round to have a reverently murmured word with as many of the mourners as he could manage, trying to share his favours equally among the faithful and the backsliders who stood more in need of his ministrations and his exhortations. The conversation was in whispers, even among the men who spilled out into the yard holding good cups and saucers in cautious hands and looking hot and uncomfortable and trapped in their good dark clothes. Mr Ferrier came out and drew Meg aside, and the others moved away gratefully enough, to give them room to talk in private.

'You're not much changed, Meg,' he said.

'Oh, I'm older, Mr Ferrier.'

'And a wee bit wiser, you think?'

'Not very much.'

'It's not a good place, that Glasgow.'

51

'It has to be borne.' She was conscious of a trace of hypocrisy that worried her, of falling into pious platitudes to avoid saying anything that mattered.

'I couldn't wait to get away from it. Oh, I could see the temptations there all right, and the drinking, and the blasphemy. A godless place.'

She couldn't believe Mr Ferrier had ever been tempted into anything, except long sermons. And maybe long sermons were tinged with the sin of pride too. She was astonished at the irreverence of the thought.

'I keep myself to myself,' she offered weakly.

'And there are the children.'

'Five.'

'Just so. Just so.'

If he didn't know she had married twice she didn't intend to go into long explanations.

'And you're bringing them up in the light of the Lord.'

'I do my best.'

'He is the only bulwark against the temptations of life, especially in Glasgow. He is our refuge and our strength. You'll be a busy girl with five wee ones.'

'Yes. I find some time to read.'

It was a mistake, her unthinking assumption that a man of God, a man of learning, would be pleased at this.

'As long as your Bible is to your hand, it is all the reading you need.'

'Yes.'

'You do not want to be wasting your mind on the trash that passes for books today.'

'There are some books worth reading, Mr Ferrier.'

If he had known her better he would have known that he had touched steel.

'All they can do is take your thoughts away from the Bible, and God himself. Beware of secular temptations, Meg.'

'I think when God gave us minds he meant us to use them, Mr Ferrier. There is so much to learn.'

'There is little we need to learn that is not already there in the word of God.'

'I disagree. The more I understand about . . . well, the more I understand . . .'

'You're confused, Meg. I hope you remember my words

about the sin of the intellect.'

'Yes.'

'Ah, you're young yet.'

'That's true.'

She had a revelation about herself. As a little girl she had been bored and bored and bored by Mr Ferrier's monotonous outpouring of sin and misery and hell-fire, but she had known that that was her own error and her weakness. Now the conviction came to her in an instant that all along, her feelings had been right and her conscience had been wrong. He was a narrow, boring old man.

'It was a great comfort to hear you, Mr Ferrier.' She told the rare lie with a straight face, and he nodded in satisfaction and went to offer comfort to somebody else. The men in the yard furtively backed away as he moved about.

After a long half-hour he had to leave on a visitation of mercy, and the atmosphere changed at once. Billie brought whisky from the cupboard under the dresser, and the male mourners started to loosen their ties and unbutton their collars. Even some of the most unctuous women let themselves be cajoled into taking a small refreshment, as a matter of courtesy.

It still puzzled Meg that so soon after a funeral, even this funeral, celebrating the tragic end of a young life by drowning, hilarity started to set in. She mentioned it to Henrietta.

'Life goes on, Meg, life goes on. You can't be moping forever. It's just a natural . . .'

'Reaction?'

'Oh, you were always one for the words, I suppose that's the right word. Have a wee dram yourself, it'll dull the pain.'

'No, I've never liked it, I don't understand it.'

'By Joves, Old Biddy Ewing is fair getting carried away with it, it's a good job the minister isn't here to hear her cackling. She'll be in the front pew on Sunday nodding away like a gorilla about the sins of the flesh. I suppose she thinks that means too many home-made scones.'

'Or using scented soap.'

'I wouldn't like to think the last time she used soap at all, Meg. She's got the odour of sanctity.'

'Is that what it is, Henrietta? You know, when I was a wee girl and I had to sit near her in the church, I always thought she must be carrying a few raw herring in her handbag, the smell was that strong.'

'Raw herring my bottom, she hasn't washed in thirty years. And I've seen her standing outside the Post Office window, looking holy, and the piss running down her legs, and her nodding and shaking her head at the sins of mankind while she did it.'

'She's a good faithful churchgoer, we shouldn't be laughing at her.'

'Och, it's good to talk to you again, Meg, and you living in that great sink of iniquity of Glasgow. His Nibs is often on about it and the terrible temptations of the flesh. Thank God for them is what I say.'

'It's good to be back on the Island, but I could never come back to stay. I couldn't be doing with Mr Ferrier at all now.'

'The man is a shite, Meg. A year ago he dropped in on a visitation and started on and on at me about Billie and men, and the bairns, and the drink, and the duties of holy matrimony and self-restraint, and I was very nearly telling him the truth, but it would have killed him on the spot for sure.'

'What was the truth?'

'Och, it's too rude.'

'No, tell me.'

'Well, Meg, I was – oh my God, I was thinking it right enough. I was nearly going to say, "And what would you know about marriage, after thirty years of humdrum fucking with Mrs Ferrier up at the manse?" I've shocked you, Meg.'

'Yes. But I wonder lately why some words should be shocking. I used to think God was a Bad Word. Since I started reading books in Glasgow I'm not sure of things so much. I don't like the word, but then, I think, how can an arrangement of letters be sinful? If I listened to Mr Ferrier I wouldn't read books at all, except the Bible.'

'Oh, there's plenty in the Bible, Meg. I've listened to the old fraud reading the Song of Solomon, and you can nearly see the slavers running down his chin. It is a silly place, Duna, you're better out of it. I know what I was going to say – old Biddy Ewing, my word, she is the one for piety. There was a terrible thing happened at Dod Baxter's funeral, you mind old Dod. Well, the minister was well into it in the kitchen, and ninety-thirdly and so on, when a cloth hanging on the mantel caught fire, and Billie went out and ran in with a pail of water and threw it over the range before the house would burn to the ground. Biddy was terribly affronted. She thought it was terrible bad taste to interrupt the service, a decent Godly man would have let the house burn to the ground and everybody in it. Mr Ferrier never even noticed anything had happened.'

'I miss Duna all the same. I was happy here.'

'Och, you can be happy anywhere, Meg, if you want to be. Thank God for Billie and a warm body in bed.'

'It's a funny place, Glasgow, too. I was walking home from the Public Library the other week, and there's this wee street, with nobody about, except a wee boy of about four, and I couldn't help watching him. He was standing there, in the middle of the street, and looking round to make sure nobody could hear him, and then he shouted . . . that word, that word you said . . . and giggled and ran away. Oh, I think he was telling the world he knew about sin, and was fair enjoying it, as long as nobody knew about it.'

'He was shouting Eff?'

'Aye. You know, I thought, the wee devil, somebody should tell his mother. And then I thought, och, it's a wee tiny boy defying the universe. I think I'm very sinful, Henrietta. I sometimes worry about myself.'

'You were always a wee worrier, Meg. It's all the fault of people like Mr Ferrier, if he's not having any pleasure in life he wants it stamped out for everybody. Young Eileann is at home.'

'Young Eileann?'

'The Laird's boy, you know very well. A very quiet odd young chap he is, you remember him.'

'Oh aye.'

In the evening, she went for a walk over the old paths she had known. The hypocrisy was terrible, and there was complicity in it as well. Henrietta's youngest, wee Sheila, had wanted to come with her, and Henrietta had told the child that it was too late for her and that Auntie Meg wanted to be by herself. You're a silly old woman, Meg told herself sternly, and then told herself, You're only going for a walk of old times' sake, there is no harm in it. You are an old married woman with five children and if you want to go for a walk there is no harm in it.

But she tramped a third of the way round the island without meeting anybody, and there was a sad heavy feeling of disappointment on her. Then he suddenly appeared on top of the hill and shouted, 'Hello', and he was a terrible bad actor too, making out that he had just appeared there by chance and didn't know who she was.

But maybe he didn't, after so many years. Still, there was just something wrong and false about his surprise, and the awkward way he trotted down the hill to the path. He remembered all right, and her heart leapt at the sight of him.

'I've been rehearsing this accidental meeting for half-an-hour,' he said.

'My name is Meg Macrae.'

'I know your name is Meg Macrae. Oh Meg. Oh God.'

'That is blasphemy,' she said primly. 'Why would you be following an old woman?'

'You're twenty-eight, Meg.'

'Yes. An old woman.'

His laugh rang across the hill.

'Oh, lass, lass.'

Now she laughed.

'Oh, that word is so funny in that odd-like Englified tongue, Eileann.'

'That's something, Meg, to be able to make you laugh. It's better than nothing. Are you well, Meg?'

'Why shouldn't I be well?'

'I've often thought about you.'

'Have you now?'

'I don't suppose you've ever thought about me.'

'I've been busy.'

'Yes, of course. And you're well?'

'You repeat yourself.'

'It matters to me.'

'I'm well enough. And you're well yourself? Oh, I hope you're well, I want you to be well. I'm married, Eileann, I'm married twice.'

56

'Oh God. Would that I were both of your husbands. I'm sorry, I shock you.'

'I am not easily shocked. Yes, would that you were. I never expected to meet you again. You're married yourself?'

'Oh yes. For some time.' He threw the question away. 'What a young fool I was.'

'That is hardly a compliment.'

He stared into her eyes.

'You are a woman, and you're a doughty woman, Meg, I would have expected it.'

'I am only a simple peasant girl.'

'Meg, don't cry, or I will too, and a man isn't supposed to cry. Why didn't I ask you to marry me?'

'Your mother would have cut you off with a shilling, Eileann. Things are as they are.'

'The old lady had a shilling specially sharpened for the job, but I'm ashamed, ashamed.'

'You have a guilt complex, Eileann.'

'Eh?'

'No, that is not accurate, it is not a complex. You simply feel guilty. Dear man, don't be ashamed or guilty.'

She started to walk, and he fell in beside her.

'We are looking at each other sideways, Eileann,' she said. 'I would rather look at you straight, because there is not much time.'

'I have never met a woman who talks like you, Meg.'

'Life is too short for folk to be oblique, and I want to look at you, because there is still a silly young girl inside me, inside this old woman.'

'At the risk of being trite, Meg, I must tell you I will love you till the day I die. I think of you all the time.'

'I don't think of you all the time. That is silly. I have things to do and my children to raise.'

'I am suitably snubbed.'

'I think of you in between times. But there is no sense in it. And what we did was a sin. At least, I thought it was a sin. Now I am not sure of anything.'

'It was the great experience of my life, Meg.'

'Well, if it is any comfort to you, if it was today, and me seventeen years old, I would do the same again, and I don't care.'

'You know you're more beautiful than you were when

you were seventeen?'

'I love your kindness, Alan. It is the only thing that matters in a man, I think. I am greatly surprised. I didn't know what to expect, you might well have forgotten me, and it is a great joy, and I may well cry, so I will leave you now.'

'Yes. Thank you, Meg. Will I kiss you?'

'Oh, oh better not, I am trying to be a sensible old woman and live my own life.'

He did, all the same.

'Ah, Alan, Eileann, I'm glad you wouldn't take no for an answer, for I would have died of disappointment, and now you had better go away from me, for now it would be a sin and a treachery.'

He didn't look back, and she walked down the hill and stared at the Sound till the tears stopped flowing and she could dry her cheeks. It would be a relief to rejoin the McGillivrays in their house of mourning, where her emotions would be reasonable and legitimate; to be away from the past and the ridiculous clinging to adolescence. She found herself stroking the skin on her neck, searching for the stringy muscles of old age; and almost persuading herself that she couldn't find any.


The house of death was easy. The pious mourners were long gone. Billie had got himself thoroughly drunk, and wept, and raved, and wept, and got things off his chest and finally gone to bed.

'That's not the end of it,' Henrietta said. 'Maybe it's worse for Billie than for me, and he's a great softie.'

'Billy a softie?'

'Ah, they're all the same. So is your man.'

'Who?'

'The man you're married to, Meg, don't look so guilty. I've never met your man, Meg, but you're the kind of girl that softies would want to be leaning on.'

'You don't know everything, Henrietta.'

'Och, away with you. Did you meet the wee lairdling, as if I didn't know?'

'And why should I?'

'He's on the Island, and you're on the Island, and Duna is not as big as Australia.'

'You always know!'

'I know now. Mind you, I don't think that one is a softie. But a girl couldn't be hard on him.'

'Oh Henrietta, I don't know anything. I don't know what it's all for.'

'Och, one foot in front of the other, Meg, that is all life is about, and wear tacketty boots if you can, and now Billie's asleep I'm having a dram anyway.'

# 8

Meg kept a tidy house. It would be difficult, she sometimes thought wryly, to lose a set of false teeth in it, even if she had a set of false teeth. The tidiness was an act of assertion. If she couldn't change her life, she could control the area of life around her. Beyond that area she was powerless, and in rare moments of depression she could find herself bitterly angry at being powerless; and then ashamed of her anger.

Life in Glasgow wasn't good enough, but it was the same life for everybody. Rich people were rich and poor people were poor. The poor had to suffer short commons even if they had work, and if they had, they were better off than others. She bought end-loaves because they were squashed out of shape and a halfpenny cheaper, but they tasted the same whatever their shape. She looked for bargains in vegetables and made a lot of soup because it was cheap and good. Often it was the entire midday meal.

She mended and improvised, unpicked whole garments and remade them so that young Andy's clothes could be passed down to John, and from John to Bobby, and eventually maybe from Bobby to Peter if the cloth still had any strength in it.

She had a natural knack with a needle, and her luckiest possession was an old Singer that Andrew had brought from his first marriage. She could sit happily at the treadle listening to the needle for hours. Accuracy was natural to her. She could work nearly unconsciously while her thoughts went in every direction, and not feel guilty about wasting her time thinking, because she was doing something useful at the same time.

But she tried not to be impractical even in her thoughts. She sternly stopped herself when thinking merged into dreaming. Dreaming was for children and not for grown matrons with families.

Sometimes, all the same, things came into her mind unasked and she was foolish enough to let them linger for a few minutes before she forced herself to more sensible things. The sewing machine was even luckier because it made money. A small circle of neighbours had found her out, one by one, and she could earn a few coppers or even a few shillings for doing alterations. Then she advanced to making new dresses and even coats. There was a story she had read in a book from the library . . . no, not a sewing machine, the story had been about a typewriter and no, it wasn't a story, it was a theatre play. The Twelve Pound Look, it was, about a woman with a domineering husband and how she got a typewriter and freed herself. The sewing machine was nearly as good.

Not that Andrew was a domineering husband, or that she wanted to free herself. It was just an interesting thought, and what was done was done.

If only a few blades of green grass could grow in the back courts, in place of the slate-grey dusty earth. This was no place for children. They scooped out little holes in the earth and played a game with marbles. Well, true enough, they could never have played that game on Duna, on a heather hill. They never complained because they knew nothing better. She saw herself on a heather hill, with the clean wind whistling in from the ocean, and she put the thought away.

She was lucky to have Andrew, and his boys, and not be alone, trying to survive with Henrietta and little Peter, and no man in the house. A softie, a softie. She was going to put that thought away, but she couldn't until she remembered who had said it. Henrietta McGillivray. It was odd how her thoughts kept coming round to Duna. Billie McGillivray was no softie, but Henrietta had said that *Meg was a girl that softies would always be leaning on.*

Well, so. If that was the way of it, that was the way of it. Andrew was a plain man with little in the way of dreams, for all he was handsome and well-set and thoughtful enough every now and then. Henrietta McGillivray would have said that he had the best of the bargain, a hardworking girl to take his dead wife's place and take care of his boys, but bargains were chancy things and a wise man, or even the wise Henrietta McGillivray, might not know who was getting the better of one. Andrew was not one to complain, at least. He was happy to be what he was and where he was, with a job of a kind in the stickyard and no notion of improving it. As she drove the treadle she shook her head impatiently at that, because there had to be something better, folk couldn't just stay still where they were forever.

And Andrew's sister Alice; a sly, in-turned wee woman,

with no resemblance to Andrew at all, always picking at the edges of other people's lives and other people's happiness. It was not nice to think it, but Alice was not a nice woman; and always her wee sideways questions about the Com Pen, she was fair obsessed with the Com Pen. Andrew himself had never brought up the subject of the compensation Meg had got for Paul's death, he had positively said, right at the start before they were married, that that was in the past, and no business of his. No, it had never entered Andrew's head, she was sure of that. It was to stay by for Henrietta and little Peter, to help them get on.

Ach, the city was too crowded for human beings, but it was a good enough life and they were all in it together. And it was quite nice to have the tramcars clanging past the close and be able to go into town now and then without a long walk in the rain. And she liked fine going with Andrew on a Saturday and being able to have an afternoon out without his having to pay; it was her sewing money treat; a wee joke between them, and he wasn't daft enough to feel bad that his wife was paying for it, the way some men would have been.

She always opened the tin box and handed him the money, out of sight of the children, and it was all nice and easy. And it meant he didn't stay too long in the pub on a Saturday on his way home from work. But that was an unkind thought, because he wasn't a hard-drinking man like some. She was still trying to get rid of her infancy horror of drink, and accept that it could be all right in moderation; like most things, even if Mr Ferrier might disagree.

Mr Ferrier. His name took her back to the Island too. She was glad she had Mr Gillan now, in Glasgow, at the United Free Church in the Gallowgate. He was a strict man of God, but cheery with it, and not always on and on about damnation and misery. Oh yes, strict enough – he allowed dancing at the church social, but when the Eightsome Reel was on, he suddenly appeared on the platform and shouted, 'There will be no hooching.' It was hard to know why God would put up with dancing, but be offended if the dancers shouted 'Hooch'. But there was a lot Meg still didn't understand, even as an old married woman.

Her own mother would whirl in the grave if she could

have seen some of the books in the Public Library; especially that doctor, Freud (Meg pronounced it Frood in her mind), and what he said about things that decent people had never even put a name to. The very word he wrote about sounded strange, because she had found that it didn't refer only to male and female, but to what men and women did to each other.

Sex.

It had been just an ordinary word when she was a schoolgirl. Now, maybe, it was another Bad Word.

Sex.

She blushed, sitting alone in the kitchen. It really wasn't proper. She was ashamed of the way she sometimes thought, lying in the box-bed at night beside Andrew, and wishing he would do something, wishing that this handsome powerful man would do something with her; ashamed of wakening sometimes to find herself taking liberties with his sleeping male body. Neighbour women often confided in her their complaints that men had That One Thing in their minds all the time, and she agreed and sympathised, and wondered what was wrong with her, or Andrew, that it was she who had it in *her* mind. She wondered if Doctor Frood had turned her mind in wrong paths.

In the meantime, life had to be lived. There was the business of young Andy that had to be settled, and she wasn't looking forward to it, so she brought it up with the man of the house that evening, to be done with it.

It was quite simple, Andy wanted to leave school and get a job and make money, and Meg wanted him to stay at school and make something of himself. Andy was doing a newspaper run for Convery's and he couldn't see past Convery's. He was a young fool. She would get Andrew to see that.

It was hopeless. Maybe Henrietta McGillivray on Duna might be right, maybe Andrew was a softie, but he was soft in his own way, and arguing with him was like arguing with a jellyfish, that changed shape and slid away every time you got your hands on it.

'You don't want the boys always to be stuck in the same place, Andrew, never to get out of the bit.'

'There's plenty of good men can't get a job at all. What's wrong with Convery's shop?'

'It's no job for a man, Andrew.'

'Andy's only a boy.'

'He'll not be a boy forever, Andrew.'

'Ach, leaving school, that'll make a man of him. Everyone has to start somewhere. All that school just puts ideas in people's heads.'

And that is where ideas ought to be, there is no other place to have ideas, she thought, but she knew it was useless, and the only thing to do was let it go. Young Andy wanted to leave school, and be a man, and wear long trousers, and smoke and swear, and Andrew was on his side. Andy would be what he chose to be, and she could do nothing about it.

'Well,' she said, 'after the exams next year, Henrietta will be going to Whitehill School.' Whitehill School was the Big School, it was the springboard to real education, to things she had never learnt. And as she spoke, the door opened and John and Henrietta and Bobby all tumbled into the kitchen, and young Bobby caught up her words.

'Whitehill pup, with your tail tied up!'

Andrew looked sourly at the children, and said, 'We're not splitting up the family – Henrietta at one school and John at the other.'

Certainly John looked stricken. He was fond of Henrietta, he sometimes seemed to feel towards his stepsister as if she were his mother, or his daughter, rather than a girl of his own age. Henrietta, the transparent one, was ecstatic.

'Am I going to Whitehill, Mother? And shut up, Bobby, you're a silly little boy.'

'. . . With your tail tied up,' Bobby persisted.

'John will go to Whitehill as well.' Meg was as positive as granite, and Andrew's brows came down.

'John will go where I bid him. He's my son.'

'He's my son too.' She was done with wheedling. 'Would you like to, John?'

'Oh, could I, Ma?' The whipped puppy look fell from him. 'Is it all right, Da?'

'Oh, somebody's asking for *my* opinion. You want to be better than your brother? You want to get above your family?'

Young John recoiled, wounded again, and Meg cut in, very very coldly.

'No he doesn't want to be better than anybody. He just wants to be as good as he can be himself. And he will go to Whitehill with Henrietta, if he passes the Qualifying Exam.'

'Oh, he will, Mother, he will. He's the best in the class,' Henrietta cried. 'He's better than me.'

'Is he?' Andrew was startled, and then recovered. 'I think these books turn kids' brains. But I don't count, of course. Anyway I promised to see Dick Murchison for a wee while, it's time I was off.'

As the door closed behind him, Meg thought she actually hated him. But she would win for Henrietta and John, and Bobby and Peter too. They would make something of themselves, and get to know things she would never know.

She waited up, in her nightdress with her old coat over it, for Andrew to come home, and he was as cheery as she expected. Quite cocky even. She had the sudden intuition that he had been boasting to Dick Murchison about his two kids going to Whitehill School. She was impatient with him, with his narrow little view of life and his determination to stick in the mud and never move. And that was the night he turned to her wordlessly in bed – wordlessly because Henrietta was in the other box-bed only a few feet away – to do what men do with women; the one night in weeks when it was the farthest thing from her mind. She forced herself to appreciate him, with her eyes closed and her mind fixed on somebody else, and another part of her mind accusing her of committing adultery in her heart.

# 9

Peter came home from school every day an hour earlier than the bigger ones. Meg was already dressed for the street. She left the key under the mat in case the others came home before her, and whisked him with her to the Public Library.

She was worried about the weather. The weather was just as important in Glasgow as it had ever been on Duna, because Bobby was at school in his sand-shoes, and his feet would be soaked if it rained. She had his boots in her basket, with the heels worn down nearly to the uppers and they would have to be mended before they were past mending. It would have been fine to buy him a spare pair, but he was growing so fast that he would just have outgrown two pairs instead of one. She could have squeezed the price of a pair out of her sewing money, but it would have been a waste, and there were plenty of other things to spend money on. If she could get the worn pair to a cobbler, and maybe plead with him to have them ready for next day, everything would be fine.

The need for hurry diminished her pleasure in the Library; it was a place to be savoured slowly. And she always felt a pang at leaving little Peter sitting like an idol, stricken to silence, while she scanned the shelves. A girl, one of the staff, approached her and spoke in the reverential murmur suitable to this cathedral of learning.

'Would your wee boy not like to go into the Children's Department?'

'You know, I never thought of that, I am a fool. He would just love it, and I could stop fretting about him as long as he didn't get lost.'

'He'll not get lost. Do you want to apply for a ticket for him?'

'Oh yes, yes, it's the great ideas you've got. A library ticket would be the very dab, as good as a present.'

'I'll make out the form while you're looking for something.'

It was great, right enough, having a big library just down the street. The *Rover* and the *Wizard* were all very well, but for a boy with a curious mind, the Library was an Aladdin's cave. And a good book to read at home might take his mind off climbing dykes with Bobby and his pals, and ringing doorbells, and stealing potatoes from Blaney's shop – games that mothers never got to know about, of course. She smiled a little smile as Peter took the librarian's hand, slid down from his chair and went into the Children's Department. He was a lot of things, but he was a wee devil as well. She looked at the clock and decided that she could slow down and enjoy just exploring.

When she was leaving, Peter had a book gripped under his arm, and looked dazed.

'Here's the form,' the librarian said. 'It'll have to be signed by a ratepayer before he gets his ticket, but I've let him have a book while we wait. You can bring the form back next week with your husband's signature.'

'My husband's signature?'

'Yes, it has to be a ratepayer.'

'Oh. In that case I can sign it myself.'

'The house is in your name?'

'Yes.' She hid her irritation as she signed. The last thing Andrew had ever wanted when he moved into her house in Cumbie Street was to be the ratepayer. Coping with money and bills was women's work too.

'What have you got, Peter?'

He held up the book. The Water Babies.

'It has very good pictures,' the librarian said. 'Mrs Margaret Mason? He told me his name was Cassidy.'

'My first marriage.' It was always a tiresome thing to explain. 'Isn't The Water Babies a wee bit . . . a wee bit frightening for a young child?'

'You know the book. Well, I don't know, Mrs Mason. I think we worry too much about children being frightened with books. They're tougher than some people think.'

'Now I think you're right, and I should have thought of it myself. If it's too much he'll just stop reading it.'

The librarian glanced down at Peter, his face turning from side to side to follow the conversation; and she muttered, 'I don't think it'll be too much for that one. He's been here before.'

'I was here last week,' Peter said. He didn't understand why they laughed.

There was a shoemaker's on the way home, one she hadn't used before. It had the dark look and the mixture of smells of a real shoemaker's, and a man was sitting behind a bench buffing the edge of a boot-sole on an electric wheel.

'Two minutes,' he said. 'Have a chair.' He was on his own. Peter went close to the bench and gazed at the work, and the man gave him the odd half-nod, half-shake that meant an informal hello in Glasgow. He finished the buffing and began to rub black wax into the pale leather sole.

'It's my other boy's boots.' Meg took them from her basket and brandished them. 'It would be nice if I could have them for tomorrow.'

'To get back to school?'

'No, no.' Meg blushed. 'He's at school all right, but . . . he needs his boots.'

The man nodded, took the boots and examined them.

'Heelplates?'

'If they're not too dear. Oh aye, heelplates will save money in the end.'

'And they're good for slides.'

'That's what wears them out, slides.'

'More work for the cobbler. I'll do them now, if you like.'

'This very minute?'

'Aye, while you wait. My sister does ear-piercing the same way. Ears pierced while you wait.'

'That's very convenient, but I don't think I would like my ears pierced. You're making fun of me.'

The cobbler looked at her, under his brows. He thought her smile of pure pleasure was like sunlight; a girl who found delight in little things. Peter watched, absorbed, as the cobbler ripped off what was left of the heels.

'If I was ever to do it,' Meg said, 'I think I would just leave my ears and come back for them after.'

'You're Meg Macrae.'

'Mason.'

'Cassidy that was.'

'That's right.'

'I'm Paul's cousin. Dan Cassidy.'

'The Red Cobbler! Here, I don't know if I should be in this place. Paul used to say terrible things about you.'

'They're all true. I once met you with Paul, but you'll not remember.'

'You've got black hands,' Peter said.

'Aye, son, the calloused hands of the downtrodden proletariat. Your mother will explain that to you.'

'Indeed I will not, Mr Cassidy. It is a lot of nonsense.' He merely smiled, a private smile. A nice easy man, Meg thought, and nothing like what she had imagined. So this was the terrible Red Cobbler, the apostate, the bloodthirsty Communist. He had a fine style with his pliers and his hammer, a man who put himself into his work. And that quiet wee smile, as if he knew everything. Little Peter was staring at his clever hands, completely entranced.

'It is good of you to do the heels straight away, Mr Cassidy, Bobby is in sore need of them.'

'Aye, it's not funny being barefoot proles, Mrs Mason. But the day will come when the meek inherit the earth.' He laughed out loud. 'Now you're thinking the Devil can quote Scripture for his own ends.'

'But you are not a devil, Mr Cassidy.' Her face was alight, she was enjoying the argument just fine. 'You are only a cobbler.'

'Aye, and they're the great destroyers, you know, because they're at the bench all day, with nothing to do but think about life and society and man's inhumanity to man. The French Revolution was absolutely jammed wi' cobblers.'

'And knitting women.'

One of his eyebrows lifted.

'You've read your Dickens? Oh. If you want real blood and thunder and the rising of the oppressed masses, try Barnaby Rudge.'

Oh, this accidental meeting was a real treat, even if the cobbler was a dangerous subversive with a head full of nonsense.

'I'll read Barnaby Rudge,' she said. 'I'm surprised, I thought you wouldn't have read anything but Karl Marx.'

'Have you read him?'

'Karl Marx? I wouldn't give him house-room.' She glanced at Peter. 'I think we should talk about something else.'

'Aye, all right. I talk too much. I think too much as well, that's my trouble.'

'Oh, Mr Cassidy, I'm right glad somebody else has the same trouble. I sometimes wish I could turn my mind right off.'

He had a way of letting a smile slide over his long-boned face, very slowly, as if he was chewing something tasty and making it last a long time.

'If there is a God, Mrs Mason, he gave you your mind to use.'

Meg was startled.

'You know, I once said the same thing to a minister, and a Wee Free minister at that. He was not at all amused, Mr Cassidy, not at all amused.'

The Red Cobbler laughed quietly in his chest.

'You never did. We'll make a Red out of you yet. Giving up cheek to Wee Free ministers. We'll have you on Karl Marx yet, if you can stomach a German Jew.'

'Ah, now that is insulting, Mr Cassidy, a man is what he is, and I have been reading another German, and he's a Jew as well. Frood.'

'Froid. In German they pronounce it Froid. Oh, you're in deep waters there, but Nietzsche said Live Dangerously.'

He busied himself at the boots, and he knew he had an audience. A touch of style, a touch of pride. She could see the resemblance to her dead Paul in his face, but this face had none of the nervous innocence of Paul's, it was well-tanned leather over matured bones, although he was not an old man. Something like wee Peter, a man who had been here before.

'I have never heard of Nietzsche,' she said.

'I read him in the original. He's supposed to be a Fascist reactionary, but he wasn't daft.'

'You speak German?'

'Aw, Mrs Mason, the war's been over for ten years. I taught myself.'

'You never did!'

'Well, I started to learn fretwork, but the blade broke.'

'Stop teasing. That is a wonderful thing to do. I would like fine to do something like that, I am so ignorant, I never thought you could teach yourself a foreign language.'

'Ah, ignorance is a great beginning. One and thruppence.'

'One and thruppence is ridiculous, it would be two shillings along the street.'

'Family discount. And here's a sooker for the young man.'

He picked out of a rusty tin full of water a sodden circle of leather with a string knotted through the middle, and dropped it in a paper bag and handed it to Peter, who took it, uncomprehending. Meg was confused and embarrassed, first at being confronted with the Red Cobbler she had heard about and imagined to be a roaring beast, and then at the speed of everything and the unsettling conversation. No. What was unsettling was that it had not been unsettling, it had been so comfortable. She couldn't remember talking to anybody about books for years, except young Henrietta. And as she left the shop, Dan Cassidy just looked at her and smiled, and she could do nothing but smile back, and he laughed out loud.

'Oh, if they could put that smile in a bottle, they could sell it for a fortune.'

'Dan Cassidy, I think you are a wicked man.'

'I try, Meg Macrae, I try.'

Peter was holding her hand and dancing on the way home, and shouting, 'What will I do with my sooker, Mother, what will I do with my sooker, what will I do with my sooker?'

'Ssh.' She waited till they had turned the corner off the main road and into Cumbie Street, and took the thing from the paper bag.

'If you hold the end of the string, and stand on the leather, it'll stick to the ground.' She flashed a glance round again to see that nobody was watching her foolishness, and pressed the leather on the stone flag with her foot. She was laughing to herself. Peter took the string and pulled, but the leather was stuck tight. He looked worried.

'I want to take it home, Mother.'

'Don't fret, Peter. I'll get it off the pavement.' She stooped and picked at the edge of the leather disc till she had loosened its grip.

'I mind one day,' she said, 'I saw four wee boys with a sooker at each corner of a flagstone, and they pulled it right out of the pavement, the wee devils.'

'Oh Mother, I want four sookers, I want four sookers.'

'So. You will have to wear out your boots, then, won't you?'

'Why, Mother?'

'Never mind. It is time we were home.'

The rain started as soon as they reached the close, and by the time they were upstairs it was a downpour, bouncing inches off the street; and Bobby in his sand-shoes and not home. It stopped after half an hour, but the pavements were running inches deep.

She was tempted to put on her coat and run to the school with the boots, to catch Bobby, but he might be coming home in any direction, and even if she found him, he would be ashamed about being chased by his mother. There was nothing to be done. He came in an hour later, very jaunty.

'Oh Bobby, your poor feet!' Then she saw his sand-shoes slung round his neck by the laces, with his socks inside them. He was nonchalant.

'I came home in my berries, Ma.'

'Say bare feet, Bobby, do not say berries. Oh Bobby, you never did. It is only the scruff that go in their berries.'

'We all did it. It was rare, Ma. There was puddles miles deep. Miles! You missed yourself, Peter.'

'I've got a sooker, Bobby.'

'Oh, give us it a minute. Great.'

Bobby was trying the sooker on the tiles of the hearth when John came in.

'I think I've got a hole in this shoe, Mother,' he said. 'My sock's wet. I'm sorry.'

'Take them off, John, son. Oh, you are sodden. Never mind, I have got a good cobbler that can fix them fine if tomorrow's a dry day.'

She blushed. But there was no harm in knowing a man who could talk about books, so there was no need to blush. So if there was no need to blush, why was she convincing herself there was no need to blush?

The cat swished its stupid tail towards the hot bars of the fire, but she caught it without thinking and tucked it under him.

She felt wicked.

# 10

'Hetty's French teacher wants to see me,' Meg told Andrew. He glowered, and thought his own private thoughts.

'What is this Hetty business? What is wrong with her real name? It's that school. It gives the kids a lot of toffy ideas.'

A conversation with Andrew nearly always wandered into side streets and dead ends. He clamped his jaws and considered the matter.

'So she's in trouble wi' the French teacher. It's her own blame for taking French, what do we need wi' that foreign rubbish? The French are dirty, you know. We knew them in the war. Dirty. You don't want anything to do wi' that lot.'

'No.' Meg was very calm. 'No, Andrew, she's not in trouble. She's one of the best French pupils in the second year. Her teacher wants to talk to me.'

'Rather you than me,' he said darkly. 'I don't know what good French is to a lassie in this town. She'd be better learning Jewish, the place is rotten wi' Jews.'

'Andrew, I don't know any Jews in Glasgow except the Cowans, in the sweetie shop.'

'Cowans? Cohens, more like. What for do they have to change their name, if they're not up to something? Answer me that.' He chewed over his experience of life. 'Ask anybody that was in the war and they'll tell you. You canny trust the French. We would rather have had the Gerries any time. They fought clean.'

It was impossible to follow the wild flights of his logic. She abandoned it. In any case, Bobby and Peter came in from the Band of Hope, and she took the permanently simmering kettle from the range to make cocoa for them.

'Was it good tonight, Bobby?'

'Aw, just the same,' said Bobby. Everything to Bobby was Just the Same.

'It was great, Mother,' Peter said. 'It was Lantern Night. They put the lights out, and you get throwing things.'

'Oh, kids,' said Andrew.

'It was a story about a man that drank whisky, Mother.'

'Damnt lucky he could afford it,' Andrew muttered.

'And then his wife got sick, and the baby got sick, and everything, Mother.'

'He should have given them a swig.' Andrew laughed uproariously.'

'Your father's only joking, boys.'

'I'll never drink whisky,' Peter said pompously. 'Honour thy father and thy mother and abstain from strong drink as a beverage. What's a beverage, Mother?'

'A drink, Peter.'

'What's blasmy?'

'Blasmy is bad words, son,' Andrew explained. 'Don't you let me hear you using bad words.'

Meg found herself floundering in the thought processes both of Peter and Andrew.

'The teacher said I was a blasmy, Mother. It was because I said I knew God's name.'

'Ach, everybody knows that,' Bobby dismissed him.

'Be quiet, Bobby,' said Meg. 'What did you tell the teacher?'

'I said God's name was Harold Wishart. Because it says, Our Father Wishart in Heaven, Harold be thy name.'

'He's stupid,' Bobby snarled. But Meg found laughter bursting from her, and to her relief Andrew was guffawing too. Peter was baffled.

'That boy'll be the death of me,' Andrew cackled. 'I'll have to tell the boys at the stickyard that tomorrow.'

The prickly topic of French was forgotten.

He silenced her conscience in the matter of calling in at the Red Cobbler's shop on her way from the Public Library. Once or twice, she had taken in a pair of shoes that he had looked at, and then said, 'If every pair of shoes was like this, I would be in the gutter, Meg Macrae. Are you trying to give me charity? Because charity is a Capitalist trick to keep the proletariat in its place.'

'It was just an excuse for a chat, Dan.'

'Oh, Meg Macrae, you're blushing. And it suits you. Come on, lassie, even your Presbyterian God canny kill you for having a chat. And your faith might be in peril when you come in here, but your virtue is safe.'

The word virtue made her blush again. She felt she must be a wicked woman, seeking out a man to talk to when she had a husband at home. But she wanted reassurance from the cobbler before she visited Hetty's French teacher.

'Oh aye, aye, aye,' Dan Cassidy said. 'So you're helping the lassie wi' her French homework and you fancy learning it yourself. And why the hell not? Education, education! The working classes have to rise to their full stature, and education is the wee boy that will do it.'

'Well, I thought . . . you taught yourself German, Dan. Och, I'm just a silly old woman with daft ideas.'

'Ah, Meg, Meg, we'll have you on the barricades yet, when the Revolution comes.'

'You'll have me shouting war cries in French, I suppose. You and your class war.'

He gave her one of his little lopsided smiles that made her feel warm, and went on hammering sprigs into a shoe. She wondered why such an easy man had never married again, but she put the thought out of her mind.

Dan's encouragement wasn't quite enough, all the same. After church that Sunday, she sought the counsel of Mr Gillan, the minister, because she still feared that her notion was silly and childish.

Mr Gillan was no help. He was in a hurry after the service, and he was in a solemn Sabbath mood. Education was a great thing, he said, of course, and we should all be learning, learning, all the time. On the other hand, there were things of no great practical value and we had to be careful to choose the right things and not fritter away our energies. On the other hand learning was a fine and noble thing. On the other hand, it might take up time that should be given to our essential duties. And of course, the first thing was to pray for guidance. That was it, pray for guidance and it would be given.

She was downcast when she left him to collect the children, waiting, bored, outside the church.

'Is there anything wrong, Mother?' Hetty asked.

'No, no, Hetty, it's all right.'

'You're sad, Mother,' said Peter and took her hand.

So she would pray for guidance. Then she had a revelation, and it might have come from God.

Mr Gillan was halfhearted about her learning French because *Mr Gillan didn't speak French*. He was just a man, and he was jealous. And she laughed, and little Peter looked up and laughed with her.

'No, Peter, I am not sad at all, at all. I have just been

getting guidance from God, and I hope that is not a blasphemy.' She was striding proudly along the Gallowgate, and Peter had to break into a trot.

Miss Fairhurst, the French teacher, was a daunting woman. Her coat was good, but a bit showy, she was tall and thin, with strong face bones, her skin wrinkled under her face-powder and rouged to an angry red. Her red hair was blatantly dyed, with iron-grey at the roots. Meg knew about that, from Hetty. The children said they could check the calendar by Miss Fairhurst's monthly visits to the hairdresser – grey roots on the last day of the month, red roots on the first day of the next.

They met at the school gate; Miss Fairhurst hearty and confident, Meg twitching with nerves. They went to a Tally's shop and had coffee. Even coffee was an unusual experience for Meg, she never had it in the house.

'You're sitting there like a frightened schoolgirl,' the teacher accused her.

'I do feel a bit silly, Miss Fairhurst.'

'What's French for a cup of coffee?'

'Une tasse de café.'

'Go to the top of the class. And call me Vickie. Jesus.' Miss Fairhurst lit a cigarette. There were dark nicotine stains on her fingers. 'You don't know what it's like to meet a pupil who *wants* to learn the damn language.'

'Och, I feel so selfconscious about it. And it is daft, trying to learn a language when I could only squeeze in half an hour a day, it is silly and I am a foolish woman.'

'Havers. The brats in school have their bums on the seats, but I'm lucky if their brains are with me for half an hour a week. We'll have you speaking like a Parisian. Your kids are okay, incidentally. That John sounds like an impersonation of me, and I learned my French in Paris.'

'Oh, Paris.' Meg's eyes went misty. 'Och, that must be a wonderful place, although . . .'

'Ah, ah, yes, sinful, eh? Well, it's true. Oh, I was a bad girl in Paris.'

'I don't believe that.' Meg looked at the older woman to see if she was being teased, and all she got in return was a cheerful smile.

The meeting itself was an education to Meg. Teachers

had always been another kind of people, removed from ordinary human beings. They would never do ordinary things, like going to the pictures; they certainly wouldn't use coarse language, and they certainly would never have behaved shamelessly in Paris or anywhere else. But Miss Fairhurst, for all her university degree, was no more remote than Annie Miller. In a strange way, the discovery made Meg even more like an ignorant schoolgirl, because it made life still more surprising. And there was no doubt who was boss in this conversation. The woman's kindly smile, her private amusement, were maternal, and Meg was the bright surprising child.

'Listen,' she was saying, 'it's good to get away from bloody shop talk. How would you like to make this a date every week, and I'll check on how your French is coming on – if you stick it, that is.'

'Oh, I will, I will, I'm quite stubborn. But oh no, I couldn't – the wee one's home from school at three o'clock, and I couldn't leave him on his own every week.'

'Ah, a bit of neglect's good for them. All right, I've got two free periods on Tuesday mornings, we could meet here at ten.'

'Yes . . .' the idea was so appealing that Meg felt it must be sinful. 'All right, I'll try.'

'You'll do it. Here's a present for you.'

She handed a French grammar over the table.

'Oh, I couldn't.'

'It's all right, I stole it from the school. So you have a French book of your own. And here's a jotter. Hetty can bring your exercises to school, and I'll mark them.'

Meg clutched the French grammar and stared at it, with dreams in her face. She walked home in a dream. She opened the drawer that was used for sewing scraps, and never touched by anybody else in the house. She slipped the books under a piece of gingham and closed the drawer with a thud.

Life was still one thing happening after another, and some of the things were quite good.

# 11

Life did change; it moved, and they were moved. It had taken a lot of quiet determination to drag Andrew into the move, but it was impossible to live a civilised life in a room-and-kitchen with children growing into adults, and as long as he wasn't involved he was willing to let the thing happen. The new house still had a box-bed in the kitchen – the Master Bedroom was a phrase she had heard in a film, and it amused her to think that their Master Bedroom was a recess in a kitchen wall. But although the four boys still had to share a room, Hetty had a tiny room of her own, her own castle. There was even a bathroom with a bath, though there was no hot water system to make it the luxurious bathroom of the films.

And instead of a narrow dark lobby there was a square hall so big that it seemed a waste of space. But there was a use for it.

Hetty and John were learning ballroom dancing, with young Andy and his girlfriend Tina as their teachers, and Bobby and Peter getting in the way. Andy had a portable gramophone borrowed from Mr Convery, and it was playing on the floor on a corner of the hall. The hall was the only place in the house where they could move without bumping into furniture. *Whispering*, and *I'll Be Loving You Always*, and *Girl of My Dreams*, old songs on scratchy records. Bobby and Peter took turns at winding the gramophone.

It was funny to watch Andrew's confusion. He couldn't decide whether to join in the fun or dismiss it as a lot of nonsense, so he compromised; sitting in his chair humphing at the newspaper, but with one ear cocked towards the hall door. Meg stood candidly at the open door, fascinated by a kind of dancing she hardly recognised as dancing. The waltzing was all right, but the quickstep made no sense at all, one-two-chassé, one-two-three chassé, one-chassé; there was no pattern to it. But when young Andy and Tina swooped round the hall together, they knew what they were doing all right.

'It is not like *Strip the Willow* or the *Eightsome Reel*,' Meg said. Young Andy was contemptuous.

'Ach, these are for tacketty-boot dancers, Ma. You want to see the tango?'

'We don't get tangos at the school dance,' Hetty told him.

'Huh. Right outa date, that dump. Okay, take partners for the foxtrot. And mind, John, don't let Tina shove you about – you're supposed to lead. You're the man.'

John let Tina shove him round the floor all the same. At fifteen, he was taller than the girl, but unassertive and unaggressive; and Tina was a very positive wee girl. Meg wasn't sure about this girlfriend of Andy's, with her tightly waved hair and noisy lipstick, and her dress a wee bit too smart and tight and aggressive. But she was good-natured enough and laughed a lot, and it was Andy's own business.

Hetty seemed to learn the strange dance by instinct. It was as if each generation grew up knowing its own customs and its own tricks without having to study them. She was already a young woman, with the shape of a woman, and, Meg thought, a beautiful woman. Life was beginning for Hetty; and she would surely find more in life than her mother had.

When they had danced enough there was tea ready.

'Or you can have coffee if you like, Tina,' Meg said.

'Oh hey, sure, just the game, Mrs Mason. See in the pictures? Myrna Loy and Richard Dix and them? It's always a cuppa coffee they drink, you never see tea. My old lady never has coffee in the house.'

'Right you are,' said young Andy. 'You have your coffee. I've got a coupla bob, Da, you and me could nip down for a pint, eh?'

'And desert your guest?' Meg complained. But Andrew was already out of his chair and reaching for his jacket.

'See men?' Tina asked nobody. 'They treat you like conveniences.' She sounded complacent, all the same.

Meg was glad that young Andy was able to enjoy his father's company. She was sorry that it usually happened with drink, but that wasn't very different from the men on the Island, it was the way of the world. Young Tina was evidently not worried, and in a few minutes she had forgotten she was a sophisticated young woman and was working with Peter on a jigsaw puzzle, laughing constantly.

It was only half an hour before Andy came back with his

father, and ordered Tina proprietorially to get her coat so that he could walk her home. She lived only three streets away, but it would be a long time before he came back.

Andrew sat heavily in his chair, but quite soberly, with something on his mind.

'You two are getting quite hoity-toity,' he said, with thin joviality. 'Think you're quite the old jiggers, eh?' Hetty and John nodded cheerfully.

'Just watch it,' he warned them. 'You don't know everything yet.'

'No, we don't know the tango,' Hetty offered.

'That's not what I'm talking about. I mean to say, there's a lot you don't know. Life. Life. You don't want to get too big for your boots.'

'I'm getting too big for mine, Da,' Bobby announced.

'Kids!' Andrew complained. 'You can never get a word in.'

'They're squashing my toes, Da,' Bobby insisted.

'A lotta funny things can happen when you start on the jiggin',' Andrew intoned. 'You want to watch your Ps and Qs, don't think you know everything, that's all I'm tellin' you.'

'It's only a school dance, Da,' John protested.

'Aye, and the rest of it, and don't give me your lip. Anyway, Hetty'll be all right, you'll be taking her, and bringing her back. Now. That's enough.'

Hetty looked vague and uninterested, but John lowered his head and blushed and said, 'A girl doesn't want to go to a dance with her brother, Da.'

'What a girl wants and what she gets is two different things. That's your job, you take her there and see she gets home without any . . .'

'Without meeting any strange men,' Hetty suggested helpfully.

'Aye, you can laugh, but I've had my say. Enjoy yourself, mind, but I've had my say. You're only young once,' he added obscurely.

'I don't mind if Hetty doesn't,' John said, and Hetty smiled and patted his hand. Was she reassuring him, or telling him to let the subject drop? Meg felt undercurrents that worried her.

## 12

To John, the junior dance was a lot of noise and confusion as he dutifully got up for every dance with any girls who happened to be near, without seeing their faces.

Hetty's mind was absolutely clear. She danced when she was asked and made polite friendly remarks, and dismissed partners' apologies for clumsiness by taking the blame herself. When the first Ladies' Choice was announced, she was standing a yard away from Dick Smith. She turned to him, wasting no time but looking vague and unconcerned, and held out a hand.

'Me? You're asking me?' he asked.

'Yes. Well, why not? Unless you were expecting somebody else to ask you.'

'Eh, no, it's all right. I mean, fine. Eh, I suppose, right enough, a lot of other girls are quite anxious.'

'You must be awful popular.'

'Oh, you know, eh . . . yeah. That's right. I suppose.'

'It's because you're so handsome.'

'Aw, quit the kidding.'

'Well, you are, Dick.'

'Here, chuck it, you're putting me off my step.'

'You're a nice dancer, Dick.'

'You're pretty good yourself.'

'Thank you.'

'Don't mention it.'

He concentrated on dancing. He didn't try to hold her close, the way wee Archie Watson always did. He had a white hankie bunched in his right hand, to avoid getting her dress dirty. His left hand was sweating.

'I never thought you noticed me,' he said.

'Oh, everybody notices you.'

'I'm useless at maths.'

'You're good at football.'

'Oh, yeah, I'm pretty good. I never knew you noticed.'

'Are you enjoying the dance?'

'It's okay, for a school dance. You enjoying it?'

'Mm. I've never been to any other dances. It's nice.'

'Yeah, it's nice. It's quite nice.'

He was flushed and hot. In her brand-new blue dress she

felt cool and poised, and apprehensive at the same time. When the music stopped he took her to a seat and lingered in indecision.

'Do you, eh, fancy the next one, Cassidy? I mean Miss Cassidy?'

Her hesitation was minute.

'All right, Smith. Mister Smith.'

Yes, she was cool, and poised, and delirious and triumphant, and hardly surprised when he said, 'Eh, I suppose you're booked for the last waltz.'

'No, actually, I hadn't thought about it.'

'Would it be all right?'

'Well, it's a bit early yet to think about it. Well, all right.'

Before the last waltz, John sought her out. He was worried.

'Listen, Hetty, Maisie Strang asked me for the last waltz. *She* asked *me*.'

'She's got good taste.'

'But I mean, she lives away out Alexandra Parade, miles away.'

'That's all right. You can walk fast, and I'll walk slowly, and I'll meet you at the house and we'll go in together.'

'All right, I'll run back all the way. Funny, that. She asked me. I don't get it.'

In the cold night air, Dick Smith was wordless and nervous, shuffling awkwardly to keep to the outside of the pavement, his hands bunched in his pockets. Hetty tucked a hand in his arm and he spent a long time clearing his throat.

'You're good at French,' he said finally.

'So is my mother. I'm not as good as John.'

'Is your mother French?'

'No, she's just learning French.'

'Gee. You all right? You cold?'

'No I'm fine.' She glanced up at him. 'Were you going to offer to put your arm round me?'

'No, nothing like that, Hetty, honest, I'm not going to try anything.'

'I'll not break, you know.'

His arm came slowly out of his pocket and he laid his arm across her shoulders. She put an arm round his waist, and they walked rather uncomfortably, till they reached the house.

'Well,' he said.

'Well.'

'Well, goodnight, I suppose.'

'Right. I thought you might be expecting to kiss me goodnight. But people would see us out here, I suppose.'

'It's all right, honest, Hetty, I mean, I'm not suggesting we should go into the back close or anything, honest.'

'But it's not a bad idea,' she whispered. He followed her through the gaslit close to the darkness at the back. She turned towards him. He bent forward and kissed her nervously on the cheek, but he felt her arms moving over his shoulders and he put his arms round her waist. The thickness of their winter coats felt enormous. He imagined her in her pale blue dress, and the firmness of her body through the fine material. Her lips were against his and he was terrified of crushing them.

'You're awful nice, Hetty, I mean it.'

'So are you.'

If only it was summer and they weren't wearing thick coats. But in summer there would be no darkness to hide in.

Andrew was in his pyjamas and the patchwork dressing gown Meg had made for him, but he was determined not to go to bed until John and Hetty were safely home. Meg, still dressed, was sitting with a newspaper on her knees, polishing boots.

'It's nearly eleven o'clock,' he complained.

'That's not late, and they're perfectly safe.'

'It's nearly eleven o'clock. I'm going down to look for them.'

'You'll do nothing of the kind. It would only embarrass them.'

'I'll give them embarrass.'

'Oh, I'll go down if it'll satisfy you, for all the good it can do.'

She got up before he could argue and hurried out as she was, in cardigan and skirt and slippers. Just before she reached the bottom flight, she heard a hoarse whisper.

'Hetty! Hetty, are you there?'

'Ssh.'

Meg peered through the gap between the banisters. Two

83

figures, one of them Hetty, were advancing from the darkness of the back of the close to meet John. She could hear them whispering from below, and felt mean and sneaky.

'Sorry, Hetty, I ran all the way.'

'It's all right, John. Goodnight, Dick.'

'Goodnight, Hetty. Goodnight, John.'

'Goodnight, Dick.'

The unknown boy Dick left then, and Meg had the impression from the lamplight shadows that he was dancing. John and Hetty paused before starting upstairs.

'Did you have a nice walk with Maisie?'

'No she slapped my face for trying to take her arm. She said she wanted to be escorted home, not attacked in the street by a maniac.'

'Oh, the wee bitch.' Hetty started to giggle, and John joined. Meg, afraid of being discovered as a spy, backed quickly upstairs, then coughed quietly and walked back down.

'Oh, you're there. Your father was getting anxious for no reason, so I popped down to look along the street, for no reason. Did you fair enjoy yourselves?'

'It was all right, I suppose.'

Well, at least one boy must have enjoyed himself, even if it wasn't John. She walked ahead of them into the kitchen and spoke with determined briskness.

'The wanderers have returned. Now say goodnight to your father and off to bed, the hot water bottles are there already.'

'Goodnight, Da.'

'Goodnight, Father.' Hetty leaned over Andrew and kissed him on the brow before she whisked away.

'Aye, it's all very well.' Andrew was loth to give up his grievance. 'But a girl of that age out at this time of night.'

'Oh, havers, Andrew. Come on, the boots are ready and I'm tired.'

She turned off the gas after he was safely in the kitchen bed, and changed by the fire. It was fine having the big house, with a bath, and a room for the boys, and a tiny room for Hetty, and not having to share rooms. In the faint light from the fire she saw the glint of Andrew's eye, watching her. And why not? She was his wife, and she would have undressed in the full gaslight if he himself didn't think it was embarrassing. It should be a consolation that he should want to watch her at all. But this night, it troubled her.

In the luxury of her own little room, Hetty knew she would never sleep. The music kept repeating itself through her mind, again and again; the music, and the words, and everything. She didn't want to sleep.

# 13

Meg did not need to tell Andrew that Hetty was getting mixed up with Some Boy. Hetty had never told her. She knew. The girl had simply become different. She had always been sweet-natured and happy in herself, but the change was luminous. She was living on a cloud, and Meg was happy for her.

Andrew wasn't. He reported that he had seen Hetty, when he was nipping out of the stickyard for cigarettes, walking as bold as brass with some yellow-haired kid and holding his hand.

'Right in the street. Public spectacle. I'm not having any of that.'

'There's nothing anybody can do about "that". It's been the way of the world since time began.'

'A kid of fifteen? It's going to stop.'

'Oh, no doubt it'll stop, Andrew, it often does.'

'I'll make damn sure it does.'

A snatch of poetry came into Meg's mind, and she couldn't identify it. *Care, mad to see a man so happy* . . . It was strange, how some people resented other people's happiness, instead of enjoying it with them. It was true, there was some sadness in her own enjoyment of Hetty's happiness, but it was a gentle sadness that was almost happiness itself.

'We'll just leave well alone,' she said gently to Andrew. She was beginning to talk like him, in ready-made phrases. Clichés. She even knew now how to pronounce the word. 'It's only puppy love.'

'I'll sort that pup out. We know what he's after.'

'Yes, Andrew, he's after a nice girl to talk to and walk with and imagine that it's the great romance that'll last forever. It'll all blow away, no doubt. More's the pity.'

'I'll punch his jaw.'

'Don't be foolish, Andrew.'

Andrew was not to be pacified. She forced herself to be patient with him, but the real anger she disliked in herself was growing.

'It's that school,' he muttered. 'Putting funny ideas in their heads. I was again' that from the start.'

'Do you think Hetty wouldn't have met any boys if she had gone to work instead?'

He didn't listen.

'I'll sort that young lady out.'

'You will not bully her, Andrew, you will leave her alone. I'll not have that.'

Her tone stopped him dead. She hardly ever resorted to strength, but when she did, there was no doubt about it.

'Have I no rights in my own house?' he complained.

'Yes, you have, Andrew. But so has Hetty. All right, maybe she is a wee bit self-willed, but if she is, this kind of thing will only thrive on opposition. We'll not exaggerate it. It'll go away by itself.'

And she patted his hand, in a sympathetic gesture that was so hypocritical she was ashamed. So that little tussle was over. Nothing was settled.

Hetty and Dick Smith lived in a dream. Soon nobody at school even troubled to talk about them. Her girl friends forgot their envy and were eager to become her confidantes, to enjoy the lordly Dick at second hand. When she was alone with him, there was nothing lordly about him. He was simply perfect, and so was she. They left home early in the morning so that they could meet and walk to school together. Dick brought sandwiches to school, so that he could walk Hetty home at lunchtime, wander the streets eating his sandwiches, and walk back to school with her. They both liked all the same things.

He worked doggedly to improve his French so that they could talk to each other in the language of love. Life was perfect.

One day, as they were walking home together, she suddenly pulled him aside to stare into a shop window.

'Do you want something?' he asked. 'Sliced sausages, sixpence a pound. Very interesting.'

'No, I just saw my father.'

'Oh.'

'I don't want him to see us.'

'Right.'

'He's a bit . . . old fashioned.'

'Oh. All right.'

A shadow had fallen on his pleasure. They became

cautious, and when they went to the pictures once a week, they went with the crowd. The rest of the crowd carefully didn't notice the way they held hands, and kissed when the screen was dark.

He was big and burly for his age, and his mind reeled at the slender delicate perfection of his true love. He was terrified of hurting her. He was worried about some of the thoughts he had about her. He couldn't connect her with the things that kept coming into his mind.

He went by himself to see *Song of Songs* because it was about a sculptor making a nude statue of Marlene Dietrich, and he was frantic to see a naked woman. The movie was a cheat. They showed the nude statue all right, but in the scene where Marlene stood with a blanket in front of her in the artist's studio, she suddenly dropped the blanket, and the picture instantly changed to a close-up of her face and nothing else, not even her bare shoulders.

Another thing worried him. He and Hetty were in different classes for maths, and in the maths class he couldn't help looking sideways at June Delaney. She always wore tight sweaters that showed her little pointed breasts, and she was friendly with older boys, in the fifth year, and there were stories about her that turned into pictures in his mind and made him feel ashamed and unfaithful.

Hetty, with her sweet soft lips and cheeks and her warm little hand, belonged in another kind of reality. There were the hot sweaty feelings he got about Marlene Dietrich standing stark naked, and the outline of June Delaney's breasts that had him fidgeting painfully in the maths class; and there was the gentle delight of Hetty, and there was no connection between her and them.

That night, he couldn't get to sleep for the blazing pressure in his belly. He tried to ignore it because it was bad for football training, but finally he slipped out of bed and went to the toilet to release it. He thought of Hetty, and wondered about her, and tried to keep her in his mind. To his astonishment, she was blotted out by June Delaney.

# 14

## PETER

At that time I was more on my own because I was the only member of the family still at Thomson Street School. Bobby had got through the Qualifying and followed John and Hetty to Whitehill. That must have been another small victory for Mother over Da. I think I knew even at the time that that marriage was a permanent skirmish. Looking back now I see it clearly, but even at ten years old I felt it. I think I spent most of my energy just looking and listening.

Sometimes I felt there was something lacking in me. Other people did things. I looked at them doing things. If I had known the word I would have called myself a passivist. I didn't even talk too much, although I always had a lot to say; because I got tired of being attacked for being a smartie.

Like the time in Miss Johnson's class, when I got too smart. Miss Johnson was quite nice. The lesson that day had something to do with France, and she asked if anybody knew any French. Ella Greenlees shot her hand up and chanted, 'Comment allez-vous ma petite demoiselle?'

'Very good, Ella. What does it mean?'

'How are you my little miss, Miss.'

'Very good.'

I was afraid of Ella Greenlees. She was a girl. But as well as that, she had fair hair and a tilted nose and she was sure of herself. Her father was a tramways inspector. She was beautiful. I think I was in love with her.

'Anybody else?' Miss Johnson asked. I put up my hand and said, 'Oui, Mademoiselle, je parle quelques mots.'

'Yes, you would, Peter Cassidy,' she said drily. I didn't know what I had done wrong. Ella Greenlees was glaring at me. She hated me. I couldn't understand that.

'Eh, comment?' Miss Johnson asked me.

'De mon frère et mon soeur, Mademoiselle Johnson.'

'Hm,' she said. 'Maybe you're getting ahead of yourself. Right. Arithmetic jotters, please.'

Hughie Dickie was sitting next to me. He dug his elbows into me and snarled, 'You!' in a whisper. It was as if he thought I was to blame for bringing on the arithmetic lesson. At playtime I passed Ella Greenlees in the corridor. She curled one beautiful lip and said, 'Smartie.' I had ruined my chances with Ella Greenlees.

In the boys' playground, Hughie Dickie was still annoyed about the sudden arithmetic lesson, and maybe about other things. He danced round me yelling, 'Frenchie, Frenchie, Frenchie!' A little gang joined in and took up the shout. Some of them were boys I usually played with. I couldn't get used to that. I could never understand why people were always so quick to join a mob and shout at somebody.

They stopped when they saw Miss Wales at the door, looking in our direction. I don't think they needed to worry about Miss Wales. They could have torn me limb from limb and set fire to me, and she would have let it rip till I was fried before she interfered. She had never assaulted me again after that first experience in the Penny Buff, but every time she saw me I could tell she hated me. We called the baby class the Penny Buff.

But what I was saying, about speaking French and so on, was that I got cautious about doing anything too clever. In fact, it was a rule of the tribe that you shouldn't be too clever, or too good at lessons. It was all right for the girls, but not for us. It was like going over to the enemy side.

I was learning a bit of French, because it kept happening, when Mother was going over the lessons with Hetty and John, and I was just there at the time. That was a brave adventure for Mother, I can see that now. It was dead against Da's philosophy of not changing anything and not getting fancy ideas. But Mother was always brave.

She was clever too. She didn't try to talk Bobby into going to Whitehill School. She just altered John's old school blazer and put new buttons and a new school badge on it, and once he had tried it on and strutted around the kitchen in it, he was sold, and Da was outnumbered.

What I'm remembering about Active people, compared with Passive people, is the day I was going home from school alone, and thought a war had broken out. There was a crowd of people in Ardyne Street, mostly women, and there was a table, and chairs and other bits of furniture on the pavement, and a bit of scuffling going on, and a lot of shouting. The women were doing the shouting, and using words I had never heard women using before. I asked a man what was going on, and he got quite angry, though he was just looking on, like me, and told me to get away home.

I didn't, of course. He wasn't a teacher or a policeman or anything. I drifted away from him and kept on looking. It was all exciting and confusing. There were three men among the crowd of women, and they seemed to be organising a flitting while the women were trying to stop them. As the men brought furniture out of the close, women wrested it from them and dragged it back into the close, and screamed at the men. Fuckin' rotten Bastars, and Scum Whoremaisters, and Bloody Guttersnipes, and Away and Fight the Fuckin' Germans.

That's what made me wonder if another war had broken out. One thing I knew is that I wouldn't ask Mother what whoremaisters were. I would ask Bobby.

The men were pushing the women aside, quite roughly, and shouting back at them. A woman fell in the gutter, and everything got worse all of a sudden. Another woman, a big fat woman, screamed something and drove her fist into the nearest man's face. He staggered back, and two other women dragged him down and beat at him. Another woman raised a foot and brought it down right on his balls. He yelled and rolled over and over, and when he got clear he got half upright and shambled down Ardyne Street with his hands between his legs. The women screamed in triumph, and one of them, in a flowery overall and bare feet, rushed out of the close waving a sweeping brush and smashed it down on the second man's head.

'Get stuck in, Aggie! Go on yoursel! Lib the bastar!'

It was no wonder I was afraid of girls.

The man had three other women flailing at him and clawing at his face, and another one trying to get a kick at him. He threw himself free and bolted. Just then, the third man came out of the close carrying a coal scuttle. He had quicker wits than the others. He threw the scuttle at the crowd and darted back into the close to the back court to find another close for escape.

Then it all turned into a carnival. Everybody was laughing and cheering, and weeping, and carrying the furniture back into the close. Then it was all over. The excitement had stopped, and they were all standing about on the pavement waiting for something else to happen; but it was finished.

I had to tell Mother about it, though I didn't mention any

of the words the women had used. Bobby was mad that he hadn't been there. Mother started crying straight away. Although she was really quite strong, she always wept at other people's bad luck, and she told me the men were factor's men trying to throw out some poor soul for not being able to pay the rent.

Da said he wasn't surprised. They were a raggle-taggle crowd in Ardyne Street, and mostly Papes at that.

'They're still God's creatures, Andrew,' Mother said.

'Idle-onians, Meg.'

'Well, jobs are hard to get.'

'That crowd'll neither work nor want.'

I saw another fight, on Glasgow Green, worse than the battle of Ardyne Street. Unce Red took me to it. Uncle Red Cassidy was something else I never mentioned at home. Nobody had told me not to, but I knew. I knew, the same way I knew I shouldn't call a prick a prick, or call balls balls, in front of adults; not to call them anything at all, in fact. You had to pretend there were no such things.

That was something else I had noticed about myself, but I only talked about it to Hughie Dickie. We were friendly most of the time. When I read about something sad, my eyes got wet, just like Mother's. But when I read about cruelty, like Red Indians torturing women, my prick got hard. He said he was the same, and I wondered if girls were the same as well.

'That's stupid,' he said. 'How could their holes get hard?'

It had never occurred to me that girls had holes, but it was something I had always known without knowing I knew it. It helped to explain the mysterious quality of girls, going about with something hidden and secret.

'Ella Greenlees as well,' I said. It was like suddenly having a hold over Ella Greenlees, knowing her secret.

'Sure thing, every tart.'

'Even Miss Wales!'

He had never thought of Miss Wales like that. We laughed till we were in agony, spluttering Wales' hole, Wales' hole.

Hughie was resentful about girls. They had an unfair advantage, because they knew all about boys, because they saw them peeing in the street, but boys never saw anything. He thought we should go on an expedition to some scruffy streets where wee girls sometimes were out with no knickers on, and have a look at them; but nothing ever came of it. Hughie was a man of action, but he was a coward as well.

The way I got to go to Glasgow Green with Uncle Red Cassidy was that when Mother and I were in his shop one day, he said I should go with him on the May Day procession, it was part of a working-class boy's education. She agreed and disagreed at the same time.

'But it's on a Sunday afternoon, Mother,' I said. 'I would miss Sunday School.'

'Oh yes,' she said. 'And you never miss Sunday School, Peter. You never just go for a walk and spend your collection money on ice-cream.'

I stared up at her.

'How is it you know everything, Mother? It's not fair.'

'I don't know everything, but God does, and if you go with your daft uncle, He will know. But I don't want to know anything about it.'

Actually, Sunday School was all right. Miss Forbes wasn't much older than Hetty, and quite pretty. She was guaranteed to blush if we asked her how her boyfriend was, and it was fun making her blush. I quite enjoyed the Bible lessons too. I thought the ancient Jews were a bit daft, the things they got up to, worshipping golden calves and drowning the priests of Baal and so on, but I was always on Christ's side against the Pharisees and the Romans, and the stories about scourging had that funny effect on my loins. We sometimes dug through the Bible for discoveries, like the Jews eating their own dung and drinking their own piss, and the word 'womb'. I used to go about muttering womb womb womb to myself, and looking innocent, knowing nobody could hear me.

But anyway, I skipped Sunday School and went with Uncle Red to the May Day procession. It was great. We stood on the pavement for a while just watching, and listening to the pipe bands and looking at the banners, and then Uncle Dan took my hand and we slipped into the march.

Some of the people watching waved, or cheered, and others booed. One woman shouted, 'If you don't like it here, away you go to Russia!'

Uncle Red answered people like that with a smile and a nod, and to this woman he said, 'Gladly Madam, if you'll pay my fare.' That drove her insane, and she nearly lashed out at him with her handbag. She was worse than the women in Ardyne Street.

When he wasn't waving regally to the spectators, Uncle Dan told me he was going to teach me the Theory of Surplus Value. Other men in the ranks turned round, smiling, and cried, 'That's right, Comrade, catch them young!' I felt I was among friends.

A mounted policeman trotted back and forth, and somebody shouted, 'Capitalist lackey!'

They didn't like him. I thought he was great. I was crazy about horses. I dreamed all the time about having a pony. One day, I was sure, an old gentleman would stop me in the street and say he was going to Australia and he was looking for somebody to take his little pony. But it never happened. I was crazy for a pony, though. One night, in my sleep, I had an actual dream that I myself was a pony, and I could hear somebody shouting, 'And now for the bareback rider,' and when I turned my head, Ella Greenlees was riding me, with nothing on, and I could see everything, jogging up and down on top of me. I wakened up all sticky, and I thought I must have been sweating in my sleep.

By the time the procession arrived at Glasgow Green, I knew all about the Theory of Surplus Value. Capitalism owned a factory, and Labour worked in it to produce goods, worth a million pounds. But Capitalism existed for profits, so it sold the goods for a million and a half. But it only paid Labour three quarter of a million pounds. So Labour, which was also the customers, could only buy half of the goods. So there was a glut. Simply by insisting on a profit, Capitalism had ruined itself, because the factory had to close down because there weren't enough customers. It was the classic Capitalist crisis of overproduction.

Also, millions of tons of wheat were thrown into the sea because nobody could afford to buy it, while millions of people were starving. Starvation in a world of plenty.

I absorbed all this like an eager sponge. Uncle Red was delighted with me.

In Glasgow Green, the marchers were dividing into groups round portable pulpits and speakers were shouting at them about wage cuts and unemployment and injustice and war. We wandered from group to group. It was like a carnival.

One speaker was funny, I remember.

'Yes, Comrades and Friends! In this great city – did I say great? What is it great for except betrayed promises and evictions and hunger? In this great city of ours the gracious Town Council, with the gracious help of a capitalist newspaper which I am too polite to name in mixed company . . . held a festival of unemployed music. A festival of unemployed music! That's what we're reduced to. We sing for our supper, when we never even got breakfast. What was the winning song, I wonder? Christmas Day in the Workhouse? I'll tell you all you need to know about music, Comrades. The Capitalist system is the biggest fiddle since Rome burned down!'

I liked him. It was while we were listening to him that the fight started at another platform. There had been a lot of noise and shouting at the beginning, but this was different, a mixture of roars and frightened screams, and people began to run. Uncle Red hoisted me on his shoulders to look, and tell him what was happening. A crowd of men in brown shirts, with armbands, were bunched together, pushing their way through the crowd and lashing about with sticks. The crowd fell back in a hurry and the Brownshirts were there in a cleared space, moving towards the speaker on the platform.

Then another crowd of men, this one in red shirts, ran up to surround them. Some of the Redshirts were using their fists. Others had broken-up banners and fence staves.

The Brownshirts formed a ring to defend themselves, but the Redshirts burst into it and both colours got completely mixed up. I was yelling a commentary to Uncle Red, and he was jumping up and down to try to see. It was like being on a pony's back.

In the end, the Brownshirts were split up and they began to back away. As they separated into twos and threes the crowd surged in towards them, and they started to run, like the men in Ardyne Street.

Uncle Red told me I had been an eye-witness to a historical event, and that Nazism was the last brutal resort of a dying economic system. I thought it had just been a fight. I didn't like it.

# 15

Meg still enjoyed visiting Dan Cassidy's shop, for the talk about books and arguments, but she didn't do it too often because it seemed disloyal to Andrew. It was more and more difficult to talk to Andrew about anything, and that made her calls on Dan seem even more disloyal, like a criticism of her husband. Months might pass between the visits, but Dan never commented on her absences. He was easy as always.

'Family all right? They must be shooting up. Peter certainly is.'

'Hetty's a young woman, Dan, it makes me feel ancient. So Peter is still seeing you, the wee tinker. Yes, they're all healthy. Thank the Lord.'

'Aye, plenty would be content with that. There was a whole family in Scarba Street wiped out with tuberculosis.'

'Oh, no, Dan.' Her voice broke, and he smiled.

'Ah, you would take on the troubles of the whole world if they'd let you, Meg. Illness is endemic to Capitalism, Meg. Illness, and crime, and unemployment. Your man's job's all right, though?'

'I hope so. I don't know what we would do if it wasn't, with four bairns still at school, and the big house rent to pay.'

'Never mind, Meg, when everybody's on the dole they can join the Boy Scouts.'

'Oh yes, Andrew would look fine with short trousers and a pole. What are you blethering about, Dan Cassidy?'

'Do you never read the papers? Baden Powell says that all the crimes of violence show that the spirit of adventure is still alive in Britain, and all we need to do is put the criminals in the Boy Scouts, and everything will be hunky-dory.'

'I think you make these things up to annoy me, Dan.'

'Honestly, I don't know, Meg. You can believe that an old guy with a beard made the world in six days, but you refuse to believe what you read in the papers.'

'God made the world in his own time, Dan. Maybe his days were longer than ours—'

'—By God, a Jesuit as well as a Presbyterian. Meg if you're changing the Book of Genesis to suit yourself, everything else in the Bible collapses as well, in the final analysis.'

'Och, I have no time for you, Dan. Your Russian Revolution was made in ten days, but it's still just a mess.'

He smiled over his steel-rimmed glasses.

'Oh, you're on the slippery slope with your Genesis, Meg. We'll convert you yet.'

She couldn't be angry with him.


There was an alarm clock on the mantel, with twin bells on top, but the alarm was never set. Meg awakened at the right time every morning. She slipped out of bed without disturbing Andrew and filled the kettle and went silently to the boys' room to waken young Andy, with a light touch on his shoulder, for his early start at the paper shop. On this morning he wakened instantly as usual, blinked and shook his head.

'I'll not bother today,' he said.

'You'll have to, Andy. You have to open the shop.'

'Not today, I've got a cough and Convery's doing it himself. I'll be all right, Mother.'

It was a mystery. She went back to bed to sleep till it was time to wake her husband, but she lay awake. After Andrew and the children had left, young Andy emerged, dressed, and said,

'I'll just take a run out now, Mother.'

'Are you sure you're well enough? You look a bit peaky, Andy.'

'No, it's okay, honest.'

But there was something puzzling about him.


Hetty and Dick took a long way home at four o'clock.

'Not too long, though,' she said. 'It's French homework today.'

'You don't need to do French, Hetty, you're too good at it. Tu es merveilleuse.'

'Et toi. Et tu es si beau.'

'Vous deux.'

She slapped him playfully.

'Don't make fun of it, Dick, you mean toi aussi.'

'Yeah, okay. Are you going to France?'

'Oh, I would love to, some day.'

'No, I mean the school trip.'

'What trip? What trip, Dick?'

'It'll be on the notice board tomorrow. A week in Dinard. Eight pounds.'

'Eight pounds!' Her smile faded.

'It's cheap.'

'Mm.'

'It'll be great, Hetty. We could be . . . we could spend every day together.'

'Oh, it's too good to be true. Une semaine ensemble en France. It's nice to think about it, anyway. I wish Mother could come too.'

'What, as a gooseberry? Oh, have a heart, Hetty.'

'I've got a heart, silly. You can feel it.'

'I couldn't do that, Hetty!' She squeezed his arm hard. He could almost feel the firm soft edge of her breast against his biceps.


Young Andy sat in his father's chair, slumped and defeated.

'I never had the nerve to tell you this morning, Mother. But what's the use?'

'But you were doing well, Andy, you were working hard.'

'Well, the shop's not doing too well, Ma.'

'You could take a cut in your wages, Andy. Maybe I could speak to Mr Convery.'

'No, no, don't do that!'

She looked at him in sudden certainty.

'Andy, there's something you're not telling me, and you'll have to tell me.'

'He thinks I was dipping in the till.'

'That is a terrible thing to suggest, Andy, I will speak to him.' But Andy was quietly weeping. 'Oh, Andy, it's true, it's true.'

She moved towards him, and he cowered back, but she put an arm round and pressed his head to her shoulder.

'Oh, Andy, my poor boy, oh, how could you do it?'

'I thought you would be angry.'

'I am angry at myself. I'm your mother, it must be my fault.'

He burst into painful sobs and stood up, but she still held him.

'We will not tell your father, Andy. You will get another job. And you will never be silly again, Andy Mason, as long as you live.'

She felt his head shaking as he put his arms round her, and his tears mixed with her own. Her own head hardly reached his cheek. But in her arms he felt like a child.

# 16
## HETTY

I try to think it was only a childish disappointment, like a little girl not being able to go to the circus or something of that nature, but it is not at all true, I can still feel the awful sense of doom. I don't think I exaggerate in describing it as a sense of doom. Dick had been walking home with me, and simply talking of this and that, the way people do. That occasion was particularly exhilarating because of the really rather wild and impractical impossibility that emerged that we might go to France together. Now, after mature reflection, one realises all too clearly that the idea was indeed impractical and childish for that matter, and that therefore the height of the exaltation was consonant with one's childish sense of being totally bouleversée afterwards.

On ascending the stairs towards our home I encountered my stepbrother Andy descending the same staircase; an event which was in itself somewhat unusual, since his employment at Convery's newsagent store customarily kept him busily occupied all afternoon. However, he merely greeted me courteously and continued on his descent of the staircase and I thought no more of the matter.

Soon I arrived at our home, to discover my stepbrother John had preceded me and was preparing a slice of bread and jam as a temporary repast before the evening meal. Mother was also present, but of Bobby and Peter there was no evidence, they being presumably out of doors engaged in some childhood pastimes.

In view of its being Wednesday, and therefore one of the occasions for our communal study of French, I placed my French books on the table, where John's were already in evidence, and poured a cup of tea for myself, with milk but without sugar. Mother was somewhat laggard in joining us, so I withdrew her French textbook and jotter from the drawer where they habitually repose and berated her jocularly for being late in class. She appeared to be a little distrait, and averred that she 'did not feel like French' on this particular occasion, but both John and I joined in cajoling her into cooperating in what was, after all, and I presume still is, one of her favourite pursuits, and she acceded to our request.

Accordingly we devoted ourselves to an exercise in free translation, but I remained preoccupied with the matter I had so recently discussed with Richard. After an interval I could not forbear to introduce the topic, first by an apparently casual remark that it would be pleasant to visit France and experience the pleasure of conversing with the natives in their own language. Mother and John naturally agreed, Mother appearing to be especially enthusiastic, doubtless because for her a visit to France would also be a relief from the toilsome burdens of housekeeping, sewing and maintaining a family.

I then thought it expedient to reveal such information as I possessed vis-à-vis the projected school excursion to Dinard, at a cost of eight pounds; admittedly a substantial sum when compared to the economic situation of an ordinary Glasgow family, but nevertheless remarkably reasonable for such an excursion. My stepbrother John, who had not yet been apprised of the plan, displayed much excitement, but pointed out that the sum involved would be not eight, but sixteen pounds, for the joint expenditure of John and myself.

This of course I had foreseen, and it should have prevented me from indulging in such a fantasy. No doubt I had tried to dismiss it from my mind. John, however, immediately and spontaneously declared that he did not require to go, though it might be 'quite nice', to use his own rather euphemistic description. One could judge, however, that he was as fully enthusiastic as I, and was merely curbing his emotions from generosity, a characteristic for which he is undoubtedly distinguished. He is beyond question the most unselfish young man of my aquaintance, save perhaps for Richard (and one realises that one's assessment of Richard is possibly rather partial, though his generosity is there for all to see).

Mother took the standpoint that strict fairness was essential in a family, but revealed that the discussion was nugatory, since my stepbrother Andy had been dismissed from his employment, which explained my unexpected encounter with him on the staircase.

Such information, naturally, rendered the excursion to

France null and void, and indeed made it pale into insignificance beside the more serious financial straits which it would inevitably entail for the household since, in view of the prevailing situation, it would not be easy for Andy to find alternative employment.

I have to confess to a terribly selfish response, which I trust I managed to conceal. I believed that, but for Andy's misfortune, my mother would have contrived by some means to find sufficient money to permit both John and me to journey to France, and I was angry at Andy for losing his employment at so inopportune a moment. I knew this was an unworthy thought, since his plight was worse than mine; but I cannot deny that I thought it.

But worse was to come, or so it seemed; for when Father was informed, he was at first very angry and considered the possibility of physically assaulting Mr Convery to make him change his mind. Such threats, in my limited experience, are but vain and empty, and indeed the proposal was soon abandoned due to Mother's ability to divert him gently from such purposes. He then declared, however, that the event 'put the kybosh' on the continuing education of John and me, and that we should perforce find employment to repair the ravages to the family budget. The possibility of being prematurely removed from the educational process I found quite horrifying and so, I am sure, did John.

Mother, always diplomatic on such occasions, persuaded him that it would be wiser to defer any decision, and Father agreed with some reluctance, adding cryptically that the Com Pen might come in useful. (This reference was to the compensation paid to Mother by the General Omnibus Company following the death of my natural father, and rarely mentioned aloud in the family circle.) The matter was not pursued at the time, because to my astonishment, Father made a sudden and unprovoked attack on the absent Richard (not by name, which he evidently did not know) and suggested that my continued attendance at Whitehill School was merely a pretext for consorting with young men; though he did not describe them in such polite terms. In my total discomfiture I was thankful that Mother diverted his wrath and convinced him no more should be said on the topic. He left the house, considerably out of patience.

All in all, an eventful day, and perhaps one should be

grateful that the even tenor of one's way is sometimes rudely disturbed, though it is not easy to adopt such a philosophical attitude at the time. Perhaps inevitably, I was not inclined to sleep that night, and was still wakeful when I heard Father returning, and was aware of a discussion in the kitchen, followed by the opening of my bedroom door; by Father, I divined by the alcohol in the atmosphere. He sat on my bed in the dark, and declared his contrition for his words earlier in the evening, explaining that he had been naturally perturbed by the news about Andy. He assured me he knew I was a good girl and that he only wanted the best for me. I assured him in turn that it was perfectly all right and that indeed I was very tired and anxious to go to sleep. I was glad when he at last made his goodnights and left me, since my bosom was quite painful where his hand had been resting on it, he being somewhat uncoordinated through the effects of alcohol.

But still I did not sleep. Left to myself I was permitted to indulge in the bitterness of my disappointment, and I was further tortured by unworthy thoughts, imagining that Richard would be resentful at my failure to join him in the excursion and that, even more poignantly, in the holiday atmosphere of France, so far from Glasgow, and in my absence, he would undoubtedly be attracted to other girls. I was certain that Sally Colvin and June Delaney would go on the trip, and both had always held an ill-concealed admiration for Richard.

My rather bruised chest reminded me that Richard had always been the very parfit gentil knight, and had never essayed to go beyond the bounds of propriety in our relationship. That very day I had held his arm and turned to press myself against him, perhaps to prove that I trusted him and would not upbraid him if he indicated his affection in, shall we say, a slightly bolder manner than heretofore. This was doubtless wrong and forward of me; but since I was quite noticeably bruised, I almost wished that the bruise had been inflicted by his own dear hand, rather than be caused quite accidentally by Father.

You will never read this, nor will anyone else. But Oh Dick, I was so miserable and lonely for you. I cried all night.

# 17

Life was so full of small things that had to be done that Meg's weekly date with Miss Fairhurst had dwindled to a monthly date. But there was more to it than that. Meg mentioned the meetings because she felt she was using the French teacher as a dump for her own troubles, and she was afraid of exhausting her goodwill. Vickie Fairhurst was nearly outraged at this suggestion.

'You make me feel young, Meg. It's bloody kids that exhaust my goodwill. Pour out your troubles, they're a helluva lot more interesting than mine. Bring me your huddled masses and all that nonsense. Anyway, you want to know what I think about Hetty and this kid Dick Smith. There's nothing anybody can do about that.'

'That is my own opinion, Vickie, and I am happy for her but I worry about her because I am a silly woman.'

This provoked that quiet inward smile of Vickie's, the smile that made her look like a wise old parent listening to the prattling of an entertaining child. It was unsettling how directly she gazed at Meg's face, as if she were trying to memorise it. And she was. The older woman wasn't completely sure about her own feeling towards Meg, but a lot of it was quiet satisfaction in watching some kind of progress towards the light, the opening of a flower. She saw an immense potentiality in this unlettered Highland girl, climbing up through her ignorance and discovering new wonders, the routine wonders of existence, and envied her the innocence that went with a kind of invulnerable strength of will.

'And you're not saying much,' Vickie said, 'because you're a silly woman and you would never think of wondering if this boy is going to impregnate your daughter.'

'That is a terrible thing to say, Vickie Fairhurst, and it is exactly the thing I am wondering, but there is nothing I can do about that. I could never find the words to talk to Hetty about that, she is so happy and I don't want to make it all sound dirty.'

'No. Well, your Dick Smith is all right. To tell the truth, he's mostly bone and muscle and football, but he seems decent enough. Christ, since he got Hetty on the brain he's been working like a Trojan on his French. If it got them all that way I would have an easy life. It's Sally Colvin you're thinking about.'

'I am trying not to think about Sally Colvin, Vickie. It makes my heart sick. The poor daft lassie.'

'Meg, if Hetty told you about Sally Colvin, if Hetty could find the words to tell her mother about Sally Colvin, Hetty is not a daft lassie.'

'You know Vickie, you are right. She knows more about life than I give her credit for.'

And it was true. It was astonishing how easily and simply Hetty had told her about the girl who had to leave school because she was pregnant. She had been upset and slightly tearful as she told the story, but surely it had been important that she had told it at all, there must have been a signal hidden in the telling, a signal that Hetty knew the dangers of life and that her mother shouldn't be worrying about her. Vickie was looking at her again. That look followed her thoughts, and Meg laughed.

'I knew that, Vickie, I knew it all along. I was just waiting for somebody to tell me what I knew already. I just hate the idea that I'm prying into Hetty's life.'

'Oh, shite, Meg.'

'Yes, I suppose I am a fool. Oh shite.'

'That's the first time I've ever heard you swearing, Meg.'

'I am old enough to swear. Anyway, shite is not a swear word, it is not blasphemous.'

'No, but it gets something out of your system, especially if you're constipated. But there's nothing anybody can do about Hetty anyway. She's young and healthy and beautiful. Christ, she's so beautiful I detest her. She's nearly as good-looking as you.'

'Don't be stupid, I'm an old woman.'

'Jesus, you're thirty-three. If I was your age and had half your looks I would be in some man's bed every night, and having odd afternoon sessions in the headmaster's office as well.'

'You are talking nonsense, Vickie, pour épater les bourgeois.'

'Go to the top of the class, the accent is fine. Hell and damnation, the young think they invented sex yesterday. They're no bloody good at it. It takes twenty years to learn

105

how to do it right, and by that time nobody wants to do it with you.'

'I am closing my ears to this.'

'You've never closed your ears to anything. And let an old woman tell you something. When you get to my age you'll be sorry for all the temptations you resisted.'

'Indeed I shall not, for I'm not likely to have any.'

Vickie laughed aloud, and Meg frowned primly before she laughed too.

'You know,' she said, 'I would never have thought that proper educated people even thought things like that, I always thought the strange things that went on in my own head were because I was ignorant and not very high-class, they were disgusting things that decent people wouldn't even mention. Is that what education is all about? Saying rude things out loud that ignorant people pretend are not there at all? I suppose that is what Sigmund Freud is all about.'

Vickie stared at her in a moment of wild revelation, and said, 'Christ, it's you.'

'What?'

'It's you, Meg Mason. My God, there's been a story going round the staffrooms for years, about some ignorant woman who burst her way into a headmaster's office and accused one of his teachers of being sadistic. He thought she meant seditious because he had never even heard the word sadistic. Tell me it was you.'

'Yes, yes, it was me. I remember being disappointed that an educated man had not read Sigmund Freud in that day and age.'

'My God, this is like meeting Christopher Columbus.'

'Och, don't exaggerate, I am only an ignorant woman who likes going to the library.' But she flushed with pleasure.

'I don't know why anybody of your metal should come to me for advice. There's nothing I can do for you.'

'You have done it, Vickie. You have listened to me. It is a great comfort having an intelligent woman to talk to.'

'Oh well. My university degree hasn't been in vain.'

# 18

A new boy arrived in Peter's class, Harry Cooke. He had a wonderful confidence that Peter recognised as the badge of a man of action. He even had the nerve to argue with Miss Johnson, and she actually let him. When she was giving a lesson about the conquest of India, Harry put up his hand and said, 'Please miss, my mother says that the Indian Empire is just colonialism.'

'That is true enough, Harry,' Miss Johnson said, quite politely. 'But history tells us that it is benevolent colonialism. Britain did bring its superior civilisation and industrial knowledge to the colonial peoples.'

'Yes, Miss, that's what I meant.'

'Very good, it's a very interesting point, Harry.'

Peter was astonished that Harry had got away with it, and thought it would never have worked with Miss Wales. He was flattered when Harry Cooke chose him as a companion. He discovered that Harry knew everything. He was quite positive that Great Britain was no good. Peter had always had a quiet satisfaction in being British, because the British had always been right, and had always won every war, and made all the great inventions. But it was obvious that Harry knew what he was talking about.

'What's the greatest country in Europe?' he asked Peter. Peter soon learned that Harry was a bit like a schoolteacher, always asking questions that would produce the wrong answer, so that he could brush it aside.

'France?' Peter suggested.

'Russia.'

'Oh.' There was no questioning it.

'You know there's no poverty or unemployment in Russia? And you can get a divorce if you just ask for it. And there's no crime or anything. It's an ideal state.'

'How do you know?'

'My mother's a Town Councillor.'

'Oh.' There was no answer to that either.

'Isn't it cold in Russia?' Peter asked.

'That's only propaganda.'

107

'What's a divorce, Harry?'

'Did you know the Viceroy of India gets paid £80,000 a year?'

Peter goggled. 'That's nearly one thousand six hundred pounds a week!'

'It's more than that. And he's got a palace, and servants, and Rolls Royces. While the Indians are starving. Do you like girls, by the way?'

'Aye, a bit.'

'I don't. They're stupid.'

'Well . . .' Peter couldn't find a way of disagreeing, '. . . some of them are a bit stupid.'

'I'm not going to have anything to do with girls. They just get in the way.'

'I suppose so.'

Peter found his mother less impressed when he reported that Russia was the greatest country in the world, and accused him of listening to Uncle Red Cassidy. She was quite impressed to learn that Harry's mother was a Town Councillor, and thought she must be a brave girl.

'Everybody in Russia can get a divorce if they just ask for it, Mother.'

'What would they all be wanting a divorce for?'

'I don't know. I don't know what a divorce is. Harry Cooke's got a Platignum pen.'

'Lucky boy. Do you need a Platignum pen?'

'No, Mother. Anyway, the nib's broken.'

'Oh well, that is a shame. I suppose in Russia the nib would never break.'

'How?'

'I'm making a wee joke, Peter.'

'Oh.' Peter smiled to himself. 'I'll tell it to Harry.'

It was comforting to feel that his mother probably knew even more about everything than Harry.


Hughie Dickie collected songs and poems. Peter didn't always understand them, but most of them were marvellously rude. They were Hughie's way of establishing his importance, as some other boys used their skill at football, or breaking the glass on lamp-posts with their catapults, or being able to pee right over the wall of the roofless school lavatory.

*Too late, my love too late my love*
*He's got me round the middle*
*His Union Jack is up my crack*
*And you've lost your bloody fiddle*

Hughie could always keep an audience round him with his recitals, wide-eyed and sniggering. He was a peeing champion too, and had a trick of squeezing his foreskin till it bulged with water and then forcing the water up in a thin straight jet. Peter didn't even try that trick. He taught himself to snap his fingers with both hands, and learned to move his ears, and he was sometimes asked to do both tricks at once.

Harry didn't like Hughie's dirty poems, and after admiring Peter's tricks a couple of times he got bored and irritated with them, and sometimes even angry if he saw Peter's ears moving unconsciously. Now and then Peter noticed him furtively trying to snap fingers with his left hand, and failing.

Harry and Hughie came together in their taste for cinnamon stick, which Peter had never tried. Harry often had money to spend, and he was generous about sharing his purchases. He bought three sticks of cinnamon for a penny, and the three of them found a quiet spot on the lane overlooking the railway and lit up. The smouldering cinnamon had a nice smell, but no matter how hard Peter sucked, it kept going out, and when he did get some smoke into his mouth it tasted hard and acrid and made him cough.

'Look at him, Harry.' Hughie and Harry were united against him in their superior sophistication. 'He's *blowing* it. You're no' supposed to blow it, stupid.'

'I'm trying to keep it lit.'

'You'll never get the knack,' Harry told him. It was Harry's revenge for not being able to snap his fingers. A woman suddenly came round the corner into the lane, and they started in guilt, but she only shook her head and laughed and said, 'You'll stunt your growth, silly wee beggars,' and walked on.

'Ach, what does she know about it?' Hughie scoffed. 'Stupid old bitch. They tell you the same thing about rubbing your thing.'

'That's stupid.' Harry sounded less than confident.

'My big brother says,' Hughie announced, 'that if you play wi' it too often, you get warts on your hand.'

'That's absolutely stupid.' Harry was unobtrusively glancing at his palm as he spoke, and had a sudden fit of coughing.

One day he invited Peter to his house on the way home from school. Peter was interested and reluctant at the same time. He had found the word reluctant in the *Daily Record*, but he had never heard it spoken and he pronounced it reluctulant. Boys of his age were hardly ever taken into other boys' houses. Any time he went to ask if Hughie was coming out to play, he waited outside the door till Hughie came out.

'That's all right,' Harry assured him impatiently. 'You'll get a biscuit or something.' The biscuit settled the matter.

Harry's house was quite grand, and had a big living room separate from the kitchen, a big carpet on the floor instead of waxcloth, and a couch and two armchairs. The couch fascinated Peter. He had never seen one before. Mrs Cooke was quite grand too, with a nice dress and no overall. She had been a schoolteacher before she married, but had to leave because it was against the regulations for married women to have teaching jobs.

She gave them milk in tumblers and put a little wooden barrel full of biscuits on a little low table for them. There was a cut-glass bowl on a sideboard, full of apples and oranges and a banana.

'Are they real?' Peter asked.

'Yes.' Mrs Cooke smiled. 'Would you like one?'

'Oh, no thanks, Mrs Cooke.'

She smiled as if he had said something funny and asked, 'And how are you getting on at school?' They always asked that.

'Just the usual, Mrs Cooke.'

'You know education is the greatest gift we can have, Peter.'

'Oh aye, I mean, oh yes.' He was anxious to impress this daunting lady. 'I know the theory of surplus value.'

'Do you indeed?' He wondered if he had been too smart. 'It's more than I did at your age. Did Harry tell you?'

'What's the theory of value?' Harry asked in fierce irritation.

'Maybe Peter will explain it to you, Harry. Is your family Socialist, Peter?'

'I don't know. We go to the U.F. Church.'

She laughed, at one of those private jokes only adults understood, and left the room.

'You always have to be so smart,' Harry accused him.

'Sorry.'

'And you're always saying sorry as well.'

'Sorry.'

'You could have had an apple if you'd wanted.'

'It's all right.'

It was certainly strange to think of living in a house with a bowlful of fruit and not bothering with it, as Harry didn't. Through the door to the hall Peter could see Harry's father coming in, carrying an attaché-case. Mrs Cooke met him and kissed him, the way wives did in the pictures. He came into the living room and nodded briefly at the two boys, incurious about Peter's presence, opened his case and put papers on a desk, and Mrs Cooke came in with a tray with a lace cloth and tea-things on it.

'This is Peter Cassidy, John. He knows the theory of surplus value.'

Mr Cooke's smile was amused, but friendly.

'You can never start too young.'

Peter said nothing, for fear of annoying Harry again. In any case, Harry was making signals for him to leave, so he stood up.

'Well, thank you very much. I'd better go home now, Mrs Cooke.' He wondered if he should shake her hand, or even bow, but she was just smiling and Harry was jostling him towards the door. They went downstairs together.

'My father's got work to do, you know. You're not supposed to interrupt him.'

'Okay.'

There was an Austin Seven standing outside the close.

'That's ours.'

'It's a beaut. A motor!'

'It's not a "motor", it's an Austin Seven.'

'Oh. Well, see you at school, I suppose.'

Harry turned to go back into the close. Peter walked along the street and didn't turn round to stare at the car till he was sure Harry was out of sight. It was beautiful. Maybe one day he would get a ride in it; but he would never suggest it to Harry.

Next time he visited the cobbler's shop he told Uncle Red

111

he had met a Town Councillor.

'You'll be chatting to the King next. Lizzie Cooke, eh? Oh aye, I've met her. She's got a mouth like nippy sweeties.'

'She's quite nice. What do you mean?'

'Never mind me, Peter, I've got a twisted mind. So you're going over to the Reformist camp, eh? Revolution, boy, revolution is the only method. Capitalism is never going to tolerate peaceful change.'

'They think Russia's great.'

'I should bloody well hope so.'

'The Viceroy of India gets one thousand six hundred pounds a week.'

'Poor sod. How does he manage the rent?' Red pushed his glasses down his nose and smiled at him. 'I'll say this for Lizzie, she's all for town planning. We should have done it years ago, like the Germans, before that Capitalist lackey Hitler took them over. Modern flats right out in the country. Smash the tenements down and house the people right.'

'I suppose so.' Peter found a space on the ancient bench and meticulously hammered a sprig into it.

'Standard houses, modern methods, every one the same, mass production. It's coming all right. A place in the sun for everybody.'

It was Red's enthusiasm rather than the words that created a picture of a shining new city full of sunshine and happy people. Maybe everybody would even have an Austin Seven. Peter was now torn between an Austin Seven and a pony.

'Will the workers get ponies?' he asked.

'Oh, you're full of daft notions, Peter. I've never liked horses since the Cossacks rode down the Russian peasants. They're an instrument of oppression.'

'I would love a pony.'

'They'll probably do it this way. There'll be a place put aside with a supply of ponies for the communal use of the workers so that everybody has an equitable share. There'll always be facilities for healthy recreation.'

'Oh.' It was better than nothing.

# 19

Peter was living in a bombardment of strange ideas, mostly from Harry Cooke, who explained that religion was superstition and the opium of the people and that the story of Moses splitting the Red Sea was just a fairy tale, and that the Capitalists used religion to keep the working classes from seeing how they were being exploited. As long as Catholics fought Protestants, they would never fight the boss class.

But there were other curious discoveries unconnected with Harry. He had often heard grown-up people saying that a girl had 'a fine leg for a kilt', and couldn't understand it, because girls didn't wear kilts. His father had said it about a girl in a photograph in the *Daily Record*, and his mother had laughed and slapped him playfully. When Peter looked at the picture he couldn't see anything noticeable about the girl's legs, either of them.

Suddenly he discovered what it meant. He had never noticed anything particular about Ella Greenlees' legs, but he looked at them from the back one day in school and saw two strong rounded calves tapering to fine ankles, and her gym slip swinging and flicking at the backs of her knees, and he couldn't stop looking at them. She had a fine leg for a kilt. He looked at Emily Reid's legs, but they were not interesting at all. Ella had a fine leg. She had two.

It was no good telling Harry about his discovery, because Harry didn't have any time for girls. He just started looking at girls' legs and enjoying them, but looking just casually, not staring.

In summer the boys wandered the streets, ran along the dykes and dreeped from wash-houses in faraway back courts, or played King if they had a ball, and Tig if there was no ball. Peter found himself hoping they would run into a group of girls, and he sometimes nudged the gang in the direction that might lead to a street or a back-court where girls played. He was cautious and hypocritical about this when Harry Cooke was there.

Harry didn't completely approve of these games, even without girls. He thought it was more important to go on explorations to study social conditions, and sometimes

Peter went with him, willingly enough, on long hikes to the People's Palace Museum, or even away out East to the Tollcross Park Museum. It had a huge glass case of stuffed birds illustrating Who Killed Cock Robin.

Life at home was changing too. Mother and Da still went out on Saturday afternoons to Town, window-shopping and going to the pictures and sometimes bringing back French cakes. But the performance of Saturday night tea had disappeared because Andy was out working at Donnelly's Bar, and John sometimes liked to go away for the whole day, walking, and Hetty was always in a hurry to go out with her own crowd, to the café or the pictures. Bobby was wearing long trousers, and always impatient to get out too.

But some things were better. On a Saturday, Andy often slipped him as much as threepence to add to his regular penny, a secret transaction that had to be kept from Mother. So if he did go as far away as Tollcross Park with Harry he could suggest going home on the tram, and even pay Harry's fare as well as his own.

When they did wander with the gang, and ran into a crowd of girls, Harry was always particularly discontented, but he played as hard as anybody. In private he told Peter that although he had no time for any girls, he disliked Ella Greenlees especially. Maybe that was why he always tried to catch her at Tig, running straight past other people. And maybe it was because he could hardly ever catch her. The legs that were fine for a kilt could run like the wind.

Peter could catch her. She got furious at how often he could catch her, or she pretended to be.

'You're just a perfect nuisance, Peter Cassidy.' She was panting and shining.

'I'm playing the game.'

'You always have to catch me.'

'You're the best.'

'Oh, you!' But she was half laughing, teeth white and pigtails swinging. He had come to accept the pigtails. He suddenly remembered a moment from infancy when he had played ropes with the big girls in Cumbie Street and kissed a girl called Jeannie. Only infants could do things like that without getting slapped.

'Oh, get on with the game,' Harry shouted. Peter darted away, and Ella ran in pursuit of Harry.

Sometimes they bought lemonade and buns and walked to Alexandra Park to play on the grass and watch the model yachts hungrily. If they had enough money they clubbed together to hire a paddle-boat and trundle round and round the tiny lake, sometimes bumping into boats full of girls.

One Saturday he missed the others and was walking aimlessly in the direction of the park in the hope of finding them. Half-a-dozen boys approached him in a bunch.

'A Billy or a Dan or an old tin can?' one of them asked, in a threatening shout.

'None of your business.' They were bunching to surround him and he remembered it was the day of the Orange Walk. Flute bands and anti-Catholic songs and people chanting Twelfth of July the Papes'll die; and gangs of enthusiasts roaming the streets looking for an enemy to attack. If the crowd were Catholics it was wise to say a Dan. But there was no way of telling.

'Tell us,' the leader shouted.

'An old tin can.'

'He's a bloody Pape,' one of them shouted. 'Get the wee Fenian!'

'I said an old tin can,' Peter insisted. 'But anyway, I'm a Proddy.'

He recognised Hughie Dickie, who looked disgusted, and said, 'Uch, he's no a Pape, he sits beside me at school. You're a right stumer, Cassidy. We're looking for Fenians. Twelfth of July, the Papes'll die.'

'That's a lot of shite.' From fear, Peter had graduated to anger. 'What if you meet twelve Papes?'

'We'll massacre them.'

'Cassidy is a Fenian name,' the leader shouted; but Hughie shoved him aside and said to Peter. 'Come on, you're in the gang.'

Peter apathetically trailed along with them, hoping they would meet no Fenians. But they did. At the top of Ardyne Street they surrounded a lone figure and chanted the question.

'A bloody Dan,' the boy shouted. 'Come on, just try it.'

They bounded forward joyfully, but a much bigger boy suddenly jumped out from a close, waving a boiler-stick and yelling, 'Right, Terry, into the Proddy-dog bastars.'

The gang scattered in panic, but Hughie Dickie had been

gripped by the first victim and was trapped. Peter first ran with the others, and then came back to see what would happen. He thought the big boy was going to smash the stick on Hughie's skull, but he only breathed hard and said, 'Right what do you want?'

'Nothin', honest,' Hughie wailed. 'We were just out for a walk, honest, mister.'

'You want to fight him, Terry?' the big brother asked.

'Who's lookin' for a fight?' Hughie bleated. The big brother glared at Peter.

'I'm his pal,' Peter said.

'Beat it.'

'No.'

The big brother glared again, and decided to ignore Peter. 'Awright, keep out of it,' he said.

Terry released his hold on Hughie. Peter kept an eye on the big brother, who was still clutching the boiler-stick and looking ready to use it. Terry and Hughie squared up. The rest of the gang had found their way down the other side of the street and were spectating from the distance, backing steadily away.

Terry got close to Hughie and shoved him with his shoulder. Hughie staggered back, crouched, his fists clenched in the famous killer punch, with the thumbs poked through between the first and second fingers. He advanced and butted Terry with his shoulder. Terry shuffled and returned the shoulder-butt.

'Come on, give him it!' The big brother was thirsty for blood. Terry threw away caution and short-armed Hughie in the chest with his palm. Hughie backed, duck and weaved, and gave Terry a shoulder charge.

'Punch him,' the big brother roared. Looking perfectly terrified, Terry swung a punch at Hughie and struck him on the cheek. Hughie clapped his hands to his face and wailed.

'He's broke my teeth, he's broke my teeth!'

'I'll break your bloody skull, you wee Proddy shite,' said the big brother. But Hughie was already bolting down Ardyne Street. The big brother stared at Peter.

'You want it as well?'

'No.'

The big brother stared at him, puzzled.

'Well, get to hell or you'll get it.'

Peter backed away to the other side of the street and trotted down to the gang at the corner. Hughie's teeth were gritted, fists clenched again.

'I would have massacred him if that big bastar hadn't shoved me. Fenian bastar.' He looked to Peter for support. His friends were muttering, 'Sure, you could have basted him easy. Big bastar. They never fight fair.'

'That's right, innit, Peter? Well, isn't it?'

Peter was still thinking. Hughie became belligerent.

'I notice you never done nothing.'

'I never ran away.'

'Huh. You weren't much help. I could have massacred him.'

'You couldn't fight *Ella Greenlees*, unless you had a gang,' Peter said, astonished at himself.

'I'll batter you,' Hughie warned him.

'Baloney.'

'*We'll* batter you,' the leader said.

Peter ran. He ran well. They started to chase him, but the spirit had gone out of them. They yelled Dirty Wee Crapper after him. He slowed down and walked home. He thought he might have to fight Hughie Dickie the next time he met him; but on the Monday they were playing leave-oh in Cumbie Street and Hughie ignored him till he couldn't avoid him any longer, then said, 'I fixed that wee Fenian all right, didn't I?'

'Aye, sure.'

A few days later, Peter wandered innocently in the direction of Ella Greenlees' back court. She was there, in a striped dress, playing a meaningless game of throwing a ball to another girl, and Harry Cooke, and Peter stood on the side, ignored, until the other girl threw him the ball.

'Did you see the Orange Walk?' he asked Harry.

'Who cares about the Orange Walk?'

'It was on Saturday.'

'Oh, we went on a run to Largs on Saturday and had high tea.'

Harry lived in a separate world. As they spoke, Ella Greenlees hurled the ball and struck Peter on the side of the head. Harry caught it on the bounce and threw it at his head again. Peter caught it and hurled it into Harry's stomach, and Harry doubled up.

'Can you not take a joke?' he demanded. Ella Greenlees

117

was glaring at him with her lips pursed. The other girl was laughing. He left, feeling stupid, suddenly having to remember how to walk again. He found Hetty in the kitchen at home, and he slumped down in Da's armchair wondering what was wrong with him.

'You feeling sorry for yourself?' Hetty asked him. He shrugged.

'What happened?'

'Oh, nothing. I'm fed up.'

'Well, everybody's fed up. Mother's going into hospital.'

'What's wrong?' He was in terror.

'Nothing serious, but you'd better put a smile on your face.'

'All right.'

She leant over him.

'Poor wee Peter, did somebody steal your scone?'

'Aw, shut up, Hetty.'

'There there.' She kissed the top of his head. 'Hetty kiss it better.'

'I'll murder you.' He giggled.

'It's only for a few days, it's all right.'

'Can I have a piece and jam?'

'If you make it yourself. Oh, all right. See men? Useless, absolutely preternaturally useless.'

'What does preternaturally mean?'

'Look it up yourself, I'm making your piece. But you'll have to wash the dishes for the next few days.'

'Okay. What kind of jam is it?'

'Rhubarb and ginger.'

'Great. What's wrong with her?'

'None of your business.'

'Okay.'

# 20

It had happened. Something had happened and Meg was sure it was It. When she got back from hospital, everything was fine. The house was as clean as it had ever been, and the table was brightly set with tea and fancy cakes for her welcome. Hetty was bright and even hectic, talking too much, being too busy; natural nervousness, possibly, after the strain of being in charge for four days.

She went on like that, but between spells of being bright and chatty she would sit with a book, and Meg was sure she wasn't even reading it. She spent a lot of time in her room alone, studying. At least, she had books open. When she was asked how she had managed to cope she would sometimes gaily laugh, a bit like that Tina girl of Andy's, who had meanwhile disappeared from his life. When Meg got her alone, she asked her plainly if something was wrong. Hetty waved a hand wildly and cried, 'No, no, what could possibly be wrong, Mother, everything is preternaturally splendid and you're home I've got to read these books.'

'But you've finished school, Hetty.'

'Just in case I ever get into university, ha ha ha or become a personal secretary to some great public figure, work work work ha ha ha.'

There was no way of getting to her, but whatever it was, whether it was It or not, it was bound to come out. But weeks went by. Then Meg found consolation in remembering that the time had come and gone for the great school excursion to Dinard, and Hetty was at home while her boy was in France. She cursed poverty, she could nearly agree with Dan Cassidy that the time for a revolution was ripe.

If only she had thought of it earlier, or if it had happened earlier, young Andrew could probably have produced the money to let both Hetty and John go on the excursion. He was certainly always, nowadays, well supplied with money, which she hoped was honest, and he would never refuse to help. If only, if only. But even if they had had the money, Hetty would have had to cancel the trip because of the terrifying order by Dr Black that she had to go into hospital, 'for a clean-up'. She detested polite phrases to describe impolite things. Andrew and the boys could never have been left to manage by themselves. A woman was always needed.

She convinced herself that the girl was suffering the pangs of frustrated young love, and that was no more than a part of education. Young love was always frustrated, and the end of the frustration would be joyful. Peter asked Meg privately what was wrong with Hetty. She told him Hetty had things on her mind and that people were entitled to have things on their minds without being bothered by other people.

'Why, when people are afraid to fight when they're just themselves, they want to fight when they're with a crowd, Mother?'

'That is bad grammar.'

'Oh.'

'We're all cowards, that's why.'

'Oh.'

'Do you fight when you're with a crowd?' she asked sharply.

'No, not much. I don't like hitting people.'

'You mean you don't like people hitting you.'

'People don't hit me.'

'You're lucky.'

'Are you feeling all right, Mother?'

'Yes, I'm feeling just grand. Leave Hetty alone.'

'Is it Dick Smith?'

'You are a very nosy young man, Peter.'

'I know.'

'Well, stop it.'

'Okay. All right.'

But he was no nosier than his mother. She asked John if he knew anything.

'I don't know, Mother. Girls of that age are often funny.'

'Listen to Granddad.'

'So are boys. But it's harder for girls.'

'You *are* Granddad. Most men of eighty don't even know that.'

'It stands to reason, Mother. The female sex goes through larger physiological changes than the male. There are bound to be psychological effects.'

'Where did I get this collection of intellectual infants?'

'You got landed with me. Andy and Bobby are too sensible to be intellectuals.'

'Don't get above your brothers, or yourself, young man.'

120

'I try not to.'

'You are making fun of me.'

'Why shouldn't I? You've often made fun of me.'

'Oh, I've never, John Mason, I have never made fun of you.'

'I always liked it.'

'Why is young Andy like young Bobby, and you are a bit like Peter, and you not even related?'

'It must be the influence of maternal environment.'

'Oh dear oh dear, I don't know if I've ever influenced you at all, you've always been so much yourself, as if you didn't need anybody.'

'That's not true.'

'You remember the night a lassie called Maisie slapped your face on the way home from the school dance?'

'I'll murder Hetty.'

'No, I was a bad woman, I was standing on the stairs when you told her, eavesdropping. I couldn't help it.'

'You know, Mother, I've always thought you knew everything, without having to eavesdrop. I thought it was a talent innate in mothers. You see, I'm very ignorant and adolescent. I didn't know you were a detective as well.'

'I think Hetty is sorely worried about something. Maybe that young boy, maybe something else. Be nice to her.'

'You can't help being nice to Hetty. All right. But if she tells me a secret, I couldn't tell you.'

'No. You are a comfort, John.'

He flushed and looked stupid. She had a wild notion, looking at him, and she wondered why it had never occurred to her before, that maybe he wasn't a Mason at all, that maybe Andrew's first wife had known another man before Andrew. Before she could stop herself, she had said, 'John, what was your own m— No, never mind.'

'My own mother. I hardly remember. She was nice. I don't think she was happy.'

'No. I shouldn't have asked.'

'I was only five.'

'Yes. I'm glad I got you.'

'I'll be nice to Hetty.'

There was something ugly and fearful hanging over the house. But life went on, the men had to work, Meg had to calculate and clean and cook; the inescapable routine helped to keep things bearable. Everybody was affected by something, all the same. Peter and Bobby talked less and stayed out more, as if the air of the house silenced them and scared them away. Andrew was surly and snappish. Hetty herself got over her hectic false laughter and became demure and remote. Only young Andy was unchanged, but he was never much at home anyway, with his work in the pub in the evenings and his mysterious occupations during the day. Meg kept herself fiercely busy, almost building a wall round herself. The unbearable became bearable by becoming normal.

She was positively relieved when the worst became open reality, when Hetty's silence broke and she told her.

'You're sure.'

'I think so.'

'It's young Dick.'

'I don't want Dick mixed up in this. He's just started . . . anyway . . .'

'But maybe he'll want to marry you.'

'No. He's only seventeen. Maybe he would, but no. I'm not doing that to him.'

'But he *is* mixed up in it, Hetty. Anyway, we can't be sure you're having a baby.'

'I'm sure. I don't even want Dick to know.'

'He's entitled to make up his own mind.'

'No.'

She was as quietly stubborn and immovable as her mother. Meg thought of the poor girl Sally Colvin, and was consoled that Hetty at least wouldn't be cast out in the cold.

'We'll manage,' she said, and cradled the girl in her arms. Hetty remained quiet and tearless, and Meg grimly controlled her own urge to weep.

Andrew went insane when she told him. She knew he would take it badly, even stupidly, but she wasn't ready for his explosion. He was slightly drunk. He had been drinking more in any case. But drunk or sober, he was berserk.

'She'll leave the house,' he raved. 'I'm not having her in this house, I told you before she would go to the bad, Jesus Christ, fuck bloody whore she'll not stay another day under my bloody roof.'

'She'll stay with her family. This is the very time when she needs us all.'

'Out, out!' He banged his fist down on the table and smashed a plate. A broken piece flew across the kitchen and broke against the sink. Meg found herself looking at it, neatly separated into three equal pieces.

'She'll be out of my sight by the time I get home tomorrow.' Now he was muttering, but there was literal froth on his lips, spittle on his chin. 'Fucking filth fornication bitch whore.' Deliberately he swept the few other dishes on the table to the floor. He got up, swaying, climbed into bed and turned his face to the wall. Meg silently picked up the dishes and put the broken pieces in the pail. She sat down with a newspaper on her knees and polished the shoes. She turned out the gas and spent the night fully dressed in Andrew's chair.

In the morning she wakened him with a touch on the shoulder. He got up, looking past her with nothing to say, ate hunched over the table, closed and untouchable. She left the house and walked till he would have gone.

That was the end of that. The words went through her mind endlessly till she realised she had been walking for nearly an hour without even thinking of what could be done.

Annie Miller Annie Miller Annie Miller. This was a meaningless chant in her head too, but it was all she could think of, and she was brokenly relieved when she went back to the old close in Cumbie Street and found Annie at home, wearing an overall over her nightdress, a cigarette hanging from her lips, inhabiting the comfortable clutter that was never cleared.

'Christ, you look as if you had found a penny and lost a quid, Meg, there's still some in the pot but not a drop of milk in the house. Sit down in the name of God.'

Meg told her about Hetty and she responded in her own way.

'Aw, the poor wee soul, Christ, you never know the minute. The things kids get up to, we would have got the high jump at their age. Times change, that's a fact, what the hell am I blethering about, it's been the same since the world began, men have always been getting lassies up the kyte. That's no' much consolation when it's your ain, is it, though? I'll tell you no lie, Meg, I had to get spliced myself in a wee bit of a hurry and then it turned out to be a false alarm.

Well, I could have done worse. Will the fella marry her?'

'She'll not have him. Anyway, she's only seventeen, Annie, it's too young.'

'Ah, Jesus. Sixteen, me. Is there anything against the fella?'

'No, it's not that.'

'Women are bloody queer, aren't they? I mind a woman in the next close when I was wee. Jenny McIvor. Oh, a real slummock, never gave a damn. Four weans without a ring on her finger and never gave one teetotal damn. And they were all to the same wee chap, you could tell wi' the red hair. So my mother asked her once if he wouldn't marry her, and Jenny said to hell wi' that, she didn't like him.'

Meg let the words flow over her like a warm river.

'So,' Annie said at last. 'What's to do?'

'Andrew will not have her in the house.'

'Aw, a belt in the jaw'll make him see sense.'

'Never.'

'Right enough, he was always a dour bastard. Between you and I and the gatepost he done very well for himself when he got you. Three motherless weans and a ready-made mother, good-lookin' wi' it, boy did he land right on his feet? But grateful? Never look for it, give the bastards a hand and they'll chew off your bloody arm. I hope he never got his paws on your Com Pen. Jesus. What a life, who would be a lassie? I'll shove some hot water in that, it's like tar. Sorry about the milk.'

'Where can we go, Annie?'

'Christ, I'm blethering like an eejit when it's help you're needin'. Aye, where can you go right enough? You mean where can the lassie go?'

'Oh, she'll not be going anywhere without me, Annie. That is all over with Andrew Mason. There was never a very strong feeling between us, but there is nothing now. I'll never look at his face again.'

'Christ, you're in trouble. You'll be taking wee Peter as well.'

'Yes. Don't fret, Annie, I'll think of something all right. I just wanted to sit down and talk to a friendly body while I think.'

'I would take you in a minute, Meg, but . . .'

'Och, there could be no question of that, you've hardly

room for yourselves. I just have to think.'

'A squat.'

'No. But I could manage to pay rent if I could only get a place. Not a lot.'

'They'll no' take it there. They're trying to clear the lot out, the bastards want to ding the whole tenement down and build a factory. You just have to be quick before their bloody storm troopers get wind of it.'

'I couldn't Annie, I couldn't face the shame.'

'You want your lassie sleeping in the bloody street?'

'No.'

Annie Miller, her old neighbour who couldn't keep her tea caddy filled or remember to buy milk, or find her husband's false teeth, had powers of organisation in matters away beyond Meg's experience. Almost numbly, Meg let her take control of everything.

When she went back home the children were up, and young Andy was sitting in his father's chair, wearing his showy Tootal dressing gown and reading the racing section. They all realised that an announcement was going to be made, and she had rehearsed her words with care to avoid any suggestion of warfare or even grievance. But there was no way of softening the first blow.

'Hetty is going to have a baby.'

It was hard to tell how they took that. Nobody said anything. Young Andy, looking at his newspaper, froze.

'This is quite unfortunate, because she is not married, and she is not going to get married, and,' and in spite of her preparation, the words started coming out at a gallop, to be finished with it, '. . . and many people think that is a disgrace and a sin and of course it is wrong and it should never have happened and as a matter of fact your father is so ashamed that he will not have Hetty in this house any longer, so she is going somewhere else.' Hetty herself was suddenly stricken. 'But she cannot go away by herself and she needs her mother and I am going with her and so is Peter.'

Now Bobby burst into sobs and threw himself at her, just as she had feared.

'Are you going for good, Mother?' Andy asked, and she nodded.

'Don't go without me, Mother,' Bobby wailed. She was gripping herself tightly. It was John who pulled him away

125

and patted him awkwardly.

'I cannot take you away from your father, Bobby. But you can see me any time.'

Bobby threw himself from the kitchen and ran to throw himself on his bed.

'Where are you going? You'll need help.' Young Andy was quiet, stiff, not looking at anybody.

Annie Miller's powers of organisation were magical. Joe Muldoon materialised at the close with his fruit barrow and the boys carried down Hetty's bed and the sewing machine and clothes wrapped in sheets and the few possessions she wanted to take away. Andy wouldn't let her go with the barrow.

'Keep out of the way,' he muttered. 'You don't want anybody looking at you. You can come when it's all fixed. Oh, the old man's a stupid bugger.' He still didn't look at her. A door on the lower landing opened a crack and an eye peered out. There would be other people at their front windows to see the show. Meg clamped her jaw and walked along the street with Hetty, staring straight ahead of her. Worse things were happening all the time to the poor black people in Africa and India. She could have wished she was black, and in Africa, where nobody would notice anything out of the ordinary. She couldn't stay completely out of it. She and Hetty stood on the other side of Ardyne Street, looking in a shop window and seeing reflections. Hetty was made of stone.

The barrow, pushed at a run by Joe Muldoon and Andy, with the boys trotting alongside, stopped at a dingy close where Annie Miller was waiting, with two other women; bedraggled women, members of what Andrew called that Ardyne Street mob. The stuff was taken from the barrow and into the close at a gallop. A scruffy woman stopped at the shop.

'Is it your stuff, hen?'

Meg nodded and turned her head away.

'Holy Mary Mother of God, the terrible things they do to God's children. I hope all goes well.'

Annie Miller signalled from across the street and they moved over, stiff-legged, sightless. She was half-aware of women in the close patting her and saying things.

The house was on the ground floor, a tiny room-and-

126

kitchen with splintered floorboards and the stench of wet ashes and cats. The front window was broken and boarded over. The back window was broken and covered with a bit of sacking. The door was hanging on one hinge.

'It's no' exactly a palace,' Annie said. 'Jesus.'

'I'll get the door fixed and get you a bolt,' Andy muttered, and left. There was a broken crucifix hanging above the range. The neighbour women were still there. They were so kind and so curious that she wanted to scream to them to leave her alone, but they left at last. Peter was examining the house with wide fascinated eyes.

'Oh, Mother,' Hetty said; her first words all day. Meg nodded. It was no time for words, or sentiment.

'I never even thought of a scrubbing brush,' she said at last. 'We've got a lot to do. Are you there, John? Bobby?'

'You'll need help, Mother,' John said.

'It's like camping, isn't it?' Peter said.

'That is just it, Peter, we are away on a holiday at camp and we are going to enjoy ourselves just fine. We'll not need another bed, a mattress will do.'

'There's one in the box-bed.'

'And it is coming right out of the box-bed for a bonfire. We haven't even got a dish in the house, we'll have to buy everything.'

'There's no water, Mother,' Peter told her.

'You don't get tap water at a camp, you have to carry it, Peter.'

The shame cut into her, but shame was not practical or useful, compared with the need to keep life going, and the thing that mattered was to be busy and make things work. At least the miserable little house was on the ground floor, and Hetty would not have to go up and down stairs when the baby came, or when she was far through pregnancy. Meg stopped herself at that thought, it was so stupid. They could never live more than a few days in this illegal squalor.

She was afraid to go out with the children and leave the place empty, in case the factor's men came in their absence and threw their wretched possessions into the street. But even as she was thinking that, there was a quiet knock at the door, and it was surely a friend, for the factor's men would have kicked it down with one blow.

'It's all right, it's only myself,' a voice said, and the woman

127

from across the close came in with a tray, or a board, with a teapot and a milk bottle and a little pile of sugar and a spoon and two cups and three jamjars.

'You'll be needing a cup, hen,' she said. 'I can let you have a chair, it's a bit broken, and a stool, and come to me for water any time you need it.'

Don't cry, don't give way.

'The door's never locked,' the woman said.

'You are very good.'

'Ah, it's the poor that helps the poor, and that is not a word of a lie. When Pat comes home he'll fix the Primus stove and you can have it till you get yourselves sorted out. But you'll need paraffin and methylated spirits.'

'Oh God in Heaven.' Meg was speaking below her breath.

She wrote a list of things people needed on a camping holiday. Even Bobby had got over his tears. The woman across the close, her name was Bridie, told her never to worry about the factor's men, there were lookouts and the factor's men didn't fancy Ardyne Street after all, they had learned better.

Meg went first to the bank and drew some of the precious money, and the children joined her in a spending spree, tin mugs and plates and cheap knives and forks and spoons and a scrubbing brush, and soap and candles and paraffin and methylated spirits; and a mattress and a new bed-board and two pillows. By the time they came back, the ruined hinge on the door was replaced and a bolt fixed, but no sign of Andy. But there were three pails of water in the kitchen and a fire burning in the grate.

'Bobby,' she said, 'you will come out with me and we will buy a wireless and you will carry it home.'

'Oh, great, Ma. Can I come and listen to it?'

'You will have to, Bobby. I bought one of these mugs specially for you, it has got to be used.'

Hetty was on her knees, scrubbing the floor.

If it had not been for the smell of cats, it wasn't too different from life on the islands. Water had to be fetched. Light came from candles. Meg threw off her shame and threw herself into work. The neighbours were kindly, but they respected her privacy too. A woman from two closes away arrived with kitchen chairs and reassured her about her security.

'They're feart to come near Ardyne Street, missus,' she said. 'The bloody rack-renters. We shot some of them dead in Ireland in the old days and still they put us out, but they'll not put us out of Glasgow. The blessed saints are on our side.'

Meg took down the broken crucifix from the wall, washed it and put it back. If it was a Papist image it was still entitled to be there, where some other woman had wanted it and respected it before she was driven out of the house. A mysterious man appeared at the kitchen window at the back and fixed new panes in it, and wouldn't even take a shilling for his trouble. He said Andy had sent him, and he gave her a letter to prove it. He wouldn't put glass in the front window, he explained, because that would just let the bastards know somebody had moved in.

There was no letter in the envelope from Andy, only four pound notes. Peter slept in the kitchen, on Hetty's little bed, and Meg and Hetty slept in the box-bed in the front room, holding each other like sisters. They went to the Barrows and bought a table, and brought it back on the driver's platform of a tramcar. Two women at the closemouth carried it into the house and nearly gave a little cheer. It was a scruffy street and some of the language was terrible but there was no malice in it. Peter was fascinated.

'Why do they say Holy Mary Mother of God and then say a bad word as well, Mother?'

'What bad word? They never say a bad word about God, Peter.'

'No. They say Holy Mary Mother of God and they say where has that f—ing brat got to.'

'It is only a word, it is only a habit, and don't let me hear you saying that word. Or Holy Mary Mother of God either. Anyway, they don't all talk like that.'

'No.'

But oh Holy Mary Mother of God, she thought, we can't go on like this, it is not fitting, and Hetty is still closed up in herself and I don't want her to get married, God knows I don't want her to do what I had to do, but we cannot go on like this, it is no way for my children to grow up when they are entitled to a better life.

It seemed that Hetty and Peter had settled into the miserable little house in Ardyne Street. Peter had, anyway, and was picking up odd, strange, Irish ways of speech. Hetty was living her own private life. Meg had the courage to ask her what was ailing her, because they couldn't go on forever being private from each other; but there was never any answer that meant anything. Whatever was going on in the girl's body, she was not well in her mind, and Meg could find nothing to do about it. They had to get out of this place. She had the superstitious idea that if they were able to get away, they would leave their worries in Ardyne Street; but whether it was superstitious or not, she was resolved to do it.

Old Mr Cowan died, the only Jew she had ever known, although Andrew had always insisted the city was overrun with them. He had the sweetie shop in the Gallowgate near Cumbie Street. His children were grown up and away in their own shops, and old Mrs Cowan had no heart to carry on without him. She gave up the shop and went away.

Meg was trembling with fear at the idea that had invaded her when she saw the empty shop, but it wouldn't go away. She couldn't go on forever living in a condemned house, with no money coming in and the precious savings trickling away, and a shop was a shop. It was what that funny wee man said in H.G. Wells' book, she thought. Keep a shop and a shop'll keep you.

Not sweeties, though. Clothes; and repairs; and alterations; and bits and pieces on the side, pins and needles and ribbons and braid. And if they were not as cheap as Woolworth's, they would be handier than Woolworth's. And if it swallowed up the bank account it was better than letting it dribble away week by week. But the prospect of a business was so novel and mysterious that she had a kind of paralysis of the will. She walked past the empty shop constantly. When she saw anybody else looking at it, even idly, she was stabbed with despair in case the casual passer-by was making his own calculations and getting in ahead of her. This was foolishness, she knew. Cowan's wasn't the only empty shop in Glasgow and if she really meant to do something there were plenty of others. But the plan had come to her because of Cowan's and it was all wrapped up in Cowan's. Cowan's was an idée fixe. She didn't discuss it with the children. It was enough that her own head was full of trains and rails, without filling theirs with fantasies that wouldn't come true.

She was sure that if she went to the factor's office to ask about renting the place, she would be recognised as an impostor, an ignorant working woman who had no right to be posing as a person of business. She would be chased from the office. They would laugh at her.

That was foolishness too. People weren't *born* to business. Everybody had to begin some time, take the mad leap at a venture. But she couldn't throw off the fear of humiliation, the recognition and the exposure.

But the tension of looking at the shop every day, and seeing other people look at it, seeing it being stolen from under her nose, was even harder to bear. She took the address from the To Let notice and went to the office, breathing deeply to fight her nervousness.

It was a dingy place, one stair up in a dingy tenement, and it reminded her unpleasantly of a pawnshop. More than a dozen people were queuing at a counter with a frosted glass window running along its length and one small pane in the middle.

A sour woman with her hair in a bun was behind the counter, taking money and marking amounts in rent books. There was very little talk among the customers and what there was, was in whispers, as if the woman with the bun might look up and tell them to stop talking at the back; or as if they were in church; but more as if they were in a pawnshop and their business there was shameful and humiliating.

She arrived at the head of the queue, nervous herself and feeling like an imposter.

'Well?' The sour woman was irritated by silence.

'Cowan's shop in the Gallowgate.'

'Speak up, speak up.'

'Cowan's shop in Gallowgate.'

'What about it? What's it got to do with you?'

'It is to let.'

'I know it's to let.' She was so snappish that Meg's gorge rose. And that was a curious expression, she thought. Who had ever seen a gorge rising? But she was too angry to be nervous any more.

'If you want to let it, then, you had better learn some manners.' She spoke loudly and clearly and looked the contemptible biddy straight in the eye. Somebody in the queue behind gave a little whooping laugh and then they fell

131

silent. She felt that she was in the role of the White Knight, slaughtering their dragon.

'Perhaps,' she added, 'I should discuss it with someone competent to talk business.' Oh, very cold, very hard, Meg girl. A man in a dark suit popped out behind the sour woman, who muttered, 'It's about Cowan's shop, Mr Livingstone.'

'Ah. If you'll just come this way, Madam.' He vanished and reappeared at a door at the end of the counter, stepped aside politely to let her through and made little gestures with both hands to usher her into another office.

'Please sit down. You're in the, ah, confectionery trade?'

'No, I am not.'

'Yes?' He was so eager to be friendly that she abandoned her idea of glossing over the reality, and told him that she was in no trade at all, but that she intended to try. He looked doubtful, but still eager, and she knew, she knew for Gospel truth, that there was no mad rush of tenants for Cowan's. He nodded encouragingly as she explained her idea, and managed to look interested and eager and doubtful at the same time. What was he worried about? If she took his shop and failed he would just throw her out and be losing nothing. He was a silly man, she decided, and probably not too honest.

'You would certainly be, ah, an attraction in the shop, Mrs Ah . . .'

'Mason.'

'Aye, aye. Mason of course.'

Why of course? Now he was straight on about what a fine location it was, splendid passing trade, a very good record, one of the finest properties on his books. Was he trying to hypnotise her, making it sound like Woolworth's and Marks & Spencers rolled into one? It was only a shop. It took him a long time to get round to anything practical. Three pounds a week? It was a fortune. Sorry, that was the rent. They could even get more for it from some other clients. Oh, no doubt. They had had many enquiries.

No doubt.

'You'll be telling me all these people queuing at the counter are wanting to ask about the shop.'

They shared a smile at her little joke.

'One of the multiples has expressed an interest, in point of fact, and they could pay over the odds.'

'Oh, in that case it would be bad business to give it to me, Mr Livingstone.'

He jerked into a half-standing position as she looked like leaving.

'First come, first served, of course, that goes without saying, in point of fact.' And he was eyeing her slily, running his eyes up and down without looking, as it were.

'Payable monthly, in advance, of course.'

'That would be quite satisfactory, if I decide.' She wondered why she had ever been nervous at all. 'But if it were paid monthly, that would be twelve pounds a month, which is less than three pounds a week.'

'Yes, of course, that's understood.'

'It is a lot of money. I will think about it.'

'Don't think too long, of course, eh ha ha.'

'We'll see. I am looking at a few other places.' Well, that was not an actual lie.

'Perhaps you'll leave your address, of course . . . in case, well, we do have other properties on the books, just a few.'

'It's Mrs Margaret Mason . . .'

She was abruptly terrified. In all the days she had been in Ardyne Street she had never thought to discover the factor's name. It might be this very office, and if she gave her address they would be there in a twinkling to throw her out:

'I don't have a proper Glasgow address yet.'

'Ah, I thought you were from the Highlands, the lilt of course. Staying with relatives? We *might* be able to be of assistance there too, of course.'

'Yes.' She stood up positively, frantic to be away from the place and safe. 'I'm not sure where I am from day to day at the moment. I'll come back in if I make a decision.'

He was equally frantic to delay her, not quite laying hands on her, but quite anxious to, she thought. She had to stop in the close and breathe deeply again. She *was* an imposter, and she could have been publicly shamed. She fought down a bitter anger at the injustice of the world, and society, and poverty, and landlords, and other people.

It was not the same factor, she learned from Bridie next door. She had worried for nothing. In her relief, she was able to tell the children about her mad scheme. Hetty was gravely pleased – there wasn't much excitement in Hetty these days.

Peter was wide-eyed with the audacity of it. They both shared her terror of the moment when she nearly gave her address.

'Tell us everything you said, Mother.' Peter was enchanted. 'A whole shop! Tell us every word.'

'But maybe all the factors have . . . I don't know,' said Hetty. 'A list?'

'Heaven help us, Hetty, I never thought of that, maybe they all get together. Oh, it is just terrible having my two bairns here like criminals.'

'It's my fault, Mother.'

'It is nothing of the kind and we'll have no more of that. Oh, we'll get the shop and we'll get a decent place to stay and hold our heads up, it will all be just sublime.'

There was a thundering knocking at the door and she gasped in shock.

'Have they come already?' Peter whispered. She went to the lobby.

'Yes, Who is it?'

'The Red Terror, that's who. Open up, in the name of the Revolution.'

'Oh, Dan Cassidy. You're a tinker, I could have fallen dead with heart failure, I'll never forgive you as long as I live.'

'Well, you'll not live long here. Hello Peter. Hello Hetty, I would never have known you.'

'No.' Hetty offered a wan smile.

'Well, the Red Dawn has dawned and poverty and oppression have perished from the earth. You're crazy, woman, you're crazy, and you're no friend of mine, bringing your huddled masses to this slag-heap without even asking my permission. Come on, the carriage awaits without.'

'Without what, Uncle Red? Wheels?'

'That boy will end up in Peterhead, Meg.'

'Look at the carriage, Peter – it's Rice's scrap-iron cart.'

'What in Heaven's name are you up to, Dan Cassidy?'

'I'm a knight on a white charger, can you not use the eyes God gave you? Or Karl Marx gave you? You're about to flit, woman.'

'And to where, may I ask? Are we going to live in your smelly little back shop?'

'You're going to live in my bijou residence in Dennistoun,

that's where. God knows it's empty enough with nobody but me rattling round in it.'

'No, Dan, Positively no.'

'I'm not taking no, Meg. I'm ashamed of you, forgetting your friends.'

'It just would not do.'

'Aha. Bourgeois morality, is that it? Can you not throw off the shackles of Capitalist convention, after everything I've taught you?'

'A widower and a married woman, Dan. It would not be right.'

'You've got two chaperones, and I need somebody to dust the place. And that's all I need, Meg, that's all. You understand me.'

'Can I go on the cart, Uncle Red?'

'You can drive the horse, Peter.'

'Oh, Mother, he's letting me drive the horse!'

Dan Cassidy laughed and took her hand.

'You'll never deprive Peter of that, will you?'

'You're nothing but a tinker, Dan Cassidy.'

'Come on, Peter,' said Dan. 'Give us a hand. Out with everything. Now what are you thinking about, woman?'

Her hand was squeezing his fingers painfully, and she bit her lip painfully, but it was no good, the tears blinded her and it was hard to speak.

'I'm thinking, Dan Cassidy . . . I'm . . . I'm thinking there is a God in Heaven.'

'Ah, there is for sure, and the saints be praised for your good fortune.' Bridie had been at the open door all the time.

## 21

She had always had the notion, even unconsciously, that one day things would settle down, like the oceans after the Flood, one day the irritations and the troubles and the problems would be over and everybody could relax. She wondered about it now and decided that it was a superstition and that it must have been Heaven she had been thinking about; and she wasn't ready for Heaven, in the unlikely event that she was good enough to qualify for it. There was no such thing as Life, only an endless succession of incidents and surprises. Everything led to something else, and the something else could never be imagined ahead. That was Life. So be it.

Young Andy had gone into politics. She knew because she met him in the street, since he never visited them. He was working for a nomination for the Town Councillor elections. She wondered about a Town Councillor who was a publican and a sinner.

'It's only a job, Mother. Oh, I'm a sinner all right, but at least I know it. Remember when Convery caught me dipping the till?'

'I never think about it, Andy.'

'Oh, I do. Oh, you were the goods that time, Mother, you were the goods. But do you know why I did it? Because I'm a born rascal, I'll always be a rascal. I've just learned to be a rascal without breaking the law.'

'Running for a bookie is breaking the law.'

'Ach, there are laws and laws. Fools will always gamble, Mother. If I didn't take their lines they would find somebody else. I'll not stick it too long anyway, I'll get myself something respectable. If I get the nomination I'll call myself a shop assistant. That's true enough.'

'I wish you had never got into the liquor trade either, Andy.'

'Ach.'

'And will you get into the Town Council? Oh I would fair love to see you there, Andy, I would like to see my boys getting on.'

'Not a snowflake's chance in Hell. If I get a nomination, it'll be for some ward like Kelvinside, where the folk think the Independent Labour Party is a mob wi' horns and bloodstained scimitars.'

'What is the sense of it, then?'

'Have to start some place. It gets my name in front of the comrades.'

'Comrades? You're not a Communist like Dan Cassidy?'

Dan's name always made Andy look uncomfortable.

'Ach, they've got no future. And you canny trust the Communists.'

She was going to say that she could trust Dan Cassidy with her life, but she let the name drop. She suspected that Andy might do well in politics, and it was just a pity that he approached them like a bit of a rascal, even if Dan Cassidy said that every non-Communist political *was* a rascal.

Andy's approach to politics was something he could hardly have defined himself. He saw it as a way out of the drab streets and into another kind of life, but he was getting excited too by the idea of changing the world and getting rid of the drab streets for everybody, and the logic of Socialism was irresistible. He read the *New Leader* every week and everything in it made sense; the treatment of the unemployed, and the callousness of the Means Test, which refused a man benefit till he spent his savings, and the growing success of the great Russian experiment in spite of mistakes and setbacks, the brutality of Hitler's Germany condoned or supported by the international conspiracy of Capitalism; and the savagery of Fascism in Italy, the suppression of India's legitimate aspirations to be free of British rule, the legal fraud of Tom Mooney's trial in America, Sacco and Vanzetti. He was amazed at his own ignorance and hungry for knowledge to feed his enthusiasm.

He hoped to make sure of a good place for himself in a brave new world, but he wanted to see the brave new world too. He made his way cautiously in the Party branch and listened more than he spoke, made contributions with generosity but caution in case he might incite envy and resentment, sized up the other members and chose friends and allies with care. When the branch treasurer fell ill he was willing to substitute for him when nobody else was. He found the books in a mess when he finally persuaded old Willie to hand them over, and he sensed from his own rascality that the old man was terrified of being caught with

137

glaring losses in the tiny funds. Andy made up the losses and cooked the books back to health and promised never to mention it, and made a friend who would never let him down.

When he spoke at all at meetings it was always an opinion taken from the *New Leader* and absolutely acceptable. Some of the comrades, he realized quite early, didn't read the literature too thoroughly, or didn't remember it well. From being nervous and humble in face of their long experience he steadily assessed their talents and their failings, and found a technique of disagreeing while seeming to agree.

'Comrade Kinney is absolutely right when he says the plight of the Indian masses must be a high priority in our propaganda campaign, and I can only add that, as Jimmy Maxton himself pointed out at the rally last month, we canny do much to help starving Indians if the British workers have starved to death before they can give our Indian comrades a gee-up. But I'm sure Comrade Kinney had that in mind anyway.'

He studied the speaking or the oratorial styles of the older hands, and discarded Stan Kinney's intoxication with language, his mannerisms, his constant iterations of favourite phrases, like the Municipal Elections – not Municipal, but always Munic*IPI*al elections; and the Challenger of the Exchequer. Stan was a tolerated joke as well as an embarrassment, and he never uttered one of his ringing, wrong phrases, without repeating it at least once for emphasis and style.

Andy sometimes spent an hour in the public benches in the City Chambers to watch municipal politics in action. There were few flights of oratory there; it was more like a scrappy committee meeting, sometimes more scrap than meeting. But the rules were still the same, he decided. Say nothing till there was something worth saying, say it loudly and clearly, and think fast. And some of the City Fathers were quite as stupid as Stan Kinney.

All in all, he could see his way ahead. A few election fights in absolutely hopeless wards, no complaining, no pushing, and something would fall into his lap in time. In the meantime, he was managing to put some money away. It might go towards a pub of his own, or maybe better, a sleeping partnership that didn't show. Political connections were an asset in the Trade, where a livelihood depended on the renewal of the licence by the magistrates every year.

He regretted a little not having more time to spend at home. But he couldn't do much there. Da was very morose, and drinking more, and liable to fits of temper, and his moods drove the boys out of the house, which gave him an excuse for more bad temper. John was old enough to stand up for himself, and although he was never aggressive, he would take no bullying. But Bobby was still angry and hurt at losing Mother, and he was always liable to provoke the old boy without thinking.

It was a hell of a life with Mother away. But he couldn't blame her for that. He wondered how she had put up with the old man for so long. He wondered what was between her and Dan Cassidy.

After Ardyne Street, Dan's narrow little terrace house in Dennistoun was sumptuous. It had even two toilets, one in the bathroom upstairs and another tiny one off the narrow hallway on the ground floor. There was a tiny overgrown walled garden at the back. The floors were carpeted and so were the stairs. The house had the unkempt look of long neglect, but it was a cheerful dilapidation, and Peter found it enchanting, with a room of his own for the first time in his life, even if it was so tiny that there was hardly room to walk beside the single cot, and the drawers in the chest at the end of the bed couldn't be fully opened.

He missed Bobby, with his scratchy toenails, but he liked the feeling of his own place. Hetty had the little back bedroom upstairs and Uncle Red was in the front bedroom. His mother slept downstairs at the back in what had been a dining room when they arrived.

It wasn't only the house, and the grass, which Peter himself was doggedly cutting, in small instalments with a pair of scissors. Everything else was different with Uncle Red, who was so easy-osy and unworried and never lost his temper, who made jokes and talked all the time, unlike Da completely.

Hetty came back to life, at least a little, with the shop. Dan laughed out loud when Meg first talked about it.

'You in a shop? You would be giving everything away and going bankrupt every week. Folk don't like paying money, you know, even when they've got it, and a lot of them haven't got it. They'll run up bills, they'll ask for tick and run up bills sky-high if you give them a chance, and to hell with you.'

'There would be no tick. I never asked for tick in my life and I would not encourage people to get into debt. Is it a silly notion?'

'You'll have to do something, Meg. The rent here is going to be astronomical. Now I'm in the rentier class I'll be a real vampire.'

'Yes, and we'll have to talk about that this minute.'

'Oh, don't bother me with business, woman. I'll send Peter out to work, as a sweep's boy maybe, or dragging wagons down a mine.'

'They've got pit ponies for that,' Peter corrected him. 'It would be great.'

'Do you not think I could do it, Dan? I can sew, I've had to depend on it for a few extra shillings for years. And I can count.'

'Aw, do it, Meg, while you're young and crazy.'

'I could maybe make hats as well. Anything, I don't know.'

'Where will you get the money to start?'

'That is my business, Dan Cassidy.'

'The arrangement here is, I buy the food and you cook it, or Hetty cooks it.'

'And what other arrangement?'

'That's all the arrangement. You keep the house, I buy the food.'

'Indeed you do not, it would turn to ashes in my mouth.'

'Oh, shut up, Meg Macrae, and do as you're told.'

It was wonderful how Dan could say something brutal and it didn't sound brutal at all.

'Three pounds a week?' Dan said. 'They saw you coming. You'll get a cheaper place than that.'

'I just have a kind of feeling about Cowan's shop. But I'll take your advice, you are a proper businessman.'

Dan roared with laughter.

'I've been buying dear and selling cheap all my life. But I'll come with you next time you see that bugger Livingstone. A pasty-faced Uriah Heep. I'll threaten him with the Revolution. And I'll buy the first hat you make.'

'I've never made a hat in my life, but I'm sure you don't

have to be an Einstein to do it.'

'Even if you do have to be an Einstein, you'll manage it.'

'Och, your head is full of broken bottles, Dan Cassidy.'

Dan beat Mr Livingstone down quite brutally, the man was putty in his hands. He even said they would take the key at once, but they wouldn't open for a month, so they wouldn't start paying rent until then. Meg was flabbergasted at his cunning. They inspected the shop in a dream, took out the stuff from the back shop, where the Cowans had cooked the home-made sweets. There were plenty of shelves, but they were narrow; and plenty of useless sweetie-jars, but not much else. But it was intoxicating. Dan found an out-of-work painter, a Communist of course, to paint the front and write 'Meg's' in fancy script in what nearly looked like gold leaf. She had wanted to clean the house from top to bottom, but it had to wait while she scrubbed the shop instead.

She had never met a wholesaler. She had to go to the Gorbals. She had never met so many Jews. After her first few nervous inquiries she discovered that they were all pleased to see her. Some of them would have sold her enough stuff to fill the Public Library. She had to pretend that she was a genuine businesswoman, and take notes in a new notebook of prices and descriptions to compare with other places. It was not insulting, she realised. People expected her to be firm and take her own time. One of them put her on to a dress shop in a slum building that was to be demolished, and she was able to buy four dummies and an armful of little display stands for the counter for practically nothing.

She nearly grew devious. She would go to other shops, well away from the Gallowgate, and buy something trivial like a bobbin of thread or a yard of elastic, and then waste time in small talk while she inspected the stock and displays. She soon realised that it was better to be plain and honest and admit that she was opening her own shop. It was wonderful how ready people were with advice, they enjoyed giving it, especially when they found that her shop was so far away. She got a joiner to saw the long counter in two and move the halves to different places so that the place would look more like a salon and less like a sweetie shop, and got two long mirrors at the Barrows to hang in the tiny lobby between the front shop and the back shop, to turn it into a fitting room, with two electric lights in the ceiling. Electricity itself was a delight, so immediate and easy and no danger of fire. It was one of the things that had pleased her in Dan's house, after all the years of turning the gas up and down, and the inverted mantles that would break if a bluebottle landed on them, nearly. It was a great adventure, and Hetty was really looking forward to serving in the shop, practising her techniques, cooing, 'Can Ai help you, Moddom', in a mincing voice and sweeping from door to counter like a mannequin.

There was no sign or word of the boy Dick. He was probably lying low and hoping everything would blow over. Meg had the irreligious hope that it would too, that something unfortunate but not harmful would happen to Hetty and she would lose the baby. But that was in God's hands, and for the moment God was good, God was very good. She hoped He hadn't been reading her mind.

At church on Sunday Mr Gillan was kind enough to speak to her particularly after the service.

'It's some time since I had a wee visit to you, Mrs Mason. I'll be in your neighbourhood, let me see, oh yes, tomorrow, so I could look in then. I understand your daughter hasn't been well.'

'Oh.' She was a little dashed. 'She is just fine in herself at the moment. But I'll tell you about that tomorrow. Oh I'm not in that neighbourhood any more, so that's no good. I'll give you my new address and you can drop in some other day, maybe.'

'No, tomorrow will be very suitable. Mm.'

There was something going on there that made her apprehensive; and it was inconvenient to give up an afternoon of work at the shop. But she stayed at home and spent the morning cleaning the house instead, and sent Hetty to the shop in the afternoon. If the minister knew about the girl's condition . . . it was probably silly to conceal the truth, The Truth Shall Make You Whole. But equally there was no need for Hetty to undergo an inquisition, if that was what Mr Gillan had in mind. And there was no need to tell anybody about the visitation either. She ordered Peter out to play.

Peter's enthusiasm for the shop had worn down. He wandered back to his old haunts and met Hugh Dickie, alone and bored. It was the Fair Fortnight, and nearly everybody was away on holiday.

'Look,' said Hughie. He had a grubby folded paper in his pocket, with typing on it.

'My big brother gave me it, it's typed.'

Book Titles, it said. The Nail in the Carpet, by R. Scott. The Nail in the Banister, by R. Stornoway. The Bare Naked Woman, by Major Coxstand. The Chinese Turd, by Hoo Flung Dung.

Hughie watched anxiously, like a doting mother whose child is being inspected, and Peter obligingly tittered and snorted. 'Hoo Flung Dung. Hee hee hee.'

'Major Coxstand! Great, that, innit? That's my favourite. Oh here, see a bare naked woman?'

'No, where?'

'Ach, you. I mean, see a bare naked woman, it must be great. Hey, that's funny, see a bare naked woman, no, where. Hee hee.'

'I've seen one.'

'You have not.'

'I have sot.'

'You lucky dot! Where? Did it Major Cockstand, I bet?'

'Well, a picture.'

'Och, a picture. Right enough? Bare naked? They've always got bathing suits or corsets or something. Right bare naked?'

'Sure. My uncle's got a book, the Universal Home Doctor and there's a picture in it.'

'Christ. Can you see everything?'

'You can see her diddies.'

'Christ. Can you see her thing?'

'No, she's standing up with her feet together.'

'That's right rotten. Right enough, you can see her diddies? Can I get seeing it?'

'Oh, we'll see,' Peter said grandly. His picture was more exciting than Hughie's list of books. Hughie was wriggling and adjusting his trousers at the front.

'Is she hairy?'

'No, she's a woman, stupid.'

'My big brother says women are hairy the same as men.'

'That's stupid. They don't have moustaches.'

'Right enough. But he says they've got hair there. Maybe she shaved it.'

'Aye, maybe. I never thought they had hair. That's funny.

143

Miss Wales as well?'

'Hee hee. Hairy Wales. Good morning Miss Wales, I fair like your hair style.'

They giggled their way along the lane by the railway.

'If we had a fishing net we could go to the canal,' Hughie said sadly.

'I've got a penny.'

'Great. I'll go up to the house and get a jelly jar.'

They spent the afternoon at the canal and caught four baggy minnies, and Peter generously let Hughie keep them, because they had only one jar. But three were dead by the time they got to Hughie's close.

Mr Gillan was clearly going to spend his visitation with his lips firmly pursed, and Meg found this exasperating. She was glad to see him, she was sure, and she was grateful for any counsel he might give her, but she detested pursed lips. She was impatient too with his painfully roundabout approach to the subject of Hetty, and cut it short by telling him straight out. He had the grace not to feign surprise, but nodded in melancholy satisfaction.

'Yes. The sins of the flesh.'

'Are always with us.'

'Not always, among Christian people, I hope.'

'Christians are sinners, like other people, Mr Gillan.'

'How true that is. Well, there can be no question of a church marriage, but I'll be happy to arrange it in the vestry.'

'She is not getting married.'

'But that is very serious. The child must be born in wedlock.'

'Yes, it is serious. But it is the truth.'

'She should have been here, I must reason with her.'

'You would be wasting your time, Mr Gillan.'

'But you've reasoned without avail.'

'I have not. My daughter has made her own decision, and it is her decision. I will certainly not persuade her into a marriage she does not want. There is no worse thing in the world than that.'

'There is illegitimacy.'

'Yes, and it is not very nice, but Mr Ramsay Macdonald is illegitimate, and it didn't stop him from being Prime Minister.'

He didn't want to know about Ramsay Macdonald.

'Rebellion is as the sin of witchcraft.'

'That is a very strange remark, Mr Gillan. I do not understand it.'

'I was referring to rebellion against God.'

'It is no rebellion to consider my daughter's happiness.'

'Even if you are living out of wedlock yourself, Mrs Mason?'

'Oh, it is that too, is it? My cousin took me into this house when I was in sore need, and there is no scandal in this house. And you are wasting your time, Mr Gillan. I will not be moved.'

He clamped his jaws, and then had to unclamp them to speak.

'If that is your attitude, Mrs Mason, I think it would be best if you did not attend my church.'

'Your church, is it? And here was I thinking it was God's church. Well, you need have no fears on that score, Mr Gillan. And I think it would be wise to end this conversation before harder things are said; because I know to my shame that I can be a hard woman.'

'So be it.'

He had to have the last word, and she let him. He left before she could open any doors for him, but he did not slam them. Oh, he would be fair tempted to slam them. She could see him through the window, getting into his car and not slamming that door either. Quite a nice car, dark blue.

Store not up riches on earth, she thought. It really was a very nice car.

She would not tell Hetty about the little stupid battle. She would not tell Dan, for it would only confirm him in his contempt for religion.

She would not be able to resist telling Dan.

Once in a way she had to have somebody to share her little adventures with, even if he did turn it against her and her faith. And when she was telling him she found herself remembering years ago when she had fought the battle of words with young Peter's headmaster, and she told him that too, the first person ever to hear the story from her.

'But plenty heard it from the headmaster,' she said. 'It went round the schools like a gorse fire. When I met Vickie Fairhurst the French teacher she recognised me as the woman in the story.'

'Ah, you're a tartar, a proper tartar, Meg.'

They were sitting companionably in the kitchen over yet another cup of tea – Dan was a real tea-Jenny, he would drink gallons – while Hetty and Peter sat in the living room listening to the wireless.

'It's true,' she said wonderingly. 'I've always thought I was meek and mild, and anything for peace, but I suppose I suffer from the sin of pride too. Especially when my bairns are touched.'

'Ah, when the barricades are up you'll be a Boadicea. I hope to Christ you're on the same side as me.'

'I notice, and I shouldn't be saying this because it'll just start you off, I notice that you haven't told me Mr Gillan proves you're right about religion.'

'He doesn't, Meg, he doesn't, worse things than that have been done in the name of Jesus Christ and I would never hold him responsible for them, he was one of the first Communists. Your Mr Gillan is just a petty bourgeois whippet wi' no more idea of Christ than that teapot, and it's empty I notice.'

'You and your tea. When the revolution comes you'll be paddling to it in a boat on a river of tea.'

'Christ, that sounds like a blueprint for the ideal society. Make it thicker this time.'

She turned the gas up under the kettle.

'It's a fair treat to have a wee crack. You're very good to us, Dan. Oh, I must see Vickie Fairhurst. I've neglected her, and she always said I should go to her if I ever needed help. I'm a scatterbrained woman.'

'You've got a grasshopper mind, and nobody's "very good" to you. You know, I like your kids, Meg, I honestly like them. John and Bobby as well. But it's nice having Hetty and Peter about the place when I get home. I missed that. I'm worried about the lassie, though.'

John and Bobby visited them at least once a week, on Sunday afternoons. She suspected that they were on the pretext of being at Sunday School but she never asked. She had feared that it might have been embarrassing, but nobody ever mentioned Andrew that she knew of. They sometimes passed the time in going for a walk with Hetty and Peter, and what they said with them she never asked. They seemed well enough.

She and Dan took their last cup into the living room. Hetty and Peter were listening to unfamiliar music on the wireless.

'Bellamy predicted it, you know,' Dan said. 'He thought people would need a special room full of equipment to listen to messages from far away. We only need a wee box, but he predicted it all.'

'Funny music they play sometimes.'

'It's a part of our education, Meg. Mind you, that thing is going to destroy conversation.'

'Ach, away you go. Most of the houses I've ever been in never had any conversation at all, and not even a wireless to fill in the silence. Funny music, that. Do you like it, right enough, Hetty?'

Hetty nodded without speaking, and smiled. It was a patient, brave smile, rather than happy. But any smile was better than none.

# 22

It was a time for learning. Meg was learning the novel and sometimes frightening facts of business. The first frightening one was the boredom of sitting in a shop while the world walked past and nobody thought of coming in. Hetty, still slightly remote from life, was a determined comfort all the same.

Neither of them knew anything about bookkeeping on the business level. Hetty cursed herself for having opted for German at school instead of the commercial course; but business was not too different from housekeeping. It was a matter of knowing exactly how much money went out, and how much came in. Hetty kept her company in the shop, and was charming to the occasional customers, and they passed the idle time in inventing systems to account for every penny, ruled out a big notebook to divide life into weeks, with the proportion of rent and rates, and the electricity, and every purchase on one side, and every sale on the other. The answers were depressing, the debits were enormous and the credits a sad trickle.

Jerry Sterne, one of the wholesale travellers who called oftener than the others and stayed longer, laughed at their techniques and brought proper cash-books which he seemed to find lying about free. It was no good, he explained, buying a gross of something and marking it down as a debit for one week and balancing it opposite a sale of three pieces. It wasn't supposed to be cleared in a week, it was money in the bank, and if they sold no more than three pieces in a week they could calculate how many weeks the gross would last, and debit each week with three pieces at wholesale and credit each week with three pieces at retail. Meg's head swam slightly when she was confronted with cash-books and daybooks and ledgers and stock-books, but Hetty took to them like a child learning a new game. There was a little money coming in; a little.

Meg moved her sewing machine from the house to the back shop, because it was foolish to take work home when there was so much free time during the day, and she could even do alterations almost while the customers waited, like Dan and his boot-heels or his sister and her ear-piercing. She was sure she charged too little for alterations. Jerry Sterne told her she charged too little. he told her she had to pay herself a wage, enter it as a debit, and charge enough for her time to pay herself.

Meg jibbed at being so completely commercial. If there was no work to do, and nobody buying anything for the moment, it was better to be at the machine making a shilling or two than not be making anything at all. Jerry laughed and said she would learn. He cheered the place up and there was always a cup of tea for him in the back shop. Sometimes he would bring his sandwiches and have lunch there. He was the smooth-tongued salesman she had heard about, and she had no objection to that. He was always very gallant with Hetty, but he flirted with Meg, and if it was hard to tell whether he was flirting from mere habit or had something more positive in mind, it passed the time very nicely. Nobody had flirted with her before. Her first husband Paul had simply been worshipping and besotted, which had been nice in its way, and Andrew was practical and uncommunicative. Paul had been so young, of course. Flirtation was a pastime for mature people, past the gaucherie of adolescence; and a bit of flattery brightened the day. She liked Jerry.

'If you were my daughter, with legs like that, I would have put you on the stage.'

'Your daughter indeed. I'm old enough to be your . . .'

'Sorry, I meant niece.'

Hetty, listening to this kind of talk, would smile quietly to herself, like a mother smiling indulgently at children, and pretend to be working at the books. But business was quiet. Meg had had the innocent idea that once she had put so much of the compensation money into the shop, the world would beat a path to her door, and in a few weeks, the little fund would be restored, and ready for its real use, whatever that was. If things had turned out differently, it might have stretched to getting both Hetty and John to university, and she could have worried about Peter when the time came; but all that had to be forgotten. There could be no question of university for Hetty, at least not that year, and John had gone uncomplainingly into a clerking job with the Corporation. Well, he might make something of that, and be a department head one day.

When the baby came, she would take on the burden, even

if she had to keep it in the shop all day. It might even be an attraction. Every woman liked babies, and folk might come in just to see it, and buy a packet of pins as an excuse. Then, the following year, Hetty would be free to go to university; unless the shop swallowed up all the money by then and was a failure. Meg fretted constantly about this, but she kept it to herself. Other shops stayed in business; though she now suspected that some of the shopkeepers she had sometimes envied for their prosperity had been living fretful lives just like her own.

She had a disagreement with Hetty, an open disagreement, about business. In her spare time, she still studied other shops, spied on them, looking for the secret of success. She announced that she was going to clear out the window and pack it with stuff – pins, needles, ribbons, thread, hooks-and-eyes, button cards, elastic, all the trivial things that people always needed. Hetty was downcast and rebellious. It was a good quality shop. The needles and pins were all very well, in discreet little showcases inside the shop or in drawers, but the *idea* of a shop should be high-class, to attract people of taste, people looking for elegant dresses and a sumptuous atmosphere, a place where it would be an entertainment merely to enter.

'You'll be having Axminster carpet on the floor next, Hetty.'

'Yes! Oh, just think of it, Mother. A salon, like the ones in the pictures.'

'And two women in it, starving to death and wondering how to pay for the carpet and the rent and the light. When we move to Sauchiehall Street we will have proper carpets, and a doorman with white gloves.'

And a chamber music orchestra.'

'Och, we'll have a full pipe band, and men tossing cabers all over the shop, and the ladies having cups of coffee off wee glass-topped tables.'

'And cabers flying past their ears. Oh, imagine having a shop in Sauchiehall Street!'

'Aye, that would be just champion. But I have been having a wee keek at other shops, not in Sauchiehall Street, and you know a funny thing, Hetty? It's fine having a nice window, with a couple of nice dresses to make women's mouths water, but I get more fun looking in a window with just a whole clamjamfray of wee things, and the prices on them, and thinking, now these buttons would go fine with my old coat, or that reminds me I need some hooks and eyes, and I'll just go in there and spend a shilling.'

'I suppose.' Hetty was sad at the loss of her Hollywood salon. 'And maybe when they come in to spend a shilling they'll buy a dress too.'

'Oh, we'll bar the door and not let them out. But we have to get them in first.'

The elegant window dressing scheme was given the heave, and Hetty set herself to printing scores of little price cards to go on trivial little things.

Jerry Sterne was the first to applaud. Shove the stuff right in their kissers, he said. SPQR.

'Senatus Populusque Romanus?' Hetty inquired.

'No, small profits quick returns. Oh, isn't education wonderful? She's as clever as she's beautiful.'

'Now which one of us is it you're after?'

'Both of you, both of you. The beautiful Mason sisters, or the Cassidy sisters. If I saw you both on the stage doing high kicks I wouldn't know which way to turn.'

'It does come out like a gramophone record, doesn't it, Mother?'

Peter sometimes came into the shop to help, but he felt out of place in a woman's world, and once, when a customer asked him for a yard and a half of pink silk knicker elastic, the words set off an explosion in his mind and he had to run into the back shop, holding in hysterical laughter till it snorted down his nose. He was excused counter duty after that.

In any case, the summer days were still long and the school holidays were running out, with only two weeks to go. It was funny – a two-week holiday at Easter was long and expansive, but the last two weeks of the summer holiday shrank to an instant. At the same time, he sometimes secretly wished for the holiday to be finished so that he could start the adventure of the Big School at last, with lessons like French, and algebra and geometry, which were just strange words to him. He didn't tell anybody he was looking forward to school. It would have been an act of treason to admit it.

But it was difficult to find anything exciting to fill the dwindling days of freedom. He and Hughie convinced themselves it was fun to put a halfpenny on the tramlines and get it squashed out to the size of a penny. All they got was a bent halfpenny with the design obliterated.

They walked all the way to the West End of Glasgow, an interminable trek that felt like twenty miles; and found the West End a strange foreign country, pregnant with the sight and smell of wealth. They were intruders. They found a pond on Great Western Road, with a wood-built cafe, like a ranch-house, beside it, where rich families had ice-cream and ginger while other families rowed about the pond in little boats. Other kids, invaders like themselves, squatted at the side fishing for minnies, but they couldn't because they hadn't brought the net. They threw stones halfheartedly into the pond, to splash water on the rich in their rowing boats, and were chased, as usual.

They found the Botanic Gardens and walked through them, always alert for the sight of a parkie. Parkies hated boys, and their whistles were always ready for a threatening blast. There was a big glasshouse and a parkie guarding the entrance, but they waited till his back was turned and slipped inside to stare at trees and exotic flowers steaming in the heat, and birds flying about under the glass roof. They dodged adroitly among the strolling crowds to keep out of sight of another parkie, gazed at huge goldfish in a pond and tried to drop pebbles on them.

'Quick, Peter, quick, here.'

He followed Hughie and stopped in awe.

'A bare naked woman,' Hughie whispered. They were confronting a marble nude that dazzled Peter.

'Look at these diddies,' Hughie muttered. 'Major Cox-stand.' Peter went on staring, wondering whether he was excited or not. It was beautiful.

'See?' he whispered. 'She's got no hair.'

'Ach, you don't get hairs on stone. Jesus, she's bare naked.'

A well-dressed woman passing by with a little girl hardened her face and actually pushed Peter viciously in the back. He slipped round to the other side of the pond without complaining and drifted back casually to inspect the nude out of the corner of his eyes. Then the parkie chased them out.

Down a side street on the way back they chased a big black

car decked with white ribbons, chased it hopelessly for three blocks and saw it turn a corner far ahead. When they caught up with it, parked outside a front door in a red stone tenement, they had no breath.

'A scramble, a scramble,' Hughie gasped. Oh, the magic possibility of rich people at a wedding throwing out enormous amounts of money from the bridal car. It was too good to be true.

'Maybe rich people don't have scrambles,' Peter panted. 'If they've all got money, they wouldn't bother.'

'Maybe they fling out half-crowns and pound notes!'

'Ach, I'm jiggered,' Peter said. He hung on to the railings and sank to his knees. But the taxi waited a long time while people gathered on the pavement, and a few came out of the house, all dressed up and carrying boxes of confetti. Other children joined them, eyeing Peter and Hughie with cold hostility, recognising them as foreigners. Hughie bunched his fists, but not in the Killer Punch. They had outgrown that. You could fracture your thumb, using the Killer Punch.

A vision of a girl in white silk, a long veil trailing out in the wind, came out of the house with a fat man in a black clawhammer coat, and floated into the car in a rain of confetti, and they jostled their way through the crowd for a good position. The other kids were elbowing them angrily and pushing them from behind. The car started, very slowly, to move.

'Hard up, rusty pockets!' Hughie screamed. One of the local boys looked at him and sneered. It might be that the people in the West End, where everybody was rich, didn't shout Rusty Pockets. In fact, they might not even have scrambles; because the car window was still shut and the car was gathering speed. Peter and Hughie ran alongside it, outstripping the local boys and wondering if it was worth it. The fat man in the car was glowering at them as if he wanted them to disappear.

But then the car window slid down a few inches, the fat man's hand appeared, and a shower of coins appeared, aimed high over their heads.

They checked and turned and dived downwards in one movement. They were practised old hands at scrambles. Peter found himself cannoning into three boys. He got three pennies in one hand and a threepennny bit in the other. A booted foot came down on the hand with the threepenny bit, but he refused to open his fist. He threw himself against the leg to move it, and jumped upright. He was facing a bigger boy, who wore a school blazer and a furious face.

'That's mine, you little scruffy shit,' the boy said. 'Hand it over.'

'No, it's mine.'

The big boy grabbed for him, and Peter leapt back, knocked into somebody else, and found himself standing beside Hughie. Hughie's fists were still clenched, and the big boy in the blazer, who kept licking his lips, shouted, 'Get them!'

His friends moved to surround Hughie and Peter, and Hughie lashed out to kick the large boy on the knee. The big boy shrieked.

'They don't fight fair,' one of his friends shouted.

'Bloody scruff,' the big boy wailed. 'They don't know how to fight fair.'

'Izzat fightin' fair, four against two?' Hughie demanded. 'Just bloody try it.'

'Get them.'

'Hey, there's a half a crown,' Hughie yelled, pointing at the gutter, and threw them into confusion.

'You boys!' A thin sour man in a dark suit appeared among them. 'Get away from here, you don't live here.'

The other boys milled about, torn between robbing the invaders and finding the half-crown, or something else. Hughie and Peter backed away from the thin man, grateful for the intervention but still watching the others.

'And don't let me see you back here again,' said the man. He sounded like a teacher who was sorry he had forgotten his strap. They kept backing away.

'Think you're bloody posh!' Hughie yelled, and they bolted.

'Posh bastarts,' Hughie panted. 'I got a shilling. And a penny and a halfpenny.'

'I got sixpence.'

They were trotting down a steep hill, with no pursuers.

'Come on we'll come back here every day,' Hughie said. 'They fling shillings. That big hoor. I hope I broke his knee.'

'We can have an iced drink and go home on the car.'

'We'll go halfers. What's half of one-and-sevenpence-halfpenny?'

'No, no, I've got enough, and it was you that kicked him.'

'Big hoor. Think they own the street or something.'

'I think I'll have American Cream Soda.'

'I'll have Tizer.'

'Tizer's all right.'

'You can taste mine and I'll taste yours.'

It was a great adventure. Peter thought of it as being the Red Indians who beat the cowboys. He quite liked cowboys, but he was always on the side of the Red Indians. And they went back to the West End once, but it wasn't the same. There were no weddings, and he had seen the bare naked woman in the glasshouse, and he didn't know what to think about her.

They filled in the rest of the holidays in their native haunts, sometimes playing Liney and other games with marbles, or just playing bools along the gutters. Hughie was a champion bools player. He had a pair of woollen gloves with the fingers cut off, and they made him a champion. He wouldn't lend them to anybody. They gave him more distance and accuracy when he knuckled a bool along the gutter. Peter was inexperienced at bools, and he was nagged when he tried to roll the bool underhanded.

'No sheavies, Cassidy.'

The game was as much concerned with getting in the first shout as with skill. If somebody screamed High Pots, you had to stand upright and lob the bool, but if the player was quick enough to scream Low Pots he could aim from a crouch. Two spangs and a knucklie, two spangs and a knucklie. That was two lengths of a hand then a knuckled shot. It was more foreign than French or algebra.

There was an upsurge of enthusiasm for Cowboys and Indians. It was started by Danny McIvor when he turned up one day with two wide strips of sacking tied round his legs. They were cowboys' chaps. He galloped across the coup beating his right calf raw with a newspaper. Suddenly, you were nobody if you didn't have canvas chaps.

You could get a sugar bag from Blaney's for tuppence. Peter got one and took it, a little shamefacedly, to his mother, to get it tailored into cowboy chaps. She scoffed at the idea, and in a few minutes at the sewing machine she converted the bag into a pair of genuine baggy trousers.

Then everybody had to have baggy trousers. The skyline of the coup was dense with cowboys in sugar bags galloping across the prairie and blazing off cap-guns or shouting Bang. Hughie Dickie's mother made him a pair of cowboy trousers from a Cooperative grocery flour-bag. Even when turned outside in they still displayed the blue and red printing, and no amount of rinsing would get rid of the flour. It flew in clouds every time he ran. It was a laughing-stock for days until everybody got used to White Cloud on the warpath.

If sugar bags or packsheets could make trousers, they could make tents too. The coup bred a township of teepees made from sacks, and poles or garden canes, held down at the edges with stones. Warriors huddled under the canvas, uttering strange oaths in Cherokee and sometimes smoking cinnamon stick. They tried to smoke it in a clay pipe of peace, and coughed a lot. Some of them brought Woodbine cigarettes, and got dizzy. Peter tried smoking tea-leaves in a pipe, because they looked like tobacco. He got very sick.

Then the squaws joined in the rites.

Peter was interested to discover yet again that other people were doing things while he was only watching. One day he arrived at the coup and found a sniggering group of boys clustered outside a teepee. They all knew something he didn't know. Harry Cooke was just home from a touring holiday in Yorkshire, and Harry was the leader. Something interesting, and probably dangerous, was going on inside the teepee. It was probably dangerous, because the boys kept scanning the horizon for hostile adults.

A boy came crawling out of the teepee, giggling and breathing deeply, and another boy was shoved in. There was a lot of muttering and squealing inside the tent, and the boy came out, pink, buttoning up his trousers.

'You'll be next,' Harry told Peter.

'What is it?'

'You'll see.'

'You mean they'll see,' somebody else tittered.

For once in his life, Peter didn't like the idea of the unknown.

'It's the initiation,' Harry said impatiently.

Three of them seized Peter. They were very brave, he

thought, as long as there were three of them. He was pushed into the teepee and found two girls, vaguely familiar, kneeling on the ground and giggling. One of them reached for his trouser buttons. He protected them with his hands and bent over.

'Come on,' one of the girls said, 'we've got to see it.' She tried to pinion his arms while the other girl tore open his trousers and grabbed him with hot fingers.

'He'll not lie down' she shouted, and somebody else dived into the tent. It was Harry, his friend, snarling, It's the initiation ceremony, lie still, Cassidy.'

The first girl grabbed one of his hands and said, 'It's your shot now,' and pushed his hand up her own skirt. He felt something wet and pulled his hand away and she snorted.

'I'll have a shot,' Harry said.

'You've had yours, Harry Cooke.'

But Harry pushed his hand under her skirt and she wriggled and gasped and pushed him away. Nobody was holding Peter. He tried to clamber past Harry, and bumped his head against the tent pole. It parted from the canvas, and there was a yell from outside. Peter was still crawling and trying to button up his trousers while bodies threw themselves on the heaving canvas and hands groped all over it for something to touch. Finally it was pulled off. Harry got up, looking absolutely exasperated. The first girl, smeared with dust and bits of grass, her ribbon hanging over one ear, was throwing boys off in every direction. Her name was Marie Rennie, he remembered.

'Get your hands off,' she shouted. 'And don't let him in again, he's useless.'

That was strange. Harry hated girls, but it was Harry who had arranged everything. Peter thought about the girls, and didn't resent them at all, though he knew Ella Greenlees would never have carried on like that. It would have been different, he thought, if nobody else had been there except himself and the girls, nobody forcing him to do things. It was Harry he was puzzled about. Harry didn't like girls.

He remembered a dream that he had had more than once. He was walking along a wall, and there were girls below, and he jumped down, and realised too late that he had no trousers on and his shirt was flying up and showing everything. But if the girls in his dream had all been Marie

Rennie, they wouldn't have screamed or looked shocked. Some girls had funny ideas too.

And so had Harry.

## 23

Meg had a start of fear when Andrew came into the shop. She had put him so thoroughly out of her mind that he was like a ghost from another life. It was early in the afternoon, but he looked drunk. He leaned against the door and stared at the floor while she measured out and cut some ribbons for a customer. She was glad Hetty was at home.

The cluttered window in the shop was working. People did find an attraction in a display like a bazaar, and they did drop in for the little things, and she gave them as much attention as she would have given one of Hetty's imaginary clients looking for a Paris gown. She was a born shopkeeper, she thought, she enjoyed customers.

The books were beginning to make sense and there was more money coming in than money going out. If she had written off the entire stock, as she thought she should at the beginning, as the expense of a single week and never to be endured again, the takings would have looked great for every week thereafter. Secretly, she *had* written off the stock in her mind, because she had bought it with her own money. But Hetty and Jerry Sterne would have reminded her that the stock would have to be replaced and that the weekly takings had to include a debit to pay for re-stocking.

She didn't really care. If people were always coming in and she wasn't sitting idle, or reading a book, she felt that the shop was a success and she could stop fretting about going broke.

But in the meantime, Andrew was here, swaying against the door. The customer left, glancing oddly at Andrew, probably smelling his breath. He looked quite drunk, when he should have been at work at the stickyard. He was going to be difficult.

'Uhuh,' he said. He walked stifflegged and leaned on the counter. 'We've had enough of this nonsense, eh?'

'I don't know what you want, Andrew, but I have nothing to say to you.' But she was trembling and she was afraid. He took his hand from the counter and turned round to look at the shop. She saw him with terrible clarity, a drunk man being determinedly sober, and failing; a man she had desired, physically, because he was there, and she was a creature of desire. Now, he was a stranger, and she was ashamed to discover she hated him.

'What am I supposed to do?' he demanded.

'Whatever you choose to do.'

'A wife's place is in the home. The home, see?'

'My place is here, Andrew, and you will leave me alone.'

'A shop. A shop? It's all right, Meg, so we made a coupla mistakes, no harm done, water under the bridge, I'll take you back, no harm done, we'll say no more.'

She was glad the counter was between them. The shop door opened and a woman came in, but she took one look at Andrew and left.

'Andrew.' She tried to be quiet and removed. 'Please leave this shop, and don't bother me any more. Everything between us is finished, so go away.'

'Oh, that's your attitude, is it?' He became bellicose, and then changed his mind., 'Well, fair enough, don't blame you, but fair's fair. Come on, what about me, eh? What about me, eh?'

She hated drunkenness, and the way drunk people repeated themselves without sense, and he was very drunk.

'What about me, eh? Kids need a father, eh? Well known fact, I'm supposed to be mother and father to these poor weans, can't be done, can't be done. 'S your job, 's your duty. Love honour and obey, that's what sez love honour and obey. 'Ats whole sum and substance, eh? No jiss a minute, kids need a mother. You made a vow, you made a bloody vow, eh?'

'Andrew, go away.'

'Go away. Go away. Go away.' He was staring down at the counter, working out something in his mind, and suddenly it became bizarre and horrible. He straightened up, still supporting himself with one hand and started to sing.

*Why did you make me care,*
*Why bring me dreams so rare*
*You told me that sweethearts should never part*
*Why go and leave me, and break my heart . . . ?*

'Andrew,' she said, 'please leave this shop.'

His jaw was slack, but his eyes were vicious.

'You lost me my job. You. Lost. Me. My. Job. Oh, very hoity-toity, you've got a shop, you're awright. You don't care about the poor working classes, you're awright.' He turned angry again. 'You are my wife. I've got rights, and I'll bloody well get them.'

Frightened, and disgusted, she looked at him and wondered how she had ever married this stupid man. From fear of being left alone, maybe, from gratitude that a good-looking man had wanted her, and he was still a good-looking man in his way, and he had arrived in her life when she was lost and frightened when Paul had died.

'I didn't lose you your job,' she said. The whole marriage had been a disaster. The burly handsome man was not looking for a wife, only for a mother and a housekeeper.

'I haven't got a tosser to my name,' he bleated. He tried, and failed, to turn a trouser pocket inside out to show its emptiness. She knew it was unwise, but she was desperate to get rid of him, and she opened the drawer and offered him a pound note.

'Take this and leave me alone, Andrew,' she said. He inspected the money and crammed it in his pocket and muttered, 'How long is that supposed to last?'

'Get out.'

'Don't you worry, I'll be back. And you'll be back.'

'I will not, I am quite happy where I am.'

'Oh, is that it? Your fancy man?'

Her hand came up in automatic anger and he shuffled back.

'You'll bloody crawl back,' he muttered.

'Get away from me.' Her face was stony hard.

'Bloody Fenian fancy man,' he muttered, and then repeated it in a shout. 'Bloody Fenian fancy man.' And as he moved away, from a safe distance he shouted again, 'She talks about me? She talks about me? Off wi' a bloody Fenian fancy man.' Meg had never felt so exposed, but she wouldn't go back inside the shop in case he should turn back if she stopped looking at him. She refused to notice the faces of the people passing by.

'She asked for it,' Andrew yelled, and lurched in the direction of Donnelly's Bar.

She went back into the shop and stood trembling. Everything she had planned was in danger. It was true, the unexpected was always what happened. She had thought that part of her life was ended, had been glad it was ended. Was it possible he had lost his job because she had driven him to drink by leaving him? Was she to blame? Worse than that, although she had seen him the worse for drink before, he had never been like this, he seemed to have deteriorated into another man in a few weeks.

Perhaps he would be different when he sobered up, but there was something worse in him, something dissolute, that she hardly recognised. Whether it was her fault or not, she would never go back to him; but she thought she might never feel secure again, talking to customers and selling her buttons and pins and counting the takings. He was there, somewhere, and his resentment was festering in him. She wished she had paid more attention to Mr Livingstone at the office, and found another place for the shop, miles away from the Gallowgate.

If she had still been a church member, she might have thought of going to Mr Gillan, for comfort, if not for help; but Mr Gillan she now dismissed as a man of straw, and though there must be better, more Christian-minded ministers, she had never persuaded herself to take her lines to another church and join.

Sometimes she went to the Tent Hall on a Sunday morning, because she needed evidence for herself that she was keeping her faith intact. She enjoyed the simple sermons and the old Gospel hymns, so much more spirited and innocent than old Mr Ferrier's brand of fire and brimstone on Duna, though there was plenty of hellfire in them, and a great enthusiasm for washing in blood, which had never appealed to her. But the old fashioned, unquestioning Gospel raised her spirits and sent her home cheerful. She doubted, however, if fiery little Mr Conrahan the preacher would be of much help to a woman who was worried because she had left her husband and was keeping house for an ex-Papist. Mr Gillan had disapproved, Mr Conrahan would probably have a stroke.

She kept it from the children, but she told Dan over their fourth cup of tea in the kitchen.

'The drink, Meg, it's the drink, that's all.'

'That is not a consolation, Dan.'

'No.'

'I do not know what to do.'

'Neither do I. I'm not much help.'

'It helps to talk.'

'I could bring a last round to the shop, and sit among the fancy underwear hammering in sprigs, but I doubt the customers would like it.'

'Not very much.'

'Anyway, I never had a great talent for what you might call the violent arts.'

'I wouldn't tolerate any kind of violence, Dan.'

'Oh, I'm with you there, Meg. That's for the lower animals and the Capitalists and the Nazis. But you know, sometimes I catch myself thinking there's some people would be better off with a belt in the mouth.'

'Oh, Dan, it is a terrible thing, the drink.'

'Aye, aye. That reminds me, I've got a bottle of sherry in the press. We'll have a wee glass while nobody's looking.'

'Don't you dare, Dan Cassidy.'

But he poured two glasses, and she sipped the dangerous stuff.

'It is quite nice, Dan,' she said. 'I never tasted but whisky before, and that was that hot and bitter I didn't like it at all.'

'Oh, you're right, whisky's not ladylike. Of course, in an ideal society, folk will not need the artificial comfort of alcohol, but until we have an ideal society we have to do the best we can.'

'Dan, you are worse than a Jesuit!'

'You know, I've never met a Jesuit? At school it was always Dominicans, or the Marist Brothers. Have another wee drop.'

'It makes you feel quite warm, doesn't it? I had better beware of it.'

'Aye, not a word to the children.'

Peter missed the reckless scruffy companionship of Hughie Dickie when Hughie went from the junior school to Onslow Drive and Peter to Whitehill School. They promised to keep playing with each other, but they knew they would be wrapped up in their own classsmates. Peter was slightly surprised when the girl Marie Rennie appeared at Whitehill too. He had assumed that girls who enjoyed unbuttoning boys' trousers would belong on a lower social plane. When he found himself sitting across the aisle from her in the English class, she first put out her tongue to him, and when he did the same, she winked, and then put her hands under the desk and mimed the act of squeezing a phallic object. He put a hand under his desk and mimed the act of poking a finger into a hole, and she sneered and shook her head. He shrugged his shoulders and put a lot more energy into not knowing she was there any more.

He fell into his old acquaintance with Harry Cooke and found that Harry still considered that girls were useless and should be ignored. The scramble in the tent on the coup and Harry's determination to have 'another shot' had passed out of memory. Peter felt some guilt about feeling superior to Hughie Dickie, on the inferior social level of Onslow Drive. He knew Onslow Drive was not inferior, and he envied the woodwork classes, which sounded more adult and casual than filling blank maps of Canada with Industries and Products, with a fine-pointed Gillot Fine Nib. But he couldn't dismiss the feeling of importance and even loftiness that went with being a Whitehill Pup with His Tail Tied Up, and the cachet of teachers who wore academic gowns all the time. Even copying out the timetable had a feeling of importance.

He remembered to be unobtrusive in French class, and discovered in any case that some people were picking up the language easily, so that he needn't look too much of a smartie. His first year French teacher was Miss Jamieson, quite young and very chic, with tight pencil skirts he enjoyed looking at. He had no difficulty in recognising Sugar Plum Fairy, Miss Fairhurst, from her hair of blazing unnatural red, and the first time he met her in a corridor he bowed in what he believed was the French manner.

'A galant?' she was amused and not quite derisory. 'do I know you?'

'Cassidy, Miss.'

'Ah, the other Cassidy. Et comment va-tu, monsieur?'

'Je vais tres bien, mademoiselle, et ma mere me dit de vous donner ses meilleurs souhaits.'

'Ah oui, tres bien, tu a bien travaillé, mon vieux.'

'Vieux, mademoiselle? Je suis agé de douze ans.'

'Ah, trop agé pour moi. Et ta soeur, comment va-t-elle?'

'Assez bien, je crois.'

'Bon. Au revoir.'

'A bientot.'

'Saucy wee tinker.'

'Oui, mademoiselle.'

Yes, Whitehill was full of moments of importance. Ella Greenlees was standing behind him.

'Big mouth,' she said.

'Can I help it if I'm very good?'

'Oh help.'

'You're very good as well.'

'Thanks for nothing.'

They were eyeing each other like boxers sparring for an opening.

'Oh, you,' she said, and pushed him in the chest. He peered at her, and she recoiled, but he didn't push her. He wondered about it, but he didn't push her. She blushed, which pleased and interested him. She was so confident that a blush was a novelty.

'You're violent,' he said.

'Oh. You. You're an annoyance.'

'You're not bad, for a girl.'

'Thanks for nothing.'

Why did everybody say thanks for nothing? She swirled away. She did have a nice leg for a kilt.

Some of his mental energy was absorbed in calculating a hierarchy. The idea was absurd in itself, since he now agreed completely with Harry Cooke that all people should be equal, and even if he had never met Harry, Uncle Red's philosophy would have seeped into him because it fitted exactly what he read as the meaning of the new Testament. All people were equal because God had created them equal; sinful, maybe, but equal. Little children were equal to adults, or even better. Black people were equal because God made black people. Women were equal because God made women.

In another sense, he wasn't too sure of that. He suspected that women were superior. His mother had been superior to Da, and nearly everybody else. Ella Greenlees was superior to him because she knew something he didn't, and it had nothing to do with her being good at French or having nice legs. And there was some kind of superiority, some kind of scale, that had nothing to do with being rich or tall or short.

165

Teachers he left out of it. They didn't belong to that scale. But Ella Greenlees was superior to Marie Rennie, partly because Ella Greenlees would never unbutton anybody's trousers or drag somebody's hand up her skirt. He occasionally imagined Ella Greenlees doing exactly that, and dismissed it as incredible.

Harry had a kind of superiority because he knew everything. It had nothing to do with his father having a car. Well, it did have something to do with his father having a car. People whose fathers had cars had access to a different kind of experience from ordinary people. But Harry had a superiority inside him. No, it wasn't that he really knew everything, but that he *felt* he knew everything, and that was just as good.

Alastair Barr had his own rung on the ladder. Yes, that was because he was rich. He wasn't very good at lessons, but he was quite good at football, and he was rich. His father had a garage and a car sale-room only a few blocks from the school. The boys often detoured to stare through the windows and wonder how it would feel to have not one car, but a whole shopful of them; even second-hand cars. Morris Oxford Tourer, £30. Hillman Minx, £50. Austin Ruby, £17.10. They gleamed in the window. They were so cheap, but even £17.10 was more money than most people had ever seen. And Alastair's school scarf was of a dull texture that looked cheap beside the artificial-silk scarves that other people wore, but there was a subtle richness about the way it didn't wrinkle. It was pure wool.

And Alastair took piano lessons. He hated them. Every day, nearly, he moaned about having to go home and practise. Peter couldn't understand him. To have an entire piano at home, and be able to go home and practise playing it, sounded like heaven. Alastair couldn't sing. In the music class he was always flat, and if there was a song with a long pause, he always cut the pause short. But he was learning to play the piano. And the fact that he detested and despised it made him even more enviable.

Alastair didn't have to worry about anything, and when he left school, whether he passed any exams or not, he would go into his father's garage and never worry about anything.

Ella Greenlees was superior to Marie Rennie, of course. On the other hand, now that they had stopped putting out their tongues at each other, he got on easily with Marie and dismissed the memory of her curious assault on him.

Marie laughed at jokes, while Ella usually just looked suspicious and disapproving of them. This indicated some mysterious kind of superiority, or maybe not. The scale of individual superiority was hard to define, but somehow there was one there. Some people were much better than others.

He didn't put himself on the scale at all.

There was the strange case of Billy McKinnie, who didn't seem to fit in at all at first glance because he wore a Parish suit, made (apparently with a hacksaw) of ugly thick dark grey cloth. A suit suitable for charity cases. And he wore Parish boots, which were nearly always issued a size too big. A good fault, he had heard women say – the kid will grow into them.

Parish suits had been common in the junior school, and they often went with the low-class haircut, the hair shorn off, right into the wood, except for a tuft at the front. Some boys would grease the tuft and comb it into a little wave to impersonate the front end of an ordinary haircut, but it was still a Parish haircut.

In fact, when he arrived at Whitehill, in his Parish suit and boots, Billy's head was covered with short bristles like a scrubbing brush, trying to grow back to normal length. He didn't seem to suit Whitehill, but he did, and the boys were careful not to make any remarks about his hair, at least not to his face. It also seemed that he had no parents, but lived with his grandparents and his auntie.

For Peter, he took the place of Hughie Dickie because Billy also knew a lot of dirty jokes and rhymes, like *It was the good ship Venus, by God you should have seen us, the figurehead was a hoor in bed, the mast was the captain's penis.* There seemed to be a great store of these poems and songs somewhere, but only particular individuals had access to it. So people forgot about Billy's suit and haircut.

But, considering it was a Good School, there was a lot of ignorance about. Most of the girls thought Charles Darwin was a fool. Peter could hardly remember when or where he had encountered the theory of natural selection, but its logic was so obvious that it was hard to believe anybody could doubt it.

'It's against the Bible,' Ella Greenlees said positively, during an aimless discussion in the English class while Big Joe the teacher was out somewhere and they were supposed to be reading Clive of India on their own.

'Whales have an appendix,' Peter pointed out.

'So you say, smartie.'

'So the World of Science by Sherwood Taylor says. I can show you the drawing.'

'Thanks for nothing.'

'How would all the mammals have the same bone structure,' Harry Cooke demanded, 'if they weren't all related?'

'Maybe your grandfather was a monkey, Harry Cooke, but mine wasn't.'

Charlie McIlvanney, who got restless when anybody talked seriously about anything, went into one of his chants.

'Oh yeah, and how, said the monkey to the cow, if it wasn't for your liver I would throw you in the river, oh yeah, and how.'

They ignored him. Charlie was designed to be ignored. And yet Ella Greenlees was quite intelligent and got good marks.

On the other hand, John Taylor, who was clever and read a lot, and was useful for intellectual discussions, reported to Peter that somebody had done an experiment with fruit flies, had bred dozens of generations of fruit flies in total darkness to discover if the species would eventually discard its power of sight, and at the end, the youngest generation could see as well as ordinary fruit flies. This seemed to cast serious doubt on evolution.

'Maybe they didn't go on long enough,' Peter suggested. 'It must have taken thousands of years for giraffes to reach up for food before their necks grew any longer.'

'Maybe.'

One of the good things about the senior school was that you could sometimes argue with teachers, instead of listening and nodding and believing everything. They took the problem to Smiddy the science teacher, and Peter approached it as Devil's Advocate.

'Recent experiments have disproved the theory of evolution, sir,' he said innocently.

'That takes care of that, then,' Smiddy barked. They had

to be cautious with Smiddy because his temper varied with the weather. It was well known he had got one of his legs full of shrapnel in the war, and the pain came back when the wind was in the east, so he would snap at everybody and get the belt out at no provocation.

'Generations of fruit flies raised in the dark could still see, sir.'

'And that proves what, Cassidy, apart from your unfathomable ignorance?'

'That evolution doesn't work, sir.'

'You're talking Lamarckism, Cassidy, your undersized brain is living in the Dark Ages, isn't it? Answer me, boy, yes no or I don't know.'

Peter was silenced.

'What are you smirking at, Taylor? Are you a member of this superstitious heresy too, boy?'

'It was me that read about the fruit flies, sir.'

'Which demonstrates your equal ignorance, doesn't it? Answer me Yes No or I don't know.'

'Yes No or I don't know, sir.'

'Insolent thug.'

'What's Lamarckism, sir?' Peter asked.

'None of your business, Cassidy.'

'I'm trying to learn, sir.'

'You're trying to waste the time of the class and get out of a lesson on the specific gravity of metals, Cassidy. Look it up, boy, I'm not your wet-nurse. Where did you read about fruit flies, Taylor, when you should have been doing home exercises?'

'The *Reader's Digest*, sir.'

'God, the pea-brain's Bible.'

'It's very educational, sir,' Harry Cooke said stoutly. Harry didn't like thick books. He was devoted to the *Reader's Digest*, and believed that every book could and should be condensed into four pages.

'You are an ignorant lazy thug, Cooke, living on pap. You remind me of the fool who said to the Duke of Wellington, "Mister Brown, I believe." And what did the Duke reply, boy?'

'I don't know, sir.'

'No, he did not say I don't know sir. He said, If you believe that you'll believe anything. Now get on with the experiment, and anybody else who mentions fruit flies or the *Reader's Digest* will get six of the best.'

It was always possible that he meant it.

It was easier to bait Piggy, Miss Hogg the geography teacher, who had spent two years teaching in South Africa and knew everything about every foreign country. She would seize any excuse to talk about her South African experiences, and an innocent question about South Africa could waste half a geography period. She adored the British Empire.

'I read an article, Miss,' Harry Cooke said, 'about the movement of power from East to West. It said there was the Chinese Empire and then the Indian Moguls and then the Romans and then the Spaniards and then the British Empire.'

'That's quite true, Cooke. You missed out the Persians and the French, but there does seem to be a pattern in these things if we learn to see it.'

'So it said that power would keep moving till it got to America next, Miss.'

'No doubt it was an American magazine you were reading.' Her lips tightened.

'Yes Miss.'

'There's a big difference, Cooke. All the other Empires were built on tyranny, and for greed. The British Empire is purely for the good of other people, to bring them Christianity and prosperity. It will last forever.' One of the wall maps behind her was the political map of the world, with the areas of the British Empire coloured in red. 'The sun never sets on the British Empire.'

'Why, Miss?' But she saw through the trick and brought them back to the British railway system, a wonder of the world.

Although he didn't like reading long books, Harry was enthusiastic about education, and sometimes dragged Peter at weekends to the Barrows, to listen to hucksters selling linoleum and fancy goods and non-slip floor polish, and he was quite cheeky at heckling them, and quite shrewd. When the non-slip polish man demonstrated his stuff by trying to slide his fingers along a piece of polished wood, and failing, Harry shouted, 'You never slip in your bare feet. Try it with socks on.'

'You'll get a sock if you don't get to hell out of here, sonny.'

They always drifted away at that because Barrows people always looked tough, and even violent. Another man was selling a magic new brand of toothbrush by scrubbing sets of macabre false teeth from dark brown to gleaming white.

'This brush is the only brush that brushes where other brushes never brush,' he shouted. 'Because it's prophylactic. Prophylactic means that every single bristle is inserted singly, for life.'

'No it doesn't,' Peter muttered.

'What does it mean?' Harry whispered.

'I can't remember.'

'It doesn't mean that at all,' Harry shouted.

'Oh, we've got a college professor here,' the huckster shouted cheerily. 'And what does it mean, Professor?'

'It means something else, that's what.'

'Just you go and ask your nanny to change your nappy, Professor, I can smell it from here. Now then, ladies and gentlemen, as I was saying before the professor here gave us the benefit of his ignorance and stupidity, this brush is prophylactic.'

The crowd was on his side.

A huge negro turned up every Saturday to sell his own corn cure, made from a secret African recipe. They admired his cunning in having a placard bearing his name, which looked like Dr Phillips, but was actually a very large D and a very small R, merely his initials, so that he couldn't be charged with false pretences. His tale was that Zulus running through jungles never had corns because they had never made the white man's mistake of cramping their toes in badly made shoes, but if they had trouble with the soles of their feet they went to the witch-doctor for his secret formula, which Dr Phillips had now smuggled into Britain at the risk of his life.

He had a tray with genuine extracted corns, grisly pieces of human skin, and would pick one up with a pair of tweezers and wave it gruesomely in the air.

In spite of Harry's contempt, Peter paid twopence for a tin of the secret formula. He didn't have corns, but on the underside of one big toe there was a little white ring on the pink skin that sometimes throbbed painfully, and he didn't want to bother his mother about it. He secretly applied the secret formula, and the skin gradually turned white and dead and could be sliced off with a razor blade with no sensation; but he was puzzled to find the white ring was still there, under all the layers of skin, as if it went right through his toe like the letters in a stick of sweet rock. In the end it went away, but whether because of the secret formula or for other reasons he didn't know.

On a Saturday, sometimes on a Sunday, as many as four public speakers set up in shouting distance of one another in Braefield Street, a cul-de-sac with the railway at the top end, and harangued anybody who would stop and listen, and heckled one another at the same time. The Economic League, the Socialist Party of Great Britain, the Scottish National Party, the Unemployed Workers' Union, and sometimes the Judge Rutherford group proclaiming that Millions Now Living Would Never Die. Harry and Peter moved from platform to platform, bombarded with facts and promises and threats. There were sideshows too; an escapologist, stripped to the waist, wrapping himself in yards of bright steel chain and then lying down and writhing to get free.

The chains made angry red patterns on his skin and sometimes drew blood and spectators dropped pennies in the cap lying beside him. An ancient brown man with a turban brought a tattered pram bearing a gramophone with a curving horn on top, put a wooden board on the street, wound up the gramophone and put on a record of *Keep Right On to the End of the Road*, and clog-danced mournfully on the board. The only time he showed emotion was when another entertainer came too near, and then he shouted angry gibberish in a high thin voice. There was Woodbine Annie, a tiny woman with a leathery face and a fur coat down to her ankles. She wore it in all weathers. There was always a cigarette hanging from her lips, even when she played the mouth organ.

It was educational, Harry said, his mother had told him it was educational, a demonstration of Capitalist exploitation, Peter thought it was just a show.

Dick Smith called at the house when Hetty was at home alone. She recognised his shape through the frosted-glass door and was able to look composed when she opened it, to

172

find him shuffling on the mat; was able to smile in surprise and ask him in. He nodded a lot and did awkward things with his hands, putting them in his pockets and taking them out and clasping them, but he didn't try to kiss her. She sat him in the living room and insisted on making tea, so that she could have a few minutes alone.

'And how have you been?' he asked. Not looking at her. She looked more beautiful than ever, with a flush like a bloom on a peach.

'Fine, Dick. Very well.'

'Yes. Good. I'm at Jordanhill Training College.'

'Oh. That's nice, Dick.'

'Physical training course.'

'You'll do well at that, Dick.'

'Yes. It's quite hard work.'

'Oh, it must be, Dick.'

'Yes. In fact, it's, eh, it's . . . '

'I've got a lot to do too,' said Hetty. 'Well, I mean to say, it's quite difficult. We'll not be able to see much of each other now.'

'Well, it's quite hard work. The parents, you know the kind of thing, oh, they keep saying keep the nose to the grindstone sort of thing, you know what they're like. It is quite hard work, actually.'

'Well, we're both a bit older, Dick, we have to get on with things.'

'That's what I was thinking, that's funny. I, eh, did I hear you hadn't been well?'

'No, I've been fine, just fine.'

She let the silence die till he spoke again.

'Well, it's nice to see you, actually. It's a pity and all that.'

'Well,' she said, 'I've really got to get on, there's a lot to do. It was nice of you to drop in, Dick. I'm sure I'll see you again, some time.'

'Oh, sure, sure. Well . . . '

She got him to the door and he got out, paused to wave awkwardly, and went away. She gently closed the door and went into the living room and sat down and wept silently. It was soothing. When her eyes were dry, she went to her room, took the science notebook in which she had once written a long secret letter to him, or to herself. She pulled out the pages and tore them in small pieces and burned them in the

173

living-room fireplace. Then she washed her face and started to peel potatoes. She always enjoyed dull jobs like peeling potatoes and washing dishes.

'At least,' she said to the empty kitchen, 'I'll never have to polish anybody's boots.'

After midnight that night, she was jolted from sleep by the doorbell and an urgent knocking. She started up from a dream with the sudden image of Dick hanging from a tree, and for a moment she didn't know where she was. There were noises downstairs. She jumped from bed and ran down to the middle landing. The light was on in the hall, and at the front door was her mother, and a policeman towering over her. Hetty gave a little moan, and her mother turned from the policeman to see her pitching downstairs.

## 24

Hetty was aware of being the centre of a lot of trouble and confusion. She was lying on the couch in the living-room, and her mother wouldn't let her sit up. The policeman was there too, and Uncle Dan, and Peter.

'There is nothing wrong with Dick,' her mother said. She stopped trying to sit up. The policeman was saying something muffled and her mother was saying to the Devil with the shop, it doesn't matter.

Doctor Black was there, and two men were carrying her somewhere. She felt that she wasn't in her own body and wondered if she was dead, but it didn't matter.

Meg went with her in the ambulance. She was asked not, she was ordered not to. She went. Peter, torn between fear for Hetty and the excitement of emergency, helped Dan to carry some planks through the deserted night streets to the Gallowgate. The policeman went some of the way with them before he left them to call in from a police box.

'I'm right vexed,' he said to Dan, 'about giving the girl a fright like that, it was the farthest thing from my mind.' His voice was soft and musical, like Mother's.

'You're not to blame for that, man. We're grateful to you for coming so soon.'

'It's on my mind nevertheless, and I just hope the lassie is all right.'

'She's young and strong, she'll be all right.'

'I'll just look by in a day or two and see how she is going, if you wouldn't mind. I'm just afraid of scaring her again.'

'No, that would be fine, officer, any time.'

'Capitalist lackey, of course,' Dan said when they had left him. 'But they have their uses. Who the hell would throw a brick at a haberdashery? If it had been a jeweller's or even a ham shop I would see the force of it.'

'One of those juvenile delinquents you're always saying should join the Boy Scouts, Uncle Dan.'

'Aye. Maybe one of them did join, and then stuck his pole through the window. I mind a story about one of those Highland polis trying to catch a bookie's runner with the goods on him, but wee Hughie always foxed them, so Sergeant Hector got dressed up in plain clothes, to be an agent provocateur. An agent provocateur is—'

'I know what it is, I'm not a child.'

'No, you're a cheeky gnome. Anyway, he got on his kilt and his good tweed jacket and sidled up to wee Hughie in Dumbarton Road and said "Psst, take this," and offered him a betting slip and a bob. "Not on yur life," said Hughie, "I'm not a bookie, and anyway, you're a polis." "How do you make that out?" said Hector, and Hughie said, "You've still got your helmet on".'

'Is is true?'

'It doesn't have to be true. I laugh when you tell jokes, Peter.'

'Maybe I tell better jokes.'

'In an ideal society you'll laugh at my jokes or you'll go to the salt mines.'

'Okay. The salt mines might be funnier than your jokes.'

'The salt mines are a myth, Peter, an invention of Capitalist propaganda.'

'What do the Russians put on their fish and chips, then?'

'I'm giving you up, you're ineducable, you're the lumpen proletariat.'

There was another policeman waiting by the shop, and he stood by agreeably, but without offering to help, while Dan and Peter hammered planks across the broken window. So Dan asked him in for a cup of tea. He seemed willing to spend the rest of the night till Dan asked him what time he usually called in to the station.

'The greatest job in the world, that, Peter,' Dan remarked. 'Long legs and a teak skull and you're fixed for a lazy life and a pension.'

'What's the lumpen proletariat?'

'Ah. That's the mistake some of the comrades make. Never sentimentalise the working class. There are a lot of eejits among the proles. The eejits ye have always with you.'

'Even in the ideal society?'

'Sure. Education will cure crime and disease, but eejitism is incurable. That's the lumpen proletariat, Peter. Even after the Red Dawn you'll get them, and all you can do is fling the buggers a bone and make sure they don't ram it in their ears instead of chewing it.'

'Will I stay in the shop all night?'

'The ghost will get you.'

'Don't believe in ghosts.'

'Have you never heard of Flannelfeet?'

'Sure, he's up a close in Bellfield Street. Who is Flannelfeet, anyway?'

'Damned if I know, I never had the nerve to ask. All right, if you can stay here I'd better get back to the house for your mother coming home.'

'That's terrible. I forgot about Hetty.'

'I think she'll be all right. You know what's wrong with her?'

'Of course. She's pregnant, and she's hurt.'

'Good. Use plain language and no bloody euphemisms. Call a spade a spade.'

'You call it a bloody shovel, Uncle Red.'

'That's my privilege. Well, she's maybe not pregnant any more.'

'Ah.'

'So. You guard the premises and I'll get back. Tell Flannelfeet I was asking for him. Of course, you don't see him, he just comes up at your back and drapes his big soft hands over you.'

'Sure.'

Peter was pleased that Dan recognised his maturity and his right to stand guard. When his uncle had gone, he went to the shop window and picked out the broken glass and took it into the back shop, then sat on one of the two hard chairs for his vigil. There was no way of getting comfortable and he was suddenly very sleepy. He tried lying on the floor, but it hurt his bones. He wished he had gone back to the house and left Dan to guard the shop.

Meg came home by an early tram towards dawn, and was slightly shocked that the boy had been left alone in the shop, but she too recalled that he wasn't a child any longer.

'He'll be aching in every bone,' Dan said callously. 'Good for him. Good training for the Revolution.'

'You and your daft revolution.' She touched his face fondly. 'She's all right, Dan.'

'Good. Did it, eh . . . ?'

'Yes, couldn't you tell that from the blood.'

'I admit I was kind of half-hoping, Meg. As long as she'll be all right.'

'Oh Dan, I nearly sinned my soul hoping that something

177

like this would happen.'

'I believe you. Did you insure the window?'

'Och, to blazes with the window.'

'Maybe Livingstone did. Never mind, I'll talk to him in the morning.'

'What makes folk get up to such stupid destruction?'

'The distortions of Capitalism, Meg.'

'And a good belt in the mouth would cure them, you said so yourself.'

'You cast my own words in my teeth. Would you like a sherry now?'

'You know, I wouldn't mind at all. Wicked, wicked habit.'

'Aye, right. Down with virtue.'

'Stop that. Oh here, Dan, we're in the house all by ourselves, it's not right.'

'Well, you can walk the streets if you like, Meg, I'm not giving up my bed for your bourgeois morality.'

'I know, I'm just being silly, You're a dear man, Dan, I don't know whatever I would have done without you.'

She took his arm as they went to the kitchen, and they had to jostle through the narrow door. She felt the blood rising to her face.

'Here, I don't think I should have a sherry, Dan, not at this time in the morning, I'll just away to my bed.'

'What's wrong?' The face he turned to her was innocent and concerned, and she hoped he couldn't see her breast heave.

'Nothing, Dan, I just feel tired all of a sudden, if you don't mind.'

'No no, I'll see you in the morning, Meg.'

She escaped to her room, her hand at her throat, distressed at what she was nearly thinking, and her poor daughter in a hospital bed. Perhaps it wasn't entirely a good thing to be sharing a house with a man, perhaps Mr Gillan in his narrow stupidity had not been so far wrong.

She concentrated on the trouble at the shop because it was the least troublesome thing to think of. Stupid boys, or drunken men. There was no way folk could feel safe from the stupidity going about in the world. There was no way folk could feel safe from the stupidity going about in themselves.

## 25

Meg had a long talk with Hetty when she came home from hospital, and held back nothing. It would have been a sin, she said, to have hoped for such an accident, but it couldn't be sinful to accept it and make the best of it and even conclude that everything worked out for the best.

'I did hope for it, Mother, I'm sorry. But I'm glad it was an accident. I had a vision that night of Dick hanging from a tree, but I think I was mixing him up with myself.'

'Oh, there is no way of stopping strange thoughts from coming into the mind, Hetty. But you surely never wished such a thing on Dick.'

'No, never. I'm sorry for him now. It's so sad and stupid. He came to see me the other day.'

'Well.' No comment, Meg thought, say nothing either glad or sorry.

'He seemed so young, Mother. I think he felt he had to come, but he was so glad to get away.'

'And your heart isn't broken.'

'Oh no. I'm not myself yet. But no, no, it was as if everything had happened years ago when I was a wee girl.'

'You're still a wee girl.'

Hetty gave her a sad wise smile.

'Anyway. I think his parents wanted it all stopped. They heard, I know they heard, and they didn't want Dick mixed up . . . he's only seventeen, he's just started college. You can't blame them.'

'You're taking too much on yourself if you start forgiving everybody in the world, Hetty. There is a bit of callousness there in these people. Och, maybe you're right to be sorry for them, they're just frightened of real life, they want everything awkward shovelled under the carpet.'

'I never met them anyway, and now I don't have to.'

'Yes, but it's all very well for them to be worrying about their child, and him starting college. I'm worried about mine too, though I don't know how we would have managed to pay for university anyway.'

'Oh, that.'

'Yes, madam, Oh that. You have your whole life ahead of you and all this has only been a wee interruption. If God spares us you will go to the University next year, if they'll let you in, if we can afford it.'

'I'll go to night school.'

'Whatever for?'

'I can learn typing and bookkeeping. French and German aren't much use in a shop, unless we open a branch in Paris.'

'Oh, we might just do that. But you could go to a day school, one of those colleges like Skerry's.'

'It would cost more money. Anyway, night school would keep me busy in the evenings.'

'You'll find better things to do with your evenings than that.'

'No.'

There was no arguing with that. The girl was right when she said she wasn't herself yet, and she would have to find her own way back to herself. Meg had her own things to think about, with fools throwing bricks at her window; because no sooner was the window repaired than it was smashed again, and she had to keep Peter from school for a day to run about and find the people who fitted wire mesh guards on shops and get one in a rush, rather than be picking up broken glass every day and being called out by the police every night. Hers wasn't the only shop to suffer, but there was no consolation in that. Everything cost money, everything ate into the credit-and-debit balance (which she thought of as a seesaw, with her at one end, a load of debt getting bigger and bigger at the other end). Nothing ever settled down.

That Sunday, Bobby arrived by himself, hours before the usual time. He had a rucksack on his back, and he came into the house without a word. He didn't put the rucksack down.

'Can I come here and stay, Mother?' he asked, and there were tears close behind the words. She was stabbed by his look of helplessness, and the shame of maybe crying in front of people, a big strong boy of fifteen. She tried to be calm and conversational.

'Well, I don't know if your father would approve, Bobby.'

He didn't answer. She guessed that he was afraid to speak again in case the tears came in earnest. She saw Dan walking past the open living-room door and pausing, and he answered her look with a wave of both hands, nodded, stuck up his thumb.

'Have you asked your father?'

Hetty picked up her book and drifted out of the room, but Peter stayed, fascinated.

'He says as far as he's concerned I can go to – he says he never wants to see me again.' The voice broke completely. She waved Peter impatiently out of the room, and he closed the door behind him, looking cheated.

'Don't be afraid to cry, son, if you have tears they're better out than in.' She put an arm across his shoulders and he turned to her and spoke in jerking sobs.

'He was hitting me, for nothing, and I said I would run away, and he said it was time I had a job and there would be no more of that school and then he started shouting about the Cassidys, he said terrible things about everybody, Peter and Hetty and you, and then John came in and got between us and he started shouting at him as well but John didn't bother, and Da said he could see me far enough and I said well I'm going and he said I'd better not try to come back or he would kill me and I didn't know what to do.'

'Well, you came here.'

'I don't want to leave school, I like it.'

'All right, all right, Bobby, it's all right.' They sat on the couch and she patted his arm and murmured meaningless repetitions till his fit had passed.

'Stupid,' he muttered. 'Greeting in front of people.'

'Stupid indeed? There's older and bigger men than you are not ashamed to cry, so we'll have none of that.' Her voice was brisk and bracing, and he wiped his eyes and nodded. 'Now we'll just have to see what we're going to do with you and yes Peter Cassidy you can take your ear away from the keyhole.' Peter appeared instantly.

'My bed's only this width,' he said seriously.

'I can sleep on the floor, Peter.'

'The floor's only *this* width.'

'That's okay.'

'You can wear a jacket with a coathanger still inside it, and hang yourself up in the wardrobe at night.'

They both started to snigger.

'You can sleep head to feet if you have to,' Meg said.

'Oh help,' said Peter. 'That means I get his scratchy toenails in my mouth. Come on up and see my room.'

The rainstorm was over and the sunshine out in seconds. Oh, to be young. But she was worried about laying a fresh burden on Dan Cassidy.

'As long as he doesn't break into the sherry, it's jake with me, Meg. It's his father that worries me.'

'Aye, he worries me too, and I don't want you to bear any of the brunt of him. It's nothing to do with you, Dan, and I wish Bobby had never come.'

'You can't send the kid back.'

'It might be best for him. I mean it. We all have to put up with things, it's a part of growing up, and he's getting big enough to take care of himself.'

'Right. We'll send him back.'

'We'll do nothing . . . you wouldn't, Dan, would you?'

'Oh dearie-me, Meg Macrae, oh aye, you're the hard one, send him back and let him get knocked about for his education. Don't be daft. We've got no choice. I've told you before, the family is an obsolete institution, and that poor kid is the proof of it.'

'Oh yes. What about uncles? Are they out of date as well?'

'I'm not his uncle. We're nothing to each other but fellow-citizens. I would do the same for an escaped murderer.'

'I've no patience with you, Dan. The time has to come soon when we all get out from under your feet and get a place of our own.'

'Aye.'

She looked at him quickly, his solemn nod, and had a twinge of alarm.

'But not this week, nor the next, or any I can think of just at the moment. By God, I think you were expecting your notice there, Meg.'

'You'd be quite in your rights.'

'Aye. I just hope we're wise. Or lucky. I prefer lucky.'

'So do I, for I've hardly done a wise thing in my life.'

'That's true, you're known for a fool the length and breadth of the Gallowgate, people talk about nothing else.'

John arrived at his usual time, his usual quiet unobtrusive self.

'Is Bobby here?'

'Yes.'

'Is it all right, Mother?'

'Yes, it's all right.'

'He's upstairs with Peter tearing the house apart,' Hetty

said. 'Do you feel like a walk, John?'

'Mm, sure, Hetty.'

And John was out of the house almost as soon as he was in it. She found herself looking at Dan, both of them thinking probably the same thing, and they went to the window to watch the two children strolling up the street. John had his hands in his jacket pockets. Hetty's hands were taking up half the width of the pavement as she talked and talked and talked. They could see John's face half-turning to her, half-nodding, half-smiling, as she rattled on.

'Now she is telling him things she would never tell another girl; or her mother.'

'He listens a lot, your John.'

'You know, there is something very deep about that boy, Dan, and I don't know what it is because he doesn't talk much unless you provoke him to it. But I've always trusted him. Whatever Hetty is telling him, nobody else will ever know.'

'He's well made.'

'Ach, that has nothing to do with it, because there is no aggression in him.'

'I'm with him there.' Dan laughed. 'I sometimes think I'll hire a substitute when the barricades go up for the Revolution.'

'Oh, the girls John could have, If he could just be bothered, if he knew what it was he had, it's a thing a woman can't resist, whatever it is, and I don't know myself.'

'Ach, if he's got something, and he knew about it, he would be unbearable, leave him alone.'

'I will, I will. I would just fair love to be a fly on his shoulder and hear what Hetty's raving about.'

'Shame on you, Meg Macrae.'

'Aye.'

By the time the two came home from their stroll, Bobby and Peter had been ordered to prepare the little afternoon feast. Dan left the family to it and went to the kitchen to sit on the floor at the open door and look out at the little garden with a great pot of tea at his side and contemplate the mysteries of society and economics and the historical process. John unexpectedly came in and asked if he could join in.

'Yup. Sure. Give me your cup.'

They sat side by side for several minutes, and Dan saw what Meg had meant. The boy, and it was not easy, looking at him, to tell what age he was, seventeen or thirty-seven, was comfortable in silence, quite unlike young Peter, who was receptive enough but had talk boiling up in him all the time.

'Can I talk to you, Mr Cassidy?'

'Yeah, sure.'

'There could be trouble in this. Bobby being here.'

'No trouble to me.'

'My father is . . . he's very difficult, Mr Cassidy. It's hard to say this, but he's violent. He's more violent. Maybe it's losing his job. He's difficult.'

'Mhm.'

'I'm glad Bobby's away from him. But I'm worried.'

'I'm surprised you haven't left, yourself.'

'Oh, he needs somebody there. Andy's out a lot of the time. Da needs somebody there.'

'You mean your mother?'

'Oh no. I mean me. There's nobody else.'

'Doesn't he strike you?'

'Oh no, Mr Cassidy. I don't like violence. He's felt me holding his wrists, he would never try that. He's a bit vain. Everybody is, I expect.'

'Uhuh.' Dan realised more and more clearly why Meg hadn't been able to define what it was that John had. It was a bit frightening.

'What I mean is, I don't want to talk to Mother about this, I don't want to worry her. But Da is a wee bit dangerous. He's changed. It's Da that broke the shop window.'

'Aha.'

'Yes, I caught him at it the second time. But what can I do? I'll not let him do it again, but he's got a grudge against Mother.'

'Thanks for telling me. I feel great now.'

'You had to know, Mr Cassidy. I don't know. Mother should never have married him, they're the wrong types.'

'But you're glad she did.'

'Oh yes. I'm glad. But not for them.'

'Well, is there anything else?'

'No. But he'll have to be watched. Especially when he knows Bobby's here.'

'I feel even better.'

John smiled suddenly, then laughed.

'I'm probably talking a lot of rubbish, I've read too much psychology. Don't pay any attention.'

'No, I'll not. I wonder how much a Great Dane costs at the Barrows.'

## 26

The two Misses Newton next door were crazy. They dressed in long clothes and extravagant hats with a lot of decoration and veiling. Each had a small Cairn terrier, and when they emerged from their house it was always separately, to walk their dogs in separate directions. Sometimes Meg could see them, from her upstairs back windows, hanging out clothes to dry in their little garden. They each had a separate clothes-line, and if they did chance to be in the garden at the same time they kept their backs to each other and hung up their separate washing without speaking. Dan reckoned that they were the kind of people who ended up committing axe murders, but any time Meg met either of them in the street and offered a courteous good morning, Miss Newton – it wasn't easy to tell which one – would respond gravely, or with an embarrassed titter, sometimes the hint of a curtsey.

They belonged in a museum, Dan thought. Meg's theory was that they were a museum in themselves. They didn't dress, she suspected, to look like old ladies in old-fashioned clothes. They dressed to keep looking young, in the clothes that had been bright young fashions in their long-ago youth. Neither of them liked Hetty. Meeting her outside, on their separate travels, they would turn their faces away and look affronted, and very nearly sweep their skirts aside as she passed, to avoid contamination. Hetty was puzzled but not concerned. If her mother was right in thinking that they were still living in their youth, the sight of a young woman in the style of the thirties, with her high-heeled shoes and her calves visible, was probably shocking.

Peter began, and Bobby soon joined in, to invent legends about the strange life the Misses Newton lived behind the blank front door and the curtained windows of number 23. They dressed very formally for dinner, and always began with Grace and then a toast to Dear King Edward and Mr. Asquith, in Madeira wine. Dinner was served by an ancient maidservant, never seen outdoors because they kept her chained to a ring in the cellar when she wasn't working, and threw her the scraps that the dogs wouldn't eat. If she spilled anything or broke a dish, one of the sisters pulled her hair while the other stuck pins in her.

'We could hear her screaming,' Bobby objected. It took Peter only a second to dispose of that.

'She's deaf and dumb. That's how they got her cheap from the orphanage a hundred years ago.'

'No, they've got an iron clamp on her head, like the Man in the Iron Mask.'

'That's right, that's right! So that she can't steal a mouthful of the fresh salmon and . . . and caviare . . . and crêpes Suzette while she's cooking their dinner.'

'You don't cook fresh salmon and caviare, silly,' Hetty corrected him. 'You shouldn't talk about the poor old souls like that.'

'What are crêpes Suzette anyway?' Bobby asked.

'Pancakes.'

'Made of cloth?'

'No, not made of cloth, you ignorant boy.'

'Listen to that,' Bobby said. 'She sounds like Miss Wales again.'

'And they have gentlemen guests, with stiff collars and medals,' Peter said.

'Nobody ever goes in or out, silly.'

'I know, I know. They keep them chained in the cellar as well.'

'No, they don't.' Bobby was seething with discovery. 'They're mummified.'

'You're right, you're right, Bobby. They came for dinner years ago and the sisters liked them so much they wouldn't let them go so they, eh, they . . .'

'They let them kiss their hands, and they were wearing wee rings wi' needles in them.'

'Like the Borgias, the Borgias. Great. And suddenly . . .'

He held out a hand. Bobby bent over it, stood up, and staggered round the living room clutching his throat and croaking horribly before slowly collapsing. After a lot of athletic convulsions, he lay dead.

'But they had to get them on to the chairs,' Peter rushed to drag Bobby into a chair, 'before rigor mortis set in.' Bobby froze into the posture of a diner, and then muttered through clenched teeth. 'But once a year, at the full moon, they come to life.'

'No, sit where you are, Bobby. I'm Miss Marguerite. Ah, my dear Lord Muck, would you care for another spot of the

187

old caviare if I shove it in your gub with this gold fork?'

'That's right, the *old* caviare – it's still the same dish of caviare they were eating sixty years ago.'

'Yugh, it stinks.'

'No, it's mummified caviare. Try it, Sir Lord Duke Viscount.'

'Any mummified chips going, Miss Newton?'

'Chips are for the lower classes.'

'Well, I'm a lower class lord. If there's no chips, you can keep your smelly caviare. Is that right. Hetty? You mean the King never gets chips? That's a right swizz.'

'The King,' Hetty explained, 'gets pommes de terre frîtes.'

'Ach, foreign muck. Then they dance a cotillion, eh?'

'They've got a mummified orchestra.'

'They would never get room for an orchestra in a house this size. Just a minute, they've shrunk them as well, like the Jivaro Indians.'

'That's it. They've got wee totty violins this size, and a wee totty piano this size, and they're stuck on the mantelpiece so they can never escape to tell the tale.'

'And so the dogs canny eat them.'

'Ach, imagine eating a mummy.'

'Maybe the dogs are mummies as well. You notice they walk funny. And as soon as the dawn comes up, they have to rush back to a coffin full of their native earth.'

'Ach, that's stupid, Peter, that's vampires.'

'Well, some of them are mummies, some of them are vampires. The Misses are vampires maybe.'

'But they go out during the day.'

'Maybe their clock's stopped and they don't know the difference.'

'Maybe,' Meg looked up from her book, 'Maybe they're Australian vampires.'

Bobby looked puzzled.

'When it's night-time in Australia,' Meg started to explain, and everybody shouted, 'It's Wednesday over here.'

'You've got me as mad as yourselves,' Meg complained. 'The terrible things you're saying about these poor women.'

'I went stark staring mad half an hour ago,' Uncle Dan declared. 'What have I got myself into?'

Coming home from school one day the boys were taken

aback to hear an imperious knocking at the front window of the Misses Newton, and see one of the sisters there, the curtain drawn back with one hand and the other hand beckoning them.

'They want to mummify us as well,' Bobby muttered without moving his lips.

'But we can't dance a cotillion.'

'Will we run?'

'They're only old women.'

They advanced warily up the front steps, and the door was flung open.

'Little boys.'

'Yes, Miss Newton.'

'Will you run to the shops and fetch me a quarter-pound of Cooper's best tea?'

'All right.'

She held out both hands with a shilling in each.

'And a quarter-pound of Mazawattee tea for Miss Amanda. Don't get them mixed up, now. Cooper's Best, for me, and Mazawattee for Miss Amanda. She prefers Mazawattee,' she added, with an incredulous sniff. 'And if you hurry back you may come in for a dish of tea and a sandwich.'

'Yes, Miss Newton.'

They were hugging themselves as they trotted to the shops, to two separate shops.

'We'll see the mummies, Peter.'

'And the wee orchestra.'

'And the coffin full of native earth.'

'Mind, now, don't kiss anybody's hands, or Krrrrk, away wi' the goalie, thud bang wallop.'

'A dish of tea? Does she mean a soup plate full of tea or something?'

'Aye, maybe they give it to you already saucered and blown.'

'We'd better not laugh.'

'Oh God. Do you think we should ask Mother first?'

'She'll not be home from the shop.'

'Oh Jesus.'

The door was open before they reached it, and Miss Newton waiting for them. She accepted the two packets of tea and the separate handfuls of change and ushered them into the front room.

'The kettle's just on the boil,' she said. 'We'll be with you in a moment.'

She left them to stare at a quite ordinary roomful of old-fashioned furniture. The only novel thing was that the fireplace contained little ornamental fans of red crepe paper instead of a fire, and the curtained room was dim. Peter saw Bobby clap his hand to his mouth and start to choke as he looked at the mantelpiece. Ranged along it were eight little coloured china figures; monkeys, dressed in old-fashioned clothes and holding musical instruments. Peter could feel his lungs heaving. They sat down in chairs facing the other way, bit their lips and dug their nails into their palms, and sprang up when the Misses appeared, each carrying a tray.

'Now I am Miss Marguerite, and my sister is Miss Amanda.'

'I am Bobby, and this is my brother Peter.' The boys found themselves bowing, and waiting till the sisters were seated before they sat.

'We don't usually hold with neighbours,' said Miss Marguerite.

'—with neighbours,' Miss Amanda echoed.

'She always repeats everything I say.'

'Not always, Marguerite.'

'Nearly always.'

'—always. No I don't.'

'But you seem like quite nice little boys.'

'—little boys. I was just going to say that.'

'Well, I said it. You seem like quite a happy family.'

'Oh, I'm sure you're a very happy family,' Miss Amanda said, quite independently.

'Now, do you prefer Cooper's Best, or Mazawattee, Peter?'

'I don't know the difference, Miss Marguerite.'

This was a blow to both ladies.

'Never mind, you shall have a cup of each.'

'Yes, a cup of each, please.'

And indeed, there were three cups and saucers on each tray; fine China cups that made Peter feel apprehensive. The china on each tray was of a different pattern. And there was a little plate of tiny thin sandwiches on each tray. The boys went through a curious ritual of drinking from two cups, with two pairs of eyes on them, and the feeling that they were on trial.

'They're both very nice,' Peter said, before the question could be asked.

'Yes, I suppose they are.' Miss Marguerite wasn't too disappointed.

'I just prefer Mazawattee,' said Miss Amanda.

'And you're quite right to choose it,' said her sister. 'What is the sense of putting up with somebody else's choice?'

'That's what I say, Marguerite.'

'So do I. We're a funny old pair, aren't we, Bobby?'

'No, Miss Marguerite.'

'We are a funny old pair,' Miss Amanda insisted. 'People laugh at us, because we don't really hold with people.'

'We don't see any young people, that's the trouble. We're out of touch.'

'Well,' said Miss Amanda, 'young people are the worst. They do laugh at us.'

'We don't, honestly, Miss Amanda.'

'I am quite sure you do, Bobby. When we were younger we were always laughing at people. Now speak the truth and shame the Devil.'

'We nearly laughed,' Peter admitted.

'I told you so.'

'No, not at you, Miss Marguerite. See, we sometimes wondered what you did in the evenings, and I thought—' Bobby was shaking his head violently, his cup rattling dangerously in the fine china saucer, but Peter couldn't find a way of stopping.

'It was a silly idea. I thought maybe you sometimes danced, but there wasn't enough room for a real orchestra, so you would have tiny wee musicians, sitting on the mantelpiece to keep them safe from the dogs. And then . . . '

He wished he had never opened his mouth. But the Misses were shocked into laughter, holding napkins primly to their lips but quite helpless. Miss Amanda seemed in danger of going into a polite paroxysm and choking genteelly to death.

'Oh dear or lor,' said Miss Marguerite, 'we never hear anything funny these days.'

'—these days. Ladies aren't amusing on their own, of course. Oh dear, tiny little musicians . . . '

The Misses voted afternoon tea a resounding success, quite resounding. They conducted their guests round the ground floor. The two terriers were in the kitchen, living in separate baskets and with separate dishes. Miss Marguerite explained that when two people lived together it was very important to retain their individual personalities. There were two of nearly everything. The boys agreed.

They would visit again, of course, since they lived so conveniently. Bobby said the Misses must come to tea too, and both shook their heads very doubtfully.

'You must,' Bobby persisted. 'You must come and meet us all.'

'This young man is bullying us, Amanda,' said Marguerite, and Bobby nodded happily, wondering what Uncle Dan would say. But they could come while he was out.

Meg and Hetty had come home. Bobby was diffident about describing their experience, but it turned out to be a hilarious story, and Mother agreed that the old ladies should be asked 'to tea'.

'It is a sin not to know our next-door neighbours, and it would take them out of themselves, the souls, they must come in while we're still here.'

'Are we going away?'

'I don't think we can ask Uncle Dan to keep us forever, Peter, it's a lot to put on a man when he's hardly a relation at all.' When Peter looked glum she added, 'But there is no hurry to think about that.'

Dan never complained, it was true, and she hoped he wasn't just being polite when he said he was happy to have them all. It must have been lonely on his own, but on the other hand, people need privacy too. At least he wasn't being exploited, the word he would have used. The shop was beginning to pay, and she bought all the food in spite of his objections, and paid a share of the electricity and the coal.

She was happy about the shop. She felt she should be happy about everything. Andrew was still a shadow in the background, partly of fear, partly of guilt. No matter how good, how irresistible her reasons had been for leaving him, it was worrying to think that she might be to blame for everything that was happening to him now.

It was a Tuesday, the early closing day at the shop, when he appeared again, at the house. She recognised him through the door, and told Hetty to stay in the kitchen out of sight. He was slightly drunk again, but only slightly, and when she let him in, his attitude was a mixture of defiance and unease.

'You should never have come here,' she said. 'It is not my house, and it is only an embarrassment.'

'I'll keep the head,' he muttered. 'I know damn well whose house it is.'

'And don't say a word against him.'

'Uhuh. All right. All right, I'm willing to take you back.'

'I am not willing to go back. This is a waste of time, Andrew.'

'I mean I'll take the lot of you back.'

'The lot of us are not coming back. Can you not understand?'

'You only left because I lost the head about . . . her. Well, all right, least said. I've changed my mind. I just lost the head.'

'I am not coming back.'

He wasn't listening.

'Anybody would have done the same, no self-respect, man-mad, her mind never off it, she was asking to get herself into trouble. But all right, that's all finished with.'

'She didn't get herself into trouble. She was got into trouble.' Meg heard her voice rising, in her furious impatience and anger at the glib injustice to the female sex. 'A girl doesn't "get herself" into trouble. She is got into trouble and you know it as well as I do.'

His face was twisted in confused anger.

'She's a liar, a born liar. What has she told you now?'

'What has she told me?' Bells were clanging in her head. She felt dizzy. 'What did she have to tell me?'

'Don't you look at me like that, it's got nothing to do with me, she got herself into it.'

'What are you telling me, Andrew Mason?' She was hearing herself from a long way off.

'Nothing, I don't know what you mean.'

'You are telling me something. You are not telling me but I hear you telling me. What have you done to my girl?'

'She'll say bloody anything.' He was roaring.

'I asked you a question. God in Heaven, Andrew Mason, you will answer me.'

'It was none of my doing, do you think I'm . . . what do you think I am?'

'I am trying to find out.' She was blazing, and blind with

revelation, and cold as ice, and trembling with horror, and she saw him crumbling before her, slavering.

'In the middle of the night, aye, oh aye, oh aye, she'll tell you anything, but saying she had to take her mother's place, I never even knew what was happening, I was sleeping, nothing happened, it had nothing to do with me, the bitch, they're all the same at that age, Christ . . . I never did nothing, it's all they ever think about. Meg, I need my wife, people laugh at me in the streets, I came to say we can forget all about it, just come back.'

Now there was no anger, only ice in her.

'I don't know how I can look at you, Andrew Mason. God in heaven. Leaving your own wife neglected, and ravishing a poor lassie you were supposed to protect. No wonder you wanted rid of her, to get rid of your shame.'

'It was her, it was her, don't look at me. Who the hell do you think you are?'

'I don't want to look at you. I am amazed I am talking to you when I should be at your throat.'

'She was dreaming.'

'You could go to prison for the rest of your life, and I am not sure I would care if you did.'

'I did nothing, she's a lying wee bitch, man-daft, thinks about nothing else.'

He was backing towards the door, and a good thing, for she could have killed him.

'You took my son away from me,' he bleated.

'Aye, and I'll keep him away from you. You are a drunken pig, Andrew Mason, not fit to be with human people. Maybe I'm not finished with you, Andrew Mason, but by the living God in Heaven, you had better be finished with me and mine and keep away from them, or you'll be sorry you were ever born. And go, go, before I am sorry for what I might do to you.'

She stalked after him into the hall, saw him groping in his mind for words or sense. There was a scream that froze them both. Hetty was leaning against the kitchen door. The sound seemed to go on for hours. She stopped, and screamed again. He fumbled for the handle of the front door, opened it and shambled out, leaving it wide open. Hetty started on another unearthly scream. Meg went to the door and quietly closed it. When she went to Hetty the girl was still screaming. Her eyes were wide and blind. Meg took her by the hand and led her into the living room and pushed her down on to the couch. She still screamed. Meg sat beside her and held her rigid hand and did nothing. In time the screaming stopped.

She was still wide-eyed and absent, but her face slowly relaxed and she sank back, staring in wonderment at something.

'That is a good loud noise you make when you feel like it, Hetty. You could fair call the sheep in from the other side of the Island with that noise.'

Now the girl stopped staring and began to tremble, and Meg let her get on with it.

'Brrr,' she said. 'I was screaming.'

'Oh, weren't you just. And it sounded to me like something breaking. Like a dam.'

'Brrrrr.'

'You've had it all piling up inside you all this time and never let it out. Will you be all right, I wonder. I'm not sure what to do for you, Hetty.'

'It's all right.'

'I'll make you a nice strong cup of tea in a minute.'

'No, don't go away.'

'I'll not go away. I know. I never meant to shout. You heard every word.'

'I heard every word.'

'What a time you have had, Hetty. And you couldn't even tell me. No, how could you tell me that, it would be impossible.'

'I wasn't even sure if it was true, or just a nightmare. And I wasn't even sure who it was, it might have been young Andy – he was awful strange and quiet after it. I just wakened up and it was happening to me. But there was blood on the sheets in the morning. But even then I thought it might be the period.'

'Now you will tell me all about it, Hetty. You've been carrying a poison in your mind all this time.'

They went to the kitchen and had tea, and talked, and talked, about everything and nothing, and she could see the girl relaxing as if she was getting over a cramp.

'I think you'll be all right, Hetty,' Meg said at last. 'As long as you don't believe this is you finished with men for all your life. That would be a shame and a waste.'

Hetty managed a shaky laugh.

'I'm not very interested at the moment, thanks very much.'

'No, by Jove, you've had a wee overdose, it'll take a while to get that out of your system.'

Hetty gazed into her face as if she was looking for the first time.

'You take everything in your stride, don't you, Mother?'

'Oh, I fall on my face now and then, girl. I've had troubles I thought would be the end of me, but we have to go on, Hetty, we have to go on.'

'Mother, you're crying!' Hetty put her arms round her to cradle her, and Meg shook her head, impatient with herself.

'I'm a silly old woman, Hetty, and that will be quite enough of that. From now on I want to see some smiles about this house, or I'll know the reason why.'

'Yes, Mother.' Without knowing why, Hetty was in a flood of tears.

When the children had gone to bed she sat up to keep Dan company with his tenth cup of tea.

'I do not know how you can ever get a night's sleep with all that tea in you, Dan.'

'No, sometimes I think I should pour the last three cups down the toilet to save getting up at three o'clock.'

'You're a terrible creature, and crude, too.'

'There's something on your mind, Meg. What's wrong?'

'Oh, just private woman's business, nothing to worry you with, and it's all right. You always know when there's something on my mind.'

He shrugged.

'Oh,' she said, 'I've had a sore travail thinking about men, and women, and the awful things they can do to each other.'

'Blame God for that, Meg, it had nothing to do with Karl Marx. I don't think the old fellow was bothered much with sex, to tell you the truth.'

'He was lucky. Maybe. Dan, you're not really a saintly man, are you?'

'The exact opposite.'

'I'm not sure you're right about that. But I've been thinking, about this thing and that thing, and how odd it is to be a woman. And I was wondering if you would be shocked, if I was to ask you, if you would ever like to keep me company in my bed tonight.'

He spilled his tea.

'You are shocked.'

'No. Aye, I'm shocked. No, I'm surprised. No, I'm flattered. No, I'm flabbergasted.'

'And what would your answer be?'

'Would I ever throw your generosity in your face?'

'I don't think you ever would.'

'My God, you're cool, Meg.'

'That is very far from the truth. But you might think I was a calculating woman if I said I suddenly had the notion to be with a man, and the comfort of him, because I decided it myself, I decided the time and the place and the man, and oh Dan, you are a dear dear man to me. That is not very womanly, is it?'

'Meg, in the name of Marx, I don't think I'm ready for the philosophical disquisitions. God. That's my tenth cup of tea. Is it all right if I go upstairs, and, eh, wash my hands?'

'Take your time. I'll be in there when you come down. And I'm grateful, Dan, you didn't turn me down.'

'Godalmighty, *you're* grateful!'

He was diffident, he was cautious, he was nervous, he was kind, and she wondered if she had forced him into something he didn't want, but her body was ablaze and what she felt for him was some kind of love, and sweetness. In the night, in the dark, he said, 'Thank God for that, Meg. I thought I might not manage it.'

'Oh Dan, Dan, maybe it is just a physical appetite I should be ashamed of, but you are a dear man. And it is early yet, I think you'll manage it again in a wee while. You are so good to me, Dan Cassidy.'

'Aye, that'll be right, Meg Macrae. We'll not be making a habit of this, I think.'

'Well, Dan, it wouldn't be right, for the sake of the children anyway. But I am not sorry. And sometime, if you feel the need, you will ask me and I will refuse you nothing. It is a man's place to ask.'

'I'll ask, Meg. If I don't have the nerve, I'll send you a wee note.'

'All right. And dammit to hell.' She giggled under the sheet. 'I said dammit to hell, I swore. I'll be smoking next.

Dammit to hell, Dan Cassidy, if everybody thinks you are my fancy man, I may as well have the benefit of it now and then. Oh Dan, Dan you are ready, aren't you?'

'I would never have believed it. What do you mean, you'll be smoking next? You're a hell of a woman.'

'That is true, I should be ashamed of myself.'

## 27

And now that was all over, and so simply. It could not have gone on, living scandalously, and with the feeling that she was using Dan for her selfish comfort, when she suspected that he didn't need physical excitement as she did. Her own fierce appetite put her at a disadvantage.

Anyway, when Dan heard that his sister and her husband were coming back from America, broke and homeless, the decision to move out became inevitable. She was able to get a big flat in Alexandra Parade from Livingstone the factor, and although it was still in the grubby city, grass grew in the back court and the trees and the greenery of the park could be seen beyond. Things were going well enough. Things had to be taken as they came.

And although it seemed a terrible risk, she had expanded into the shop next door, at the insistence of the Misses Newton.

The Misses Newton were the most astonishing change of all. From the first audacious step of having Bobby and Peter to tea, they had graduated reluctantly to visiting Meg for tea, and were steadily emerging from their cocoon.

They got over their suspicion of Hetty, who represented the youth they had lost. They read her fashion magazines. They visited the shop for new clothes and let Hetty choose them. They finally offered, very nervously, to put some money into the shop as a Wee Hobby, and work in it, to get them away from their recluse.

They still insisted on being independent of each other, and worked on alternate days in the shop, with two dog baskets in the back shop. They were quite grand with the customers, who couldn't tell them apart.

'Oh no, Moddom, that was the other Miss Newton who served you.'

'It was you.'

'I sincerely beg to differ, Moddom, but I am sure I can give you satisfaction. The other Miss Newton is a wee bit out of touch with modern styles.'

Dan came in several times a week at his lunch break and flirted outrageously with either or both of them. They twittered and upbraided him, and loved it.

He was having a bad time with his sister.

'It's not the same as having you there, Meg,' he admitted. 'You made me feel like a boy, though the . . . the you know . . . that's never really been my hobby, all my energy went into the intellect, I think.'

'You were good to me, Dan, in everything you have done.'

'Never as good as you've been for me, Meg. But my sister's a boring bitch. Look at her sideways and she's off on a string of Hail Marys and flinging beads about. She's got the place stuffed wi' Madonnas and Sacred Hearts.'

'They're a comfort to her, Dan, you have to realise that some people need that comfort.'

'She disapproves of me. She's living in my house rent-free and she disapproves of me.'

'So do I, you recusant pagan.'

'Aye, all right, Meg, but when you disapprove, you do it wi' a touch of class. Teresa's as common as the pigs of Docherty.'

'Listen to the champion of the equality of man.'

'Oh, I'm still for that, Meg. And I think the final struggle is about due. This Fascist rebellion in Spain is the wee cloud the size of a man's hand. It's the rehearsal for the big blow-up everywhere.'

'Away with your bogey-men, I will not have it. I do not want to hear about Spain.'

'Oh, you will, Meg. You will.'

And she did. John came to the shop on a Saturday, full of tidings, and apologised for his long absence. He was spending his weekend on homework for his night classes in engineering, and Meg was happy about that. But he was such a good-looking boy, and she wondered if he had no time for girls at all. To her very offhand questioning, he looked his usual relaxed, unworried self, and admitted that there were two or three girls in the office who were quite nice, and one of them had asked him out once or twice.

'Brazen hussy.'

'No, she's quite nice. Da's gone away. I didn't know if I should mention it.'

'Why not, John. You mean with another woman?'

'Aye . . . well, he's . . . actually, she's a widow with two daughters. The three of them are all . . . I don't know, it's none of my business.'

'You mean they are loose women.'

'That sort of thing, I think. Andy's going to Spain.'

'He is not going to Spain, I will not permit it.'

'I wondered if Hetty would like to come out with me tonight, to the Palais or somewhere.'

'Stop jumping about, John Mason, I have not finished with Andy yet. That is not much fun, having a date with your sister.'

John shrugged.

'She's easier to talk to than the girls in the office. I never know what they expect me to do. Andy's talking at a rally in the Central Halls on Monday. He sent you these two tickets.'

There was nothing more to be said. She was terrified. But she went, alone, to the rally in the Central Halls and discovered that Andy was actually acting as chairman.

She could have shaken sense into him, but she was proud of him at the same time, and nervous for him. There was no need for nervousness, he was completely in control, the cocky young devil, and he knew all about chairing a meeting. And she could feel the enthusiasm, and anger and exhilaration, all round her in the crowded hall as he introduced the three speakers and they reported on the civil war in Spain, and the feeble treachery of the British Government, and the dress rehearsal of the Fascist conquest of Europe, and a lot of things she could hardly believe, though she could feel herself lifted with the enthusiasm of the crowd and tried not to be.

When the last speaker was finished, Andy stood to close the meeting, utterly confident, and cried 'No pasaran!' The audience roared in return.

'I hardly feel fitted,' he said, 'to occupy the chair with the great speakers we have heard tonight, and I ask you to express your appreciation again.' They did.

'If I need an excuse for being in this chair,' Andy cried, 'the only one I can think of is that I'll not be having much chance to chair any more meetings in Glasgow for a while. I'll be with our comrades in P.O.U.M., in the International Brigade in Spain. Goodnight, comrades.'

The tinker, she thought, saving the touch of theatricality to the end and stealing all the thunder. There was a perfect uproar of enthusiasm. People were trying to get to him to carry him shoulder-high. She laughed in spite of herself, and found a hand gripping her arm. She turned.

'I didn't like to stare,' the man beside her said. 'But when you laughed, there was no doubt of it. Nobody else ever laughed like that, Meg.'

She did stare.

'Eileann. Well I never.'

## 28

He wanted to talk politics, but she wouldn't let him. She was more immediately concerned with the experience of being in a superior restaurant for the first time in her life, was looking round at it with the candid curiosity of a child. It was an adventure.

'Never mind your politics, Eileann, my daft lovely son is going to Spain and I am not going to think about it. Ce que je veux savoir, puisque le menu soit en français, est qu'est-ce que c'est, ce Steak Tartare?'

The waiter leaned over.

'Raw beef, Madam, minced with an egg folded in, and various other flavourings.'

'Raw? That seems a dangerous way to eat meat, with so many germs about. I usually have my mince stewed, with plenty of carrots and onions and a nice thick gravy.'

'Moi aussi, Madame.'

'Ah, courage, courage, je vais avoir une experience. Nietzsche said Live dangerously.'

'Congratulations, Madame.'

She was suddenly shy when the waiter left.

'He probably thinks I am a silly woman, never to have heard of Steak Tartare.'

'Meg, Meg, the man is already half in love with you because you are honest as well as beautiful. Would you like Chianti?'

'That is an Italian wine. I have never tasted it. It will be another adventure.'

He nodded. He couldn't stop smiling, he couldn't stop looking straight into her face, and she looked back into his and took happiness in it. It was strange and almost shocking that the aristocratic Eileann should be a Socialist, but it didn't matter, and his presence was a joy, even if it was only for an hour. His hair was thinning at the temples, but he was all the better for it – or maybe, she thought, she would think he looked the better even if he were totally bald, as long as he was himself. He was strong, and confident, and ageing suited him. She had feared she might be nervous, but it was impossible to be anything but happy.

'You should not be looking at another woman like that,

Eileann, or even having dinner with her, and your wife sitting at home.'

'I have no idea where she is sitting, Meg, so stop being moral. We're only having dinner.'

'I am sorry you are not happily married.'

'Who said I wasn't happily married? Well, it isn't very important, Meg, we'll not talk about that.'

'I am just sorry because I would have wanted happiness for you. But all right, we will not talk about other people, we will just enjoy our dinner if I have the courage to eat raw mince. What are you doing with your life?'

'I lecture at the London School of Economics.'

'Well, I am glad you have made something of yourself, Eileann, there is too much in you to waste in just being a laird.'

'And what are you doing with your life, Meg?'

'I am doing whatever I am doing and it doesn't matter. I am having dinner with a handsome man who is a lecturer in the London School of Economics, and oh, I am sure you are a wonderful lecturer, the girls must all be crazy about you.'

He laughed aloud, and she laughed with him, though there was no real joke. She kept control of herself, because he really was so handsome that she could have wept. But the important thing in life was to enjoy the present time, and she was having dinner, her first meal in a superior restaurant with strange food, and waiters in tail coats, and strange sour Italian wine, and with Eileann, and she concentrated her mind on these things. And the waiter was absolutely charming, and so friendly without a bit of superciliousness although she was so naive and inexperienced.

Eileann too had a son. He didn't want to talk about absent people, but she sensed that he had a son he loved, whatever he felt about the boy's mother. She held back from asking too much about the son, because the thought of the boy started too many useless thoughts in her mind; and she diverted him from asking about her family. There were too many useless thoughts there too. She devoted herself to enjoying an adventure that had been dropped in her lap by the gods, and so did he.

'Meg, where in God's name did you go after you were seventeen? The silliest thing I ever heard is this imposture of yours about being a simple girl from the Islands, and quoting Nietzsche and throwing in bits of French to the waiter. You know more about everything than I do, except political economy.'

'Ah, Eileann, I have a good teacher in political economy too, and I think it is a great deal of nonsense. I think you suit being forty.'

'I like being forty. And looking at you, looking the same as you did when you were seventeen.'

'Ah, it is a lie, but I like you for it, Eileann.'

'If you even like me, I am a man greatly blessed. Can I take you home?'

'No, Eileann, I shall take a taxi.'

'I can take you in a taxi, Meg.'

'I can afford my own taxi, Eileann. I am in trade.'

'You make it sound so superior I am humbled. Meg, Meg, does your Presbyterian faith forbid you to let me take you home?'

'Oh, as for that, I cannot remember Jesus saying anything about sharing a taxi with a person of the opposite sex, but then, I suppose it was not a problem that was common in Galilee. Maybe Saint Paul said something about it – Paul was terribly down on nearly everything. But let us not be in a taxi, Eileann. It is a question of dignity.'

'I give in. I wonder if I'll ever see you again, Meg.'

'Eileann, I can think of you any time I choose, without having to eat raw mince or drink Italian wine. Though I did enjoy the raw mince.'

'Meg, you drive a man mad.'

'A laird, and a lecturer at the London School of Economics, driven mad by a simple girl from the Islands? Away with you.'

His laugh rang through the restaurant, and the waiter looked over and smiled as if he was in a conspiracy with her, and she laughed to the waiter too.

'Yes, Eileann, I mean it, away with you, dear Eileann, because we have had our hour, and that is the end of it. And oh, thank you Eileann, but we are not children, and we have had our hour, and we have our dignity.'

'Oh God. I mean, God bless you, Meg. We will meet again.'

He put his lips lightly to her cheek.

She was glad she had chosen to go home alone. For her peace of mind, and her dignity. If there was nothing left but dignity, it was at least something.

# 29

## ANDY

Nobody who hasn't done it knows what a war is like, and as far as I'm concerned nobody is going to find out. The whole Spanish thing was a bloody disaster, but you couldn't tell anybody that kind of thing, because for a start, it was the big fight against Fascism, and we had to be the goodies fighting the baddies. If I had started spilling the real beans when I got back from Spain, it would have made me look like a dummy for getting mixed up in it, when I could have been running a pub in Gallowgate.

Now, I've got to get this straight in my head. I wasn't a dummy, and I wasn't a load of rubbish. I meant it, I was being absolutely honest, when I stood up at meetings and got a big hand for saying I would be away any minute to join the International Brigade. I enjoyed getting the big hand, okay, but I meant it anyway. These Right-wing thugs had to be stopped, and Andy was the wee boy who would do it. God I was young.

When I was in a daft mood I could see myself jumping over walls with a machine-gun and spraying the Fascist sods with lead and saving Madrid single-handed, and coming home with a medal, which would be very handy when the next election came up. But even when I was in a daft mood, *I was bringing the medal home*. I wasn't planning to have it stuck on a bloody tombstone to congratulate a dead hero.

I saw quite a few quite nice guys out there rushing to die a hero's death, and I always thought, Sod that for a caper, Mason, keep the head down, mind your back, there's another bottle of wine under the bed and a tart on top of it if you're lucky, and you don't want to disappoint either of them.

But honest to God, it was a bloody pantomime, and I suppose that's what history is like. I bet the Battle of Waterloo was a bloody pantomime as well, a lot of half-cut Jocks running bayonets up their sergeants' arses out of habit and Napoleon losing the game ten-nil because his Frenchies were even drunker than the Jocks.

It was fine at Glasgow Central Station when the mob

came to see us off. You would have thought we were just nipping down the road to knock hell out of the Fascists and coming back for fish suppers on the Monday. They had a piper playing Scotland the Brave, and a few half-bottles making the rounds, but not many because the comrades were a bit down on the booze. I didn't touch a drop. A lot of these people seeing us off would be voters, or election workers, and be honest, Mason, one of the reasons for going to Spain was to get a passport to the next election for Parliament. What I did have was a full bottle in my kitbag, to help to pass the time on the train to London.

There were only about a dozen of us on the train headed for death or glory. Six in our compartment, so I could start getting acquainted with my comrades-in-arms. I shared the bottle round. Two of them didn't drink. One of these was a boring little poultice called Dan Murphy, who had Got Socialism just a few weeks before, the way some people get acne, and he tried to give me a lecture about the Dictatorship of the Proletariat. I begged him, politely, to shut his face.

Another guy I don't forget is Bob Rankine, and I honestly don't know what to say about him. He was just bloody great, he was so straight he made me feel a bit of a chancer. His father had been one of the big men in the coal mines, and the union, one of the real guys because in those days it took a lot of guts to fight the bosses. You were on your own and they could squash you like a flea. Young Bob was a chip off the old block, I suppose. He didn't say a lot, he listened a lot, and he was nice to everybody, even to Dan Murphy.

You know these smiles that make you think the guy actually likes you and means it? That he would comfort you in your travail and lay down his life for you and all that rubbish? Bob was like that, and when I think of what happened to him I want to destroy the whole bloody human race. But he wouldn't think like that. He was a kind of saint, but not pious or anything, just jake-easy. I didn't know how a man could get to be as good as that, and nice with it. He didn't even hate Capitalists. He thought they were only protecting their own, the same as the workers, and you couldn't blame them for that. That man Rankine made me feel very small, but he made me feel good as well. I mean, if we've got human beings like that, the human race can't be too rotten.

It took years to get to Paris, and a French comrade led us to the upstairs room of a pub, and this skinny old English lady – I mean, a real Lady, with a title and everything, Lady Something, formally recruited us, and after a couple of nights in a doss-house, we got on a train for the Spanish border. The next easy stage was climbing over the Pyrenees, at night, and it was freezing. I had expected Sunny Spain, like a summer holiday. I thought a lot about that pub in the Gallowgate while we were staggering about in the dark, walking up precipices.

Barcelona was another thing. I fancied Barcelona in my dreams. It was hellish. There was nothing in the shops. No meat, no fish, no nothing. I mean the country is surrounded with fish, and they keep killing all those bulls, but there wasn't a sausage. Wine, yes. Meat, no. I kept trying to tell myself I was having a fantastic experience, I was Abroad, but the funny thing about being Abroad is that you're still there yourself, the same as you were in the Gallowgate. And of course, I was at war, I was a working-class hero, qualifying for his seat in Parliament. I had the war.

I couldn't find the war. We couldn't find the Fascists. We did have the Anarchists, who were my comrades. They took over the telephone exchange, an action which would stamp out Fascism for sure. The Government sent a crowd to persuade them to get to hell out of it. The Anarchists shot them up. The Government came back with more guys and kicked out the Anarchists. We sat in cafes and drank that pissy tinto wine. We were all the left-wing heroes thirsting for Fascist blood, but most of the time we were fighting each other.

We, the gallant Scottish lads, lived on wine and gossip. The gossip was not very hopeful. What I heard about our comrades, like the gallant Durutti column of the Anarchists, who went to war with no food because they were willing to fight, but not to cook, put cold shivers up me.

The natives were friendly, including a tart called Dolores, who got me to sleep at night, and a guy called Manuel Ortiz, who couldn't have been nicer, and spoke English. He was one of the PSUC, the Communists, and he didn't talk a lot of English, he just listened. I had him figured for a suppurating scab after a few minutes, and when Bob Rankine warned me not to say too much to him, I knew what he meant, because we discovered that the PSUC, our Communist brothers, were arresting Anarchists and flinging them in jail. These guys actually had private prisons. Not for Fascists, because there weren't any Fascists handy. Just for freedom fighters they didn't like.

After a while we actually got organised for war, under an English Communist called Charlie Miller. His first trick was to confiscate everybody's money, and pay the troops ten pesetas a day, which would buy tinto wine. I kept my money in my boot. The comrades might have abolished money as a Capitalist symbol, but they weren't going to abolish mine. They were not too keen on giving us guns, either; just taking our money.

When we finally moved to join the British Brigade at the Cordoba front, your hero felt like a half-hearted Christian being tossed to the lions. I got pally with a couple of Yankees who had lost their way and joined us for lack of a better idea. They were all right. Jim Sears was one of those guys who just likes a fight. He was constructed like a granite shithouse two storeys high. His pal was Gary Walsh, but everybody called him Roebuck because he went with Sears. Roebuck was a funny wee number, passionate about politics but not such a bore as Dan Murphy except that he wrote poetry, all the time. I even remember one of his poems.

> *The sky is the colour of blood*
> *And blood is the colour of blood*
> *And on Spain's wine-dark fields there springs*
> *The crimson surge of liberty*
> *The surgeon's knife*
> *Of revolution spurts a gory fountain*
> *And a torn land drinks deep, deep*
> *To drown the dying throes*
> *Of Tyranny.*

Some of the boys actually listened to that kind of stuff and cheered, as if it was Shakespeare or somebody. I thought it was shit. I knew that the Spanish poet Lorca had been executed by the Catholic Action mob, and after I heard Roebuck's poetry I wondered if the Catholics had the same taste in poetry as I had.

We got some real training in a dump called Albacete, and I

began to feel nearly like a soldier, but that's when Bob Rankine went sick. There was something wrong with his guts, and I knew it wasn't that he was yellow, he would just keep doubling up and collapsing. We had to leave him with one of the Communist PSUC comrades to find him a doctor. I hated that, and I hated the comrade too.

But we were finally in the fight. We were stuck on a hill in this place called Lopera, and we were going to save that hill for democracy. I was with Sears and Roebuck, and Dan Murphy, and the way I saw it was, the Fascists wouldn't be mad enough to attack a hill. We would sit there for the rest of the war, pick up the medals, and skedaddle.

The Fascists didn't have the sense to see we were impregnable. They shelled us to hell.

Why don't we shell them back? I inquired.

Ain't got no shells, said Jim Sears.

Bloody marvellous, I said.

Sears was actually brave, or he was a good actor. So was Dan Murphy. Roebuck had just curled into a ball and crawled back into the womb. I tried to imitate the heroes. At dawn, the Fascists were visible down there, coming up the hill. They looked like darkies.

Moroccans, Jim Sears said.

Oh Christ, I said.

Why Oh Christ?

The Moroccans scalp their prisoners and cut their balls off, that's why Oh Christ.

Oh Christ.

There were millions of them. Some of our mob started firing rifles and machine-guns at them, and the bullets fell miles short, but you have to do something to keep your spirits up. But the nearer they got, the more of them fell down. Dan Murphy leapt up screaming No Pasaran and fired at something, and I turned round to tell him to shut up, but he was lying on his back with no face. He had no face.

Now this brave officer, Charlie Miller, was running back and forth screaming at us not to panic, but to make an orderly retreat. I thought, sod that for a caper – panic. Sears and I grabbed Roebuck and bolted down the backside of the hill with him, and everybody hid in some olive trees which looked shell-proof. They started shelling the trees. We beat it.

That is my life as a war hero, and you can keep it.

We got back to Albacete, and set out to find Bob Rankine, and ran into Manuel Ortiz, our PSUC comrade, instead.

Rankine? he said, dead innocent and about as convincing as a three pound note. Oh, you would be wise to forget him.

Sears picked him up by the jacket and showed him a fist the size of a ham and asked where Rankine was.

Rankine has been arrested, said Ortiz. He is a Social Fascist and will probably be shot as a deserter.

Jim Sears gave him a belt in the mouth. Ortiz shook his head and spat out a lot of teeth and said we might be next on the list. It was quite inspiring, that, fighting for the freedom of Spain.

## 30

It was Meg's idea to have a party. They had never had such a thing, and now they could affort to be hospitable, like other people. It was for Peter and his friends, and Peter had the pride of inviting the guests.

Harry Cooke was inclined to despise the idea, on the grounds that parties were bourgeois activities unless they were devoted to discussing important political ideas.

'I thought we would have eight a side,' Peter said. 'Eight boys and eight girls.'

'You agreed we couldn't be bothered with girls, Peter.'

'I'm not having a party without girls, Harry. You don't need to come. You don't have to cuddle Ella Greenlees.'

'That's all you ever think about.'

'I know.'

'I'll think about it.' Harry yawned. When Harry was trying to hide his thoughts, he yawned. Next day at school, he yawned again and said in an insanely casual voice,

'Is it okay if I bring my cousin to your party? She's very intelligent.'

'Is she good-looking?'

'What's that got to do with it?' Harry was indignant.

'We don't want frumps at my party.'

'Oh God, you're so childish.'

Harry's cousin was a raving beauty. One look at her drove Ella Greenlees out of Peter's mind. Her cheeks were like alabaster, he thought, and she had a posh accent. Ella Greenlees hated her. The boys all tried not to stare at her, and Harry spent a lot of time standing beside her, with his arm across her shoulders.

Meg sat quietly in the kitchen, reading, and they started the entertainment with Forfeits. Peter had to be the Dreamer, since he was host.

Ella Greenlees stood behind him, since she had to be boss, and said, 'A wave, a wave, above your head, what is the owner of this to do?'

'Kiss all the flowers on the carpet,' Peter said promptly.

'Oh help, I was waving my own ring,' she wailed. 'I'm not kissing any carpet.'

'Oh, come on, Ella.' Peter was bored with Ella now he had

seen cousin Hilary. 'You know fine it means kissing the boys sitting on the carpet.' The boys on chairs slid smoothly to the floor.

'All that lot? Oh help.' She made the round with a good show of boredom and distaste. 'At least I don't have to kiss the Dreamer, because he's not on the carpet.'

Peter shrugged, just to annoy her.

'What is the owner of this to do?'

'Take Hilary out to the lobby and count three stars in the sky.'

'Nothing but kissing games at this party,' Ella snorted. Willie McKinnie gulped down his fourth cake and led Hilary out of the room, and everybody chanted One, Two, Three. When they came back, Willie was deep red and Hilary was laughing. She had beautiful teeth and a beautiful little pink tongue.

'Next forfeit,' Ella snapped. 'A lady.'

'All right,' said Peter. 'She goes down to Capaldi's and gets a pennyworth of ice cream in a chamber pot.'

'It's me!' Hilary squealed. 'Beast. I can't, and I shan't.'

But they all pushed her out of the house and swarmed down to Capaldi's to watch the fun. Tony Capaldi served the ice-cream without a smile. He knew the game.

At last they got to Postman's Knock, to groans of disapproval, and at last it happened. Peter got Hilary into the dark hallway. And she didn't kiss like Ella Greenlees. She gripped him below the waist and pressed against him, and her lips were open.

'You like French kissing?' she whispered.

'Is that French kissing? I've never done it.'

He felt her tongue in his mouth, and heard impatient shouts from the living room, and suddenly her right hand slid round to his front and squeezed, and he gasped.

'I don't do that to all the boys,' she whispered.

'Oh.'

'I'm enjoying your party.'

'Yes.'

'We'd better go back in.'

'Yes.'

Harry, for some reason, was quite annoyed and contemptuous, and muttered fiercely to Peter to leave his cousin alone. Peter shrugged, but it was obvious that Harry was not

214

enjoying the party as much as he might have. He had brought his beautiful cousin to show her off, not to have her getting friendly with other people, and he obviously felt that Peter was getting the whole idea wrong by being interested in Hilary instead of being impressed by Harry. And he took Hilary very positively by the arm, to see her home at the end of the party.

Peter tried to catch her eye, but she was looking round everywhere and at nobody.

'That was a bonny girl,' his mother said when he went upstairs. 'Is she in your class at school?'

'No, she's Harry's cousin.'

'Such a bonny girl, such a bonny girl.' There was a shadow over his mother's face, and he didn't understand it. But she smiled. 'You're not getting serious about her, are you, Peter?'

'I only met her tonight, Mother.'

'Yes, I know, Peter. Oh well, I am glad it was a nice party. Stop looking at me, I was likely thinking about Andy, away at that silly war in Spain, and never a letter from the tinker.'

'Andy'll be all right, Mother.'

'Aye, so he will. Ah, such a bonny wee girl.' And she sighed.

Peter was wondering where Hilary lived. He knew Harry Cooke would never tell him.

## 31

Peter felt that life was suddenly changing. He was growing hair on his body. It made him feel he was evolving, like a tadpole growing into a frog. Power. Virility. When I become a man, I put away childish things.

He was smug about it, he was joining an élite organisation. Grown men. He wanted to reorganise the world. He had serious talks with John Taylor, who had a Penguin book about design, and he complained to his mother that their house was a Victorian clutter of ornaments that would have no place in a properly organised, planned, clean society. Hetty told him to stop behaving like a pimply adolescent. He shrugged his shoulders and dismissed the myopia of the female sex. He thought about Harry's cousin Hilary all the time.

Harry was going through some kind of change too. He had given up his anti-girl principles, but reluctantly, and Peter had to tread carefully through conversations with him.

'Do you ever notice,' he asked Harry, without thinking, 'the way Ella Greenlees sits in the French class so that you can see up her skirt?'

'That's nonsense, Cassidy. You're obessed with Ella Greenlees.'

'You mean obsessed.'

'Obsessed. I can read, you know. Ella Greenlees isn't like that. You're thinking of Marie Rennie.'

'Well, it doesn't matter.'

It was easier talking to John Taylor. John didn't seem interested in girls, but he was interested in design, and the new world, in which there would be no ornaments on mantelpieces that needed Victorian maids to dust them, and coal and gas would be abolished and everything would be electrical. Harry sometimes joined them, because they were having serious discussions, and he approved of that.

'Electricity is clean,' he said. 'We've got it in the house.'

'Electrification equals socialisation,' Peter told him.

'Who said that?'

'Lenin.'

'Smarty. We've got all Lenin's books in the house, you know.'

'I was reading a book by Ethel Mannin,' Peter said. 'It's very good. In the new society, sex will be free. I mean, people will do it any time they like.'

John Taylor looked doubtful.

'The girls wouldn't do it.'

'We've got a book by Ethel Mannin in the house,' Harry said seriously. 'She's a famous author.'

'Here,' said John Taylor. 'I've noticed something. See in the French class? The way that Greenlees sits sometimes, you see right up her skirt. I mean, I just happened to notice it, I wasn't actually looking.'

'God,' said Harry, 'Both of you are obessed with sex.'

'It's obsessed,' said John.

'Both of us like Greenlees' legs,' Peter explained. Harry snorted with disgust.

'I'm going to the theatre with Hilary tonight,' he said, and yawned. 'She's very intelligent.'

Peter felt a knife in his heart. He had developed the habit of saying Hilary Hilary Hilary endlessly in his mind, but there was no hope of finding her again. It was unbearable. All he knew was that she went to Park School, which was very posh, very private, and somewhere in the West End.

Finally, he skipped school one afternoon and took a tramcar to Woodlands Road and waited endlessly till the school came out. He was sure he had missed her, but she came down the street with three other girls, and saw him, and looked straight through him, and got on to a tram with her friends. He threw himself aboard, and lurked on the bottom deck, and got off behind her at Botanic Gardens.

She crossed at the traffic lights and he trailed miserably behind her till she suddenly turned on him, in a fury.

'Why are you following me?'

'I don't know.'

'That is not an answer, boy.'

'I wanted to talk to you, Hilary.'

'Very well, say what you have to say and go away.'

She sounded like an impersonation of a schoolteacher.

'I love you.'

'That's silly.'

'All right.' He turned away. He had been wrong and stupid about Hilary and there was no sense in going on. But she called out to him, in a loud whisper.

'You can walk with me through the park, if you behave yourself. No, walk behind me, and don't look at me. Somebody might see us.'

She had to be obeyed. He followed her to a quiet path in the park above the river, and she turned, and said, 'You don't love me, you're just saying that.'

'I do.'

'All right, you can kiss me. Once.'

He put his arms nervously round her, and at once she forced her right hand between their bodies and seized him.

'I quite like you, actually,' she said. 'Do you like me to do that?'

'Mm.'

'But you must never do that to me. And I can never be seen in your company. I am not allowed to go with boys at all.'

'All right. Even with Harry?'

'Harry's boring.'

'Oh oh oh oh.'

Her tongue was flashing in and out of his mouth too.

'I shall have to go,' she said. 'Perhaps you may see me again, as long as nobody knows.'

'I don't think I have enough money for the tram.'

'I can led you tuppence. Are you going to come and see me again?'

'If you let me.'

'All right. I may. I'll think about it.'

'Ach, don't bother, Hilary. You talk like a schoolteacher. If you don't want to see me I'll not bother, I don't care.'

Her eyes filled with tears.

'I was just trying to behave like a lady. You don't really care about me at all.'

'I do, Hilary. I'm sorry. Don't cry, please.'

He was patting her shoulder, and she wiped her eyes.

'But I can't keep on skipping school,' he said.

'I go to my music lesson on Thursdays. You could meet me at the park gate at half past six.'

'I will, I will. Honestly, Hilary, I do love you. I'll be there every Thursday.'

'Thank you, Peter. That is very gratifying.'

His life had become a secret. The sun shone all the time. He sometimes examined his body to see if any warts were growing on it, but he found nothing except wonderment that

Hilary should want to touch him, to touch anything so ordinary.

In the meantime, after she dried her eyes she forgot to lend him the tuppence, and he had to walk home.

# 32

## ANDY

War is not boring. I'll never complain about being bored again. Being bored is okay, you can do something about it. It was quite educational though. For one thing, I had never met a pansy before. You know what I mean, I had met pansies, but they were just pansies, like Gordon Drummond, a guy I knew a few years ago, he always dressed nice and was very good to his mammy.

Sears and Roebuck were pansies. I shared a room with them in Albacete, and I realised they weren't just sleeping together, they were *sleeping* together.

Roebuck, I could see that, the poetry and everything, and going into a panic when the shells began. But Sears was a huge guy, as brave as hell. My old man, the silly old sod, used to say the only thing to do with a pansy was put the boot up his backside. He wouldn't have tried that with Jim Sears. You do not offer to boot people like Jim Sears up the backside. A heroic pansy, for God's sake. I was learning.

I was still trying to find out about Bob Rankine, and I could get nothing out of Comrade Ortiz. It was Roebuck who brought the news. Bob was in prison about two miles from Albacete, a big house the PSUC had taken over. And the way Roebuck knew was that Roebuck had joined the PSUC and was writing Party-line poetry. He even gave me a lecture about deviationism and premature revolution and all that trash, and I was surprised he was still hanging about with Jim Sears, considering what Jim had done to Ortiz's face. But at least I knew where Bob Rankine was, and I went to find out about him.

That was a mistake. My whole Spanish war was a mistake, but that was the beezer.

The guy at the gate, with a rifle, tried to wave me away, in Spanish, but I yelled Inglese Inglese, and refused to go, till this other guy came out, a Comrade Captain or Comrade Commissar or something, and he had a bit of English. He asked me a few questions, about POUM and Dan Murphy, and the big desertion at Lopera Hill, and I think I called him something along the lines of a Fascist pig. In no time I was being reunited with Bob Rankine, in a basement room with the door banged and bolted at my back.

I thought Bob was actually dead, and he wasn't far off it, but he lay on his plank and smiled at me and asked how I was. I was choked. I banged on the door and screamed for them to get a doctor. While I was doing that, Bob died. His smile didn't change, but he died.

I screamed a lot more, but nothing happened till daylight, and I think I knelt beside Bob's body and wished I could pray for him.

They took their own sweet time to come back to the basement, and they didn't seem too concerned to find a corpse there. Two of them dragged Bob out by the ankles. Two more shoved me out and dragged me up and out into the courtyard. There were three or four more there, lounging about with their rifles and looking quite interested.

One of them gave me a short lecture in Spanish, a language which I swear I will never learn or listen to again, and shoved me against the wall, and his pals started checking their guns and blew up.

I mean they blew up, like balloons full of tomato sauce. There was a bang, or maybe two bangs, and a lot of smoke, and these guys with the guns were thrown about and spattered, and I'm not sure of the exact running order of the programme now, but the house blew up as well. At least, it gave a kind of whoosh and a blast of flame came out of two ground-floor windows, and the guy who had given me the lecture did a back flip with a nasty red patch above his right eye.

Then some other guys, five or six of them, came bolting out of the front door with their trousers on fire, and rolled about on the sand in the courtyard.

And another guy strolled into the picture from the other direction. Big Jim Sears. He looked at the flaming comrades, quite entertained, and asked if I was okay. I said I was okay.

I went over and joined him, and I remember thinking, if they hadn't kept me short of water all night, I could have pissed on one of them and put his trousers out. They would know better next time. But there wouldn't be a next time, because Big Jim was going round shooting them through the head. The last one was Ortiz, and I nearly thought I would like to leave him to burn slowly, but I had no time to suggest it. That Sears guy wasn't wasting any time.

See pansies? don't ever say a harsh word to me about pansies. Including Roebuck, who was the greatest Fifth Column in the Spanish Civil War. He had got right inside the PSUC and ruined this nasty little bit of it for good. He even had a little lorry, and we got into it and got to hell out of Spain and into France, and the only damage I got was a broken kneecap when some idiotic comrade shot at the truck on general principles; and there is nothing wrong with a limp when you want to look like a war hero; and get elected to parliament; and stay out of the fighting game for ever after.

It was weeks before I got home, but okay, a pound note went a long way in France and I was entitled to a holiday. When I did get back home and went to the house, John was there and he told me he was going to America. He seemed to be apologising, as if he was deserting me, but I told him any place was better than Spain, and bloody good luck to him.

I never got very close to John. I don't mean we didn't get on, you know what I mean, he was jack-easy, always good-natured, never asked for anything, but always ready to help. I liked him. I just never knew what was going on in his head. He said he couldn't see a life in Glasgow for himself, and I said fine. I could see a life in Glasgow for me.

Mother was quite nippy when I went up to see her, because she had been worried, but when she saw me limping she burst into tears and hugged me to death. She's great.

# 33

The shop was making a living. It was hard to accept the idea
that she was a natural born shopkeeper, when she knew that
she was a frustrated woman of passion, but day followed day
and every day had to be filled with work. Her life was the
house, and the shop, and the Sisters, and she saw it moving
inexorably on; especially when one day she came out from
the back and saw a white-haired old man talking to Miss
Marguerite, and realised after an instant that it was Dan. His
white hair was a message to her about her own lost youth and
the merciless passage of time, though her own hair was still
black and full.

It was time, maybe, to accept reality and put dreams
behind. Maybe a mother's job was to enjoy the dreams of her
children, to watch her youngest change in a state of wonder
into a man, to enjoy Hetty's marvellous young sophistication.
Hetty would surely find some dreams. She was working as a
secretary for the BBC, and from the outside at least that
seemed splendidly glamorous, talking every day to famous
people and bringing home casual anecdotes about them,
and being pursued by some of them, Meg was sure, though
they probably wouldn't get very far with her very self-
contained daughter. But that would change in time.

The nearest Meg herself could come to a glamorous life
was going out occasionally with Jerry Sterne. He was good
company, his conversation was always risqué, hidden
meanings under the surface of every innocent remark. She
was old enough to enjoy that kind of talk now, and no harm
would come of it.

When she looked at Hetty, beautiful, assured, she sometimes thought back to Mr Gillan of the UF Church,
and his tight-lipped horror at her family's affairs. He had
probably been additionally outraged by her sharing a house
with a man who had been a Roman Catholic and then turned
Communist. If the poor minister knew she was going to
sinful restaurants where they served alcohol, in the company
of a Jew, he would fair disintegrate.

And a married Jew at that.

Jerry never mentioned any home life, but she was morally
certain he was a married man. When he took her to dinner, it

223

was always on a Thursday, and she decided that Thursday was his wife's night for playing cards with her women friends, or something. She didn't ask. Jerry liked her, he desired her or pretended to, he made her feel like a woman with a body.

And he was an education. She was cautious about wine, because she knew how little it took to make her feel relaxed and uninhibited, and in danger of talking too freely. But if educated people drank wine, it was good to know something about it and not be ignorant. If she ever by chance met Eileann again, and went to a restaurant, she would not be making an innocent spectacle of herself in front of a waiter.

She would not meet Eileann again.

But if she did, she would not be innocent and ignorant.

And it was the evening in the Rogano, when she had sipped a little Vermouth and tried the strange flavour of a snail in garlic butter, that she saw . . . oh, Meg, it could not possibly be true and it must be a mistake or an optical illusion, but it was real enough, she saw Mr Gillan, the Reverend John Gillan.

Oh yes, for all he was wearing a collar and tie like an ordinary mortal man, and not dressed as God's scourge of the wicked, it was him. And he was at a table for two with quite a pretty lassie with fair hair, and the two of them having a glass of wine quite the thing, and the lassie young enough to be his daughter.

Maybe she was his daughter, of course.

Meg didn't look at him after the first glance, but she did feel him glancing round now and then and oh, it was never his daughter, Meg was as sure as death of that.

'Did I say something funny?' Jerry asked her.

'Oh, I just thought of something silly, Jerry. But it wouldn't mean anything to you. You were talking about your trip to Ostend in Belgium.'

'Ah, you should have been there, Meg. Next time I'll take you with me and we'll register as Mr and Mrs Smith.'

'That is just foolishness, Jerry, the folk in hotels can read passports.'

'There are ways of getting round that, Meg. Nights of passion in Belgium. It certainly beats the Gallowgate.'

Her laughter rang through the restaurant, and Jerry

thought it was delightful, but she made herself stop, people were looking at her.

'Och,' she said, 'there is plenty of passion goes on in the Gallowgate, I am thinking. Some of them are at it all the time, they could show Belgium a thing or two.'

When Mr Gillan and his companion got up to leave, and they didn't seem to have spent very long on their meal, they had to pass her table; and she looked up incuriously and said, 'Oh, Mr Gillan. Good evening. Mrs Gillan.'

He looked like a murderer *in flagrante delicto*. She liked the phrase *in flagrante delicto*. It had a lovely musical ring to it.

'Good evening . . . eh . . . ' and he hurried the lassie past and out of sight. Oh no, oh no no no, never his daughter, nor his wife.

'All right, Jerry, I was laughing, because there yonder is a man of God who once got very stern and judicial with me about my morals, for no reason and . . . about other folks' wee peccadillos, and yon was never Mrs Gillan in her life, she is more likely a wee Sunday School teacher having a crush on the Minister, and Mrs Gillan at home all this time thinking her good man is on a visitation of mercy.'

'I have better taste than your minister, Meg. And better luck.' He touched her hand.

'You are a wicked man, Jerry.'

'Aye, but I admit it. It's my nature. I wouldn't be any other way.'

He leered so theatrically that there was no harm in it. But she was always conscious of his maleness. She had always liked thin men, but Jerry's plumpness didn't affect the sensuality that came from him; and in his absence, she had nearly committed adultery with him in her heart. The Children of Israel, God's chosen people, the Circumcised. The Circumcised.

Suppress that thought, Meg Macrae, she told herself now. But if Freud is right, suppressing it will only strengthen it. It might hide in the unconscious and then spring out.

*How are the cutlets, Meg?*

*Very good. How is your circumcision Bolognese?*

The laughter burst from her again at the thought, and this time she refused to explain it.

# 34

It was still one thing following another. Bobby had seemed happy enough in his job as clerk in the Anchor Line office, but he came home one day full of the idea of switching to a sea-going job, as a purser's assistant.

'Would it worry you, Mother?'

'Yes, it would, Bobby, but you have to get everything you can out of your own life. I would like fine to travel myself, so you can do it for me.'

There was something about Bobby, there was still something rough. He had a gallus way of walking, a cocky manner, he used too much hair-oil, and spent too much time at funny little dance-halls.

'When you get dolled up for the dancing,' Peter told him, 'you look as if you had shaved your skull and then enamelled it, wi' a wee white line of paint down the middle.'

'Style, boy, style,' Bobby said, working his shoulders and his hands. 'If you want to click wi' the dames, you gotty have style.'

'But if a dame tried to run her fingers through your hair, Bobby, they would slide off.'

Bobby's head did a strange gyrating movement, as if it was balanced on a spring. 'You'll learn, kid, you'll learn.'

Meg found herself trying to imitate the weird head movement, but couldn't. Bobby's real life was a secret she would never penetrate. He didn't go to real dance-halls, like the Palais or the Plaza, but to wee places like the Miners' Welfare, and the 'Institute', and the British Legion rooms, where it was cheaper. She visualised such places like the tin-roofed hut on Duna. She sometimes overhead him telling Peter about the bizarre life in these places.

'See, kid, it's sixpence at the Welfare, and a penny for the cloakroom, but you get these guys that try to skip the penny – they shove their coats at the back of the folding chairs. So, a bit later, they need the chairs, so the bouncer drags them out, and then chucks the coats in the middle of the hall. See gettin' a red face?'

'Then get some dames, oh real scrubbers, who fancies them? Not me, not nobody. So, natural, they are not getting their shot. So the bouncer will drag one of these birds out on the floor and shout, "This wummin has paid her tanner, she must be danced." I'm telling you, kid, that's life.'

It sounded like death to Meg, but she knew she was out of touch with Bobby's society. Everything changed. John came for lunch on Sunday, his usual quiet relaxed self, and after lunch they listened to the wireless – an indulgence Meg still felt suspicious about; the wireless, on the Sabbath.

'When I was a girl,' she said, 'we didn't even read books on the Sabbath. We didn't even cook. All the Sunday meals were made the night before.'

'Middle Ages, Mother,' said Hetty.

'I'm not prehistoric, Hetty. And there is something to be said for the day of rest. Singing psalms is one thing.'

'All music is sacred, Mother.'

'Hetty, think shame of yourself. That is the argument of a . . . a Jesuit.'

'Clever, though, isn't it, Mother?'

'Anyway, Mother,' Peter said, 'if there has to be no music on a Sunday, what about Australia?'

'What about Australia?'

'Well, it's Monday in Australia. If God doesn't mind the Australians playing music, why would he worry about us?'

'I don't know what kind of children I have reared, I must have gone wrong somewhere.'

'Talking of Australia,' John said, 'I've decided to go to America.'

'Not for good, John!' Meg had an agonising pang.

'Maybe, Mother.'

'Oh no, no.' Meg could see that Hetty was stricken too.

'I'll have my diploma in a few months, Mother, from the Technical College. I think there's more chance of using it in America.'

'But we would miss you sore, John.'

'There's nothing for me in Glasgow, Mother.' He was calm and easy as he said it, but it had a terrible bleak sound about it, as if there was more to it than the words.

Everything was changing. She still had Hetty and Peter, though there was something very peculiar about Peter these days, something secret, and although he was happy and normal, she had a sad fearful feeling about him.

'Put on the wireless if you like, then,' she said. 'I hope it's playing something cheery.'

## 35

## PETER

War is hell, but I enjoyed it. I was against war, of course, Thou shalt not kill. On the other hand, Nazi Germany was a tyranny that had to be stopped. I couldn't help feeling that war was exciting. When Mother and I heard Chamberlain on the wireless on Sunday morning, on September 3, I could see it smote her. She had lived through the Great War, of course, and she knew about the war and all its horror. And Bobby was in Canada, training as a pilot, and he might be killed.

But I couldn't help being excited.

I liked the blackout. It made life mysterious. I didn't mind when the transport broke down either. There was one morning, that winter, when it was snowy and frosty and there were no trams at all. Thousands of people were walking into town to their jobs, but it was like a big picnic. I got a lift on a lorry, and helped Marie Rennie up to sit beside me. She was wearing a maroon coat, and a tammy, and short snowboots, and her face was pink and warm from the cold. I had forgotten what beautiful round calves she had, with little flecks of snow on them and her skin shining through her stockings. She was fantastically exciting, and she knew it. It was better than a tramcar.

We all knew we were going to be called up, including me, because I was only an apprentice in an architect's office, and there was no exemption for that. So we had parties all the time. Eat drink and be merry. We didn't eat or drink, food was secondary. They were necking parties. All we needed was for somebody to have parents away on holiday or something. All we needed was premises. If you had premises, it was your duty to have a party. Any of the old Whitehill School gang who had premises was everybody's friend. We just went to the premises after an hour or two in the café, and pulled the curtains and paired off on chairs or the floor, and changed partners from time to time. It was all very innocent. There was a lot of giggling and dangerous talk in the dark, but all we did was kiss and cuddle. We knew that girls didn't want to go any further than kissing and cuddling, which is a bit funny when I remember what happened in that pack-sheet tent on the coup all those years ago; but we knew it all the same.

Ella Greenlees looked fantastic in that summer of 1940, in a costume with a tight-nipped waist and high heels and her hair piled on top of her head. Marie Rennie looked fantastic. So did the Wilson twins, who hadn't gone to Whitehill School at all, but who often had premises because their father was away and their mother often had to visit her own mother. The twins were really skinny, with practically no bosoms, and you could feel their ribs at the back and their spines, and one of them – I had to be careful to remember which, though maybe it didn't really matter – one of them would let you slip your hand right down to her pelvis and squeeze her bottom, and rest your other hand on her chest. But that was as far as it went.

No, there was one night at the Wilsons', when everybody else had to go home early and Alastair Barr and I were left with the twins. He was on the couch with Hilda, and Janet was sitting on my knees in the armchair, and absolutely by accident, just the way I was holding her to support her, I found that my right hand was round her thigh, right at the top, and my fingers were only an inch away from actually touching her.

It wasn't actually dark, even with the curtains closed, and Alastair looked over and saw the situation. Right away, he moved so that he was blotting out Hilda's view which was really very loyal, I thought, but I didn't know what to do. I thought Janet probably hadn't noticed how close my hand was, because it hadn't moved for some time. I moved my fingers a fraction of an inch, and she went on kissing me, but I was pretty sure she just hadn't noticed, and I thought that if I slipped my hand up she would suddenly notice and scream, and everything would be ruined. So I just sat there, enjoying where my hand was. I'll never know whether she hadn't noticed, or whether she was waiting for me to do something positive and was disappointed. When Alastair and I were walking home, he asked me what had happened, and I told the truth. Surprisingly for Alastair, because he went in for a lot of big talk, he thought I had probably been right not to risk it.

After these parties the boys often talked among themselves

about how necking left you with a terrible frustration, but I think that was just big talk too. Kissing was okay.

At the parties, I didn't think about Hilary, or I would have felt like a traitor. She was a completely different part of my life. Away from the parties, I thought about her habitually. It was hard to believe I had known her for years. There was a long time when I didn't see her at all, because she said she was going to the country and I wouldn't even be able to write to her because people would see the letters. I suppose, to be honest, I got used to not seeing her then, and even didn't think about her as much. But at the time I'm talking about, she had come back, and as soon as she telephoned me it was just the same as always.

She could only see me every few weeks, and she was still as mysterious and magic as ever. Actually there was something about Hilary you couldn't get to know at all, but I just sort of melted every time I saw her, and I was helpless when she touched me. I sometimes wondered if what she did to me was spoiling me for normal adult sex, but I didn't care, I just loved her, and she drove me mad with excitement.

Then, once, she didn't turn up, and I was frantic in case she didn't want me any more, in case she had found somebody else. And the funny thing is that when that happens, you feel that if she doesn't want you, no other girl will want you either. That was stupid, because there were the Wilson twins and the other girls, but that wasn't the same as somebody special. Anyway, it was hellish, it was really physical agony, and I couldn't even get in touch with her. I wanted to ask Harry how she was, in a casual way, but I didn't have the courage. But Harry told me anyway.

She had died. Suddenly that month she had died.

I didn't sleep at all for two weeks. I couldn't cry, but I lay awake at night all the time and I couldn't eat anything. Mother knew something was wrong, of course, but she didn't say anything. She probably knew it was something I couldn't talk about. I think Mother probably always knew something I didn't, about Hilary, I mean, that there was something frightening in her future, that there was something wrong with her. That's probably why Hilary would never let me touch her, because it might be dangerous.

Anyway, she died.

# 36

Now that The War had happened, it turned out after all to be just one of the things that happened, one after another. It might be a great event in history, but it was a small thing because it was only a part of her small life, it was only something that gave her fresh worries about Hetty in London, where the bombs started to fall, and for Bobby in Canada training to fly an aeroplane, and for Peter, who would be dragged into danger too. These were fears exactly like everyday fears, things to be quietly borne. To ordinary people at home, the war would mostly mean scarcities, and that's how she had explained it to Peter in the beginning.

'If food gets scarce,' he said reasonably, 'we'll eat less.'

'That is exactly what we will do, Peter and we will not make a fuss about it. There is something terrible undignified . . . terribly undignified, I mean . . . about folk scrambling about to get more of this and that just because there is a shortage of it. The lady I worked for in the Great War was a terrible greedy lady that way, at the first rumour of a shortage she would have both of us tearing round the town buying things she didn't need. She had pounds and pounds of butter in a cupboard going rancid, and cases and cases of lemonade. And sugar, oh, what is the terrible lust folk have for sugar? The Eskimos never touch the stuff and they are quite happy.'

'No, Mother, they eat whale meat and blubber, and so will we if we have to eat whale meat.'

'You and I will be just fine, Peter. Oh, I am sorry, that was a joke, I wasn't listening.'

'I'll not tell anybody about all these boxes you've got piled in Hetty's room. If things get bad we can eat buttons and zip-fasteners and bias binding and knitting wool.'

'It is good nourishing wool, you tinker.'

She had a conscience about the boxes all the same. Jerry Sterne had practically forced her to buy great quantities of little things as soon as war was declared; pins and needles and everything. He said it was a matter of social conscience and service to her customers. Even plain pins would be scarce if the war lasted very long.

'Is the Government going to fit the Germans with plain pins, Jerry?'

'A jab with a plain pin is quite sore, Meg.'

Anyway, the boxes were there and they might be useful in bad times.

She was touched at Peter's insistence on taking her out to the pictures twice a week, and she enjoyed the outings, but it was impossible to explain to him that she didn't feel deprived or forsaken, and that she didn't want to take up the time of a seventeen-year-old, the time that could never be replaced. But not always a happy time.

'You've had a sad experience, Peter.'

'Oh. Yes. Somebody died.'

'That lovely girl with the dark hair. I hoped you wouldn't get fond of her, Peter, But oh, that is stupid and cowardly, it would be a sorry grey life if we didn't get fond of people just in case something might happen to them.'

'I think you're right, Mother. I'm not sorry. How do you know everything?'

'I was seventeen too, a million years ago.'

'You never talk about being young.'

'Ach, I lost my parents when I was only a bairn, Peter, but there is no use in talking about it, it is a thing that happens. Never mind, there are plenty of other girls in the world. And I am in no doubt you are seeing some of them.'

'Is that callous?'

'No, it is life, and you have to take life in your hands, Peter, while it is there, because you only have the one life, and oh, it goes so fast.'

Peter, who had felt he should weep at Hilary's death, but could find no tears, only a dry desolation, unaccountably felt his eyes pricking at his mother's words, and changed the subject.

Dan hadn't dropped into the shop for a couple of weeks, and Miss Amanda reported that he was at home in bed.

'I made a formal call, Meg, and was received by a female person who said that he was sleeping and could not see anybody. I apologise for describing her as a female person, but she did not strike me as a lady.'

'Neither am I, Amanda.'

'Of course you are, Meg. You are a born aristocrat. I refer not to Norman blood, of couse, but innate superiority.'

'You'll be the death of me, Amanda. I don't even crook my pinkie when I drink tea.'

'I should hope not, That is the mark of the petty bourgeoisie.'

'The voice is the voice of Amanda, but the voice is also the voice of Dan Cassidy. I will go and see Dan.'

'Beard that female person in her den, Meg. You are the one to do it.'

The female person was not pleased to see Meg.

'He's as well as can be expected. I'll tell him you were here.'

'What does the doctor say?'

'Oh, him. He'll not see any doctor.'

'He will see me. I am his cousin.' Meg raised her voice. 'I will see Dan Cassidy.'

'You will not.'

A throaty voice came from somewhere inside.

'Meg. Meg. Is that you, Meg? Thank God.'

'I will push you out of the way if I have to,' Meg told the female person, who tightened her lips but moved aside. Dan was in bed upstairs, and Meg sat on his bed whilst his sister stood at the bedroom door radiating disapproval.

'Do you fancy buggering off, Cecilia?' Dan asked.

'That's all the gratitude I get.'

'She's been praying at me, Meg. And this thing round my neck is a sockful of salt. Hot salt. It bakes your jugular vein.'

'It was good enough for your father,' Cecilia snapped.

'I don't like to remind her the old bastard died, Meg.'

'That is not in good taste, Dan Cassidy.' Meg was trying to be gentle and conciliatory.

'Good taste? Christ, have you seen that plaster Madonna in the toilet?'

The doorbell sounded, and Cecilia let it ring several times before she could tear herself away.

'It's sex as well,' Dan muttered. 'She's got it on the brain. She thinks you'll be under the blankets if she leaves us alone for five seconds.'

'Say the word, Dan.' Meg giggled. 'It might be the cure.'

'You're wicked and sinful, Meg. You're just bloody great. Funny, sex has crossed my mind a couple of times. Maybe the hormones are having a last dying kick.'

She bent over him and kissed him.

233

'Oh, that's better than a sockful of hot salt, Meg. I'll live, more's the pity. I'm tired to hell. You know, I never rallied after the Stalin-Hitler pact. It was like a dunt in the ribs.'

'Oh Dan, Dan, forget your politics and enjoy being ill.'

Cecilia reappeared, and Meg turned to see her looking solemn and religious. Behind her was a tall burly priest with white hair.

'Ah, the wages of sin, Dan,' he boomed.

'What the hell is this?' Dan complained. 'A three-pronged attack?'

The priest strode into the room and sat on the other side of the bed.

'God is not mocked,' he said jovially, and ruffled Dan's hair.

'This is my cousin Meg,' Dan said. 'Father Mann. Be careful, Terry. Meg's a Presbyterian.'

'Oh, there may be many paths to Glory,' said the priest. 'I knew you weren't one of ours, cousin Meg, I can always tell.'

'Rubbish, Father Mann.'

'You hear that, Dan? Protest and rebellion. Will there be a cup of tea, daughter?' he asked Cecilia.

'He means a cup of tea for me,' said Dan. 'And a big dram for himself. And a glass of sherry for the lady. Now scoot.'

As Cecilia pursed her lips, the priest said, 'And not too much water in the dram.'

Cecilia vanished in defeat.

'A sanctimonious bitch, Terry.'

'Ah, Dan, that's no way to talk. Aye, the pious ones are hard to thole, and you'll not let anybody know you heard a priest say that, cousin Meg.'

'Not a word, Father.'

'And so, a Presbyterian. A cold colourless faith, that, and you don't look like a cold woman, cousin Meg.'

'Pay no attention to the priest, Meg. I mind him at school before he went to the bad. Girls girls girls, he had them on the brain. He should have been a Turk.'

'Ah, the fire in the young blood.' Father Mann was quite complacent about the accusation. 'We get over that.'

'Aye, Terry, you douse it in whisky.'

'No respect for man or God, cousin Meg. He'll roast in hell for sure. And you will go to heaven, Cecilia, that's a sensible dram for a man burdened with care. Now, my dear,

234

maybe I could have just a wee private word with Dan and his cousin, there are some things I want to say to her.'

Cecilia was livid, but she laid down the tray and tiptoed away.

'Don't be too hard on her, Dan,' said the priest, 'you must be a trial to her too. And so are you, cousin Meg. No wonder the family was scandalised, the black sheep throwing God away and then taking up with a raving beauty of a heathen.'

Meg found herself laughing, but she tried to be stern.

'There was no "taking up", Father Mann. I suppose you have a housekeeper yourself, and there's nothing in that either.'

'Ah, but my housekeeper looks nothing like you, and Dan isn't a priest, cousin Meg. I'm looking at you, you know, and now I know what all the gossip was about, and I hope it was ill-founded. I think I hope it was ill-founded.'

He was a handsome man for his age, a bit overweight, an ageing athlete perhaps. The high complexion might have come from whisky or simple vigour. He clearly loved Dan.

'And what do you think of your encounter with a Papist priest, cousin Meg?' he suddenly asked.

'You seem human enough. But one of my favourite writers is a Roman Catholic anyway. G.K. Chesterton.'

'A fine slim mind in a fat body! Well. I am astonished.'

'Astonished that a Presbyterian can read, Father?'

'Oh, she's very quick with the knife, Dan. Your health. I think we put ourselves in mortal danger when we let women learn to read. Right. I'll be back, Dan, to wrestle with the devil for you.'

'That's no way to talk about my sister, Terry.'

'I give you up. And I'll give you a lift home, cousin Meg.'

'That sounds a dangerous invitation, Father Mann. But Nietzsche said live dangerously.'

'My God.'

On the way home, in the priest's tiny Morris, he dropped his jocularity and said, 'Dan's all right, he's indestructible. But I think he could do with your company, whiles, as a wee corrective to his good Catholic sister.'

'He'll get it, Father. She'll even let me into the house, now I'm friendly with a priest.'

'She's just a stupid wee woman but God made her.'

'Yes, he is a versatile God.'

'Aye. I enjoyed meeting you. I need people like you and Dan now and then, for a bit of cut and thrust I don't get from the faithful. And you're a fine-looking girl.'

'Thank you, Father, I think the celibate priesthood is a shameful waste of fine-looking men.'

'Oh. I wonder, will I mention that to my confessor? Goodnight, cousin Meg, and God go with you.'

'Vaya con dios.'

'Yes, that too.'

A week or so later she made the excuse of visiting Dan to escort Miss Amanda home. The old lady, and her sister, were growing visibly frailer, and Amanda needed her supporting arm as they walked along the blacked-out street towards Bellgrove Street. Before they got there, the little dog barked in a frenzy, and Meg jerked, heard somebody coming out of the dark at a run. A flashlight shone straight into her eyes and dazzled her, and as she closed her eyes and threw up a defensive arm she was aware of a scuffling beside her. She opened her eyes to see the flashlight in Amanda's face, and in the dimness beyond, a hand snatching at her handbag.

Miss Amanda raised her police whistle to blow a blast, and a fist smashed it into her mouth and she fell out of sight. Meg flailed out with an arm and struck something, but not hard, and footsteps pelted away into the distance. She screamed, and was on her hands and knees groping for her own fallen flashlight. People were gathering round. The little dog was going mad. Miss Amanda, a hand still at her mouth, was lying twisted and undignified against a lamp post. Dear God.

Her head was tilted impossibly to one side and the little dog was crouching on her chest, howling. Meg felt a cold deeper than the night air. Miss Amanda was dead, dead for the sake of a handbag and a ration book and a few bits of loose change.

There was nothing useful she could tell the police. They called Peter from the police station and he came to get her. He was calm and controlled. He was Peter.

She wouldn't allow the police to give the news to Miss Marguerite, but she let them drive her with Peter to Dennistoun and leave them there. Miss Marguerite was surprised and pleased to see them in the middle of the week, and had just made a pot of tea.

'Saccharine,' she said. 'I no longer buy my sugar ration. It is my contribution to the national well-being. What is wrong, Meg?'

'Miss Amanda is dead.'

'Ah. Perhaps Peter will pour the tea.'

'Yes, Miss Marguerite.'

Miss Marguerite stood in the parlour, looking at the little china musical monkeys on the mantelpiece.

'She was always the frailer of the two,' she said.

'She was knocked down by a bag-snatcher, Marguerite.'

'I should never have let her go out alone in the blackout.'

'I was with her. I couldn't help.'

'No, of course. Now I have two dogs to take care of. It is very difficult. It really is most difficult.'

'We'll stay the night and keep you company.'

'No. No. It is a kindly thought. I think I should prefer to be alone. You know, I have not spent a night alone since I was a gel.'

Amanda's dog had trotted into the kitchen to eat and sleep.

'I'll stay,' Meg insisted. 'I can sleep on a chair.'

'No, I must positively be alone.'

'You won't be coming to the shop tomorrow.'

'That is kind. No, I shall have much to think over. I think I shall take my tea to bed.'

She lifted her cup and saucer and left the room. Meg and Peter looked at each other.

'Shock?' he asked.

'Yes, I don't feel too well myself.'

'I'll sleep in a chair. You need your bed, Mother. I'll phone the office in the morning and tell them, and I'll come into the shop and give you a hand, or something. Maybe we can get a taxi for you.'

She didn't feel like opening the shop in the morning. But it was something to do. There was no point in not doing it. Peter arrived at ten o'clock.

'So she's staying home today,' Meg said.

'Miss Marguerite is dead, Mother.' He was unnaturally grave, and calm, and old. 'I took up tea for her at eight o'clock. Cooper's Best, not Mazawattee, she always had Cooper's Best. She was just sort of lying in bed, dead.'

'Peter, that was two hours ago!' She hugged him, but he stood stiff and patted her shoulder.

'There were things to do, Mother, and I couldn't tell you on the telephone. I got Uncle Dan in, he says he's a lot better, and the Holy Father sends his regards and we got the doctor, and the undertakers and . . . got things arranged, and then I came down here as soon as I could. Uncle Dan took the dogs in. I don't think his sister likes dogs. She's a funny wee woman, isn't she? I mean funny-odd, not ha-ha. I told the office I would be off for the rest of the week, but I don't know what I'll be doing. Maybe I should just go in. I've never seen anybody dead before. She looked quite natural. I would never have known she was dead. Uncle Dan was very good. Of course, I've got no experience of this kind of thing.'

'No. I'll make a cup of tea.'

'Cooper's Best?'

'I've never been able to tell the difference, Peter. I don't know what to think.'

'Make a cup of tea, Mother.'

'Are you all right, Peter?'

'No. I can walk and talk and everything, but I'm looking at myself from outside. Shock, I suppose.'

'Oh, Peter. Well, I'm sure you would be of no use to anybody at the office. Just do something. Take the dog baskets from the back shop and take them to Uncle Dan. Or no, just throw them out. We'll tidy the shop and go up and see your Uncle Dan. He's a tower of strength, even if he's feeling chesty.'

'I feel guilty, leaving her all alone.'

'I know, I know. You're very good, Peter.'

'Don't talk like that, Mother, I'm not going to cry and you're trying to make me.'

'It wouldn't do you any harm.'

'Later. I'll maybe cry later.'

Miss Marguerite's body wasn't at home. Dan was there to say that the undertaker had taken it away.

'Just as well,' he said. 'Poor old lady. They were a lot of fun when you got to know them, weren't they? There was a chap here from the *Daily Record,* but I couldn't tell him much.'

'Morbid curiosity, Dan. I'll make a cup of tea.'

'Make two,' said Peter. 'One of Cooper's Best and one of

Mazawattee. Oh hell, oh hell!'

'Ach, have a good weep, son,' Dan advised him. 'It's better out than in.'

It was the Catholic priest who brought them some comfort, striding cheerfully through the open front door.

'I've no business here,' he said, 'but at least I'm professional. Your sister called me, Dan. Maybe she hoped I could snatch the two ladies into Holy Mother Church now they can't talk back. We'll have to look through the place for insurance papers and that kind of thing. Maybe there's a will too.'

'I've a feeling they were freethinkers, Father,' Peter said. 'I don't think they believed in any religion.'

'Oh well, as the Wee Free Church minister said, They'll ken noo.'

The houseful of little possessions and antiques and oddities was unbearably pathetic, and they felt like thieves and voyeurs as they moved through it in the absence of its mistresses. There was no sign of a will.

'I'm just coming back to consciousness, Peter,' Meg said. 'You know I owe the sisters hundred and hundreds of pounds, hundreds of pounds I don't possess. Who am I supposed to pay it back to?'

'Nobody, I suppose.'

'Don't be so sure. It's awful, worrying about a thing like that at a time like this.'

'We'll go into town, and go to a matinee at the pictures.'

'We couldn't. Yes, we could, it is a good idea. And if we have a wee greet in the dark, folk will think we're greeting at the picture.'

'If it's a comedy, that'll be just dandy.'

'Oh, I could go a good Laurel and Hardy picture, Peter. I don't think the sisters would object to that.'

'They would love it. Oh hell.'

'Aye, oh hell, right enough.'

# 37

It was the time of Hitler's blitz on London. Hetty found it
exhilarating and relaxing. London was an endless adventure, and the blitz heightened it. Everything important in the
world was happening in London, and she was there.

She worked for Mark Tressall, the POSPU, Producer of
Overseas and Services Programme, Unattached, and his
21C Tim Ellis. Tim was easy and unobtrusive. Mark was, in
his own phrase – in a Public School accent – the Humble
Dynamo, with his own language of favourite phrases, super
scheme, faint tinkles at the back of the cerebrum, tiny touch
of déjà vu, the Einstein of the Spoken Word, plus ça change,
wavelengths gone awry, This Spectred Isle. Not sceptred,
spectred as in ghost-ridden. He fretted at the sheer physical
impossibility of three people turning out two entire ten-
minute programmes a day, battling with unseen forces to
produce immortal time capsules. It was possibly the easiest
job in Spectred Britain.

They started early in the mornings; or at least, Hetty and
Tim started early in the mornings, for the menial labour of
combing through the morning papers for cute or interesting
news stories to be included in the capsules, and Mark arrived
later to Infuse the Job with Creativity. It was still all
fascinating. Twice a day Mark and Tim went into the little
studio in the basement, and Hetty sat in the control room
with the engineer. At the green light, Mark intoned jauntily,
'Life in Britain', and they read the stories alternately. Mark
took the funny ones.

At one of the script discussions, after the first month, Tim
said, very casually, 'Why don't we let Hetty read some of the
stuff, Mark?'

'An engaging notion, old chap, but it is a professional
chore, no offence, Hetty, but we have to maintain the
standards. And no offence, Hetty, but although we all
simply love your Scots burr, let's face it, we are the voice of
the Nation and so on.'

'That's true.' Hetty sounded unconcerned.

'There's a lot of Scots people in Britain,' Tim persisted.
'And in the Army and Navy and so on.'

'Yes, true, true. My experience, Tim, is these are the very

chaps who expect Standard English from dear old Auntie BBC. Come on now, let's go through this rubbish and Infuse it with Creativity. Sorry, Hetty, but I fear HMS would never wear it.'

A few days later, Mark remarked, very casually indeed, 'Hetty, I had a thought, a tiny tinkle at the back of the cerebrum, and I mentioned it to HMS, who for once had an answering tinkle. We'll pop up this afternoon and you could read something for him, what?'

Hetty and Tim did not smile, till Mark had popped out for a think.

'Do you think he'll expect a suitable reward?' Tim wondered.

'Of course.'

'Will he get it?'

'Tim Ellis, what a question to ask a lady. And I am a lady.'

'Of course. I always knew that. Being a fantastically nubile bint is only a temporary accident.'

'You've never spoken like that before.'

'I don't need to – you know you're fantastic.'

'Oh, do give over, Tim. Help, I'm beginning to talk like a Londoner. It must get lonely, with your wife and kids away in the country.'

'I'm used to it, it's okay, actually.'

Mark took her out for celebration drinkies when Head of Miscellaneous Services decided to try her on the programme. She talked a lot about her fiancé in the Marines.

She found the courage to complain privately to Tim that the capsules were too dull and stiff.

'You're not stiff, Hetty. You're very good.'

'They're just news programmes. I mean, anybody could do them. They're not supposed to be the news, they're supposed to be about how interesting life is in Britain. Funny, too.'

'We couldn't afford Arthur Askey as a reader.'

'No, but we could put more fun into them.'

'I can see a lot of danger ahead, and I've got a horrible feeling you're going to twist me round your little finger.'

'The only real problem is, Tim, how to implant a faint tinkle at the back of Mark's cerebrum so that he thinks it was his idea.'

'That is not a problem, Hetty.'

They hatched a plot, but they saved it for one of the recorded programmes so that they would have a line of retreat. Mark had a story about a group of schoolboys in Cheshire who had discovered that migrating frogs were being massacred by Army transports as they crossed a road at night. The boys had rounded up the frogs and carried them across in hundreds to save the colony.

Mark gave it the full solemn theatrical treatment. Instead of coming in solemnly on her cue, Hetty loosed a peal of laughter and said, 'Wonderful, Mark. It could only happen here.' And she giggled quietly through her own trivial little tale. Mark was glaring in disapproval, and it almost came through his closing announcement, 'And that is life in Britain.'

'We'll have to do it again,' he snapped. 'What came over you?'

'It was pretty funny, Mark,' Tim said.

'This isn't the Variety Department.'

'The way you read it, Mark,' Hetty said. 'It didn't look funny in the script till you gave it the treatment.'

Sam Thorpe, the engineer, came into the studio.

'Bloody good, that, bloody lovely.'

He winked at Tim and Hetty realised he was in on the plot.

'I don't know,' Mark said. 'We'd better do it again for safety's sake.'

'Not bloody on, Mark, I've another lot coming in here in three minutes. Best show you've done yet. Sounded like real people.'

'Oh well, the die is cast.' Mark walked out, heavy with responsibility. In the next few days they found him joining in the menial labour of combing the papers for stories that would get a laugh.

'PLM thinks the Forces Capsule is in danger of turning into a personality cult,' he said gravely. 'HMS cut him right off. HMS thinks the Forces need all the laughs they can get. And this, my dears, is fan mail.' He threw a bundle of letters on the desk. 'And the *Radio Times* is doing a piece on me. I shall give the troops full credit too, of course.'

It was too hilarious to imagine that he would give credit to anybody except Mark Tressall. But the *Daily Mirror* insisted on interviewing Hetty, and after a mature thought, HMS gave his consent, and patted Hetty's bottom. She begged the elderly *Mirror* reporter to give Mark full credit and he said he could refuse her nothing. She extravagantly telephoned her mother to warn her to buy the *Mirror*.

When Tim's house was bombed a few days later, Mark's response was to be testy, because it made Tim late for the office while he, Mark, was toiling through the drudgery of the script. He hadn't seen the script, and the tailpiece was a total surprise to him.

MARK: You're not your usual elegant self today, Tim.

TIM: Sorry, Mark, I've just spent a few hours in some rubble.

MARK: Oh well, every man to his own taste, eh, Hetty?

HETTY: Yes. Tim, we're always hearing stories about people finding their false teeth three streets away after a bomb. Anything like that happen to you?

TIM: As a matter of fact, yes. Four streets away, actually.

MARK: Odd that, Tim, since you actually don't wear false teeth.

LAUGHTER.

MARK: It could only happen in Britain.

SIGNATURE MUSIC AND FADE.

Always give Mark the joke lines.

There was still the problem of where Tim was going to sleep, a problem which Mark was sure would sort itself out, as he had to trot over to chat with HMS about more urgent problems.

'I can sleep in one of the Underground stations,' Tim told Hetty. 'Thousands of people do.'

'Sometimes they have sing-songs, Tim.'

'Mm.'

'Come home with me, Tim.'

He jerked visibly.

'It wouldn't be right, Hetty.'

'Would you rather sit up all night in the Underground singing Knees Up Mother Brown?'

'All right. I can sleep on the floor.'

'That is silly, Tim.'

'Christ, I'm shaking all over, I can't look at you. I didn't shake when the bomb fell.'

'You'll never know how much nerve it took to come out with it, Tim, and sound frightfully frightfully casual and sophisticated about it all.'

'I'll hate myself in the morning, Hetty.'

'You may well hate yourself tonight, I haven't really got any experience, not really. I think I'll need a stiff drink before we go home.'

They avoided each other's eyes in the pub, in the subway train, in her bed-sitter.

'I've got no, um hrrm hrrm, pyjamas, Hetty.'

'We don't need pyjamas, do we?' She asked the question in surprise.

'Eh? Oh. Aha. Good God, do you know I've never seen a naked woman? Girl?'

'And you're married for . . . Oh. Oh well, you will in a minute.'

'My God. Hetty, I've never seen anything so beautiful.'

'Are you not going to touch me?'

'Oh my oh my oh my oh my.'

'Yes, Tim. Oh my.'

They were awake again before dawn, bleary and delirious, when the blast sucked the window out of its frame and flung it across the street. The front wall of the room seemed to scream and fell outwards, and the blankets that covered them flew after it. They gripped each other fiercely while the bed rocked and slid and stopped. In the dim light from the sky she slid off the bed, holding his hand to pull him after her. Whistles were sounding outside.

'This will make a marvellous picture for the *Daily Mirror*,' she said.

'Oh God. Radio stars exposed.'

'This is a coat. And trousers, Tim.'

'No false teeth?'

'Shut up and get them on. Oh. A jacket. The wardrobe's still there. I can give you a sweater.'

'You're very hospitable, Hetty. You're miraculous.'

'Know what you are, Tim? I'm not going to explain it, but the word is catharsis. It means purging, doesn't it?'

'Is this the time for English lessons?'

He was sitting on the bed laughing. Not hysterically, Homerically. She was enjoying London.

244

## 38

So London was cathartic. Meg read Hetty's letter several times as if she was trying to X-ray it.

'There's a man in there somewhere,' Peter said.

'There is no mention of a man, and you are too smart for your own good, Peter Cassidy.'

'Cherchez l'homme, that's all I'm saying.'

'If there is a man, he is not good enough for her.'

'As long as she's happy, Mother. Anyway, you wouldn't think anybody was good enough for our Hetty, and of course, you're right as usual.'

'I will strike you, Peter Cassidy.'

'Oh Mother, you do talk awful nonsense. You're a woman, of course.'

She didn't feel much like a woman. While Hetty was doing whatever cathartic things she was doing in London, there was nothing in Glasgow but the routine of the shop, and just putting in the unchanging days, and trying not to think unsettling thoughts or harbour futile dreams. Routine was the great substitute for real life.

Then the lawyer's letter came, and things were suddenly unsettled again.

*Estate of the Misses Marguerite and Amanda Newton . . ..* Yes, there was bound to be a lawyer somewhere. *The above having died intestate . . . acting for the sole surviving kin Mrs Margaret Somerville . . . request and require you to make available all documents relating to . . .*

She called on Dan in the evening, because she had nobody else to talk to, and she didn't want to load Peter with her problems, when he was recovering from his own, out till all hours nearly every evening, and she never questioned him. Father Mann just happened to drop into Dan's house, the most blatant put-up job. She was glad of it.

Dan was just irritated when Meg declared, philosophically, that it would probably be the end of her shop, because the Sisters had put so much money into it and there was no possibility that she could pay it back without selling up.

Was there a legal agreement?' Dan demanded.

'There was no lawyer, but Hetty drew up a paper, all very exact. The Sisters didn't want any of it, and they tore their copy up, but I still have mine.'

'Well, burn it, Meg, it never existed.'

'Ah, Dan Cassidy,' said the priest, 'we are dealing with a hard mathematical Presbyterian here, there is no room for error or manoeuvre in that faith. The Presbyterian faith was invented by bookkeepers, and the audit always has to balance to the last penny. Oh aye.'

'Burn it, Meg.'

'Dan, Dan,' said the priest, 'you are inciting this woman to commit a sin. Your feelings do you credit, Meg, you're right of course.'

'I know I'm right, Father.'

'I said that. It's just a shame you weren't a bit careless, like a good Catholic, and given to losing things, a bit of paper is easily lost. Now you've infected me too, Dan Cassidy.'

'I cannot live a lie, Dan.'

'Of course she can't. You're a good woman, Meg, and that is a rare and difficult creature.'

'A good woman? Oh Father, you have no idea.'

Father Mann's eyes lit up.

'Ah, so there is sin even among the Godly? I wonder what kind of a sin that could be. It is not my concern, daughter.'

'No,' said Dan. 'But oh, you've got his mind working on it, Meg, I can see him sweating with wonder.'

'I am sweating for the lack of whisky, Dan. Oh Meg, it's a shame I'll never hear you in the confessional, that would be a treat.'

'You are a desperately wicked man, Father. I do believe you sin in your heart.'

'Every waking minute,' Dan insisted.

The priest looked complacent.

'We are all frail creatures,' he said.

They gave up trying to persuade her somehow to lose the document relating to the money the Sisters had put in the shop, and talked about sin and war and men and women instead, and she felt the better for flippant conversation with a bit of a bite to it. There was no doubt she enjoyed the company and the talk of men more than those of women. Men were a deal more civilised.

Not all men. The same evening, she was alone at home when there was a sharp knock on the door, and she opened it to find Mr Jardine, the Air Raid Warden, urgently demanding to inspect her curtains. And not only that, to be a nuisance. There was nothing wrong with the curtains, there was no light showing to break the law, but he was concerned that she never used the communal air raid shelter and it was his duty to see that the residents of the street were all right, and not maybe lying ill and alone.

The idea was absurd, and it was nobody's business whether she used the air raid shelter or not. And if she suddenly collapsed of a heart attack, it was certainly no affair of an Air Raid Warden. There was something unctuous and ferrety about Mr Jardine that irritated her.

'Duty, Mrs Mason, duty, sort of thing, we all have to pull together sort of thing, and a woman alone sort of thing. I have a responsibility in point of fact.'

She hated the way his eyes kept darting round the room, as if to memorise it. She wished Peter would come home.

'If there is an air raid,' she said, 'I am more comfortable under the table in my own warm house, and I will take my chances there and not in a cold brick shed among a lot of people I do not want to talk to.'

'Yes, yes, that's a point too, Mrs Mason, very comfortable and all right in its way sort of thing. I'll just check now and then to make sure you're all right sort of thing, don't you worry about it. And you make a flask of cocoa every night, very sensible.'

He was waiting to be invited to a cup of cocoa, or something better, but she closed her face to him and he finally went, with solemn promises to be there in any emergency.

No, not all men were more civilised than women.


Mrs Margaret Somerville, on the other hand, was not civilised at all. They met at the lawyer's office, and Meg had the powerful impression of suspicion and greed. The lawyer, Mr Scott, seemed reasonable enough, he was only doing his job, and he seemed surprised at Meg's producing the document about the shop, the only copy.

'The loans are to be paid at mutual discretion and by

247

mutual agreement,' he said. 'That's rather loose for a legal document. Not very specific.'

'I don't like the sound of it,' Mrs Somerville snapped. She was small and fat, with her hair pulled back fiercely in a bun, and her little feet didn't quite reach the floor as she sat with a purse pressed tightly against her bosom. Mr Scott ignored her.

'You have the keys to the house, Mrs Mason?'

'Yes, here they are.'

Mr Scott took safe custody of them before his client could snatch them into her purse.

'I'll give you a receipt for these, Mrs Mason, and retain them in the meantime. There are formalities with the Court before this can be settled. There may be a will somewhere in the house.'

Mrs Somerville did not like this turn in the conversation.

'We did look for one,' said Meg.

'I'll just bet you did.' Mrs Somerville had succeeded in snatching up the agreement and was devouring it. 'What's this about repayment by mutual agreement? That's a lot of money.'

'It means what it says, Mrs Somerville,' the lawyer said wearily. He was old, and he looked tired.

'Here, I never signed this. That's my aunt's money and I'm entitled to it.'

'I'll do whatever I'm asked, Mr Scott.' Meg could see his expression warning her to say nothing, but she was impatient with the whole thing.

'You mean you'll repay the loan on demand?'

'No, that is not possible, I am afraid.'

'We'll take the shop, then.' As Mrs Somerville's head shot forward, Meg could picture her on a tree branch, eagerly sighting carrion, a prodigiously overfed vulture, and she nearly laughed in spite of everything. When she left the office, she could hear Mrs Somerville muttering on and on to the lawyer, possibly accusing her of theft and barratry and even of poisoning the Sisters.

She lived through it, waiting for weeks for nothing very much to happen, but when Mr Scott called at the shop always polite and sympathetic, as if she were his client, and not Mrs Somerville, she could see her little island of security sinking beneath her. She agreed with no enthusiasm to the possibility of a partnership with the little fat woman, and of staying to manage the shop pending the final settlement of the estate.

This was a very bad idea, as she had expected. Mrs Somerville's first visit to the shop had the feeling of a Commando raid. Her husband, a mournful apologetic little man, stayed in the background and tried to be invisible while she rummaged in drawers and even tested the counters for dust, and their little boy pawed dresses on racks and vanished into the back shop to explore.

Meg held on to her dignity and tried to cope with puzzled customers as if all the Somervilles were invisible to her.

When Mrs Somerville decided to move into the shop and learn the business, it became impossible, but Meg told herself obscurely that it was probably a punishment and good for the soul, and doggedly carried on. The little woman was proud of being a shopkeeper, and she was *there*. She was more and more there when Mr Scott estimated that the stock and fittings at valuation would probably repay the loans, but leave very little over, and Meg was literally reduced to the rank of an employee. Mrs Somerville was proud of being a boss too. She poked about and read through the books looking shrewd and knowledgeable, like a monkey playing a piano. Streams of her friends visited her for tours of inspection and cups of tea in the back shop and long chats. She repelled the customers with her mixture of spurious gentility and blatant rudeness.

The little boy loved the shop. He played with the till, clanking up the No Sale sign and ringing the bell and counting the money, or sat on one of the counters staring vacuously at the customers and banging his heels against the wood and picking his nose.

When Jerry Sterne came into the shop, Mrs Somerville bustled out from the back at the sight of a male client.

'And what can we do for you today, sir?'

'I'm looking for twenty yards of half-inch blue silk ribbon.'

'Well, you'll have a hunt, there's not an inch of blue ribbon in the shop and that's a fact,' she said, in triumph. Jerry tried not to eye Meg too obviously.

'We have some royal blue,' Meg said.

'Oh, where have you been hiding that?'

Meg waved a hand towards the display.

'Huh. Well, there's never twenty yards in that, you're right out of luck.'

'Is that the kettle?' Meg asked innocently, and her employer scuttled into the back shop.

'I'll come back at six and pick you up,' Jerry said. 'My God, what zoo let that one out?'

'Sorry we couldn't help you, sir. I hope you'll call again.'

'I didn't like his looks much, Mason,' said Mrs Somerville. 'A bit of a Yid.'

'Oh? I didn't notice.'

Jerry decided to go mad and take her to the Sitting Room of the Afton instead of the café, and she was glad of a sherry.

'I heard there was trouble,' he said, 'but this is bondage in Egypt.'

'I know, and there's no sign of Moses. Unless you're him and you can find me another shop and I can start again.'

'Do you not know there's a war on?' he laughed. 'I'm out of the trade, but I can tell you the wholesalers will never open a new account. They can't get the stuff. Why don't you get a decent job? Do they not take women at Dodge City?'

'That's in Texas.'

'Beardmore's Forge, just up the road. They call it Dodge City. It's the best way to dodge the Army.'

'I would even *join* the Army to dodge Mrs Somerville. But I don't know if I could work in a factory.' But she had a twinge of excitement. Something new, something different, something difficult. Within three days she had a job that sounded menial and meaningless at Rolls Royce. So Jerry had done her another favour.

Mrs Somerville was outraged.

'You'll give me a month's notice, I'm entitled.'

'You may whistle for your month's notice, Mrs Somerville.'

'You'll get no reference, then.'

'You stupid, ignorant little woman, I would rather have a reference from Jack the Ripper.'

'Oh, it's all coming out in the wash now, is it? Eh? That's the way of it, eh? Lady Muck of Glabber Castle, butter wouldn't melt in your mouth, eh? And don't think you'll arse about for the rest of the week, you'll stick in at the work or I'll be on your top, my lady, and if I get any snash out of you you can whistle for your wages.'

Meg casually opened the till and took out two pound notes.

'That's my wages up to the minute, Mrs Somerville. I'm finished.'

'I'll get the polis.'

'You can get the Army and Navy if you like. And do you never think of having a bath? This place smells like a piggery.'

She left the little woman choking. It was unchristian to feel so pleased at having floored her, but she decided she would feel guilty about it some other time.

Peter was surprised at his own response to the news. He was worried in case his mother might be overworked. But he was bothered for other reasons. It was all right having the woman of the house doing something womanly, like running a shop, but striding about in a factory with spanners, operating great machines and making aeroplane engines, was another thing. It hurt his self-esteem. Also, the thought of his mother in a factory full of randy masculine workers, was a bother.

'I think I've got the symptoms of an Oedipus complex, Mother,' he complained. 'I don't understand it. I'm not mother-fixated or anything. I like girls. I think girls are great. I just can't help wondering what goes on when you're in the factory with a lot of men. The war has brought a deplorable loosening in moral standards, you know.'

'I don't know where I went wrong with you, Peter Cassidy. And stop psychoanalysing yourself. I am now of the considered opinion that folk can think too much about their unconscious minds and their libidos and all the rest of it, instead of just being their natural selves. I was reading Freud when you were only five years old and no sex in you at all.'

'I kissed a big girl called Jeannie when I was five. It was lovely.'

'You're an evil young rascal. You didn't ever, did you?'

'It was the day I fell on the tramrails and bled my nose.'

'It was a punishment from God, as sure as death.'

'Yes.' He looked smug. 'It was worth it.'

The work at the factory astonished her. She had pictured it as brutalising labour in an air of smoke and steam and dirt, and sweat and aching muscles. It was noisy, but it was clean and bright, and there was no strain in pushing a trolley full of parts about, and later just watching a machine that did all the work, and calling a fitter if it went wrong. The real strain was the endless journey twice a day on trams and buses, that left her no time to do anything in the evenings and not much energy to do it anyway.

'Do they whistle at you, Mother?'

'They would whistle if I was their granny. Oh, they're terrible coarse, Peter. I mean terribly coarse. And there's things go on, you know. Lassies will always be daft, and men will always know it. And the language is terrible. They will split up a word to put a dirty word in the middle. But it's meaningless, I don't notice it any more.'

She suddenly laughed. Life was a great educator, and although life in a factory was no more than an interval, a retreat from real life, it was real life too, one day following another till something different happened.

She was half-dozing by the tiny fire in the big grate (Save Fuel for Victory) when a tall young Army captain came to the door. He was wearing heavy-rimmed spectacles, which looked eccentric on a soldier.

'My name is Ferris,' he said. 'I'm a solicitor. It's about the Misses Newton.'

'I'm sorry, Mr Ferris. They're dead.'

'I know, I know, Mrs Mason. I made their will.'

'They didn't leave a will.' Only half-awake, she was confused, at the sight of a solicitor who was an Army captain, by a soldier wearing glasses, by what unlikely connection the Sisters could have had with the Army. He was very patient; an attractive young man, with a long-boned humorous Irish face. He explained slowly, as if to a child.

He was a soldier because even lawyers had to join the Army. He had been a civilian when he drew up the last will and testament of the Misses Newton. It had not emerged because, with other colleagues in the Forces and the company being run by an old uncle, an even older clerk and a silly young girl, nothing was ever done quite right, and nobody noticed anything that happened outside the office.

'It's all right now, Captain Ferris,' she said. 'I've wakened up. I am not usually so dense.'

'I'm sure you're not dense at all, Mrs Mason. Skye?'

'Pardon? Sorry, I'm dense again.'

252

'Your accent. The Isle of Skye?'

'That is very close, you have a good ear, Captain, The Isle of Duna. But this is disgraceful, you have come to my house and I haven't even offered you anything. Are you allowed to have a wee sherry on duty?''

He lay back and laughed.

'Mrs Mason, already it's a joy to meet you. Yes, Army officers have been known to take a small refreshment, on duty or off. And what a fine girl you are,' he added; in a dense imitation Highland accent.

'Ach, away, you smooth-tongued rascal, I'm old enough—'

'—to be my cousin. I'd better stop this, I'm getting married in four days. Anyway, whateffer, this iss the way of it – sorry, I'll stop the accent, I'm sure it sounds stupid. I'll leave you this copy of the will, but the gist is quite simple. The residue of the estate – and it is considerable, in good solid stocks and shares – goes to Robert Mason, Henrietta Cassidy and Peter Cassidy. For bringing them back from the dead, it says. They were sentimental old biddies, weren't they?'

'Oh Captain, I'm sorry to cry in front of you, but that was unfair. They were just lovely. Now I'm feeling dense again.'

'Don't mind me, lawyers are hardhearted beggars who ignore women's grief. Have my hankie. This is a nuisance, you know, a man with only ten days' leave and a wedding and a honeymoon, having to chase down legatees and cope with hysterical Hebrideans. Now listen, and just cry quietly for a minute. To you, a whole list of antiques and bric-a-brac, and a release from all indebtedness. I don't even know what that means, they refused to tell me anything about it.'

'They had their own little ways. They enjoyed a wee secret, Captain Ferris. And I don't want anything, it means nothing to me. It will be nice for the children.'

'Never say you don't want anything in the presence of a lawyer. Now what on earth has been happening while I was away?''

She stopped crying, and stopped being dense. She was concerned for the time the man was spending on her business when he had come home to do more important things. He listened without a word as she went through the story, but the long funny face showed impatience and disbelief and exasperation.

'Scott?' he said at the end. 'That must be Jim Scott. He's a decent man, and he was a decent lawyer, but he's old, and he's got no staff either. He should have put the word through the Faculty of Advocates. But my uncle would never have noticed it anyway, he's in his dotage. Oh dear, Mrs Mason, yes, I'll have another sherry. You can fling this person out of the shop, but the house is a different thing. The wartime regulations make it damned hard to get anybody out. I'll do what I can. At least, I'll do what my uncle can. At least we can rent for you, for the children. I wish I had more time, but I'll do what I can.'

'It doesn't matter, Captain Ferris, I'm grateful for your trouble. I hope you and your wife will be very happy. I think she's a lucky girl, that one. She'll get plenty of laughs.'

'You certainly are an unusual woman, Mrs Mason. Thank you.'

She couldn't settle. She was bursting to tell the story to Peter, but there was no telling when he would be home. He was often out till after midnight, with his friends, or girl friends, or both, and it never occurred to her to complain. He would soon be called up, and life was short, and youth was short. But she was sorry he wasn't in early for once, to hear the news. She got ready for bed, but sat in a chair by the fire with a book, and tried to empty her mind, as she had tried, and failed, every day of her life. But simple weariness began to work and she found herself nodding.

There was a sharp rap at the door. Peter, the little tinker, had forgotten his key, and it was just a mercy he was home at all, from heaven knew where, in the blackout and always the chance of an air raid. She switched on the light and opened the door.

Mr Jardine, the Air Raid Warden for the street, slipped past her like a fox and into the kitchen and over to the window. He was one of the petty irritations of wartime, a fussy old woman of a man who kept creeping round hunting for minute chinks of light in the blackout and had never really approved of her sleeping under the table instead of going down to the air raid shelter like a normal frightened citizen. He was twitching at the blackout curtain.

'Yes, it wasn't quite right, Mrs Mason.' He was breathing hard. Suddenly she thought he wasn't entirely an old woman of a man. She stood near the door, willing him to leave.

'But don't worry, Mrs Mason, it's all in the line of duty sort of thing, and I'm always here to make sure it's all shipshape. It's the least I can do for a neighbour, eh?' He moved towards her, and she glanced round at the dim-lit landing, but suddenly he was between her and the door.

'Don't you worry, Mrs Mason, I'll take care of you. I know it's hard, being a woman on your own without a man, every woman needs a man.' And suddenly he made his move. She couldn't believe it, it was so clumsy. His arms were around her, imprisoning her own arms. She was amazed that she didn't want to start screaming, and realised somewhere at the back of her mind that she wanted most of all not to make a scene; and anyway, it was quite ridiculous.

'Yes, Thanks very much,' she heard herself whispering. Why was she whispering? 'I'll get back to sleep now.'

'I'll tuck you in safe, don't you worry.'

'No. Now this is just foolishness.'

'Come on, don't be childish, we're both men of the world, we know what you want, I can take a hint sort of thing.'

And now one of his hands was inside her dressing-gown, kneading her waist through her nightdress. But although this freed one of her own arms, she couldn't bring herself to scratch his face; she pushed at him without moving him.

'Stop it, Mr Jardine.'

'Oh, don't kid me, you know you've been asking for it, it's only natural.'

As she struggled, his booted foot came down on her bare foot and she fell back gasping with the pain. Her head banged on the floor and jolted her brain, and he was on top of her, and it was going to happen, his knee was between her thighs and a hand was clawing the nightdress up, and the crazy man was actually trying to kiss her as she shook her head back and forth and tried to get breath and his groping hand was violently inside her. He seemed prodigiously strong in spite of his age, but it would not happen, it would not happen.

Far away she heard the sirens sounding the Alert. It distracted his attention, and as he raised his head, her hand found his face and she reverted to instinct and clawed the cheek. He didn't notice.

She had always thought the act was nearly impossible, but

he was sure of what he was doing, and both his legs were between hers as he fumbled and grunted and heaved up and down with his chest against hers. She stuck a finger in his eye. He only snarled, and kept fumbling.

'What the hell is going on here?'

There was a pause before he stopped moving, and got to his knees, suddenly a clownish figure, pathetic and undignified, with one hand still fumbling at his trouser buttons.

In the doorway stood an avenging angel. Vickie Fairhurst.

Meg felt her own hands automatically moving to push down the skirt of her nightdress.

She heard herself saying, 'Mille mercis, ma cherie.'

Then she fainted.


The great strength of Vickie Fairhurst was that although some things might shock her, nothing could unsettle her. She was derisive, but only gently derisive, when Meg told her of her theory, or her feeling, that there was some kind of circular pattern to life if only it could be detected. Soon after her first meeting with Vickie, some luckless girl at school had been Done Wrong, and all these years later, Vickie had materialised in time to save Meg from the same fate.

Bracing as ever, the French teacher, her hair still defiantly, spuriously, red, said that if she hadn't turned up to disturb the Air Raid Warden, Meg herself would probably have done him hideously to death, although she was a silly romantic with fey Highland notions. She, Vickie, had merely destroyed a good dramatic scene. Her only concern, and it was genuine, was whether Meg might have been wounded in her mind. Meg in turn dismissed this as Freudian mumbo-jumbo.

'I had a nasty moment, but it didn't come to anything, and now it's over I'm only thankful, Vickie, it's behind me. It is like not falling over a precipice. You don't develop terrible psychic illness from not falling over a precipice.'

'Rubbish.'

'It is not rubbish, I know who I am. Mr Jardine is the one with the psychic illness, and he had plenty of that before, but now he will not be able to look himself in the mirror for the rest of his life, and that is enough punishment for him. I don't believe in punishment except the ones we give ourselves, and I know plenty about them.'

'We should have got the police, Meg.'

'Vickie, Vickie, for an educated woman you are sometimes not entirely intelligent, but maybe I am not entirely truthful. There is the thing that, just like yourself, I like men, I think about men, you know, even in general, and if a woman has that kind of feeling it is bound to show, and a stupid little man like Mr Jardine may think it is him I am thinking about. I don't mean I give off sensuality like musk or anything like that, at least I hope I don't, but it is there all right, and I think it is hard to be too hard on somebody whose body drives him to desperation.'

'I'm a progressive, liberal-minded woman, Meg, but I would castrate him.'

'Och, och, Vickie, God made us in funny ways and we have to thole it, he even made Mr Jardine, and now I'm sounding like a Catholic priest, and now I come to think of it, *there* is a man who gives off sensuality like musk but he manages to live with it. Anyway, Vickie, there is something more selfish. What would it do to Peter if he knew this had happened? What would it do to Hetty, in the name of Jesus? She would think there was some kind of a curse on us. And what would happen if that silly little man was taken before a judge, and had to lie and lie and lie to say I put him up to it, and some lawyer questioning me about having survived one husband and deserted another, and lived in the same house with a widower? What would that do to Peter?'

'Meg, I will never argue with you again. I will walk humbly and quietly in your presence and never even make a suggestion.'

'Ach, you will, or you will be of no use to me as a friend at all.'

She was still thinking out her own thoughts. 'The wounds in the mind, Vickie, are not that kind of thing, they are the beautiful things that happened and then disappeared. And I will put that silly man from my mind . . . ' she burst into full tears, 'because I will not have sex made ugly, and stupid, and brutal, when it is not, when it can be beautiful, when once it was beautiful. I will make a cup of tea.'

'You're not telling me any more?'

'No, it doesn't matter. Living on memory is a very thin feeble way to live, Vickie, and I have had plenty of joys in my life and will have more if I have the sense to take them as they come.'

The older woman took her in her arms, and quiet weeping was a solace.

But life, Meg insisted to herself, did come in circles, because Vickie had arrived in her own life when she was reaching out for a kind of independence, and now she had returned when the great adventure of independence, the shop, was nothing but a burden. It was some kind of Providence, there was some kind of pattern, in the fact that Vickie decided just then to take her retirement because although teachers were scarce in wartime, she had had enough, and if she wanted to spend the rest of her life reading the books she had never got round to do, she preferred to do it sitting in a little shop, with people coming and going, than in an empty house. She looked forward to it. In that she was like Meg. She would always welcome a new experience.

Meg studied her own inner mind as coldly as she could, and was confident that she was telling the truth about the attempt at rape. It was an ugly incident, but it was only an incident, and it was over, and she was unchanged by it. And despite it, life was settling, unexcitingly but comfortably, again. Vickie was taking care of the shop, and if it earned no more than the rent and a few shillings, nobody was worried.

The appalling Somervilles were lodged in the Sisters' house, rightfully now the children's house, and by Dan's accounts they were maybe the worst neighbours in Dennistoun for noise and parties and squalor, but old Mr Ferris the lawyer could worry about that, and collect the rent, and Meg could put it from her mind. Hetty seemed happy enough, and well she might because she was practically a star on the radio in London. Bobby was injured in an accident in Canada, and he was very coy about explaining how it happened, but he was going to get better. Peter was still Peter. In the midst of war, she told herself, we are in peace.

## 39

## HARRY

I had a good time that summer, though I suppose in actual fact I should have spent the whole holiday in catching up on revision. The first year in Medicine is quite stiff, actually. People who have never taken Medicine don't really know what hard work is. I suppose that's why it's the top profession.

The important thing is to be mentally organised, and specialised. That's what worried me about Peter. He was supposed to be studying architecture, but he was always jumping about to other things. He had a very low taste in pictures, like *Holiday Camp*, and Laurel and Hardy, who are just for kids. He thought they were better than Charlie Chaplin, who is definitely a genius according to the critics.

He liked dance music too. I quite like it, dancing being a good exercise and an element in social intercourse, but he liked it very much. He liked classical music too. At least, he claimed to like classical music, but there's a lot of the poseur in people who say they enjoy it. He and John Taylor actually paid to get into symphony concerts, and discussed them as if they actually understood them.

Peter was very immature politically, but his brother was an ILP Councillor, and my mother agreed it was quite a good idea when Peter asked me if I wanted to go for a week to the ILP Summer School at a university in the North of England. Anyway, it was less than four pounds. Peter said he was keen because it might be instructive and because he had heard they rang a bell at seven every morning to warn people to get back to their own bedrooms. He was always flippant about things.

Before then, Peter and John Taylor and I sometimes went about together. I took them to some meetings of the No Conscription League, where you could hear really interesting talks about variegated topics, like one man Jim Jenner, who gave a talk on the point that heredity was irrelevant compared to environment. Broadly speaking, this is a correct analysis and agrees with both Marx and Darwin, and there was a blonde girl there who listened very intently and looked very intelligent. Intelligence is the most important quality in girls.

Peter, of course, always wanted to make silly jokes.

'What about Mozart?' he asked.

'What about Mozart, then?' Jim Jenner asked.

'He was composing music when he was three years old. I couldn't do that. He must have been born clever.'

'He was born in a musical environment. The potentiality of every human being is limitless if he has the right environment. Any child can do it with the right environment.'

'What about Mozart's young brother?' John Taylor asked him. Jim Jenner was annoyed at people bringing in irrelevant matters.

'He was a tone-deaf idiot,' Peter said.

'Maybe his parents were older by then, and they had stopped playing music. It was the same family, but a different environment.'

'But Mozart's older sister couldn't play the tin whistle,' John Taylor said.

'That was a different environment as well.'

That shut Peter and John up, thank goodness. I hoped to get to talk to the blonde girl, and maybe walk home with her for some intelligent conversation, but she was with Jim Jenner, so the three of us walked home together.

'I didn't know that about Mozart's brother,' I said. 'Of course, in Medicine we don't have much time to study music.'

'I don't know if he had a sister,' Peter said.

'That's childish,' I said. 'You get a scientific talk by a serious speaker and you must make stupid jokes.'

'That wasn't a scientific talk,' Peter said. 'That guy is a pompous ignorant prick. He's never even heard of Mozart.'

'That girl was quite intelligent,' I said. 'The one with the fair hair.'

'She never opened her mouth.'

'No, but you could see she was intelligent.'

'She's got great tits.'

You could hardly get a serious conversation with Peter at all.

But the Summer School was quite educational. We had a lecture every morning, and the trick was to steal a couple of cushions from one of the lounges and take them to the lecture hall to put on the hard chairs. The Independent Labour Party, of course, is only a tiny political party, really just the lunatic fringe of the actual Labour Party of which my mother is a member and a Town Councillor, and it is rather hopeless as a political entity, but they had some quite interesting people.

One chap gave a talk on international banking, which was really very informative and I wish I had taken some notes. And there was an old Irishman who spoke about the Easter Rising in 1916, a bit emotionally, really, but it was understandable. They even had a man who had been a diplomat, talking about how the Foreign Office worked. He had written several books too, and I got his autograph, for a friend at university.

We got to know some people of our own age, and a crowd of us sat at the same table for meals and called ourselves the Rising Generation. On the first day I saw the fair-haired girl we had seen at the No Conscription League. Her name was Andrea Cunningham I hoped she would be at our table, but she sat with some older people, including her father, who was actually a Baronet. Sir Robert, though everybody called him Bob.

I don't believe in titles, naturally, being a Socialist, but one doesn't get neurotic about these things. He seemed very intelligent. Peter actually agreed about this, and said that if the King gave him a knighthood, he would take it, because it would mean his wife would be Lady Cassidy, and he had always wanted to shag a titled lady. Peter could be quite funny sometimes.

We talked very frankly about things like sex, which I explained was as natural as going to the bathroom, though I did point out, as a Medicine student, that promiscuous intercourse could spread venereal disease. One girl, Jilly Reid, quite attractive physically, called me the Killjoy Professor, and after that all the Rising Generation called me Prof, which was all right, actually; but she came out rowing with me on the river and she was quite intelligent when you got her alone.

It was a pity about Andrea not sitting at our table, because I was sure she would have a contribution to make. But she seemed to be getting friendly with Peter's brother Andy, who was quite a lot older than her. But Jilly was pleasant, and quite intelligent, actually doing a course at the London School of Economics, but it was evacuated to Cambridge University. On the second night, after the usual dance, we went back to her room, to talk. She had a single room. Peter and I shared a room.

We lay down on the bed, naturally, and put our arms around each other, and had a pleasant hour talking and so on, without doing anything too advanced in the sexual sense, but it was pleasant all the same. Peter was reading in bed when I got back, and he just said hello.

'I was, eh, detained,' I said.

'You're lucky,' he said. 'I missed my chance.'

'There's always the rest of the week,' I said. I didn't go into detail about my own experiences.

'You know, Harry,' he said. 'There's a lot of hypocrisy going about. People talk about outworn shibboleths like marriage and virginity, but the corridors are crawling with parents making sure their daughters are in their own rooms. I don't call that an ideal society.'

'There are some daughters without parents,' I told him. 'You have to plan accordingly.'

'Stop looking smug and put the light out.'

'Me? Smug?' I did feel a bit smug, I suppose.

Then the next day Peter seemed to be getting very friendly with a girl called Susan Ibbotson. She wasn't really a girl, she was a woman well into her thirties. It seemed rather perverted to me.

'I would like to feel her bosom,' Peter said.

'That is infantilism, Peter. And it's ridiculous. She is twenty years older than you.'

'The human race is ridiculous, Harry.'

He always had a silly answer. Anyway, it was still great fun. We had tennis tournaments, and rowed on the river, and of course, while I was rowing the boat with Jilly, Peter was making a fool of himself lying back in his boat and letting the woman Ibbotson row him. The sillier thing is that Jilly actually shouted to them and applauded.

That evening we had a fancy dress ball, and it was actually good fun. Susan Ibbotson more or less took over the Rising Generation gang and turned us all into a sultan and his harem. We got bed sheets and she pinned them on in her room and there was no false modesty or coyness, of course, the girls were standing about in their brassieres and pants, and that didn't worry me, being accustomed to human anatomy as a Medicine student. Jilly looked very well muscled.

It was the best holiday of my life, really. I was the sultan, and Peter was the spear-carrier, in a loincloth, and it was childish, the way they were rubbing him all over with cocoa. And of course, we won the prize, and he insisted on dancing the rest of the night in his costume, but he had to hold his partners at arm's length, so it didn't do him much good. But I did overhear Susan Ibbotson saying to him, 'Now I'll have to wash every drop of that muck off you before bedtime.'

I went back with Jilly to her room after the dance, and thought, it would teach Peter a lesson if I spent the whole night there, so I suggested it was a good idea, promising not to do anything silly. She just took her robe off and got into bed. She was so casual about it that I suspected she was undersexed, but she felt really very nice. I didn't go too far, because although I had actually brought prophylactics with me, naturally they were back in my room, so I didn't want to get over-stimulated and get into danger. It was a very narrow bed and I got a bad crick, but I spent the whole night with her, that is quite a significant point in a person's life.

About seven o'clock I got up, planning to whizz back to the other building in my bedsheet, and I kissed her, although my mouth felt a bit slept-in, as Peter sometimes says.

'Thank you very much,' I said. 'It was nice sleeping with you. Actually we could have done more, because I brought precautions with me, but as luck would have it I left them in my own room last night.'

'Oh well,' she said. She didn't sound very emotional. 'I've got a feeling today is going to be the beginning of the wrong time of the month.'

'That's a shame, Jilly.'

'Can't be helped.'

I nodded and tried to be casual, but I could really have kicked myself. I don't care. It was still the best holiday of my life.

Peter opened his eyes when I went in and I apologised for being late.

'That's all right,' he said. 'I only got in half-an-hour ago.'

'Oh, you would have to say that,' I said.

263

'All right.'

He just lay there, not bothering. He was being irritating deliberately.

'What happened?' I asked him, in case he needed some sympathy.

'It was a bloody disaster. Harry, nothing happened. All my life, man and boy, if you ever got your hand on a girl's knee, you were in for a battle to get an inch farther. Even with . . . it doesn't matter. Ah, I'm not telling you, it's sneaky.'

He had turned over.

'You mean with Marie Rennie?' I yawned. I was tired. 'Not that it matters.'

'All right, naming no names. The very first time I meet someone who *wants* it, no bother, no clothes on – I couldn't do anything. I went limp.'

'That could be serious, Peter.'

'It was helluva funny as well. And the second time, by the time I could have done it, I had done it before I could do it.'

I tried to explain to him that he might have a serious condition, a guilt complex, and premature ejaculation as well, but he shrugged off my diagnosis. I couldn't understand how anybody could admit a thing like that, even.

'I didn't have any trouble of that kind.' I was yawning again. 'Not once.'

'Great, Harry, that's great.'

And the next afternoon he and this Susan Ibbotson woman went out on the river, and you could hear them roaring and laughing for miles away. I definitely couldn't understand them. And that night I was already in bed when he came in, about three a.m. but I was awake and I asked him if he had enjoyed himself.

'There are some things a gentleman doesn't discuss, Harry,' he said in the dark. He really could be irritating. I would have told *him* if *I* had something real to tell, I would have been straightforward about it. But then he said, 'You know how much you keep saying sex is a perfectly ordinary physical function like going to the bathroom, Harry?'

'It is. People put a lot of superstitious romanticism on it, but that's all it is.'

'Ach, it's nothing like going to the bathroom, Harry.' Then he laughed. 'Of course, it can be like going to the bathroom and not being able to pee.'

I had to laugh too. It really was a great holiday, actually.

## 40

Andy was happy to stand up for Peter's old school friend John Taylor at the Conscientious Objectors' Tribunal. He liked the boy and was sure he was honest, but he led him through some of the tricks of the trade to instil some cunning in him too.

'The point is, Councillor Mason . . . ' the boy was so solemn and earnest, ' . . . I don't mind being killed. Death is but a scientific fact. But I will not kill anybody else. I'll go to jail first.'

'Aw, don't be a hero, son. I've been shot at, and it's hellish, and I've been in jail, and it's hellish. I just wish Peter was a conchie as well, I hate to see him going into the Army.'

'You know, Councillor Mason, I think Peter has a charmed life.'

'Balls, John. I knew a guy wi' a charmed life, one of the greatest men I ever met, and the bastards got him. Forget it. Now, for a start, your objection is on moral and ethical grounds. No politics. And no religion, because there's a professor of theology on the Tribunal, and he would tie your guts in knots to get you into the Army for the sake of Gentle Jesus. Get your hair cut. Shave off that moustache. Wear your good suit. What would you do if a German tried to rape your sister?'

'I would try to stop him. What would I do if a British soldier tried to rape my sister?'

'That is very good, John. If they ask you that one, you can quote last week's case in Dunoon. Leading Seaman, Royal Navy. Rape. And guilty. You'll be all right if you keep your head.'

In his calm, measured way, John wasn't at all worried about the prospects of jail. It would be interesting. He might be able to write a book about it. But he had a haircut and shaved off his first wispy attempt at a moustache and wore his best suit for his appearance in the Sheriff Court. The first face he saw, in the public benches, was Andrea Cunningham, the fair-haired girl from the No Conscription League meeting, and then he realised that her friend Jim Jenner was there too, sitting in the queue of conchies. John hoped he wouldn't start haranguing the Bench about heredity and environment.

Jim did very badly. Obviously he was angry. He was probably contemptuous of the very idea of a middle-aged tribunal presuming to weigh any young man's conscience, as John himself was. But Jim let it show. He glared, he glowered, he curled his lip and dismissed all war as immoral.

When the Chairman, a thin, pale, beak-nosed judge, asked him about the morality of allowing Nazi Germany to overrun Europe, Jim snarled 'I was anti-Nazi when the British Government was supporting Hitler against the German workers, letting them take over the Rhineland and everything else. But you don't stop Nazism with war. War is a form of Nazism. To fight totalitarianism, Britain has become a totalitarian state.'

'Really?' The judge was bored to death.

'Am I free? Would I be standing in this dock if I was free? The British state has abolished my rights as a free citizen.'

The judge nodded, judicially. He still looked bored to death, and John wondered how many times he had listened to the same speech. John found himself nodding as Jim went on attacking the state, and war, and the Tribunal, and the capitalist conspiracy, and jerked awake when Jim was asked to take his seat again. There was no verdict.

Andy, seeing John's confusion, whispered to him that the Tribunal would hear everybody and then retire to consider all the cases. John nodded vaguely and watched the dust dancing in the sunbeams through the court windows.

The next two applications were appealing on religious grounds, and he was glad he wasn't. Andy had been right about the professor of theology. One of the boys was small and thin and hardly looked over fifteen, though he had to be eighteen at least. He didn't speak well. His case was a list of quotations from the Bible, and for every one, the professor could trot out three or four in opposition.

'You haven't studied your Bible very well, have you?' the professor asked, with a sympathetic smile that reminded John of a sated vampire.

'My uncle's taught me a lot, sir, and he's read the whole Bible, every word.'

'Mm.'

They didn't waste much time on religious objectors, and

John found himself suddenly angry. The boys hadn't been tested on conscience, only on the cleverness of their answers; and they had failed.

John was called. He did what Andy had told him to do. He said he had no statement to make beyond the statement he had written on the form of application, that he objected to military service on moral and ethical grounds. The professor of theology looked cheated and bored. The Judge perked up slightly, and began to lead John through questions of justice and tyranny and the right of self-defence, and suddenly John found himself calm and interested, found himself agreeing with leading questions and enjoying the game of turning them upside down.

'But modern war is not self-defence, My Lord,' he said. It sounded quite good. 'Modern war especially, because it is indiscriminate.'

The professor of theology leapt in, quietly triumphant.

'Ancient wars were indiscriminate too, Mr Taylor.'

John scented danger. While the Judge could lead him gently through an adult discussion of principles, the three other members of the bench were always there, ready to make an attack on the flank. The process, he thought, was not cricket.

'Not so indiscriminate, sir,' he said firmly. 'And not so destructive. I am not defending ancient wars either. But in modern war, if the Germans kill innocent civilians in Coventry, we don't punish the German air force, we retaliate by killing other innocent civilians in Hamburg.'

The choleric man on the bench whom John now knew to be the trade union representative, actually smacked a fist into a palm.

'These innocent civilians about which you're talking about, young man, are part and parcel of the Nazi war effort as we know it. Hamburg is an actual major centre for the industrial production of war munitions for the total destruction of democracy as we know it. Would you not agree if they support the war effort, they've got it coming to them?'

John thought the man was both ignorant and contemptible.

'That argument would justify the Nazi bombing of Coventry too, sir, and I don't think that can be justified, sir.'

He stopped himself just in time from adding, 'Do you?' and he was sure the Judge was hiding a small smile. Maybe the Judge didn't like the trade union man. But as the questions went on and on, John found his mind wandering again, found himself idly watching the motes of dust in the sunlight, found himself listening to his own voice from far away, and suddenly realised that somebody had asked a question he hadn't even heard.

'I'm sorry, My Lord, I lost track . . . .'

'We were talking about the morality of civil war. Mr Taylor.' The Judge, in fact, almost seemed as interested as John was, in having a discussion about the human condition. But it wasn't a decision between two gentlemen over vintage port. The Judge had the power to end it any time and pass sentence. John had the curious suspicion that the Judge quite liked him. He didn't want the Judge to like him. He had a conscientious objection to the Judge's liking him.

Civil war, civil war . . . ah, the Spanish Civil War. That could be a trap. He heard himself talking his way through a minefield, staring up at the high bench, for hours, though the shafts of sunlight had scarcely moved.

'You have a character witness,' the Judge said.

'Yes, My Lord.' God, it was finished. He felt like sleeping for a week. He sat down and Andy Mason got up.

'Councillor Andrew Mason, My Lord.' Oh, Andy wasn't falling asleep. What great tough confidence Andy had. 'This young man was a schoolmate of my young brother, and I have known him for many years. I have no doubt whatever of his integrity. I think he has shown he is an intelligent young man and a serious thinker. And I would submit, My Lord, that in registering as a conscientious objector he is doing his duty as he sees it, just as other young men see military service as their duty.'

The Judge looked up sharply.

'Young brother? Is your younger brother objecting to military service too?''

'No, My Lord, he has registered for the Army.'

The Judge merely shrugged. But the professor of theology jumped in.

'Surely you yourself are of military age, Councillor?'

'I really don't think that's relevant, My Lord.' Andy

269

refused to look at the professor. 'But if it matters, I served in the Spanish Civil War. I was wounded. At present I am engaged in essential war work. And I would add that Mr Taylor is an only child.'

'That doesn't concern this Tribunal,' the Judge said impatiently. 'If you're making a case for hardship, there's a separate tribunal for that.'

'I agree, My Lord. I am merely suggesting that if the Tribunal was thinking of some alternative, non-combatant service, the fact of his being an only child might be borne in mind.'

The Judge nodded and waved his hand. He seemed to be thinking of other things.

In the corridor outside during the recess, Andy said, 'A good performance, John. I think they were too wily to try the old rape question on somebody like you.'

'I was half-asleep half the time.'

'I'll see you in a tick.'

Andy trotted over to where Andrea Cunningham was talking mournfully with Jim Jenner, and John walked back and forth staring at the wall.

'You never know,' Andy was saying to Jim, 'there's always a chance they'll keep you out of the Army because you're the kind that might start a mutiny.'

'Not a chance. They've got it in for me. It'll be the Army or prison.'

'There's always the chance of a soft number in the Army.'

'I don't want any soft number.' The glower on Jim's face seemed to have fixed itself permanently. A crusading mule, John thought to himself.

'Okay, okay, sorry,' said Andy. 'What do you think of British justice, Andrea?'

'Farcical, isn't it? They'll put me in prison for sure.'

'What for?"

'I'm refusing to do war work.'

'Oh God. It must be great to be young. Will we all meet for coffee after the great minds have done their stuff? I could take you up to the City Chambers.'

'That would be nice.'

The Tribunal resumed, and John listened to the mono-tonous list of total rejections. But when his name was announced, the next words were, 'Service with the Forestry Commission or other essential agricultural work.' He was delighted. It wasn't as interesting as prison, but the idea of swinging an axe and shouting Timber and finally putting on some muscles pleased him. His father and mother would be pleased too. And if he was away from home in a forestry camp he wouldn't have to read *The Bulletin*. He would buy the *Manchester Guardian*.

In the City Chambers dining room, John and Jim Jenner immediately fell into an argument about biology. Jim wanted an argument with somebody. While they were at it, oblivious to anything else, Andy had a carefully casual talk with Andrea. In the time they had spent together at the summer school he had treated her as a pleasant companion and nothing more; especially since her father was there. He was in no hurry to change that. The boy Jenner, he decided, was fond of her but probably not very romantic, and certainly not good enough for her. But Andy kept it easy and not too familiar.'

'I don't suppose you need a character witness for your trial,' he said. 'I think you're daft, but all right. Oh, anyway, you've got your father. He would be very good.'

'I wouldn't think of it, Andy. He's really quite shy. I've told him not to come near it.'

'I would be very happy. But a trial is a different kettle of fish from that lot down the road. But say the word, if you like.'

'No, I don't think so, really. It would be nice if you would come to the trial, all the same.'

'If I have to close down Parkhead Forge for the day, I'll be there. And if they send you to Duke Street I'll bring in a file pie. You're really not bothered, are you?"

'No, not a bit.'

'You're quite a girl.'

'Thank you, sir.'


John went to a forestry camp in Argyll, where the nearest hamlet was three miles away and the general store didn't stock the *Manchester Guardian*. Jim went to the Army. Andrea stood trial and went to Duke Street Prison for thirty days. Since her father was shy and her mother had influenza, Andy met her with a taxi when she came out, and took her to lunch at the Rogano. The prison diet had made her plumper, but she looked good.

'I'm enormously fat,' she said.

'You're not fat, you're deliciously plump. I could eat you.' He made no move to sit near her in the taxi.

She was very funny about prison life. She was quite a girl. She phoned her parents in the country, they had a hilarious lunch, and he took her in the afternoon to see Bing Crosby in 'Holiday Inn'. She held his hand in a cool friendly way at the pictures.

'This is the first time I've touched a male person in a month,' she said.

'Touch away, it's all free.' He squeezed her hand but lightly.

'Mother,' Andy said, only a few days later, 'how do you fancy a baronet's daughter as a daughter-in-law?'

'Can she cook?'

'I haven't asked her'

'What have you asked her?'

'I haven't asked her anything. She doesn't know yet what good luck's in store for her.'

'Andy Mason, you're not getting round some lassie just because she'll be useful to you. You're not going to get married for the wrong reasons, no happiness can ever come of it.'

'Mother, I'm crazy about her. I would marry her if her old man was a shanty Irishman.'

'But it's more convenient having him a baronet.'

He laughed.

'Sure. But I'm telling you I'm crazy about her, honestly. Once she gets the idea that she's marrying me I'll bring her to see you. You'll like her.'

'Well, I'll try not to be too high and mighty with the poor lassie.'

'What are we going to do about Jardine?'

'What about Jardine?'

'Vickie Fairhurst told me, and you should have told me yourself. I feel like putting his teeth in. But he should go the whole way.'

'Andy, I'm not capable of sending any man to prison, I would never get over it as long as I lived. I didn't even want

272

Vickie to spread the story to a neighbour, but they all know now, and that is a bad enough punishment for a man in itself, it's just about broken him. So no prison.'

'My future wife has just come out of prison. She thought it was a lark.'

'Merciful heavens, what are you telling me? The girl's been in prison? It would kill me.'

'Nothing could kill you, Mother.'

'Oh, boredom might.'

'A helluva lot of kids in the Services wish they were bored, Mother.'

'Aye, you're right to remind me. But you're a tinker. Will the lassie have you?'

'Oh, Mother. I'm a Town Councillor. What lassie could turn down a Councillor of the City of Glasgow? Mind you, I don't know. I heard about a carter the other day in Dundas Street, looking for a wee boy to hold his horse while he shot in for a gill, but there was nobody about except a well-dressed man, so he asked him, quite politely; and the man said, "Do you realise I'm a Councillor of the City of Glasgow?" and the carter said, "Aye, all right, but surely to God I can trust you wi' my *horse*."'

'I don't believe it, and don't you joke to me about dishonest Councillors, it makes me shiver. Did the lassie do something terrible bad? Terribly bad, I mean?'

'Wait till you meet her, and I'll let you guess. Ha. You might be sitting next to a murderess and not know it.'

'Och, murder is forgivable, I've thought of it often. Do you really like her?'

'Crazy about her. She's lovely, and she's fun, and she's good.'

'I'm not going to cry.'

'Of course you're going to cry, have a good bubble. Oh, we lead you a helluva life, the lot of us.'

'Aye, and that's the life I love, Andy. I love it.'

'Christ, you've got me at it now.'

## 41

There was a sense of urgency about that summer, as if it were going to be the last summer ever. There was a frantic hunt for premises. Marie Rennie was already in the ATS, and when she was home on leave, Peter found her feminine attraction compounded in the military uniform. It was like a reversal of the sexual roles, and the sight of girls dressed as soldiers or sailors had an odd excitement. Marie was even more intimidating because she wore a brown leather jerkin over her tunic to remind herself that she was a high-ranking officer's driver. Peter, who couldn't drive a car and had always thought of it as a very masculine thing to do, was bowled over by that. It stimulated vague fantastical notions of military authority over beautiful girls, trim Army ladies giving total obedience to the Major like harem beauties, but moving crisply to numbers and saluting as they presented their bodies for the officer's pleasure. Marie never mentioned anything of the kind. Driving about in a Humber Snipe and feeling and looking important was what seemed to fascinate her.

She was still pleasantly free of inhibition, and when the question was asked about Army issue underwear, at a rather respectable party at Harry's (his parents were both at home), she laughed and pulled up her skirt to display the grim khaki bloomers with elastic bottoms just above the knee. And she winked impudently at him at a shared memory.

One puzzling thing was that on the rare evenings when somebody did have premises, nothing had changed from pre-uniform days. They were a routine of kissing and hugging and changing partners. Peter was careful never to mention his experiences with Sue Ibbotson, except very obliquely, with jokes about preferring the more mature type of woman.

'He lives in a dream world,' Harry Cooke would shout across the darkened room.

'So I do,' Peter admitted. 'A pretty damp dream world at that.'

He thought he must be a hypocrite, or a self-deceiver. What had happened with Sue gave him a secret satisfaction that he had finally Gone the Whole Way; but if he really believed he was mad with lust all the time, it was strange that he was content to hold Marie, or one of the Wilson twins, or Ella, and kiss comfortably in the dark without needing anything more. The Wilsons had both volunteered for the Wrens, and he wondered if they would come home on leave, in those exciting navy blue uniforms and with expanded appetites from life in the Navy. In the meantime it was good to cuddle them and feel their bony bodies writhing obligingly.

Harry was suddenly much easier to cope with. He was working really hard and confessing that Medicine was bloody hell, but he wasn't boasting about it, He was just reporting a fact, and he was tolerant and even enthusiastic about Alastair Barr's ambitions for air-crew with the RAF and Peter's unworried acceptance of Army service.

'Actually I envy you in a way,' he said. 'Even if it's against my principles. I mean, years from now you'll have all that experience, and I'll just be a country GP unless the war goes on forever and they take me in as an Army doctor.'

'You don't need qualifications for that,' Peter said. 'My brother Bobby told me he had heard one RAF doctor asking another one what he had been in Civvy Street, and he said he had travelled in ladies' knickers.'

'I heard that too,' Alastair agreed. 'When you go for your medical, a doctor looks in each ear, and if they can't see each other, you're A1.'

There were as many medical stories as bomb stories.

'Bobby wrote to me about this guy,' Peter said. 'He got stripped for his medical, and the doctor said he was the first darkie he had ever seen with a white penis. I'm no' a darkie, he said, I'm a chimney-sweep just back from honeymoon.'

The old arguments still sometimes flared up, but without much fury. Alastair was so bucked about being accepted for air-crew training that he had forgotten he had ever thought of escaping to Northern Ireland to avoid conscription, as he had once done, and was starting to develop esprit de corps.

'What if there was a revolution?' Harry asked him slily, 'and Churchill ordered you to bomb your own people?'

'That is crazy, Cooke. You're always on about Churchill. He's the greatest leader this country has ever had.'

'He's a Fascist.'

'Oh Christ.'

'It was Churchill that called out the troops at the miner's strike in Wales.'

'In 1926.'

'Oh, that. He was probably bloody right.'

'Do you mean . . .' Peter was fascinated, '. . . if there were riots against the Government right here in Dennistoun, you would bomb people you actually knew?'

'Sure. Your job is to obey orders without question.'

'He's a born Nazi,' Harry said sadly.

'The Nazis were right about some things,' Alastair insisted.

Alastair's family certainly had something, Peter thought. A kind of style. Partly it was a wonderful complacency. When he visited Alastair's house he was still aware that it was, quietly, a bit on the grand side. A genuine baby grand piano, for one thing, on which Alastair would still play Harlem, and even a slightly shaky rendering of Rhapsody in Blue, if persuaded. And sister Beth, who must have been nearly thirty, was still elegant and gorgeous although she was married to an officer in the Merchant Navy and expecting her first child. Peter had fallen in love with her when he was twelve and she was a remote and unattainable adult lady. Now her attraction had a different quality, and she seemed almost aware of him.

Mr Barr's car business wasn't doing much because there were no new cars and petrol was rationed, and most people had given up motoring for the duration. But he had expanded the repair workshop and had sub-contracts to manufacture components for some unmentioned military equipment, and he kept his pre-war style, with an assortment of double-breasted blazers, each worn with an open-necked shirt and a silk scarf tucked into it.

There was a picture of Churchill in the sitting-room, and a map of Europe on the wall, handy to the wireless so that Mr Barr could stick coloured pins in it to mark the progress of the war. Mr Barr talked authoritatively about the war, and Peter listened to his pronouncements without arguing. He merely repeated them later to Harry, as a joke.

Mr Barr didn't like Jews, and he knew what he was talking about.

'I know you're supposed to be tolerant, Peter, and I respect you for it, as far as that goes, but one thing you learn in business. Never trust the gentlemen from the Levant. When I was in Egypt and Mespot, the last time, you had to nail everything down. They were up for a flogging regularly for pilfering.'

'It sounds pretty vicious.'

'It's the only thing they understood. I know you don't believe in that sort of thing, and I respect you for it. But there's a big difference between theory and practice.'

'Mm.'

'Daddy was there, you know, Peter,' Mrs Barr said. Mrs Barr was a plump, kindly, silly woman who did a lot of home baking and always had a good and surprising supply of chocolate biscuits, which had nearly disappeared from the shops.

'Another thing,' Mr Barr said. 'I think America would be very unwise to send negro troops over here. It's bound to cause trouble.'

'Oh, I think the British are very tolerant of coloured people,' Peter ventured diffidently.

'That's because we've never had any. Look at places like Alabama. They know what it's like. I wouldn't like Beth walking the streets if this town was full of negroes.'

'They say the same thing about the Poles, Mr Barr.'

'I don't think much of them either. What do they carry in these brief-cases?'

'Sandwiches, probably.'

'Uhuh. Or black market whisky. They don't want for anything, that crowd.'

'I don't know, Mr Barr. They've lost their homes.'

'Well, that's a point, and they're allies. That's certainly a point.'

'And don't forget,' Alastair chipped in, 'if it hadn't been for the Jews, Germany might never have started the war.'

'Ach, that's nonsense, Alastair.'

'Aye, I think that's putting it too strongly,' Mr Barr said judicially. 'It's just something in the German character. They have to have a war every twenty years. It's their nature.'

'I'm not sure about that either, Mr Barr.'

'Not sure? Look at the evidence.'

'Mm.'

'Even though they should know they'll always lose.'

'They didn't lose the Franco-Prussian war.'

'Ah, that's ancient history. When was that?'

'It was 1870.'

'That's what I mean. Anyway, we know what the French are like. Them and their invincible Maginot Line.'

The Maginot Line had once been one of Mr Barr's special prides. He had spoken of it as if he had built it with his own hands. He was a comfortable man who adapted to circumstances. The treachery of John Taylor particularly saddened him, but it enraged beautiful Beth.

'He's got no right to drink tea,' she said. 'Or coffee.'

'I don't know if he likes coffee,' Peter said warily.

'I don't understand these people. When I think of my husband risking his life night and day to bring food to Britain, and then they've got the cheek to say they want nothing to do with the war effort, but will they stop eating the stuff the Merchant Navy has to take through the minefields and everything? Not them. Conscientious cowards and spongers is more like it.'

Peter's sadness was mixed with relief as he realised that he was falling out of love with Beth. It would give him more time to think of other girls. He felt that that was another childish thing he was putting behind him. He remembered to give Beth six little pages from a note pad, each bearing Hetty's autograph which she had promised to the other members of her sewing bee. Harry was partly right. Intelligent girls were more fun. But as well as not being too intelligent, Beth had a spiteful streak. It was quite good not to have to adore her any more.

Andy was still moving cautiously in the matter of Andrea Cunningham, though he was seeing her at least twice a week and treating her to modest meals in town. Having served her time in prison and tholed her assize she was free of obligations, and had a civilian job in the City Assessor's office. Since her department was concerned with the regulation of coal supplies, it nearly qualified as essential war work in any case, but she had made her stand for principle and didn't worry about that. She had lodgings in a quite elegant house in the West End, and Andy suspected that her father was subsidising her. It was Andrea herself who pushed the business faster. He took her home in the subway and walked with her to her door.

'You never think of kissing me goodnight,' she said.

'I do. I don't know if you want me to, Andy.' He now called her Andy, and she liked it. 'Anyway, it's broad daylight. It wouldn't do for a Town Councillor to be seen canoodling in the street.'

'I'm a virgin, you know, Andy.'

'I should hope so.'

'You're very conventional. Do you not believe in freedom of the sexes?'

'No.'

'Well, that answers that question.'

'All right, I'm old-fashioned. Do you ever hear from Jim Jenner?'

'We're not talking about Jim.'

'No.'

'Do you not find me attractive?'

'You're terrific, Andy.'

'And you're a Town Councillor. Don't tell me you think people should wait till they're married.'

'Yes. I do. Girls should anyway.'

'Oh, the double standard.'

'That's the way I see it.'

'I'm shocked at you.'

'I'm shocked at you too.'

'Oh, for heaven's sake, we're living in the twentieth century.'

Andy was still being cautious, trying not to jump to any flattering conclusions. He was extra cautious because he felt that he had reached a point of maximum risk.

'Are you a virgin?' she demanded.

'Well . . . No.'

'See? You think you're being fair to the female sex?'

'I'm just old-fashioned, Andy, I admit it.'

'Don't tell me you want to marry me.'

'Eh?'

'Have I frightened you?'

'No. Yeah, sure I want to marry you.'

'Oh well. All right, I don't mind, but it's so conventional.'

'Just a minute. Oh, I must say that's very romantic.'

'We don't believe in romance.'

'I do. I told you, I'm old-fashioned.'

'Well, there's no harm in it, I suppose. But don't you dare get down on one knee. I would kill myself laughing.'

'Bugger it, I will.' Careless of any onlookers he got down on one knee on the pavement.

'Will you marry me?'

'Yes.' She laughed beautifully. 'I told you I would laugh. But I'm glad you did it. At least you stopped looking like a Town Councillor for a minute.'

'I don't feel like a Town Councillor, I feel like a wee boy on his birthday. I'm going to kiss you as well.'

'And it's high time. Are we going to wait for the wedding night for the rest of it?'

'My God. Andy, I'm desperate for you.'

'Thank God. Will you take me to your house tomorrow?'

'I'll do it tonight.'

'Can't be done. My landlady would just die, and she's a dear old thing. Tomorrow.'

'God. Oh God. Yes. I'll meet you in Cranston's Tearoom.'

'And we'll have one of those pies with potato filling and potato flour pastry.'

'I'll have to ask your parents, Andy.'

'No, you won't. We'll have to *tell* them, that's all. I think Dad quite likes you, and Mum won't mind. Will you have to ask your parents?'

'I'll have to tell Mother. You'll have to meet Mother. And don't tell her what you were in jail for. She thinks you're a murderess and she's quite interested.'

'She sounds like an interesting lady.'

'No, I've got an early shift tomorrow. I'll meet you at your office and we'll go straight home.'

'No potato pie?'

'No.'

'I'm a bit nervous. Do you think that's childish?'

'You're nervous? *You're* nervous? Oh my God.'

He took her to Meg's house at eight o'clock next evening, and Meg looked at her candidly and said, 'He said you were beautiful. He can tell the truth when he wants to.'

'I don't know what to say, Mrs Mason.'

'Say you would like something to eat.'

'I'm starving.'

'Good.'

'Should we not have a drink?' Andy suggested. 'I quite feel like one now.'

'It really is good to meet you, Mrs Mason. He told me you were beautiful too.'

'He's a real politician, isn't he?'

'No, he can tell the truth when he wants to.'

Meg called Andy into the kitchen to help her, and wagged a finger at him.

'You couldn't wait till you married the girl, could you?'

'What do you mean, Mother?'

'What do I mean indeed. You think I'm blind as well as old? You know what I see in that lassie's eyes?'

'Stars?'

'Oh aye, those as well. I see rumpled bed-sheets.'

'Oh God. Are you shocked, Mother?'

'I have never been shocked at anything except cruelty and stupidity, and I don't see any of that between the two of you. Just don't do the girl any harm, Andy.'

'You're joking.'

'She's a fine girl. I'm not sure you deserve her.'

'I do my best.'

'You'd better, you'd better, Andy Mason.'

She watched them wolfing corned beef and chips, almost ferociously.

'Sorry, Mrs Mason, I really was ravenous.'

'Yes, a good healthy young appetite.'

Andy laughed, and Andrea looked from him to his mother in mild suspicion.

'Come on, Mother. What do you think she's guilty of?' The girl blushed deeply.

'Well, it is not murder, Andy. I think it must be something not too terrible. Like taking a photograph with an aeroplane in it. There was a man last week was jailed for two years for taking a picture of his own wee aeroplane, did you see that?'

'Judges are insane, Mother.'

'Mine wasn't,' said Andrea. 'He was quite nice, really.'

'And it surely wasn't theft, Andrea.'

'This isn't fair. I refused to do military service or war work.'

'Well, you'll not go to the bad fire for that. Or for anything else you've done, I'm thinking.' She couldn't suppress a smile, and it turned to an open laugh.

'Andy Mason,' Andrea said. 'You told your own mother . . . You told her . . .'

'Andy, I should have warned you. I never need to tell Mother anything. She knows everything. She's an X-ray machine.'

'Well.' Meg tried not to sound complacent. 'I do know something about the fire in the blood. And for all I'm a Christian, I am not against it, even if my own is cooling down. A bit.'

'Mrs Mason, you're a marvel, honestly. Can I call you Mother too?'

'You've got a mother of your own. Why don't you call me Meg?'

'Meg. You're a marvel. What a lucky boy you are, Andy Mason.'

'I know it. But I'm talented as well.'

'I'm a wee bit nervous about meeting your parents, Andrea.'

'Mother, that is a blatant lie, you're not nervous about anybody.'

'It is not a blatant lie, it is just a polite expression, Andy. And it's a wee bit true as well.'


You have to be kind, to be cruel. Hetty wondered how she had got herself into such a situation, but even as she wondered, she knew. She had been kind to herself, she had been kind to Tim, and she had created a kind of cruelty. It would never do, and yet there was no way out of it. Every day, even when he was not looking at her, she knew his eyes were on her, and she knew what it was about, she knew the awful hunger of him, and she wished she was somewhere else. He was in a situation he loved, and hated. He was in a situation he couldn't escape from.

'I'll get a divorce,' he muttered one morning when Mark Tressall had trotted off to a conference.

'You will not, Tim.'

'I hate my wife.'

'You hardly ever see her.'

'I hate her. I can never live with her again, Hetty. I can never live without you.'

'I'm trying to write this script, Tim.'

'You don't care about me.'

'Oh, Tim, I do, but I have to write this script. Anyway, we can talk tonight. You're coming home with me, aren't you?'

He looked almost ready to refuse, in order to punish her, or himself, and she hoped he would, and at the same time hoped he wouldn't, because behind her exasperation her heart still moved for his misery. She was surprised at herself, because she felt at the same time that her heart was a block of ice. She sometimes prayed for release, for some terrible incident that would leave her free; and cursed her stupidity in starting the affair.

She felt that she had discovered a universal truth about men. If a woman 'gave herself' to a man (and that was a silly expression, when the act had to be give-and-take or it was nothing) he didn't regard it as an act of affection, to be appreciated for itself. It became an endless promise. By having her once, he had established territorial rights over her body; and in Tim's case, over her spirit.

On the evenings when he did go home with her, he was importunate and helpless at the same time, he could hardly eat anything because he was frantic to get her into bed, and then so afraid of losing her that he was a poor lover, and he cried at his failures, and she had to reassure him and try to put courage and confidence into him, wishing all the time that he would just fall out of love with her and go away. She was in a trap.

It was Mark Tressall who got her half-out of it. The broadcasts in recent weeks had lost a lot of their sprightliness, and she knew why. Mark was suddenly being very Mark Tressall, fluffing cues and running over her lines, and then holding post-mortems at which he was very cold and cutting. He was working her out of the programme.

She looked forward to being out of it, in one way. It was almost a laugh. The *News Chronicle* had invited her to write a weekly article echoing the programme and reporting some of the absurdities of wartime Britain which didn't get into the programme, Britain at Bay.

It was easy, because people all over Britain were writing to her, personally, at the BBC and then at the *News Chronicle* office, with their own favourite stories. And the fee from the newspaper was nearly as much as her BBC salary. Mark didn't come right out and say he disapproved, but he wasn't pleased. Suddenly she was transferred to another department, and to a clerical job with no stardom attached to it. Mark was sorry, of course, but he was In the Hands of the Philistines.

Her place was taken by another girl from outside, one with acting training. That was life. At least she didn't have to spend all day in the heartwearying presence of Tim.

She went to the *News Chronicle* office to explain that they would probably want to drop her weekly column. The features editor, a harried Welshman, told her not to be silly.

'I don't care a damn whether you're on the wireless or not, the customers like your column. Your Mister Tressall has been here before you, offering to take it over. He is a boring English ponce. Oh, there's corruption, I could never stand the English and he has proved me right again. Us Celts have to stick together, isn't it?'

'I could kiss you, Mr Williams.'

'What is stopping you?'


Meg was deeply pleased about Andy and Andrea, though the girl was a bit selfconscious about being unselfconscious, she had the terrible compulsion of the young to be adult and to stop being young, not realising the pain of not being young any more. But it would always be so, and everybody's youth would slip away.

Vickie Fairhurst was rejuvenated. She had taken to running the shop like a navigator discovering the Americas, she said it was a permanent holiday after a life wasted on browbeating adolescent thugs. She was settled. Meg was settled, wearing out the passing days with her stint at Rolls Royce, and grieved at the prospect of losing Peter to the Army, and put up with it. Things just went on.

Dan started his lunchtime visits to the shop again, to have savage friendly arguments with Vickie, who detested Russia and democratic centralism. He had settled into the age of the elder statesman and looked as if he would stay the same age for a century. When he called on Meg on an occasional evening, she mourned his lost youth too, or the brief late flicker of it that she had enjoyed. That was clearly all behind him.

He brought reports of the Newton house and the dreadful

Mrs Somerville, who was filling it with relations, or acquaintances, or worse. If she was ever evicted, he said, they would have to tear up the floorboards to look for stowaways. Meg didn't want to think about it. Whatever happened would happen.

Vickie forced her to go out in the evenings, 'while we're both alive enough to go anywhere,' she said, and introduced her to the Cercle Intime, where it was forbidden to speak anything but French. It was a revelation. Somewhere in the drab town of Glasgow, were people insanely attached to the French language; and not because of the war, or any political alliance of the time, but for older reasons, the ancient alliance between Scotland and France against the Auld Enemy, England.

It was exhilarating to be accepted by these people as if she were, like them, properly educated and not just a simple girl from the Islands posing as something above herself. One ancient gentleman even congratulated her on her accent, and placed it in the St Cloud arrondissement of Paris, and she saw Vickie grimacing triumphantly.

And a real Frenchman, an émigré, sang. When he had a few drinks, he would not stop singing. People begged him not to, and others egged him on. He was in his sixties, but his voice was passionate and powerful, and Meg was entranced, watching and listening as he clenched his fists and the veins stood out on his brow when he drove himself to the high notes.

'Ma Normandie,' his friends shouted, and others wailed 'Oh non, nom de Dieu.'

He sang. She had heard the song before, but only from another room, among noisy shouts. Now he was there, six feet away, his face upturned and his eyes filling with tears.

*Il est un age dans la vie*
*Ou chaque rève doit finir*
*Un age ou l'âme recueillie*
*A besoin de se souvenir*
*Lorsque ma Muse refroidie*
*Aura fini ses chants d'amour*
*J'irai revoir ma Normandie*
*C'est le pays qui m'a donné le jour*

The old gentleman finished in a flood of shameless tears, and Meg impatiently wiped her own eyes.

'Facile sentimentality,' she complained to Vickie, but it was her own sentimentality she was accusing.

'He does it every time, Meg, it's his party piece. Probably never saw Normandy in his life.'

Bis, bis, people were shouting, and Zut alors, and even Merde alors. The tune, the words, the picture of the man's weeping face, had burned themselves into Meg's mind, made her almost dizzy.

Peter was still out when she got home, and she made up the flask of cocoa and went to bed. The verse wouldn't leave her alone, and she tried to make a translation that didn't sound banal, because she suspected that the original probably was banal, that its very banality was its power.

> There comes an age in every life
> When every dream must fade away
> An age when the . . . the gathered soul? . . .
>     ah, *the soul being gathered in*
>  *Must return to days gone by*
> *When my Muse, growing cold*
> *Has finished with songs of love*
> *I'll see again my Normandie*
> *There is the land that gave me the day*

And at once, her tears were wilder than the old gentleman's. Catharsis, Hetty had written. She was plunged into childhood and her tears were washing away the walls she had built against the memories, and she was weeping for Duna, and the sea, and the gorse, and the sad folly that had left her fatherless and motherless, and the magic times on the heather hill in her youth when her life was bouleversée and she pined for her childhood and her youth and her own madness. And she wept and she wept and wondered if she would ever grow up, and hungered for the Island and the magic that was gone. There is the land that gave me love.

She heard Peter come in, and was glad he had been late, for she would surely have wept in front of him.

286

'I'm asleep, Peter,' she called.
'Right, Mother. Goodnight.'

*J'irai revoir ma Normandie*
*C'est le pays qui m'a donné le jour*

For the first time she could remember, she slept without dreaming.

# 42

Going into the Army was like going to school for the first time. In some ways it was easier. Everybody knew that sergeants were bullying bastards, and sergeant-majors were Frankenstein monsters; but none of them was Miss Wales. They couldn't attack grown men with blackboard pointers.

The train to Somewhere in Britain was a night train, crowded to the point where some fiendish travellers occupied the lavatories, just to get a seat. A lot of the civilians were obviously on their way to become soldiers. Some of them carried bottled beer to show they were men. Others had sandwiches and home-made cakes to see them through the war. Beneath the manly bearing, they were exactly like kids going to a new school for the first time. Peter felt completely at home.

They arrived in Yorkshire and waited, and waited, and then waited some more, and a fleet of lorries arrived to transport them to camp.

It was certainly true that the Army had its own methods. Having filled out his form with great care and indicated that he was a student of architecture, Peter was assigned to a unit to become a wireless-operator; and there was no doubt that radio mechanics were on some other train, to some other camp, to become physical training teachers; while other athletic boneheads were going to learn draughtsmanship. It didn't matter. Miss Wales would not be there, the instructors wouldn't be twice his size, and beating recruits with pointers was against King's Regulations.

It was all right. He realised that some of the boys squashed into the lorry with him had never been away from home before. He had been away from home. He had even been in London, which made him a sophisticate. The uniform they gave him, even the boots, were not ridiculously ill-fitting. No doubt, on his first leave, his mother would do clever things with the tunic and trousers and make them look like a bespoke suit.

He didn't even mind the square-bashing. It was probably out of date in the age of the Blitzkrieg, when war would be fought in tanks and trucks and planes. But its meaningless rhythms, its toy-soldier postures, the banging of boots on the parade ground, were as simple and soothing as washing dishes, and no doubt the automatic response of limbs to orders would be useful if anybody had to march against impossible odds, like a German tank, without thinking. There was a lot of it before anybody started to mention instruction in wireless. Some of the lads got sullen and mutinous, in private, about the stupidity of forcing infantry drill on specialists. Peter kept his head down. He didn't see the drill sergeant as an enemy, but as a bit of Army scenery, a bit of audible machinery. Peter didn't call attention to himself, either by making mistakes or looking too good. He thought he might be what they called good private-soldier material, plastic stuff that could be put into any shape without complaining. He wasn't complaining. It was all new.

Among the boys in the barracks he soon made a particular friend, or rather, he was particularly befriended. Clifford Gross was thin and perplexed, with a thin voice and a strong London accent, though not the BBC accent. His pronunciation of Charing Cross Road sounded like Chawring Croarst Ryde. His adenoids worried him. Most things worried him. He had one of the cots nearest the door, and on the third day he asked Peter to swap. Peter didn't mind, but he was curious.

'I'm right in the draught over there,' Clifford explained.

'I don't like draughts either.'

'But it's not fair, I catch colds easy, I've always had this trouble with my chest. They shouldn't have put me there.'

'Nobody put you there. You were just too late to get one of the other beds.'

'Well, that ain't fair, is it?'

Peter agreed to swap, simply to stop the whining. But nothing on earth could stop that. Clifford had trouble with his boots, as well as his chest. A lot of the boys had trouble with their boots, but nobody ever had as much trouble as Clifford.

'Don't your boots hurt?' he asked Peter resentfully.

'Not much. I'm getting used to them.'

'They look softer than my boots.'

'All the boots are the same, Clifford.'

'Can I try yours?'

'No.'

'I only want to try them. If they're better than mine I'll tell Stores I need another pair.'

'No.'

'I ain't asking for them to keep. I only want to try them on.'

'Piss off, Clifford. And don't let me catch you trying them on, either.'

'There's no need to get nasty, I ask a simple question, you start throwing your weight about. I got a weak chest, you know.'

'I know. Keep your eyes off my boots.'

Clifford had a way of retiring after a philosophical discussion of this kind, and sitting staring at nothing and totting up his troubles. It amounted to a talent.

There was nothing wrong with the bed at the door, and no noticeable draught. Clifford worried about that too. When Peter said it was the handiest bed if he wanted to nip out to the bog during the night, he worried more. And he always seemed to be short of things, like shaving soap and hair cream. He insinuated himself into Peter's supplies, to the point where the other lads noticed.

'Is that you half-inching Cassidy's stuff again, Gross?'

'We're mates,' Clifford would bleat. 'Share and share alike.'

'I catch you at my stuff, you'll get a boot up the backside.'

'I don't need your lousy stuff.'

And although he did have a comb, he would try to use Peter's, as if he didn't want to wear his own out. Peter took to hiding his comb, and Clifford told him it had disappeared.

'It hasn't disappeared, Clifford. I hid it in case anybody else decided to borrow it. Is your own comb all right?'

'I was only trying to help.'

Another of the lads, Julian Tregarth, used to listen to these exchanges, but without commenting, listening as if they were entertainments. Tregarth at first glance was a lousy soldier. Even when he was smart he looked slightly sloppy.

When his hair was short it somehow impersonated long hair. He didn't worry about things any more than Peter did, although he didn't seem to fit into the crowd, with his upper-crust accent. One of the lads, Pond, thought the accent was a scream, and even that the name was a scream.

'Julian? Ohmigawd, that ain't a name, it's more like a flippin' title, innit? That really your name, then?'

'Yes.' Julian smiled pleasantly.

'Better with a number than that.'

'Mm.'

'Hark at it, the Right Honourable Julian. Whatever was his dear old mum thinking about, then?'

'Do shut up, old chap.'

'Ow. Do shut up, old chap, his Lordship's ever so bored with us common five-eights.'

'Yes, I am, actually, so do shut up.'

'Or you'll make me, eh, Julian?'

'Up to you, old chap.'

'Our Julian's getting in a temper.'

'Two things I can't stand, old chap. A fucking bore, and a fucking snob. And you're both, old chap.'

'Me? A snob? Jesus Christ, listen to that.'

'Yes, old chap, you're a snob. Now are you going to shut up?'

'Awright, awright, I never meant nothing.'

'Good.'

It had been clever of Julian Tregarth not to be the first to catch the predatory eye of Clifford Gross. But no doubt he would have frozen any advances of The Gross, even if he did it awfully politely. Tregarth was not the kind to be exploited. When Clifford was hovering about, thinking of what he might borrow next, Tregarth sometimes looked across the hut and exchanged a glance with Peter, an odd glance that suggested he and Peter were in understanding about the absurdity of human behaviour.

'There's always one,' he said to Peter one day. 'There's one in every dorm too. Soft whining leeches, on the hunt for blood to suck.'

'Dorm? Boarding school?'

'I thought the la-di-da accent would have made that quite clear.'

'I never said it was la-di-da. When you had that chat with

291

Private Pond you used it like a club.'

'It sounds quite ordinary to me, actually. Everybody at Winchester speaks like this.'

'How utterly bizarre it must sound in the mass.'

'Insulting bastard.'

'Some of the lads think my accent is a joke as well.'

'It sounds quite jolly, actually, all those rolling Rs. There were a couple of Scottish chaps in my form at Winchester, but they spoke just like the rest of us.'

'They're déraciné Scots. The primal urge of the Scottish social climber. It's a form of inferiority complex, actually.'

'My God, words of two syllables.'

'My dear Tregarth,' Peter deliberately exaggerated the rolling Rs, 'the Scots invented universal education when your lot were still wearing skins and grunting.'

'We sound like a pair of stuck-up intellectuals.'

'I *am* a stuck-up intellectual.'

'Bloody good. Shall we mount an armed assault on a pub this weekend?'

'Do you think I'll be able to dodge Clifford the Gross?'

'Tell him to get stuffed.'

'He would burst into tears.'

'Oh, I couldn't stand that. I think I would break down completely and kick him in the groin.'

'In that case, wait till everybody else is there. We could sell tickets.'

'You know, Cassidy, you are a bloody softy.'

'I take after my mother, Tregarth.'

'Your mother's a softy?'

'Now I think of it, is she hell. But she's a bit of a softy too, I suppose. I would quite like to have some drinks at the weekend.'

If he got pally with Tregarth, some of the lads, like Pond, and Gross too, would probably think he was sucking up to the posh aristocracy. He decided he could put up with that. He found the top-drawer accent no more peculiar than any of the other assorted accents in the hut, and the confident Old Wykehamist looked like being more entertaining company than, for instance, Pond or Gross.

He was back to being a passivist, and he now knew the word well; the man who looked on with interest while other people did things. He observed, as from outside, the invincible way Clifford was preying on him, drinking his blood like an adenoidal Lugosi, and responded by simply hiding things.

'What are we doing on Saturday, Pete?' Clifford asked him. He had given up insisting that his name was Peter. He was talking some inflated nonsense with Julian Tregarth at the time, and Clifford had been hovering, like a vulture on a branch, waiting to break in.

'I'm going to look at some buildings in Leeds,' Peter said, at the same time as Julian was saying, 'Peter and I have an arrangement of seduction.'

'You're just making it up. I know when I'm not wanted. I'm quite interested in buildings, Peter.'

'No, you're not.'

'What are the girls like?'

'Oh God.'

There was no way of preventing him from getting on the same lorry and then on the same bus to Leeds, sitting behind them with his head shoved forward between them, to miss nothing. At the city centre, Peter checked his street map and set off at a brisk march, with Julian in step beside him, and Clifford trying to keep in line but having to dodge on and off the pavement.

They arrived, and Peter spread out his arms, making a gift of the view.

'Quarry Hill,' he said.

'Grubby,' said Julian.

'Oh, you would say that,' Clifford bleated.

'It's grubby, Gross.'

'Well, I think it's very architectural, Peter, whatever he says. It's nice.'

'It's not nice,' Peter explained. 'It's majestic, it's visionary, it's a feat of imaginative urban planning, but it's not NICE.'

'It's *quite* nice.'

'Jesus, I wish I was dead.'

'Are we meeting the women here?'

'Oh, you scrofulous boll weevil, Gross. You are not meeting any women.'

'Maybe they've got a pal, Tregarth. I wasn't talking to you.'

'You don't even know the first law of thermodynamics,

boy. Women never come in threes, only in twos.'

'That's right,' said Peter. 'And I don't fancy the one you're getting.'

'Mean bastards. I thought we were supposed to be mates.'

Peter left them scowling at each other and trotted away to accost a middle-aged woman and a young woman with a pram.

'Morning, ladies,' he said. The older woman smiled, but the younger looked wary.

'I've read a lot about the Quarry Hill flats. Do you live here, ladies?'

'Aye.'

'Is it as good as they say?'

'Too far to the shops,' the young woman said.

'Too big,' the older one said. 'Milly here likes it well enough, but I'm not modern, never was. I'd as soon have the old back-to-back, with shop at one corner and t'pub at t'other. This place is too much like a barracks for me. And it's grubby.'

'Maybe you'll like it when you get used to it.'

'Oh, we're glad enough of any place, son. You a Scotty?'

'Aye.'

'Well, we all have our troubles,' She smiled wickedly at him and he laughed in return. When he went back to the lads, Clifford smirked and asked, 'Did they give you the brush-off, then?'

'They don't seem very enthusiastic about Quarry Hill,' Peter said to Julian, and stared hard at the massive horseshoe block he had seen so often in photographs. 'But they'll come round to it. I'm sure it's a leap forward.'

'I wonder if the architect lives in one of the flats,' Julian muttered, and Clifford turned on him.

'That's daft, Tregarth. They're working-class flats.'

'That's the first bright remark we've had from the boll weevil, Peter. Where the hell does the architect live? Probably in a converted water-mill.'

'Water mills are damp,' Clifford explained.

'An interesting question, about where architects live, Tregarth. Ça me donne à penser furieusement. And talking about damp, this sightseeing is dry work. To the tavern.'

'I don't have much money,' Clifford protested.

'In that case,' said Julian, 'you won't get much drink, will you?'

Clifford churned.

Peter was perplexed by his visit to the architectural wonder he had always admired at second hand. The stucco walls were certainly a lot grubbier than they were in photographs, but that was a trivial problem. Julian's casual contempt for the place bothered him, and the talk with the two women nagged him too. He was upset because one of his idols had been impugned. He decided he would just have to go on thinking about it.

In the meantime Army life went on, and Clifford went on, and it was hard not to be openly unkind to him, because he was impervious, like a limpet in a hurricane.

Or if he wasn't really impervious, but aggrieved, he had his revenge, even if it wasn't meant as revenge. Strolling in the camp, Peter was frozen by the parade-ground voice of Sergeant Kent; turned and marched obediently to come to a smart halt in front of the sergeant.

'You got no moral fibre, Cassidy?' Even in a conversational tone, Kent could be heard at two hundred yards.

'No, Sar'nt.'

'I didn't give you permission to speak.'

'Sorry, Sar'nt.'

Kent was all right. He was a good drill sergeant, and he didn't pick too much on people, even on Clifford. He had all the cliché insults of the sergeant, but they were automatic rather than malicious.

'You got no ambition, Cassidy? I'm disappointed in you, Cassidy. I'm not saying you're good, there ain't one good man in this whole shower of shit. But I'm not saying you're bad.'

Peter kept his face at attention.

'You afraid of responsibility, Cassidy?'

No answer.

The sergeant nearly toned down his voice to informal level.

'Why don't you want to try for officer?'

'Permission to speak, Sar'nt.'

'I'm waiting to hear from you, Cassidy.'

'I don't know what you're talking about, Sar'nt.'

'You stand there and deny you refused to try for officer training, Cassidy?'

'I deny it, Sar'nt. I was never asked.'

'Christalmighty, it was your own bosom pal told me. No, he said, you told him straight you wanted nothing to do with officer training.'

'Private Gross, Sar'nt?'

'Who bloody else? Stand at ease. Stand easy. You mean you never said no such thing to that weaselly bleedin' bastard?'

'I admire your powers of description, Sar'nt. Private Gross is what you said.'

'Christ. I'd fill him in if I was you. Your class reports are first class, you got a bit of education for what it's worth. Do I give your name to the Colonel, then?'

'Yes, please, Sar'nt.'

'Don't sound too bleedin' eager, they don't like that. Right. I give your name, but don't get your hopes up. Dismiss. Oh.'

'Yes, Sar'nt.'

'You're not too bleedin' horrible. I'm not sayin' you're any good, but you're not too bleedin' horrible. Hmhmhm. Don't let me down, right?'

'Right, Sar'nt.'

Peter wasn't surprised to find Julian with him in the little group selected to go for officer selection. And he wasn't surprised at Clifford's accusatory sulks.

'Of course, we're not good enough for you,' was the last thing Clifford said on the last day. And the last thing he said to Clifford was, 'Clifford, you are absolutely fucking right.'

## 43

Life was once more just an acceptable routine, with day following uneventful day. If Meg still hungered for excitement, the hunger was only an acceptable part of the routine. Everybody in the world had some foolish hunger. And in the meantime there were some things to be grateful for.

She was selfishly glad the blitz was over – selfishly, because she wasn't thinking of people in Clydebank or Coventry or London, but only of Hetty. Hetty doubtless had other troubles. If she was involved with a man, no doubt that would include its own troubles. But she was safe from bombing.

Bobby was invalided out of the Air Force and still in Canada, and she was disappointed for him but glad. That was all a bit mysterious, something to do with a slight accident to a training plane, and his letter seemed to hide more than it explained, but he wasn't much of a hand at writing letters anyway, and the only thing that mattered was that he was alive and getting better. She missed his scruffy cheerfulness, but she was selfishly glad he was out of the fighting.

Peter was enjoying the Army. He had gone into it the way he went into everything, had never lost that sense of curiosity and wonder at everything, and he would hold his own. He was probably doing better than he admitted. His letters were chatty and cheery and often daft.

*I got a look at the sergeant's log book while he was out. Every day for a month he had written 'Tregarth drunk today.' Nothing about me except on the last day: 'Cassidy sober today.'*

Maybe the wee tinker was drinking too much right enough, like a lot of Servicemen, but she didn't believe it. At least he would never get fighting drunk and into trouble, it wasn't his style. But under the daft jokes she had the idea he was doing all right. Maybe he was saving up a surprise for her. That was his style.

And John was in the American Army, but he was an engineering officer and he was still in America, and even if they sent him overseas, engineering sounded safe; not the kind of job where people had to run across battlefields and get shelled or bombed. Something nice and clean like sitting in an office designing bridges. She had a great hunger to see John, so long away and so quiet and remote when he left. But she could put up with that too.

Andy was a beautiful surprise. He had changed like a butterfly out of a chrysalis, his Andrea was besotted with him and even tried to imitate his working-class accent, but he was absorbing more of hers than she of his, and he didn't sound false-genteel, which Meg would have hated. He was only speaking better, and learning.

The way they looked at each other, it was surprising they hadn't started a family yet, they gave off sex like heat from a furnace. But there was time enough for a family, and it was good to be able to enjoy all that fine madness without being plunged too soon into bringing up babies. And the Cunninghams were fine too. Sir Robert was shy and sometimes awkward, but he liked Andy fine and seemed to have no reservations about having a factory worker for a son-in-law. Meg had had some apprehensions about that. It was all very well for a member of the landed gentry to be an intellectual Socialist with all the right principles about the equality of man, but it might have been a different matter when it came to his daughter. Well, it didn't bother Sir Robert. And Margaret, Lady Cunningham, was quite delightful, slowed down with arthritis and often in pain, but really a very earthy woman, sometimes as coarse as Vickie Fairhurst, in her well-spoken way.

It was odd that the women she particularly liked had a strong streak of coarseness, and she wondered if it was rubbing off on herself. She didn't worry. And even if she couldn't take Andy's political enthusiasms as seriously as he did, she had pride in a daughter-in-law who had gone to jail for her principles. That meant good smeddum and good guts, whether the lassie was a princess or a peasant. Meg's own life might be uneventful, but she could bear that.

She was walking home from the tram, in the evening summer sunshine, when she heard a wolf-whistle. Somebody whistling at a girl. She walked on, and it sounded again. She looked round and saw a soldier following her with long strides, a silly boy who had taken her for a younger woman from the back view. She smiled at his silliness and turned away. He whistled again. She turned to shoo him away and he was on her and picking her off the ground in his arms. An American.

'Are you Britishers all deaf?'

'Oh!' She was exasperated for an instant before she burst into tears. 'Oh, God is good. My beautiful boy. John John John John John.'

'My beautiful mother.'

'I could kill you.'

'It's the uniform. It gets all the girls like that.'

'Put me down at once.'

'No.'

'John, people will see us.'

'The hell with the people.'

'Yes, the hell with them.'

The routine day had exploded like a sunburst. When she took him upstairs she had a crazy compulsion to stroke his lapels, she couldn't stop touching him and his beautiful uniform. He smiled quietly and let her do it.

'You are completely ravishing, Mother.'

'You've got an American accent.'

'I can lose it if you like.'

'No, don't. I love it. I love everything about you, John, it was wicked of you not to warn me. My old working clothes, as well. I am not ravishing, you are only remembering what I was like long ago.'

'People do not quibble with a major in the US Army.'

'I will not quibble another quibble. Would you like coffee, or a drink?'

'Nothing. Put on some clothes and I'll get a taxi and take you out to dinner.'

'Oh yes, you Yankees can always get the taxis, you devils. I'm not going out to dinner, I'm not sharing you with other people. You will stay here and take pot luck and tell me every single thing that has happened to you every single minute since you deserted us. What is Boston like? What is New York like? You've filled out in the chest.' He was smiling happily. 'And the way I am going on you will never get a word in edgeways.'

'And you still sound exactly the same, Mother. Like a breeze blowing over the islands.'

'Oh, the smooth lying tongue of it.' Life was glorious. 'I think there is a wee drop of Scotch whisky in the house, if you like the stuff.'

'Here is a big drop of Scotch whisky, Mother. I can take it or leave it, but it's a historic occasion.'

'You will stay the night, John.'

'I will stay the night. The liberation of Europe can wait.'

So she drank with him, and ate with him, and talked with him, in a pleasant delirium, and tried to see the streets of New York and the yellow cabs and the Brooklyn Bridge and the Staten Island Ferry and the huge scale of the Massachusetts Institute of Technology, and it was no more use than flipping through a guide book because she couldn't see beyond himself. He seemed so big. But he was still John, the quiet one who seemed to know everything; but more so, older and stronger.

'There's always been something in you, John,' she said. 'Something very nice, and wise, and I have never been able to name it myself.'

'I'm just myself, Mother.'

'Nonsense, it is more than that. No. Maybe that is what it is. A lot of people are not themselves at all, at all. You are.'

'Maybe it's just that you love me, Mother.'

'Maybe it is, because I do. And I must let you get to bed.'

'Yes, Mother. It's good to be home.'

Something was always happening, something and then something else. Life was good.

It was after two when they went to bed, and that was the morning, in the small hours, when there was a banging at the door, and she started up thinking of that wretched Mr Jardine the Air Raid Warden. But it was two policemen on the landing. She was fully awake.

'Margaret Mason?'

'Yes.'

'You are the owner of the house at number eleven Carrbridge Terrace, Glasgow E1?'

'I take care of it for my children.'

'I am arresting you on a charge of keeping a disorderly house.'

'You'd better come into the house and off the landing. This is simply foolishness.'

'I must warn you that anything you say will be taken down

300

and may be given in evidence.'

'It is still foolishness. I don't even live there.'

'Just get dressed, Missus, and don't give us the patter.'

John appeared, in trousers and socks, pulling on his jacket, and after a glance at him the first policeman looked at his mate and said, 'Uhuh.'

'What does Uhuh mean?' Meg asked.

'You cater for the Yanks here as well, eh?'

'This is my son.'

'Oh, aye.' The policemen exchanged knowing nods. John looked them up and down, and said, 'I hope you're not suggesting my mother is a liar, officer.'

'You keep out of this, Yank.' The policeman sounded less sure of himself. 'It's got nothing to do with you.'

'It has a hell of a lot to do with me, officer.'

'Insulting language, eh?' said the second policeman.

'I'm sorry if the word offended you, officer. It used to be quite common in Glasgow. What is going on? In fact, what the hell is going on?'

'I am under arrest, John. I'll get my clothes on.'

'Okay. I'll ride to the station with you.'

'You're not riding with us, Yank,' said the first policeman.

'No,' Meg said. 'Get your brother Andy, John. It is all some kind of stupid mistake.'

'Okay, Mother.'

She could hear the silence in the kitchen as she dressed, could picture John just standing, easily, saying nothing, till one of the policemen couldn't keep quiet.

'We don't want any trouble from you, Yank.'

'You'll get no trouble from me. At this stage.'

'You threatening us?'

John laughed, his quiet easy laugh.

'Nope.'

He was actually amused. He came downstairs and stood in the close, in his stocking soles, while she had a completely new experience. She was put into the Black Maria; and not gently.

Suddenly, the policeman who had pushed her in was against the door of the van, with John's hand at his throat.

'You goosed my mother,' John said. 'I'm not sure whether I should kill you.'

He fell out of sight as the other policeman's truncheon came down on his head.

She had never seen the inside of a police station, and she tried to stay alert, to remember everything. But now she had lost her composure and her confidence, and her impressions were confused. The sergeant at the desk laboriously wrote, and accepted her valuables and put them in a drawer. John, breathing deeply and saying nothing, had been led away.

'This is simply foolishness,' she told the sergeant. 'I don't even live in the house, and I have nothing to do with it.' All the time she was standing there, one of the policemen was gripping her cuff, as if she might try to escape.

'All finished, Sergeant?' A policewoman built like a footballer was at her side. The sergeant nodded, and the woman took her elbow. There was no need to drag her anywhere. She tried to shake off the woman's hand. The grip tightened. She was half-pushed into an open cell, and as she tried to turn to speak to the policewoman she was pushed powerfully into it and the door closed behind her. The cell didn't have bars, like cells she had seen in the pictures. It was just a little room with a solid door, and a plank bed with a dirty blanket, and a chamber pot.

Well, she thought, this has certainly been an eventful day.

In the morning, the door was opened, and a man she had never seen came in.

'I expected my son,' she said.

'He got me out of bed.' The man was not in a good temper, and not too wide awake. 'My name is Makepeace. I'll represent you, if you agree.'

'I suppose somebody had better. And I don't see anybody else.'

'It's a first offence. It shouldn't be more than a fine.'

She stared at him in disgust.

'It is not a first offence, Mr Makepeace. It is not an offence at all.'

'It is a disorderly house. There's no question about that.'

'It is not my house, Mr Makepeace. I don't live in it, I have nothing to do with it. It is occupied by a Mrs Margaret Somerville, as a tenant.'

'Who doesn't pay rent.'

'Maybe she doesn't. I left all that to the lawyer. I have nothing to do with the woman.'

'Mrs Mason, let's not make it complicated. Mrs Somerville has already told the police she was only looking after the house for you, for a few days, as a favour, and she had nothing to do with whoever came in or out.'

'She is a lying bitch, Mr Makepeace. Forgive the word.'

'Well, they believe her.'

'Maybe you do.'

'I think we can get off with a fine,' he said.

'Are you supposed to be on my side, Mr Makepeace?'

'I'm doing the best I can for you, Mrs Mason. You're not helping much.'

'In the name of God, are you telling me I might go to prison?'

'It's not very likely for a first offence. We'll do our best. It's pretty routine, you know that well enough.'

'I must say I am greatly impressed with you, Mr Makepeace.'

## 44

Most of the business of officer training failed to impress Peter, and the high-pressure parade-ground exercises and cross-country ordeals impressed him least of all.

'I suppose it's a way of sickening some people into giving up,' he suggested to Julian. 'It doesn't matter whether the wrong people give up or not, as long as they reduce the numbers.'

'You're criticising centuries of experience of the British Army, Cassidy. The officer must be a super-soldier.'

'Uhuh, that's right. What this stuff does is produce super-privates. The officer has to be a different kind of creature from a private. He's not supposed to snap to attention at an order. He's supposed to give orders and watch other people snap to attention.'

'I snapped today. I think I've broken my spine in three places.'

'You are a sloppy soldier, Tregarth. Here, I like that as well. Second names all the time. That's not British. It's English. It's a fetish of the English bourgeoisie. In Scotland, where we've got a genuine civilisation, if you call a man by his second name he'll tell you to raffle yourself.'

'I'd be delighted, but who would buy the tickets? Your damned Scottish education will be your ruin, you know. They cram your brains. We English don't hold with that sort of thing. We believe in games, and the team spirit, and flogging, and fagging. Things that build character.'

'They ran out of bricks when they were building yours, Tregarth.'

'True, true,' Julian said complacently. 'Have you noticed how difficult it is to get a good slanging match with any of those other nose-to-the-grindstone peasants? By the way, do you smoke?'

'You know I don't smoke. Why, do they disapprove of smoking?'

'Heavens, laddie, no, a British officer is expected to have all the manly vices.'

'I've chucked all the manly vices. I don't want warts on my palm.'

'Egad, do they teach you that in bonny Scotland too? Astounding.'

'And you can go blind as well.'

'Yes. I don't care, you know. I can always sell matches at street corners. No, I know a chap who was dropped from the course, dropped like the proverbial, old boy, because he went to one of those jolly selection weekends at a country house, and offered a major a Woodbine from the packet, instead of from a silver cigarette case.'

'Jesus, how utterly low-class. He must have been some form of guttersnipe.'

'Probably a Scotsman.'

'A Scotsman wouldn't waste a Woodbine on a major. Let the bastards buy their own.'

'We really are rather a witty pair of swine. Cassidy, aren't we?'

'I am rather a witty pair of swine. You are my sounding board, as befits a member of an inferior race.'

'Jolly clever, that, the way you disguise your national inferiority complex.'

They went to the jolly selection weekend at rather a jolly big country house, and Peter simply let it happen. It could nearly have been a chapter from an English detective story, with a gong for dressing and a gong for dinner, and standing around before dinner with sherry. They served sparse wartime food but with a full array of cutlery. There were no jolly English girls to play tennis with, and *never mention a lady's name in the mess.* Julian warned him about that, but he couldn't think of a lady's name anyway. He did play a little tennis, neither too well nor too badly, and accepted conversation from the officers on the staff on any subject they chose. He never mentioned politics or religion or sex; though he did confess he had been raised in a Presbyterian family, and slightly dishonestly revealed that his mother's 'people' were from the Islands and that she still had connections there. 'People' was the right word, and 'connections' could mean anything from a drunken uncle to a 100,000-acre estate.

He wanted to be an officer. He wasn't sure why, but he learned, when Major Stimson casually waved him to join a table for afternoon tea, where there was nobody but Major Stimson and old Fillimore, a semi-retired major-general who had managed to hang on to the Army by presiding over the country house selection programme.

'Enjoying the weekend, eh?' Stimson asked the question in such a friendly way that it was obviously a serious interview.

'Rather, sir,' said Peter. 'A lot of very decent chaps.'

Old Fillimore just listened, and humphed and cleared his throat, in a silly-old-buffer way that was clearly a pose.

'Think you'll make a good officer?'

'I'm not sure I'm the best judge of that, sir. I would certainly try.'

'Good, good.' They drank tea and ate tiny sandwiches, and Peter didn't spill anything or break anything. He was more interested in old Fillimore than in Stimson. The old man's eyes were very pale blue, and watery, but they were sharp.

'Absolute fairness is one quality an officer must have, Cassidy. Are you fair-minded?'

'I think so, sir. Of course, most people think they are fair, so probably anybody would answer yes.'

'That's a bit evasive.'

'Yes sir.'

Old Fillimore humphed into his droopy moustache.

'Tell me, Cassidy,' said Stimson, 'why do you want to be an officer?'

And suddenly Peter knew why.

'Because my mother would be delighted, sir.'

Fillimore actually guffawed. Stimson was not amused.

'Your mother would be . . . what sort of answer is that? I've never heard that answer in all my life in the Army. I would have thought . . . you wanted more responsibility?'

'Oh, that would be all right, sir. I've never had much responsibility, but I wouldn't mind.'

'Your mother would be . . . Cassidy, are you what we call a mother's boy?'

'Yes, sir, I suppose I am. I'm very fond of my mother. I'm very fond of girls too, but I'm very fond of my mother, and she would be delighted.'

Stimson found this very hard to digest. The major-general's chin had sunk into his chest and his eyelids were drooping. Peter drank tea and looked alert.

'How does our modern Army strike you, Cassidy?'

'Quite well, sir.'

'Oh? That is really generous of you, Cassidy. You mean it's not perfect?'

'I don't think it's perfect, sir.'

'Really. Perhaps you can tell us something you don't approve of. I would really be most grateful, most humbly grateful, to have your suggestions.'

'I realise you're being humorous, sir. I enjoy the Army, really. I believe the American Army has crêpe-soled boots.'

'The American Army is hardly an army as we know it, Cassidy. Crêpe-soled boots? Do you think we should go into battle as if it was some kind of palais-de-danse?'

'No sir. But I have thought that if soldiers were running down a street looking for enemies in hiding, they shouldn't make a lot of noise, sir. I'm sorry, I realise I don't have any experience of warfare.'

'Evidently. What was your civilian job?'

'I was a student of architecture, sir.'

'Not of boots.'

'No sir.'

'Quite.'

Peter realised he was being dismissed, and begged to be excused. He could feel Stimson's eyes on his back as he left. He didn't hear Stimson snorting to Fillimore.

'Crêpe-soled boots. A bit of active service and cold steel should cure that young man of his impertinence.'

'Mphm.' Fillimore spoke for the first time. 'If you don't recognise a bit of spunk when you see it, Stimson, maybe a bit of active service would be good for you.'

'I'd like nothing better, sir.' Stimson was startled and pale.


Julian received Peter's report of the interview with derision.

'You have consigned yourself by express post to the waiting arms of Clifford the Gross,' he said. 'A mother's boy indeed. I suppose I'm one too, the old lady is rather a brick. But the overtones of effeminacy, Cassidy. Actually, the old man is all right too. He told me that when he was up in Cambridge back in the distant twenties, he was considered a bit effeminate because he went about with the girls instead of sticking with the chaps and drinking manly beer.'

'Are you going to Cambridge?'

'I'm probably going to my doom, old man, leaping out of the trenches waving a revolver and getting shot between the eyes in the first three seconds. But you're going back to Clifford the Gross. I get the best bargain, really.'

But when the weekend was over, Peter was rescued from the waiting arms of Clifford by a cryptic posting that sent him for technical training to the other side of the country, urgently.

'Lucky swine,' Julian told him. 'You'll probably spend the rest of the war in a warehouse, counting ATS knickers.'

'The posting is to advanced technical training, Tregarth.'

'What could be more advanced than counting ATS knickers?'

'True enough, especially if the odd pair still has an ATS girl inside it.'

'Swine. You could probably leave me your home address, or something, in case we ever want to get in touch, or maybe you'd rather not bother.'

'Don't be bloody embarrassed about it, I will. Come any time. You'll like my mother. I suppose she's a brick too. What a stupid English description for a woman.'

'Mm. Well, at least from now on I'll be mixing with decent upper-middle-class English chaps with no intellectual nonsense. Chaps who've been flogged.'

'Good healthy perverts.'

'Exactly so, boy. You know, I never got flogged, but I sometimes think about it, only it's being done by a girl who works in a café at home, and she's not doing it too fiendishly, she's taking a long time sort of inspecting me. I think I must have a diseased mind or something.'

'Of course you have. It's the English disease.'

'Do you really think so, Peter? Christ. I don't want to be diseased.'

Peter looked at him in surprise, and decided he was serious. He laughed.

'For God's sake, Julian. There was a girl at my school, called Ella Greenlees—'

'—A very peculiar name for a school, I must say.'

'—And I once dreamt that she was my teacher, and she was giving me six of the best on the hands, but she had opened my flies so that she could watch it jumping every time she hit me.'

'Christ, mine just jumped. You're kidding me, you made that up.'

'I couldn't make that up, except in the murky depths of the unconscious.'

'What a relief. Honestly, Peter, what a relief. You think a lot of quite normal people have these perfectly ghastly ideas?'

'Sure. We had an actual teacher at Whitehill, she wore very tight skirts and silk stockings—'

'Why the hell did I go to Winchester?'

'Because you are English, and therefore stupid, Tregarth, and kindly don't interrupt while I'm trying to recapture the magic of that teacher with the tight skirts and silk stockings, oh God, Julian, no wonder I learned French. For months I had her every night as a slave, obeying orders in perfect French. Sometimes I was cruel to her, in a refined French manner. A lot of ritual stripping went on, in French, of course.'

'My god, that's a relief, Cassidy. I'm not a unique monster of depravity.'

'You're not a unique anything, Tregarth, you're the product of an English public school conveyor belt. You know I had to go to the Public Library for a decent French dictionary that had all the anatomical words they leave out of French grammars? Phrases like "Kindly bare your left breast, girl" sound a lot more evil in French.'

'My mind is at ease, Cassidy. I wish you hadn't told me about that teacher's tight skirt, all the same.'

Camp X was very un-Army. It was really quite serious and studious, and fascinating.

'Didn't quite make the officer selection process, Mother,' he wrote home. 'The Top Brass realised that my intelligence would be a problem in the routine officers' mess where words of two syllables can cause blind panic and lose the war. Instead I have been plucked out and deposited in a job so Top Secret even the instructors are bound and gagged, and we have to wear earplugs in case we hear them mumbling. In fact, I'm being trained as Britain's new horror weapon. As soon as you've read this letter, destroy it, memorise it and then burn your head. But not at once. I haven't heard much from the home front lately. Please let me have your conventional news so that I can feel something ordinary is going on somewhere. Much love. Peter.'

Meg's letter in reply was cheery and frivolous.

# 45

The Court appearance in the morning was not like the dramatic court scenes she had seen in films. The clerk read the charge without interest ... *contrary to the Criminal Law Amendment Act of 1885, as revised ... that being the proprietor or the agent of the proprietor of the dwelling house at number ... did knowing permit or cause said dwelling house to be used for the purposes of prostitution, and that on separate occasions, namely ...*

The judge looked unwell, and uninterested too. He glanced at Makepeace, who stood up and said, 'Not guilty.'

The judge was surprised.

'Oh. Oh well, as you please.'

'These are my instructions, sir.'

'In that case you're following them. All right, remitted to the Sheriff Court.' He waved a weary hand.

An hour later, after another ride in the Black Maria, she found herself going through a repeat performance in the Sheriff Court, where the only touch of drama was provided by legal robes and wigs.

'Not guilty, My Lord.'

'Very well. Trial is fixed for . . .' There were muttered consultations between judge and lawyers. '. . . One month from the day. The twenty-fifth. Bail is fixed at one hundred pounds.'

'A hundred pounds, My Lord?' It was the first time Makepeace had sounded awake.

'A hundred pounds.'

'Thank you, My Lord.'

Andy and John were waiting for her in the corridor.

'John! I thought you were still in jail.'

'Ah, I was on before you, Mother. Choking a cop isn't as serious as keeping a house of pleasure.'

'Silly bastard,' Andy said cheerfully. 'They don't like jailing Allied officers, it looks bad. He was damned lucky to get off with a caution.'

'Andy, Andy,' said John, 'I did tell the judge I was bringing counter-charges of sexual assault. He nearly had a baby.'

She let them take care of everything and lead her out to a

taxi, in which they sat squeezed beside her, each holding one of her hands without speaking on the way home. Dan Cassidy and Andrea were waiting for them there, and there was a scuffle of hugging.

'Oh, the lumpen proles, the bloody lumpen proles,' Dan muttered.

'Thanks for coming, Dan,' Andy said awkwardly. 'It was good of you.'

'We're on the same side this time, son,' Dan muttered.

'Yep. Yep. Give us a drink, somebody, for God's sake.'

'The condemned woman drank a hearty breakfast.' Meg laughed.

'Jesus H. Christ,' John said. 'Yeah, have a drink, have a laugh.' It was the first time she could remember seeing John in the grip of a strong emotion, a boiler trying not to explode.

'Makepeace is a useless shit,' Andy said. 'I've told him to call in a barrister from Edinburgh for the trial anyway.'

'That would cost a fortune, Andy,' Meg complained. 'Nobody can believe I have anything to do with a thing like this.'

'We can't believe it, Mother, but it's other people we have to think about. If it comes to a trial we'll offer a defence of impeachment against that bloody woman. And we'll roast these bloody cops as well.'

'That I do want to see,' said John.

'Listen, why should it get to trial, Andy?' Dan Cassidy demanded. 'I know it's lousy Capitalist justice, but when they look at the evidence they'll never go on with it. I can give you half a dozen neighbours that can tell you they've never seen Meg near the place in months.'

'Negative evidence, Dan. Anyway, they'll say she could have been running the place by remote control.'

'Stop all this,' Meg said flatly. 'I am innocent, and I will put myself in God's hands.'

'Oh God,' said Dan Cassidy. 'Him? Oh all right. If he's there at all, he'll pull out all the stops for you, Meg. Maybe he'll send down a forty-day flood.'

'There is no need for blasphemy, Dan. Anyway, a forty-day flood would be terrible indiscriminate. A thunderbolt would be quite sufficient.'

'Aye. Or a plague of boils.'

Meg was laughing again, a bit shakily.

'You know, Dan, that is a wicked unchristian thought, and I am ashamed of myself for thinking what a good idea it would be.'

There was no sense in staying away from work while she waited for the trial. The charge had not been reported in the papers, and most of the people at Rolls Royce lived far enough away to know nothing of local gossip. But there was local gossip.

She once saw Mr Jardine, the Air Raid Warden, in the street, and he smirked and nodded, but if he had meant to speak to her, the look she gave him shut him up. If some of the neighbours were beginning to look at her sideways, or avoiding her, she refused to notice. It was only natural that respectable people should worry about having a whoremistress among them. But she couldn't help remembering the poor folk in Ardyne Street, 'that Ardyne Street mob', who had rallied round her as a stranger when she had been in trouble and in fear of the law. After her struggle to lift her family out of poverty and into a decent style of living, she found it painful to reflect that respectability itself might be a kind of sin because it could be a denial of compassion.

Dan agreed, of course, and certainly Dan did not abandon her. Prostitution itself, he explained, was only another symptom of the sickness of Capitalism, which put a price on everything and devalued everything, and reduced women to an economic condition where their bodies were the only means of exchange left to them.

'Oh, Dan, Dan, you are such a boy,' she said. 'Of course there is no prostitution in Russia, because every man is big and handsome and all the girls are beautiful. There is nobody too ugly to get a girl of his own without paying her. I wonder if there is another reason for prostitution, and the reason is that some girls would rather pass the time that way than stand in a factory making tractors.'

'Oho, now we have the good Christian advocating sin.'

'No, but I am not casting the first stone either. And that is a sin that did not worry Jesus too much. He did tell one prostitute to go and sin no more, but he didn't make a great song and dance about it.'

It was a time when a woman should have been able to find

comfort in her church, but she had the wrong ministers for
that. On an impulse, and a little apprehensively, she visited
Father Mann, and was warmly welcomed.

'I hope you're not seeking absolution,' he said. 'I've only
got whisky for infidels.'

'No, Father, I am not seeking either.'

'I don't want to flatter myself that you came for a word of
comfort, but if I can think of one, you're welcome to it, Meg.
Meg, man is born to trouble as the sparks fly upwards. God
gave you the strength to live through it. It's a great gift.'

'Oh, I sometimes think we get what we deserve, Father. If
I'm not guilty of this thing, and I am not, no doubt I have
plenty of other sins to make up for it.'

'I can't believe they're very black.'

'Ah, you don't know me, Father, you don't know me at
all. A woman may sin in her heart, and just not have the
courage to do it in the open.'

'I was never too worried about the sins of the heart, Meg.
They're just sent to try us. Where's the merit in virtue if
you're never tempted?'

'Very good, and very Jesuitical, Father. You are a
comfort to a wicked woman.'

'Ach, you're boasting, Meg, you haven't the talent for
wickedness. And you'll have a dram, so that I'm not
drinking alone. I wouldn't wonder you'll be playing the
harp quite the thing while I'm shovelling coal.'

'Och, I would put in a good word for you, Father. Heaven
would be a dull place without a few whisky priests round the
doors. You have cheered me up this night, and God will not
overlook that.'

But the thing lay heavy on her. *All that we know who lie in
jail is that the walls are strong, and that each day is like a year,
a year whose days are long* . . . She couldn't remember who
had written that. On Saturday, she decided, she would go to
a bookshop and buy a dictionary of quotations.

They might even let her take it into prison with her.

Three weeks passed. Andy arrived at Rolls Royce and
asked for her. He wasn't allowed inside the factory, but
when she saw him standing outside the wire gate he had both
thumbs up, and she broke into a run.

'It's finished,' he said. 'No trial. Forget it.'

'How, Andy?'

'Never mind now, I haven't got time. Tell him to open the gate and let you out. I'm entitled to a cuddle for being a clever boy.'

She went into his arms and was smothered.

'Andy Mason,' she complained, 'you came all these miles just to tell me. You could have telephoned a message.'

'And got everybody at the factory gossiping?'

'That is nonsense,' she said, 'you could have left a cryptic message, like the pursuit had been abandoned—' she giggled suddenly, '—or the lotus blossom is flying northward, or something silly like that.'

'Oh, Mother, Mother, I wanted to see your face when I told you. I wanted to see you laughing in earnest, and crying.'

'And I am doing both. But how did it happen?'

'Oh, I'm just an ordinary miracle worker. I went to see the Procurator Fiscal and he went through the roof when I told him about the Somerville bitch. Makepeace is livid about a layman interfering in the law, but stuff him. Now, Mother. I've always wanted to do something to impress you. Are you impressed?'

'You always impressed me, Andy.'

'And we're pregnant as well.'

'You are turning me into an old woman. A granny. But at least you will not have to bring the baby to visit me in prison.'

'Pity, that. It would be something for the kid to remember.'

'I will still buy a dictionary of quotations.'

'What the hell are you talking about, Mother?'

'Mind you, I was quite looking forward to reading it in peace, in a prison cell.'

'I will never understand you, Mother. I'm going to chuck trying. Anyway, we did it. I saw your lawyer, your Mr Ferris, and we got affidavits from everybody, it was all rubbish, the whole charge.'

'But what will happen to Mrs Somerville? She has been keeping a disorderly house, Andy.'

'Frankly, my dear, I don't give a damn. But we'll get her out of there pretty damn quick. You should move in there, Mother, it belongs to the kids.'

'Maybe I should. It's a sin to leave a house empty. And it might be a mercy to be away from the neighbours in Alexandra Parade.'

'Oh, hell. I just thought of something. I'll have to move in with you for a few weeks. You'll have Yankee sailors banging the door every night looking for their oats. Hey, we could put a big nameplate on the door, eh . . . the Convent of St Cecilia or something. Christ, no, that would be worse. They would all think they were onto a nun.'

It was good to laugh, a slightly coarse laugh. It possibly meant that she was growing up.

# 46

PETER

History may decide . . . I must avoid pompous clichés. What I mean is that maybe the Great War of 1914 to 1918 was a watershed. It isn't my idea at all, that's the truth. I got it from Martin Rackers, my instructor in the secret establishment Somewhere in England. We never got much about the Great War in school history, we were too busy with Mary Queen of Scots and the Battle of Naseby and the American War of Independence and all that stuff.

What Martin said was that in the Great War, troops were expendable. Martin wasn't really a sergeant, Army type. He was a boffin with sergeant's stripes. He said that in the Great War, a field marshal could decide that he would have to sacrifice 10,000 troops next morning to capture three yards of mud on No Man's Land, then throw them away and order another 10,000 from Stores. The General Strike in 1926, and the rise of the Labour movement, finished all that. Generals in this war wouldn't want casualties, because the voters wouldn't stand for it. Most of the troops in the war would never have to duck a bullet at all. Martin was a yachtsman, and he said war was about the same as sailing. You were either bored to death, or scared to death, or drunk.

Martin Rackers taught me an awful lot, actually. He hated mobs, and he hated bullies, and he said he had once been in hospital, and the nurses were nice, but some of them were a bit above themselves too, because the patients were helpless. And he had divided the human race into two types, by calculating which nurses he would want as his jailers if he lived in a police state. He was telling me something I had always known without knowing I knew it. Martin Rackers was great, actually, and he was a great teacher. I was sorry to finish the course with him, but I was needed urgently in the Hebrides. We both knew what urgent meant in the Army. They rushed you at a second's notice to somewhere and then you would wait for months till they found something for you to do.

The only thing that annoyed me was that I didn't get an

hour to stop in Glasgow and see Mother. I was needed urgently.

Now I don't believe in mysticism or ESP or anything like that; but I had the strangest feeling about going to the Hebrides, the Islands, as if there was a destiny in it, as if there were more things in heaven and earth than I dreamt of in my philosophy. No doubt because the Island I was going to was Duna, where Mother was born. I dismissed this feeling, naturally, as a temporary aberration.

Anyway, it didn't start off very hopefully. I got there in a little fishing boat that had become part of Army Transport, and there was a skinny soldier waiting for me at the jetty. He said his name was Morris Stone, but that everybody called him Ikey because he was a Jew.

'Is it all right if I call you Morris?' I asked him.

'Suit yourself. You'll only annoy the Sergeant.'

This guy was not friendly at all. But he had been waiting for me in the rain, and we had to walk back to the station in the rain, and he didn't want to talk. I just shut up.

There were a dozen men on this station, including Sergeant Wellesley. It was only a big cottage, probably a gamekeeper's house or something, with a lot of outhouses. One of the outhouses was locked, and two of the men were posted outside it with rifles, and gas capes, in the pouring rain, as if it was Buckingham Palace. That was where the Equipment was stored. Maybe the Sergeant thought that a German spy disguised as a sheep would break in and steal the Equipment.

The Sergeant slept in another outhouse, with a big open fireplace and plenty of peat to burn. The boys all slept in the cottage, except Morris, who had a cot in another shed without a fireplace. I didn't ask any questions. I reported to Sergeant Wellesley.

There had been a lieutenant in charge of the station, but he had got enteric fever, or maybe foot-and-mouth, and had been taken away, and now the Sergeant had his own command. He was off his head. Sergeant Wellesley was a career soldier, straight from an orphan home into the service, and he was Captain Bligh. He organised two hours' drill every morning, so that if the Nazis invaded we could form a Thin Red Line and die to the last man singing Rule Britannia. He didn't like foreigners, including Scotties,

318

especially the Scotties on the Island who spoke gibberish. He had served on the North-West Frontier, and I thought he fancied the occasional punitive raid on the villages, hanging the headman and keeping the natives in order and preserving the Empire.

I asked to see the Equipment, which was why I was there, and he said I was there to obey orders, I would be on cook duty next day.

He told me Ikey had his bunk in the shed because if he slept with the other lads they might give him a hard time, him being a Yid. I said I would share Ikey's room because there was more space in it. He squinted at me and probably decided I was a crypto-Jew, but okay.

Ikey didn't welcome me, but at least I knew he wouldn't be another Clifford Gross and bore me to death. I didn't care.

I did the cooking next day. That was all right. The boat brought rations for thirty men, because there had once been thirty men at the station, and the Sergeant hadn't got round to correcting that bit of paperwork. There were also local regulations. Everybody chipped in five shillings to the weekend booze kitty. No fraternisation with the natives. Take the mickey out of Yids. Stay away from the Equipment shed except when on guard. I just kept my head down and watched and listened.

In the afternoon, we had exercises. These consisted of going together to a distant spot on the island, and then being sent off in different directions to race back to the station. The Sergeant marked up the scores and pinned them on the wall.

Three of the lads didn't have to do the exercises. Rackman, Steele and Corcoran. They took turns at starting the races and then coming home by bike. They were Sergeant Wellesley's trusties. They were genuine primitives, and they didn't know what to make of me. I was simply polite to them.

About a week after I arrived, I had to do my guard duty outside the Equipment shed. I was relieved at two a.m. and went back to my billet and just walked in and found Ikey on the floor, with Elastoplast over his mouth, and Rackman holding his arms, and Corcoran raping him. Rackman jumped back, and Corcoran desisted. Morris rolled away and pulled the plaster from his mouth. It was quite

319

interesting how my basic training worked – I cocked my rifle and I had the bayonet pointing at Rackman's guts.

The Jewish bastard was asking for it, he said. And Don't try anything, he said. And, Not a fucking word about this, he said, or you'll get yours.

I left the door open, and to hell with the blackout, and I stepped aside, and told them both to get out. I didn't plan to kill either of them. I kept the muzzle pointed at testicle height. They hated that. Corcoran was still buttoning up as he backed out.

Next time, Corcoran said, you won't have your rifle, Cassidy.

Next time, I said, you won't have your balls, Corcoran, and move, this finger is twitchy.

I felt marvellously calm and cold.

Morris was still on the floor, panting and wide-eyed.

I suppose you think I wanted it, he said.

If you wanted it, I said, they wouldn't have taped your mouth and held you down. And I asked him how long it had been going on.

Just twice, he said, but I think the Sergeant fancies it as well. The last time it was Rackman and Steele. What the hell do you care?

I told him I cared because he was a mate, and Rackman and Steele and Corcoran were Fascist bastards. And I said I refused to call him Ikey because his name was Morris. And I told him that if he wasn't a yellow bastard, we were going to fix Rackman and Steele and Corcoran.

He said they were too big. I said if he wasn't willing to take them on he was a snivelling Yid and he could take what was coming to him.

They'll kill us, he said.

If they do, we'll kill them back.

Bastards bastards bastards bastards, he said, they've ruined me.

They've only buggered you about, I said. They've ruined themselves.

Next day we went out on one of our heroic exercises, and Morris and I were sent off in different directions. We joined up after a few hundred yards and lay in the heather beside the path till Corcoran came along on his bike, and I was up like a rocket with the rifle at his chest.

Don't fucking try anything, Cassidy, he said, and then gasped and fell on the bike because Morris was at his back and had given him the rifle butt across his kidneys.

Morris was smiling. He was a different Morris. If I hadn't held up a hand he would have beaten Corcoran to death. Corcoran was trying to breathe, to speak, to stay alive, and finally said We'll get you both for this.

Do what you like, I said, but if you do, and if you even mention this to anybody, we'll lie in wait for you if it takes a year and we'll castrate you. My brother's a vet, and I've helped him do it to dogs. We'll do it. And I've got relatives on this island. If anything happens to me you'll end up face down in the ocean.

But you'll be castrated first, Morris said, you filthy pervert.

We left him lying on the path and we still got back first to the billet. Morris could run like a whippet.

Next day it was Rackman's turn. We got him beside a ruined cottage, and we were starting another conversation, while he lay on his back and gasped, when a white-haired man shoved me aside, a civilian.

The one with the big ears, the civilian said, that's him.

This is a private conversation, sir, I said.

It is a free country, the old man said, and he sounded just like Mother, with the soft calm island lilt, so I will chust take part in the conversation. This is the one who was molesting my granddaughter, so I will be having my own conversation with him.

And as Rackman started to his feet, the old man drove his fist into his chest and threw him against the cottage. Rackman looked relieved to be dealing with an old man instead of two loonies with rifles. He swung two punches to the old man's face. They had no effect. The old man smashed his nose and knocked him down, and said impatiently, Get up, get up, you are not finished. Rackman threw himself forward and took a terrible blow on the side of the head and collapsed again.

I suppose, said the old man, you will have to report this to your sergeant.

No sir, I said.

So. It is of no moment to me whether you do or not. Good day to you.

I don't even know if they discussed it, but a strange thing happened. Whether Sergeant Wellesley knew it or not, he knew that his authority had fallen from under him. Morris had a new way of looking at the lads, and the Jew-baiting died away.

And in the meantime, I had an afternoon off and went to find Hetty McGillivray. I had the overpowering feeling again that something Big was happening in my life. The islanders I met were a bit cagey when I asked them for directions, but they told me, and I found the place, a really tousled croft with peats half-stacked in the yard and this great fat grandmotherly woman with frizzy yellow hair and thick glasses throwing a bucket of some stuff at the chickens.

'I'm Peter Cassidy,' I said, and she stared at me.

'You're Meg's boy, I would know you in a million, boy,' and she burst into tears, and I disappeared into her bosom.

The inside of the house was the same as the yard, with an infant crawling on the floor and a cat snarling at a dog and a canary hopping about on the mantelpiece, and she had to sweep a pile of stuff off a chair to let me sit while she was pouring a cup of tea and a glass of whisky at the same time and exclaiming to herself in English and Gaelic and reaching out to touch my face to see if I was real. I took a sip of the whisky and nearly blew my skull off. It was Macaskill's Own, fully a month old, the stuff quietly manufactured by the hotel owner and slipped in good quantities to Sergeant Wellesley in exchange for tins of corned beef.

I was choking on it when the white-haired man from the hill came in, and those great fists clenched at the sight of a soldier.

'It's Meg's boy, Billy,' Hetty said.

'God in Heaven, I should have known the eyes and known a friend, what a convergence of circumstances this is, boy,' and my hand disappeared in his and he worked me like an artesian pump with his mouth trembling. Very sentimental people, the islanders.

Hetty was rambling on about Mother, and the old days, and that silly old pastart Mr Ferrier – that's how she said it, pastart. It sounded so much more innocent than bastard, it was hardly a bad word at all. And Billy was hoping that the plutty English pastart was still feeling his pruises.

In the end I made them tell me about the old days, and little Meg. Billy was saying least said soonest mended, but Hetty said that what didn't come out would just go in and turn sour and they told me the story.

Mother, little Meg, was only five years old. Her mother Margaret was a terrible good housewife, though she was from Glasgow, and her father Hector was one of the quietest boys on the island, nearly teetotal because Margaret did not hold with drink, she was terrible keen on the church and being proper, she always had a neat peat-stack and would have scrubbed the peats if she had thought of it. Little Meg was a good little girl and did everything she was told.

Then there was the day of Gordon McGillivray's birthday, and Hector couldn't decently refuse to have a drink with the men when he came home from several days' fishing. He was in the hotel when Margaret walked to the jetty with little Meg, and met Henrietta with several of her raggle-taggle brood, going to welcome the men home. Hetty was cheerful, as usual, and said it would be fine and warm in bed tonight.

Margaret was very cold, and said that a man who stopped to take strong drink instead of coming straight home was not entitled to his wife's bed, and Hetty was amazed that a vigorous young woman should put a punishment on her man that was equally a punishment on herself, but Margaret was not the kind to be moved.

When Hector got home, late, the little girl wanted to throw herself into his arms, but she knew somehow that that would displease her mother, and she went up to her room. From there she could hear talk downstairs, and heard her father raise his voice in anger, a thing unknown, and stamp out of the house.

Hector was not a drinker, but that night he drank with the rest, and when the bar closed, he said goodnight and walked out and fell into ten feet of water at the jetty. Margaret slept in her cold bed alone, too proud to go out and look for him. In the morning, at low tide, an early riser saw Hector sitting on the dried-out sand, against the sea wall, looking quite comfortable, and called out to him, but he didn't answer. They carried him home, and Margaret just looked at him and never said a word.

On the day of the funeral, after the men had carried the

coffin away, Margaret left the women mourners and walked away in the opposite direction, and nobody had the courage to talk to her or follow her. She walked to the other side of the island and walked into the sea, and Hetty McGillivray took little Meg home and into her own bed and Billy slept on a shake-down in the kitchen.

The tears were gushing down my face, and Billy, the great burly avenger, was racked with noisy sobs, long before Hetty finished her story. I felt I was weeping not for the mother I knew, but for a dear little sister I had never met. I couldn't stop. Henrietta took me in her arms like a baby. She was lovely.

A few days later, the Sergeant went into one of his drunken stupors. Morris and I relieved the guard on the Equipment shed, broke in and assembled the Equipment. Morris, till I arrived, was the only technician in the unit. The Army is insane. Maybe it was insane to put a tracking station on Duna anyway, but it was even more insane to find a way of getting the stuff there and abandoning it.

There was a beautiful little Coventry Climax engine for the generator, and when we got the thing working, with the Sergeant still unconscious, the rest of the lads came in to wonder at it. And Morris was suddenly an important person.

When the Sergeant surfaced, he didn't blow up straight away about our interference with the Equipment. He had just had a delivery of the mail, which he always opened in case it had messages from the enemy, and found a copy of the *Architect*, addressed to me, and with my own letter published in it, and he sent for me.

You been writing to the Press, Cassidy, against King's Regulations.

It's not against King's Regulations, I told him, my letter has nothing to do with the service or the war. And I may write to my Member of Parliament to tell him you have been interfering with His Majesty's mails.

We'll see about that, he said, and anyway, this magazine is a lot of toffee-nosed balls, get it out of here.

I took it back to my billet. I don't think it was a bad letter. Too long and wordy, but I read it a hundred times. It was an attack on a lot of articles in the architectural press about postwar planning, and it said that even if a plan was good, it could become bad if it was on too big a scale, because the architect's job was to serve his clients, and nobody had thought of asking the working classes what kind of houses they wanted, and that even architects made mistakes, and if they worked on a huge scale a small mistake would be magnified 100,000 times. Totalitarianism, the letter said, was exactly what the war was being fought to abolish. And a lot more like that. I had certainly learned something from Julian and his supercilious upper-class cynicism about the Quarry Hill apartments. Maybe the Sergeant was right. My letter was a kind of subversion.

But of course, he went berserk when he found the Equipment working and said I would be court-martialled. I was really the barrack-room lawyer then.

I demand a court-martial, Sergeant, I said, at which I will explain how I was sent by High Command to assemble and operate the Equipment and was obstructed in this vital job by my Sergeant.

You'll get it, Cassidy. When I'm ready.

He would never be ready, he was licked. He was afraid of me too. But he had one last try at Morris. He put him on permanent cook duty. Oh, Sergeant Wellesley would have made a great jailer in a police state. Morris just took it. That night at dinner he served corned beef fritters. The Sergeant took a mouthful, spat it out on to the table.

Do you call this food, Ikey?

Stony stood silent.

You taste it, Ikey.

Stony stood.

The Sergeant looked at Rackman and Corcoran, he looked very happily at Rackman and Corcoran and said, Put that in the Yid's mouth and see he eats it all up.

I looked at Rackman and shook my head, and he bowed his own head to the table.

Corcoran nearly stood up, looked at Rackman and changed his mind.

Walsh, said the Sergeant. Steele. Put the Yid under arrest.

A paralysis had broken out. Nobody moved. The Sergeant got frightened, and dangerous, and said to Stony, You will come with me to the outhouse, Stone.

Now Stone spoke at last.

So that you can touch me up, you big nancy-boy?

The Sergeant jumped up and made for him. Stony threw a ladleful of steaming custard in his face. The Sergeant screamed and threw a punch at Morris that sent him flying. The rest of us sat like statues. Wellesley grabbed Stony and tried to crush him, but Morris drove his knee into the groin and smashed his forehead into the Sergeant's nose, and as Wellesley backed away, swung his foot with horrible accuracy into his crotch.

You're all for a court-martial, the Sergeant wheezed.

What for, Sergeant? I asked. Did something happen? Did anybody see anything happening?

I looked round the table, and there were all the lads, all these lovely lads, *and* the three thugs, shaking their heads.

So my trip to the Islands was a very eventful part of my war, as well as that strange prickly feeling I had about the place. It ended when another posting came for me, to a training unit in the South of England. But the posting was addressed to Second Lieutenant Peter Cassidy. I had got through Officer Selection after all, but my gazetting notice had been delivered to somebody else's spike.

The Sergeant had a heart attack, concealed behind a smart salute, and said he had guessed it all along.

I only took the commission to please my mother, Sergeant, I said very offhand. I'm a mother's boy, you see.

Oh, very droll, sir, very droll. I think that's very droll, sir.

It was quite droll, I think.

## 47

Meg was very pleased indeed. What she was most pleased about was Peter's posting to a safe billet as an instructor. His jump to officer status was pleasant too. The safe posting was prime. The war couldn't last much longer, but soldiers might be killed on the very last day. Altogether, Peter's posting leave in Glasgow was triumphant.

'I was walking down Buchanan Street,' he told her. 'Wearing the pip. And this guy saluted me. For a second I didn't know what to do.'

'It was kind of him,' she said.

'Yeah, I suppose it was. But coming up Buchanan Street was another second lieutenant, and I wasn't sure what to do to him for a minute. The Army's really a mess, Mother. The same private who saluted me was looking in a shop window, and this pipsqueak second lieutenant – that's all we are, you know; pipsqueak second lieutenants – actually bawled at him. In Buchanan Street, with all these ordinary human beings walking past. And demanded to know why he hadn't saluted. So the bloke mumbled something. And the second lieutenant caught my eye and sort of smirked, as if we were allies, and told the private he'd better mind his manners, and the bloke skulked away grinding his teeth. That's what the pip on the shoulder is, Mother. It's a licence to bully.'

'But you're not a bully. You'd better not be a bully, Peter.'

'Oh, I've done some violent things, Mother.'

'I don't believe you at all.'

'It doesn't matter, I was fighting for justice. Oh. In fact, I was violent today. When the private was away, I told the second lieutenant he was a jumped-up toly.'

'You never did, Peter, it is a disgusting world.'

'He was a disgusting man. Then it turned out he was English and didn't know what a toly meant. So I told him, and he said it was a delightful word, and he would use it himself. And then he said he admitted it, but he was just getting his own back on the Army. So I felt an idiot.'

'You deserved to.'

'Oh, I know. I know. But I'm very vain, Mother. It's great having a pip. You should have told me what happened when you were a wee girl on Duna.'

'I could never bear to tell anybody, Peter. But I'm glad you know.'

'I'm amazed you grew up without a lot of complexes.'

'Oh Peter, Peter, I have got every complex of Freud. But I'm beginning to think, so has everybody else.'

'You're probably the best-balanced woman alive.'

'Oh Peter, Peter, you're young. And you're beautiful, I love your pip and your collar and tie.'

'I must take my beauty from you, I suppose. You're not bad.'

It was true, he felt splendid, and conceited, inside his uniform, and he had to call on everybody he knew, and wear it, and pooh-pooh the absurdity of being an officer. Harry Cooke, who might have taken a tough line on workers who joined the boss class, was away from home, and his mother was alone. She didn't take a hard line at all. She thought he looked fine, and a credit to his mother. They had coffee, and biscuits from the little wooden barrel.

'The first time I came here,' he admitted, 'I thought you were terribly posh. Fruit on the sideboard for people to eat as much as they liked, and a barrel for the biscuits. And a car. Terrifying.'

'Oh you're exaggerating, Peter. You know, even as a wee boy there was something distinctive about you.'

'I was a scruffy wee urchin, Mrs Cooke.'

'Call me Liz. Everybody else does. Do you not remember you told us about the Theory of Surplus Value?'

'Oh Lord. I was a wee prig as well.'

'You were a delightful wee boy.'

'Ach.'

She had made him shy. When she saw him to the door she suddenly became emotional.

'God keep you safe, Peter,' she said. And she hugged him. He was going to peck her cheek, but she put her lips to his and kissed him firmly as she held him, till he was running out of breath.

'Come back soon, Peter,' she said.

It was a funny experience. For the first time, he felt that he wasn't only an officer but a grown man.

His mother knew what he was about, of course. He was glad she didn't know about Mrs Cooke and that peculiar little experience, but he knew that she knew he was visiting all his old acquaintances not just out of friendship but to display the magnificent pip on his shoulder, and the collar-and-tie that made him special. Meg would have been happy to have him all to herself, but she incited him to go out even in the evenings when she was at home. She knew, all right.

'I'll wear civvies tomorrow,' he said. 'I was thinking of seeing the Barrs.'

'There is no need, Peter, your old clothes don't fit very well. Yes, it is a sensible thought. There is no need to flaunt your own success when they have their troubles. You want to see them?'

'Yes, of course.'

'Ah, I'm glad. I don't know them at all, but I'm thinking not a lot of people will be bothering to see them these days. Oh, it is so silly, the lot of it,'

Mr Barr, the successful confident Mr Barr, was in prison. The Judge had told him that he was giving him a lenient sentence of only two years in view of his hard work for war production, but that defrauding the Government in time of war was not far short of treason. It was a complicated business, but the one clear thing was that Mr Barr, aside from his little sub-contracting factory making machine parts, had built up a sales business on the side for spare parts, and juggled the books to evade thousands of pounds of Purchase Tax, and he was a man in Barlinnie Prison with a family in disgrace. Peter wondered that his mother should have wondered whether he would visit the Barrs.

But at the Barrs', many things hadn't changed at all. Everything in the house still looked newer than things in anybody else's house.

Mrs Barr was still serving lashings of tea and sugar and chocolate biscuits.

'I would asked you to stay for lunch, Peter,' she said, 'but I've got a Red Cross Committee meeting. Maybe next time.'

'I was very sorry about Mr Barr.'

'The whole thing was just a mistake of the bureaucratics, Peter. Socialistic interference in business would lose us the war, Mr Barr always said. If they let businessmen run the country, the war would be over by now.'

'You're looking well, Mrs Barr.'

'Oh, the old lady never changes,' Beth said. Beth had

certainly changed. She was very pregnant, and had lost two front teeth, and Peter had a sad pang for the elegant sophisticated lady he had loved in his boyhood. She smoked all the time, with the cigarette dangling from her lips, as if pregnancy was a liberation from all the old obligations to look marvellous. 'Dad's a silly old bugger, but the business is still running. San ferry ann.' She flicked her ash in the general direction of an ashtray.

'How is Alastair?'

'Oh, he's doing very well, Peter,' Mrs Barr said. 'He decided to give up air-crew training, and now he's a lance-corporal. In the old days, you could buy a commission, you know.'

'Alastair is a bum,' Beth offered.

'And personally,' said Mrs Barr, 'I think it was a very good idea. It meant that people from good families were in charge, and that's what war is about. The best people running things. Oh, if people like Mr Barr were in charge you would see changes.'

'The Army seems to suit you,' Beth said, almost resentfully.

'Oh, it's all right, Beth. You just do what you're told and keep your head down.'

'You've grown.' He could feel her eyes weighing him.

'The open-air life.' He laughed. 'You've grown too.'

'Uhuh. That had nothing to do with the open-air life. Strictly indoor sports.'

'Beth. That's no way to talk.'

'Peter's a big boy, Mother.'

'Yes, I suppose he is. I just can't keep up with things any more. I must get off to my meeting. Honestly, I don't know what things are coming to. Well, we never died a winter yet, eh?'

'I'll have to go too, Mrs Barr. It was nice to see you.'

'Stay and have a blether,' Beth said.

'I've really got to go, Beth.'

'Oh, all right.'

She was sullen and disappointed. In spite of, or because of, her swollen belly, she looked dangerous. It was odd that she hadn't bothered to get the lost teeth replaced. She had once been a goddess.

There was a much readdressed letter from somebody called James Fraser, who had read Peter's letter in the *Architect*, and who said:

> *My dear Peter Cassidy, you are right to apologise for being a mere student and therefore probably ignorant and even stupid, but you have something of your own to say and it may be important. Received authority in urban planning can perpetuate myths of its own and the postwar world may need subversive insight, as one of the checks and balances of power structures. I have a personal and professional interest in this. If you ever find yourself in London I would like to talk to you. Yours, James Fraser.*

There was no indication of who or what James Fraser was. The paper was engraved at the top with his name and address, in Eaton Square, London, and the telephone number, and that was all.

'He sounds a wee bit supercilious,' Mother said.

'It's the first time I've had a fan letter, Mother.'

'It very likely means nothing. But keep the letter anyway.'

'I was going to, Mother.'

'James Fraser. That is a very ordinary name, and not even any letters after it. It is a kind of anonymous name, Peter, and yet I have the oddest feelings about it, there is something funny about it and I don't know what it is.'

'I've had odd feelings too, Mother. But it's a fan letter.'

'Yes, and we all need a bit of flattery now and then. There is not enough of it about.'

'It's all right for you, Mother, you don't need flattery. I mean, you're perfect.'

'If you start teasing me, Peter Cassidy, I will strike you.'

'You will not, Mother. You know very well you're perfect, but you have to be told now and then.'

'Oh, I do. I am a silly weak woman and my eyes are getting damp, you wicked wee boy.'

'You're a silly weak woman and I don't know how I put up with you.'

'There is something funny about that letter.'

'Well, if it's funny, laugh.'

She laughed.

## 48

There was nothing to complain about. Hetty could nearly convince herself that life was good. Tim was still there. With the end of the war in sight, his wife and children had come back from the country. He had invented a fictitious overnight duty once a fortnight so that he could be with Hetty. This reduction of a love affair to a mechanical timetable made it even more paltry and sordid, but it was bearable, and she concentrated her mind on the everyday pleasures of life, as Mother would have done. Mother had a great talent for taking life as it came and not wasting her energies on useless speculation.

Peter visited her, from his training unit in Luton and took her to lunch with a strangely intriguing man called Fraser, who spent the time poking gentle, humorous, almost fatherly fun at Peter and being enormously suave and gallant to her. There was something familiar and easy about him too, and he almost shook her resolve to have nothing more to do with men. She found herself oddly jealous of Peter, if he was going to work with this man after the war, in some visionary scheme to rebuild Europe, and she had to remind herself that there would be a glittering career ahead of her too, if she kept her eyes straight ahead and could be her own woman, with no emotional connections.

Peter told her the strange tale of Mother's childhood, and she wept with him.

'I wrote to Mother when I found out,' Peter said. 'And do you know what she wrote back? She said she thought she had understood it all at the time, without realising she had understood it, but as a tiny child she had made up her mind that she would never let religion, or respectability, or anything else, stop her from giving people pleasure if she could. You know what, Hetty? If Mother's own mother had thought more of pleasure and less of doing the right thing, nobody would have died at all.'

The snag, Hetty thought, was that Mother had spent all her energies in giving pleasure to other people instead of having pleasure herself. But maybe that was Mother's kind of pleasure. She, Hetty, should be glad that she herself was more selfish, but tried to give a little pleasure to other people too.

So the second Thursday came round, and here she was, in the pub, with Tim, with the noble duty of taking him home and struggling to comfort him and lie to him. And she looked across the table and saw her brother John quietly smiling down, and threw herself at him and knocked over what was left of her gin.

'You look more and more like Mother,' John said.

'Good. Tim, my brother John. Tim Ellis.'

Relief, and disappointment, and relief, and then disappointment, flashed in Tim's eyes like symbols in a fruit machine. His stricken puppy face was there again, a puppy desperately trying to behave like a grown-up doggie.

'Good, good,' Tim was babbling, 'Well, I'll have to leave you anyway. See you tomorrow, Hetty.'

She tried to feel guilty and wretched as he elbowed his way to the door, wearing a dreadful sick grin. But John's appearence had engulfed her. They sat down and just looked at each other.

'You're enormous,' she said.

'American food and the Army uniform. The doorman at the BBC told me you might be here after I tipped him a pound. I gave him a cigar too. Tim's in love with you.'

'That's ridiculous, John. Yes. It's true.'

'Quite right. You?'

'No.'

'That's sad, Hetty. It must be hell for Tim.'

'I can't help it, John. Tell me about you. Tell me everything, it's incredible. Tell me everything.'

'All right. At an early age I went to the United States of America.'

'Peter's a captain.'

'I'm a major. On arriving in New York Harbour, I made my way to a modest lodging house . . .'

He was telling her everything, but she only half-listened, his presence was enough to please her. It drew her back to simpler times, to growing up with her brothers and Mother, learning to dance, learning trigonometry, learning to live. Quiet, easy John, never ruffled, never angry, solid as a rock. She smiled at him and let the words flow over her and looked for a word that would describe him.

Good. She found the word. John was good.

'You're not listening, Miss Cassidy.'

'I'm just happy, Major Mason. Oh my God, John, you've lost two fingers.' She went pale.

'So it's the trombone instead of the piano. But you can cry if you like, as long as you're happy. Now listen. I have something surprising to say.'

'You always did.'

'I think you should marry me.'

There was a long silence, but he kept smiling, always easy, relaxed, unworried, while her mind whirled.

'Marry my brother?'

'I'm not your brother. We're not related in any degree.'

'You're joking, John.'

'I'm smiling. It's not the same thing.'

'You mean it. Now you're nodding.'

He nodded and said nothing. She stared into his face and he went on gently nodding his head.

'You're nodding,' she said, 'Just a minute . . . oh, you are infuriating, John Mason. The nod means that . . . the nod means . . . ' he nodded again. 'The nod means you're telling me I've always known it, but I never knew I knew it.'

'Mother is not the only mind-reader in the family.'

'Mother would be flabbergasted.'

'Mother will be enchanted.'

'John, be sensible. You can't just appear from outer space like this and talk like this, and anyway, I can't give up everything just when I'm getting somewhere, I have a career, I'm quite famous, you know, and I certainly couldn't leave London to . . . to traipse off into the unknown, and anyway, John, you *are* my brother, and it's ridiculous, it's probably illegal, and oh heavens John, maybe I always did know it, and it was like dying when you just went away to America, you were beastly.'

'That's why I went.'

'I really hate you now, you've got me crying again and I detest crying, and I detest you, John Mason oh my God John, what a fool I am I've never loved anybody the way I love you, I don't know how I've lived without you all these years, it's been like doing an imitation of life. You're horrible and you are really enormous.'

'It's the thick coat. You can have a career in New York or Boston.'

'Alaska, who the hell cares? Let's get out of here and get a taxi and go home.'

'I am home, Hetty.'

'I think I'm going to die.'

'Put it off for a few years.'

'Do you know that two seconds before you turned up I had decided that men would never be for me?'

'Girls are stupid, Hetty.'

'Anything you say.'

## 49

Meg had calmly considered her situation, and her analysis was that with the war virtually over, she now had to train herself for the job of being an ageing woman and living alone. There was a feeling in the country, a great surge of renewal, and Andy was riding on top of it.

The Serviceman's vote was going to do it. This was a novelty to Meg, who recalled Servicemen from that other war to end wars, and had always pictured them as men devoted to king and country in spite of what hell they might be going through; men who were fighting for the Empire and who would always stand for the Empire and the great ideals of Britain, and Parliament, and the House of Lords, and British rule, and the British ruling classes. Even as a girl she had thought that a bit daft, but it was the way things were.

This time, Andy assured her, and she believed him, the wartime experience of a citizen army had turned all these men cynical about the officer class, the Government, and the great Depression that had taken a war to cure it. They were ready for a new society and they would vote for a new society.

Andrea, of course, agreed with Andy. The little girl, Margaret, was now nearly the centre of her life. It was astonishing how motherhood had taken her over and turned her into a contented housewife with no political ambitions left for herself. She was satisfied to be Andy's wife and the mother of his children.

'Another thing, Mother,' he pointed out to her candidly, 'being married into the landed gentry makes it a hell of a lot easier to be a Labour Member of Parliament. We'll have a flat in the old folks' house in the Albany, couldn't be handier. And it's free.'

'You are a calculating tinker, Andy Mason, and you should be ashamed of yourself.'

'Do you hear Andrea complaining?'

'No, you have got that girl besotted, I just hope you appreciate it.'

'I do, Mother, I do. I'll never look at another woman. Well, not seriously. I know when I'm well off, and I'm damned well off, Mother.'

'So. I will not be seeing much of you if you get to Parliament, and I will not be seeing much of John or Hetty, and Bobby will be making his life in Canada, and I suppose Peter will be going off to rebuild the world somewhere.'

'You'll be welcome in London with us any time, Mother. Don't talk like that.'

'Ah, Andy, you and Andrea have your own life to live now, and I am not going to be a lodger in somebody else's home. I might ask Vickie to move in with me, and we'll become like the old Misses Newton, two daft old bodies making separate pots of tea and running a silly wee shop. You know, Hetty always had the idea we would make the shop a great big thing and move to Sauchiehall Street and call it a salon, but I don't think I could be bothered.'

'You'll find something better than that to do, Mother.' Andy was a little evasive. He didn't like having somebody else's troubles interrupting his confident ambitions. She patted his shoulder and assured him she would have a good time knowing that everybody had survived the war and that she had no more worries.

She was with him at the party rooms on the night the votes were tallied, and he had been right. The results coming in by the wireless from all over the country were electrifying, an explosive piece of British history. The Tories were being annihilated. Landslide was the word everybody used, and a landslide it was. Even so, Andy, standing against a sitting Conservative member with a majority of thousands at the pre-war election, was tense and twitching till his own constituency result came in. It was a runaway victory for him.

And that was that. Andy was bound for the life of London, and Peter was ready to fly the nest, and Bobby wanted Canada, and John and Hetty would live in America, and all the struggles were over, and all they had produced for her was solitude and the prospect of old age. Well, she thought, maybe that is an adventure too. There is a pattern in it somewhere even if we never manage to see it.

## 50

She was right about Peter. He came home on leave bursting with the news of his meeting with the strange Mr Fraser, though he tried to be offhand and even cynical about it, because he had brought his Army friend Julian with him, and the pair of them evidently played off each other, like a couple of music-hall comedians, those Western Brothers on the wireless who were always so bored and superior.

But he couldn't keep the champagne bubbles out of his voice when he talked of going to work in Paris with the mysterious Fraser, who was going to do something tremendously important about European reconstruction. Meg forgot her sense of desolation in the excitement of it.

'Paris, Peter!'

'And he even says I can finish my training there. I think he . . . you know. I mean, I got the idea he actually quite liked me. He liked Hetty too, he thought she was charming. He actually read her articles in the *News Chronicle*, he thought she was famous.'

'He would think Hetty was charming,' Meg said drily. 'How old a man would your Mr Fraser be?'

'Oh, Mother, he's older than you, he was really quite nice. You know, sometimes you meet people and you think you know them already, they're nice and easy. You don't mean he might, sort of . . . *fancy* Hetty?'

'No, Peter, I don't really, though you couldn't blame him for that. I'm confused, that is all, everything is so sudden. But Paris. Oh Peter.'

'He's a bit hoity-toity, of course, like Julian – these Public Schools drain the natural vitality out of people.'

'And substitute natural superiority,' Julian reminded him.

'Anyway, he wants to have a few people who don't have fashionable ideas.'

'Or even unfashionable ideas, laddie. Sorry, Mrs Mason.'

'Actually, Tregarth, it's all your fault. You opened my eyes to all my nonsense about gigantic town planning and mammoth blocks of flats.'

'Oh, cheese it, Cassidy.' Julian was deeply embarrassed.

'And you can come and live with me in Paris, Mother.'

'Indeed I shall not, Peter. I'll come and see you, oh, that will be wonderful, at last. But you're past the age for living with aged parents.'

Julian spontaneously guffawed at the phrase. It really was pleasant, in a wry way, to see the frank admiration of this elegant young man, knowing that that was as close as she would get now to knowing a man. And she tried not to be jealous of the hoity-toity Fraser who was stealing her ewe lamb from her.

'I would fair like to see this Mr Fraser of yours,' she said.

'You will, Mother.'

The telephone rang, and she started in alarm.

'It's only the telephone, Mother.'

'I know. It just startled me.'

He went to the hall, and they could hear him fairly shouting at the telephone.

'Yes, yes! No, it's just funny. I was just telling my mother she would meet you, and the phone rang, it's supernatural. Yes. Yes, of course. Oh, I have a house guest. Well, all right, if that's all right. Right. Right.'

He came back into the room dazed, to find his mother nodding.

'It's your second sight, Mother. He's on his way through Glasgow, and he wants us to have dinner with him in the Central Hotel.'

'So. That is very interesting, Peter, coincidence is a strange thing.'

'That really was second sight, wasn't it, Mrs Mason?' Julian's blasé manner had fallen from him.

'Second sight is superstitious nonsense, I think, Julian.' The boy loved to hear her pronounce his name, in the Highlands accent that made it sound like a caress. He was slightly troubled by his response to Peter's mother.

'Pardon, Mrs Mason?'

'Superstitious nonsense, Julian.' It sounded beautiful.

Julian Tregarth was quite agog with his discovery of Glasgow. He had never seen anything quite like the tenements, had never heard anything so concentrated as a million people all speaking with funny accents.

'They're genuine primitives, you know,' he informed Peter.

'So was Breughel, sonny. In Glasgow, we speak the

tongue that was spoken in the Garden of Eden.'

'And see what happened to Adam? God, have you got snakes here too?'

'By the thousand. Our dinner engagement this evening, by the way, is in a rather effete establishment built over a railway station, and our host is a bloke whose accent is even worse than yours. So don't fart about in front of my future employer and blight my career.'

'Oh, that's all right, old chap. He and I will speak English, and you can chat to your mother in your quaint patois. Oh I say, I'm sorry, Peter, I didn't mean to be funny about your mother. Her accent is actually rather beautiful, isn't it?'

'That is true, Trēgarth, that is true.'

'Peter, old chap, speaking as my psychoanalyst, and the authority on all things filthy, is there anything horrid and perverted about a chap having definite feelings of attraction towards another chap's mother? Your mother is simply electric.'

'There is nothing wrong with such infantile responses as long as you keep your disgusting English hands to yourself. Do you mean it?'

'Cassidy, she is just, oh God, there is something wrong with me. I mean, I don't feel that way about my own mother. One wouldn't, one supposes.'

'Oh, one would, in Greek mythology, old chap. But to let you into a secret, one was once embraced with unmistakable sensuality by the mother of one of one's boyhood chums, if that's any comfort to one. I mean, any comfort to the other one. Stop this bloody effete English "one" nonsense. I trust this confidence has not brought your diluted English blood to the boil.'

'It has, it has, Cassidy. You're joking, aren't you?'

'The subject is too sacred for jest. It was quite unnerving at the time.'

'But reassuring, one trusts.'

'It was quite nice; though the lady was not so youthful or dynamic as my own mother.'

'We do talk a lot of high-falutin rubbish, don't we?'

'We talk a lot of pure shite, if that's what you're trying to say. I wonder if the Wilson girls are demobbed yet. We could make a foursome some time. They were always frantic cuddlers, and they're probably more than that by this time.'

'Oh, do let's, old chap, I'm having the most fearful trouble with my gonads.'

'I'm trying to remember which twin I once nearly got my hand up, but never mind. I can put up with either, or both, We'll toss.'

'I trust you mean toss a coin.'

'Ça va sans dire.'

At the Central Hotel, Peter was careful to get the protocol right.

'Mother, may I present Mr James Fraser. Mr Fraser, my friend Julian Tregarth.'

'How do you do ... Mrs Cassidy?' The immensely assured James Fraser seemed to lose composure as he took her hand.

'Mrs Mason,' she said. 'It is a little complicated.'

'Yes. Of course. Will you have something to drink?'

'A dry sherry would be pleasant.'

'Mr Tregarth?'

'Sir.'

Fraser smiled and relaxed.

'I am neither your father nor your commanding officer.'

'I'm sorry, sir. I mean, sorry, Mr Fraser.'

'So,' said Meg. 'You are the man who is taking my Peter away from me.'

'I'm sorry.'

'I'm glad, Mr Fraser. It is a fact of life, and life is very curious.'

'Life is very curious,' Fraser repeated.

Several times Peter had rehearsed this meeting, had tried to predict how his mother and Fraser would react to each other. Their reaction was guarded, and there were awkward silences as they sat at table.

'Do they have trains actually running through the dining room?' Julian asked him.

'Frequently,' Peter said. 'The 7.15 should be through at any moment, scattering waiters like chaff. I told Julian,' he explained, 'that the hotel is a unified structure with the railway station. The pudding is actually served by the guard just as the last coach whizzes through the far door.'

'Served by catapult, one imagines.'

'Yes, actually the diners have to leap in the air and catch

the crème caramel in their teeth.'

'Rather a Scotch idea that, Cassidy.'

'One might even call it a great leap forward and upward in social engineering.'

'They talk very well for children so young,' Fraser remarked.

'Yes, they are at it all the time.'

'What if one doesn't like crème caramel hurled at one's kisser?'

'The guard is quite choosy.'

'Oh, one will positively finish one's greens, Cassidy. One would not want to be left out of the barrage. One presumes that the soup course is sort of sprayed over one's head by the train driver.'

'Not actually sprayed. Directed with unerring accuracy by a gigantic water pistol.'

'The potatoes will be delivered by some kind of ballista arrangement.'

'Precisely. One will already have noticed that some of the earlier customers had large dollops of mashed murphy embedded in their ears.'

'Well,' said Fraser, 'we'll certainly have no awkward silences. I was afraid we might have awkward silences.'

'You visit Glasgow often, Mr Fraser?'

'Not in recent years, Mrs Mason.'

'Oh.'

'I used to come to see my people, but my mother lives in Hampshire now.'

'Oh.'

'Tell me, Cassidy, what happens if the train's delayed at Beattock?'

'Starvation stalks the land, that's what happens.'

'One almost wishes one had brought iron rations along.'

'Oh, one has, one has, Tregarth. This pocket is full of nuts and bolts for just such an emergency.'

His nonsense conversations with Julian always entertained his mother, but this evening she didn't seem to hear them. There were two separate conversations at the table: his own with Julian, and the stilted exchanges between his mother and Fraser.

'You have no one else, Mr Fraser.'

'No. I lost my son, in Italy.'

'I am vexed.' Ready tears came to Meg's eyes. Fraser reached out a comforting hand to her, but drew it back. 'I don't know what to say.'

'No,' Fraser said. 'There is nothing to say. My wife . . . my wife mislaid herself, I suppose, from choice.'

'Oh. The foolishness.'

Momentarily running out of nonsense, Peter and Julian were staring round the dining room for inspiration.

'It's like some kind of conjuring trick,' Fraser said.

'What, the 7.15 train?' Peter asked him.

'Yes, the 7.15 train too. And you'll be glad to know, if we're working together, that I'm a Chesterton fan too.'

'Oh, so am I,' Meg was suddenly enthusiastic. 'In defence of nonsense.'

'Yes, Mrs Mason, in defence of nonsense.'

'And ogres.'

'Ogres too. I still feel like an object in a conjuring trick.'

'I am sure I don't understand you, Mr Fraser. Except that maybe we are all objects in some cosmic joke.'

Julian and Peter were looking from one to the other, and looking bright and baffled.

'This is some word game that one does not understand, Cassidy.'

'Neither does the other one, Tregarth. I fear we are too young for understanding, though one thought one knew everything.'

'You are right, Peter,' Meg said. 'This is middle-aged talk.'

'Personally,' said Fraser, 'I am afraid of cosmic jokes.'

'I am not, Mr Fraser.'

'Mrs Mason I don't think you are afraid of anything.'

'Oh, she isn't,' said Peter. 'Not even mice. She likes mice. She talks to them, and they go into the house next door.'

'You do not have even your wife,' Meg said to Fraser. 'You must miss her too.'

'Not really. I think my wife always had the feeling she was a second choice.'

'That is a cruel situation. Cruel.'

Fraser shrugged, and there was a difficult silence.

'My brother's been elected to Parliament,' Peter said. 'I am actually the brains behind him. I'm trying to teach him now to rebuild the world without demolishing it.'

'Yes, he has.' Meg was quietly proud. 'Andrew Mason, MP.'

'Yes,' said Fraser. 'I know the name.' Fraser turned from Meg to look at the boys. 'How is it going to be rebuilt? It is an exciting time.'

'I am an incurable Tory,' said Julian.

'Nobody is perfect,' said Peter. 'The lad will learn sense in time, if somebody beats him over the head a lot. Well, we'll nationalise the banks. And the coal mines. And the land.'

Fraser laughed, and changed back into the confident Fraser that Peter had met in London.

'And what will you do in the afternoon?' he said.

'Oh, I think we'll have a rest, like God. I myself shall continue to oppose the Government, on the principle that one must oppose every Government. But we'll never go back to the old days, which Tregarth rather enjoyed because he was a member of the upper classes feeding off the misery of the oppressed proletariat.'

'He gets that from his Communist uncle,' Meg said.

'Sounds quite good,' said Fraser. 'It has a ring to it.'

'We have to feed off somebody,' Julian complained. 'I mean to say, we are not bred to squalid toil. It is hell on one's fingernails.'

'Bully for you, Tregarth. Stick out for your rights, even if they're wrong,' said Fraser. 'And even though the tide of history is going to sweep you aside.'

'I shall go like a gentleman, sir. The fact is, I'm a secret Socialist anyway. I mean to say, all that terrible stuff before the war, unemployment and so on. It is quite ridiculous and demeaning.'

Fraser was now conducting the seminar, and Meg merely watching with amused interest.

'You mustn't laugh at us men, Mrs Mason,' Fraser said. 'We do have a compulsion to change the world, you must let us enjoy our game. Personally, I hope they nationalise the land like a shot. And the banks. And the mines. And the railways. They are the property of the people who make them work, and they'll work ten times better when the people own them.'

'I am not laughing, Mr Fraser.'

'You are smiling. But I almost believe we are moving into a new age. Now we have the atom bomb, we can never have another war. The East and the West have been brought together. We'll understand the Russians and the Chinese, and they'll understand us.'

'I don't think I could ever learn Chinese, Mr Fraser.'

'It's easy, Mother. You just make funny noises and wave your hands about, and bow a lot.'

'I know one thing,' Fraser said. 'No British government in the future will ever let a million people walk the streets for want of a job. The world has learned a lot of lessons.'

'Oh, Mr Fraser, I am not quarrelling with you, or with Peter. We need a new world, and maybe we will get it. But I think we will have a hard job passing laws to stop people from being stupid and selfish.'

'Mother, stop being a woman.'

'Indeed I will not.'

'All right, but stop thinking like a woman. We are in control of our destinies now, and it's going to be great.'

'The United States of Europe,' Julian cried.

'Exactly. Passports will be abolished. We'll all learn Esperanto or something. I don't mean we'll MAKE people speak Esperanto. We'll ask them. But they'll say yes. And we won't build great housing schemes, we'll set up this agency to build wee bungalows that look like mediaeval castles, and we'll have morris dancing on the village greens, in several languages, and everything will be just dandy.'

'You know, Mr Fraser, I've known that boy since he was an infant, and sometimes I still nearly believe his nonsense.'

'So do I, really. Life in Paris is certainly going to be stimulating.'

'You are a lucky beast, Cassidy. I have to go back to Cambridge.'

'Tough luck, Tregarth. I'll send you rude postcards.'

'I've met your daughter, of course, Mrs Mason,' Fraser said. 'She's very beautiful. I would have recognised you at once.'

'Yes. She takes after her parents.'

'My God.'

'Is there something wrong, Mr Fraser?' Peter asked. 'Do you know that Hetty thought there was something about you, and she didn't know what it was? I'm sorry, I'm just rambling. I do ramble rather a lot, but I'm trying to cure myself of the habit. I think that Chablis is rather devious, it 'sort of works on the brain cells without warning.'

'He was worse than that in the Army, honestly,' said Julian. 'One sometimes simply did not know how to cope with his verbosity.'

'I am sure you managed quite well, Julian,' Meg said. 'You are a man of great resource.'

Julian blushed and tittered.

'I had just noticed,' Fraser said, 'how remarkably alike your sister is to her mother.'

'I suppose that's true. The phenomenon is actually known as heredity.'

'I bow to your superior knowledge.'

'Thank you.'

'Your son is also a very pert young man, Mrs Mason.'

'Yes, isn't he? Quite unlike our generation. I think I shall concentrate on my food now. And see you finish your cabbage, Julian, or the guard of the train will not bombard you with crème caramel.'

'I didn't think you were even listening to that nonsense, Mrs Mason.'

'She hears everything,' Peter explained. 'And she knows everything too.'

'Loyal, too,' Fraser muttered. Peter blushed deeply.

'Well,' Fraser said in the end, 'I'm sorry the food was only served by boring old waiters, and not by express delivery. It was good to meet you all. I'll try to get a taxi for you.'

'Yes,' said Meg. Suddenly Fraser seemed lost and ill at ease, and Peter was conscious of a confusion of feelings, as well as a slight case of tipsiness.

'No,' said Meg. 'The boys may have a taxi, if they want one. I think you and I might have a wee chat about what you are going to do with Peter in that Paris place, where I have been told people get murdered in their beds every night.'

'Every night?' Julian echoed. 'That sounds rather monotonous.'

'Yes, yes,' Fraser said. He pulled a note from his wallet. 'Take this, Peter. No, take it, dammit, for the taxi and anything else you like. I do give the orders, you know.' He watched the two boys in silence as they walked away and turned to wave.

'Why do you need more than one name?' Meg demanded. 'It is not fair.'

'You have more than one name. Macrae, Cassidy, Mason. Yes, I remember your son. Andrew Mason.'

'Oh yes, Andy. He will get on. I am very proud of him. But he is thirty-two years old. I would have had to have him when I was thirteen. He is my stepson. Why do you call yourself James when you know your name is Alan?'

'Oh Meg, Meg, you know better than I do that Eileann is only the silly way the landed gentry have, of posing as bits of real estate. Eileann Mhor the father, and Eileann Beg the son, Big Island and Little Island. Meg, Meg, it is a cosmic joke. But Meg, whatever did I do to you? You're telling me that that beautiful girl is my own child?'

'Yes, and I am not proud of that, Eileann. But poor Paul was so stuck on me he would have married me if I had had twenty children. He was a good kind boy and he has always been on my conscience. But I think he was happy with me.'

'I'm sure he was.'

'Oh, but it was sore, to do such a thing to him, but I am glad he never knew it. I never told him Hetty was not his own. I exploited Paul, Eileann, and I am not proud of that at all. So. He was killed. And then I had another man.'

'And now you're widowed again.'

'I do not know whether I am or not, and I do not care.'

'Will we see each other again, Meg?'

'I am not a recluse, Eileann.'

'Good. Do you know you're more beautiful now than you were when you were a girl? Meg, I'm totally overwhelmed. What can I do for Hetty?'

'Nothing, Eileann. She needs nothing. It is all in the past and forgotten. No, I tell a lie. It is not forgotten.'

'But at least I may see you both now and then.'

'Of course you may. Wasn't that silly, not telling the boys we were . . . that we knew each other?'

'I was waiting for you to say.'

'And I was waiting for you.'

'I'm sorry, Meg. I was stunned.'

'Yes. Well.' She picked up her handbag.

'Yes,' he said. 'I'll get you a taxi.'

'Very well. I enjoyed our meeting.'

'You're trembling.'

'Yes, I believe I am.'

'Meg, I don't know what I'm doing. Do you know I've

thought of you every waking hour of my life?'

'I think that is an exaggeration, Eileann. I have not thought of you every waking hour of my life. You must have had other things to think about too.'

'You have thought of me.'

'I have thought of you. How could I not think of you, when your child was with me every day? But maybe it wasn't real. I was thinking of you as a boy of twenty-one and myself as a girl. Going back to this is only a fantasy, we are not children any more.'

'No.'

'Oh, my heavens, Eileann, you are a bit of a softy. Henrietta McGillivray on the Island warned me years ago I would always meet men who were softies.'

'I've never seen myself as a softy.' But he laughed.

'No, but you're half agreeing with me. I've no doubt you can be a strong man elsewhere, but you're a bit of a softy with me.'

'You're probably right.'

'Oh, dammit to hell, Eileann, you might at least argue the point, you might tell me I'm wrong.'

'I'm too . . . I'm too fond of you to argue with you, Meg.'

'Oh, I'm being foolish and capricious, Eileann. I know you won't argue. Maybe that is why . . .' She was trembling violently. 'Maybe that is why, and I shouldn't have to say this, James Fraser or whatever your name is, it is not a woman's place to talk like this. Maybe it is that softness. Maybe that is why I have always loved you, even if a part of my mind told me it was girlish foolishness.'

'Oh God. Oh Meg. I'm not soft, I'm terrified. I'm like a boy of twenty-one and I'm terrified of doing something wrong, and frightening you away. Peter says you always know everything. You must know that.'

She started to lift her coffee cup, but it rattled so loudly against the saucer that she put it down and put her hands in her lap.

'We should be away from all these people,' she said. 'I'm sure they're peering at us.'

'Yes. Yes. The bed in my room is hellish narrow.'

'Oh. It's bed you have in mind.'

'Damn. Now I'm frightening you away.'

'Oh, you silly man, you silly beautiful man, I'm sitting

348

among all these people and I can hardly keep my hands off you.'

'Come with me.'

'Yes sir. I'm not sure if I can remember how to walk.'

'I'll carry you if I have to.'

'So. A bit brutal and masterful after all. But do take my arm, I can't stop shivering.'

They stood for ages in the lift, beside other people, and she clutched his arm as they walked along the corridor.

'I hope I look brazen and casual.'

'You just look beautiful.'

The corridor was immensely long.

'I did develop a taste for Chianti after all,' she said.

'Chianti. God. Oh yes. You were so cool that night, so damned untouchable.'

'It was a matter of dignity. Dignity was all I had, Eileann, I couldn't afford to lose it.'

'To hell with dignity.'

'Yes, to hell with dignity. Does this corridor last forever?'

'It does. Hell must be like this. I've never been with another woman without pretending it was you.'

'You have been with many?'

'No, not many.'

'Well, now we've come this far you will never lie with another or I will cut out your heart, James Fraser.'

'You'll come to Paris. And you'll marry me. And I'll adopt Hetty.'

'I will do anything you tell me.'

The key was awkward in the lock and he cursed under his breath as he fumbled with it. When they were in the room and the door closed behind them she was kissing his face greedily and dragging his jacket down over his shoulders and he was tearing at her clothes. They fell clumsily across the narrow bed and she heard her own shaky laugh.

'My God, dignity, is it, I can do it faster myself, Eileann, let me do it.'

'I'll put the light out, Meg.'

'No, never, never, don't dare.'

'No.'

'Oh Eileann, Eileann, it's you, don't wait, don't wait, I am as ready as any woman ever was, yes, I am, and I have you.'

They lay on top of the covers and he gasped and laughed and

smiled into her opened eyes and she clawed at his back.

'Oh yes,' she said. 'Oh Eileann Eileann I can't stop saying your name, I am finally shameless and I am so grateful, Eileann my lovely Eileann it was nearly worth waiting twenty years for.'

'It was fully worth waiting twenty years.'

'Oh, I only mean twenty years was so long, so long, Eileann I have sometimes wept in my bed with the hunger.'

There were tears in his own eyes then. He kissed her eyes and stood up.

'The bed is too narrow to lie side by side. We'll have an enormous bed like the Great Bed of Ware and we'll spend our lives in it.'

'I don't care if it is an earthen floor.' She sat up and hugged her knees. 'I'm glad you're a hungry man, Eileann, for I am a greedy greedy woman, it is not a thin spiritual feeling I have for you.'

'Oh, but Meg, I love the person inside your beautiful body too.'

'I love you inside my beautiful body. You make my body beautiful, and don't dare start putting your clothes on, just walk about and let me look at you, I have waited long enough to see you.'

'Dammit, I need my strength.' He lay back in the one armchair, smiling at her.

'Thank you for curing my shivers, Eileann. If you had let me go home untouched I think I would have died of the ague. And if you are going to smoke that cigarette, do not drop any hot ash on my property.'

He laughed and stretched. There was just a suggestion that he might develop a paunch, and she was irrationally glad of it, and thought that later she might kiss it.

'We will tell Hetty,' she said. 'Maybe she saw herself in your face. And Peter told me – he was stationed on Duna, you know, it is just amazing – and he said he had a powerful sense of destiny about the place, but he knew it was silly because he is an intellectual and a rationalist and doesn't believe in such nonsense.'

She laughed. 'I was nearly going to say he takes after you.'

'Maybe you and I are related. The old lairds weren't above dallying with crofters' daughters.'

'So. This is incest as well as sin.'

'Makes it more exciting. No. Nothing could make it more exciting.'

'Are you really excited?'

'No, Meg, I'm sated. I'm satisfied. At last. Thank you.'

'You always had good manners. Maybe I should get dressed, the boys will be wondering about me.'

'I suppose so. But I'm not letting you go.'

'Ah, Eileann, you know how to be brutal and masterful. But I will have to go.'

'I'll come home with you.'

'Would that be dignified?'

'In your own words, dammit to hell. I love to hear you swear. It sounds so wicked on your lips.'

'It is not proper, I mustn't do it. Eileann, you have more experience of life than I do—'

'Never.'

'Yes.' She smiled impishly. 'You even have a university degree, so you must be very wise.'

'I have three. I must be Solomon.'

'Oh, I love a man with three university degrees, and long white legs.' He stretched them out and looked complacent. He looked damnably smug. 'It is just a silly girlish thing, Eileann. I have always been waiting for life to settle down. Like a sailor coming ashore and leaving the storm behind him. I was always hoping that one day, at last, all the turmoil would stop and I would have life in my own hands, calm and settled. Have I got it now? Instead of one thing happening after another, and every one of them what you least expected? Am I silly?'

'Yes, Meg, you're silly. What you're talking about is death.'

'You tell me. Eileann, you are wise, you are wiser than I am. Oh, I am so glad. What if I had been in love all these years with a beautiful boy who was just a ninny? I hate stupid people.'

'So do I, Meg. All the cruelties of the world are functions of stupidity. I love you, Meg Macrae.'

'You had better, James Fraser.'

'But I don't promise you a peaceful life. Nobody can promise that to anybody.'

'I am a wee bit sorry to lose that illusion.'

'Life is one damned thing after another, Meg. Lie down.'

'I thought you were taking me home.'

'I am, but not yet. Lie down.'

'Yes, yes, I am lying down. So. There is to be no rest from the turmoil for me. What a wise man you are, James Fraser. I ask for peace, and you bring a sword. Oh. That sounds rude.'

'Yes, it does, rather. You don't really want life to settle down.'

'Yes, but in a wee while. Not yet.'

THE END